A CURSED CROWN NOVEL

THE SCARLET HEIR

KITTY ALDRIN

Cover Design by Miblart

ISBN: 979-8-218-56973-0

First edition 2025

Trevor,
you saved me.

KALUTH
SOLYRUS
ROSETIA
Scarlet
Castle
LUNHAYV

sun
THE ISLES
THE EVER
Menasai
moon
life
The Fading
death
The Veil
ZANDAR

Content Warning:

This book contains depictions of grief, loss, death,

and themes of self-inflicted harm.

PROLOGUE

MY EYES SNAPPED OPEN, AND THE WORLD WAS A blur of red. The first thing I noticed was the wave of heat—suffocating like a thick blanket. The second was the smoke, thick and acrid. And then came the screams. *My screams.*

My heart pounded in my chest, a frantic drumbeat echoing the chaos around me. I clawed at my mattress, my hands trembling and slick with sweat, my nails tearing into the fabric as though that alone would save me. Even the silky pajamas clinging to my skin felt like fire, branding me alive.

The terror was a deadly beast, digging its talons into my chest, leaving my legs trembling and my thoughts caged. I couldn't breathe, couldn't think. All I could do was feel the fire closing in—hungry and relentless, licking at the edges of my vision.

"Dad!" I screamed, my voice lost in the roar of the flames. But I hoped he didn't answer. If my parents were still in here—tears streamed down my face at the thought, a futile trickle against the raging fire. The smoke scraped at my lungs, sending me into an uncontrollable coughing fit that left my chest aching. It was becoming too much. I was trapped in my own room —a space I'd always found comfort in—had become a tomb of fire.

You need to move, Amara, a voice inside my head reminded me.

I frantically searched the room. The walls, once pristine and white, were blackened and blistering. My dresser was gone—reduced to a charred, unrecognizable heap of ash. The window was too far to reach, the flames too wild, dancing and writhing like living things. I wiped at my tears, smearing soot across my face, and tried to push myself upright. My legs shook so violently they nearly gave out beneath me.

I'm going to die here, I realized.

The thought clawed its way through my panic, and with it came a fresh wave of terror so sharp it stole what little breath I had left.

Mar, move NOW!

The voice was right. I could not die like this. There was no time to think, no time to be afraid.

The bed creaked under the searing of the flames as I whirled—grabbing the thin blanket and the forgotten glass of water on the singed bedside table. My fingers burned against the touch of the hot glass, and I quickly tossed the remaining liquid over the blanket. Not that it would do much. Wrapping it around myself like a makeshift cocoon, I prayed to Nyrah for a miracle.

By the grace of the gods, a gust of rain blew through the window, patting down some of the flames. I took my chance and bolted. Glass crunched underfoot as I flew through the bedroom door, the sharp crack echoing with every step. I couldn't feel the tiny shards slicing into my bare feet—adrenaline my savior.

I squinted through the smoky haze. The door to my parents' room was open, the space empty.

They made it out. I crumbled to the floor, relief a kind brush against my racing heart.

Get out of there! the voice hissed in my mind.

Desperation fueled me and I pushed my fear somewhere deep. I tore off the blanket, took a long, ragged breath, and crawled: down the crackling stairs, through the ashen dining room, and finally, out the front door.

The cold wet night air hit me like a physical blow, stinging my lungs. Somehow, I slunk to the snow, unable to move farther as I turned, eyes wide. I watched my home burn. With each breath of fresh air, the house seemed to take a corresponding gasp, its bones groaning and crumbling.

I watched the place I called home for the last twenty years crumble—the place my foster parents, Isidore and Lettie, raised me. I watched the living room where my mother Lettie taught me to read engulf into flames. I watched the kitchen where Isidore showed me how to cook the food we hunted crumble to ash. I watched my sanctuary fall.

And as the flames died, a piece of me went along with them.

The sky cracked with thunder as I fell back on the snowy ground, squinting against the cold rain. The ash and dirt that covered me slowly melted into gray slush. I lifted my arms to assess the damage but there were no burns, no scratches. My hair, now white again without the soot, fell over my shoulder as I inspected my body. My pajamas were singed but I had no physical wounds, like the flames never touched me.

I pushed to my shaky feet, mind racing.

"Mama!" I yelled through my frenzied thoughts. The snow-coated field around our home was now melted from the heat but there was no sign of anyone. "Hello?" I screamed.

Through the haze, the silhouette of a man and woman materialized by the edge of the clearing.

"Daddy!" I shouted. Isidore's dark gray hair was undeniable, even in this storm. I ran, my legs fueled by a child-like urgency. "Daddy," I cried again. My tears mingled with the rain.

The closer I got to my parents, the louder the sounds of feet crunching over distant snow became. Hounds barking and people yelling echoed over the storm as I neared the edge of the clearing. The townspeople's torches lit up the forest in front of me, illuminating my parents.

"Mama," I cried as I fell to my hands and knees before her, my tears of joy as cold as the cool wet earth beneath me.

But she didn't move.

I froze, my breath caught in my throat as confusion overtook my relief.

I lifted my hands only to find them covered in blood. I wiped my tears, the warm crimson liquid staining my face. *Am I bleeding?* I looked back down as my vision cleared.

I was kneeling in puddles of blood.

Cold sweat trickled down my forehead. My hands trembled uncontrollably. Fear clawed at me, my breath catching in my throat.

"Daddy?" I whispered, my gaze rising.

My father, my mother, *my only family.* Both of their bodies were drenched in that crimson liquid, impaled on wooden poles.

My eyes widened as I fell into the snow. My bloody hands left a trail as I crawled backwards into the forest. My breaths were ragged and harsh, each one like a piercing strike.

From the shadows of the forest, I watched the townspeople's torches crackle as they entered the clearing, casting an eerie glow over the deadly scene. My ears rang, louder and louder, but I could still hear their distant screams.

"Over here!" someone shouted through the fog.

"Oh, gods!" a woman cried hysterically, pointing towards my family, and their voices blurred together.

"Who could do something like this?"

"Find that witch!"

"She's the *devil!*"

They raised their torches, and the townspeople searched the ruins of my home, looking for the culprit, looking for me.

I was frozen in place, frozen in time, staring at my parents' lifeless bodies.

A hand landed on my shoulder. "Amara, you need to get out of here," a familiar voice said in a low tone.

But I couldn't move.

"They wouldn't want this for you!" the man hissed. I turned to find Allen, a friend of my parents. I knew he was right. But I was too numb to process what was happening. Somewhere deep inside, I knew I should get up, run, but the thought barely registered. And Allen was too old to carry me, too old to drag me from this scene.

And I was too scared to move, too broken to try.

Allen's hounds slowly emerged from the haze of my shock, their shapes blurring at first before clearing into focus. "Come on," he whispered, tying a rope around my frozen body. The ropes burned under my arms as he yanked on them, attaching me to the harnesses on his dogs' backs.

"She's over here!" someone yelled.

Before they could reach me, the hounds started moving. The rope around my chest stung as it dug into my skin. Cold snow covered my body. I was like a dead carcass being dragged to its burial site. I watched my parents disappear between the trees. Their bodies would be forever painted in my mind.

A chilling display, a macabre masterpiece, created just for me.

1

MY MOTHER ALWAYS TOLD ME MY ATTITUDE would get me killed one day. I could almost hear the "I told you so" roll off her tongue as my captor shoved the end of his blade in my mouth.

"Shut up!" he hissed.

I clenched my teeth on the blade. The taste of cold steel mingled with the faint tang of my blood. I embraced the danger with a defiant grin and shot the man a wink for good measure.

I didn't typically find myself in these situations. For one, if someone was going to kill me, they should just get it over with. And two, I didn't want to die.

Not yet anyway.

But unfortunately, here I was, only in town to steal a *much-needed* item. No, it wasn't food or warmer clothes. This was *so* much better.

I glanced to the bookshelf built into the wall of the small cabin I'd snuck into. There, glowing in the dim candlelight, was the sequel to the book I'd recently finished. I read it in one night and I couldn't resist coming back to get the next one. It was risky, too risky I suppose—if my current situation was any indication.

The man in the corner coughed, wiping his droopy face with his wrist. His clothes were just as dirty as mine and his scraggly beard hung low under his chin. He was an older man, a drunk man. He burped and I could almost smell the booze from the chair I was tied to in the center of the room. The man before me was a bit younger. He was clean-shaven but just as dirty. He grunted as I tried to pull the dagger from him with my teeth.

Oldy in the corner fumbled with his sword, pointing it towards me. "She's a witch. We should just leave her before she curses us or kills us like her parents!"

I wasn't a witch. No, magic only existed in my coveted dreams and the books I read. But if believing I was a witch would get these men *not* to kill me, I'd take it as a win.

With a grunt of frustration, the younger man ripped the dagger from my mouth. It sang against my teeth with a sickening metallic screech. The taste lingered on my lips; a bitter iron liquid dripped down my chin. I couldn't help but watch these idiots with a sinister smile, relishing in all their discomfort. I laughed, an uncontainable uncontrollable force that echoed through the room, intertwining with the tight ropes that bound my body. I'd been accused of terrible things my whole life, and for once, I would make them pay for their lies. The laughter bubbled up from somewhere dark, a release of everything I'd been through.

The men exchanged a glance, and I shifted in the chair, testing the limits of the binding.

"We should take her to town," the old, and apparently sensible, man said.

"We should kill her. After what she did to her parents? It would be a mercy." The younger man spit on my feet. He sidled behind me, his dagger now level with my neck.

My only advantage was their belief that I was a witch, a *killer*—that they might be too frightened to act. I wasn't worthy of such a cruel title. I wasn't worthy of anything. What they didn't know was that I didn't even like hunting to survive, let alone killing a human. No, I was just a girl, one about to die because no matter how much I bluffed or taunted, I had no escape from this cabin.

The younger man's blade pressed to my throat.

The facade I'd built slowly betrayed me. Fear ate at me, a cold relentless terror. I wanted to scream, to fight, to defy fate but I was trapped, a helpless creature caught in a predator's grasp. My heart pounded, a desperate plea for mercy, and I cursed myself for believing that I could cheat death, that the thing that would bring me down would ultimately be the need for a book.

I gasped. The man's hand latched onto the back of my head, pulling at the tiny white hairs. My head snapped backwards, my eyes facing the ceiling. Tears streamed down my temples into my ears. The man looked over me, his eyes cold and desolate. There wasn't a hint of remorse, pity.

The cool blade of the dagger bit into my neck. "This is for Lettie and Isidore."

I'll see you soon, Mom and Dad.

I stared dead into the man's face and smiled. *Hello, Death.*

But my death was cut short as the wooden door to the cabin crashed open. His blade slipped, nicking a tiny part of my skin, as the man pulled back on my hair. He turned towards the door.

The legs of my chair gave out, sending me to the floor, and I blinked against the sharp jolt of pain that rang through my skull. *Ow.*

My vision blurred and I couldn't see much from the ground. Two legs sauntered into the cabin, long with well-tailored pants. My heart raced, not just because of the pain. The sound of a sword unsheathing ripped through the room.

I shimmied out of the ropes, pushing my feet. My arms scraped against the floor as I freed myself from the broken chair.

The mystery man entered my peripherals, shadowed by the low-lit candles of the cabin.

"And who might you be?" the older man slurred.

The mystery man looked down at me, emerald eyes piercing through the darkness. His voice was smooth and velvety as he spoke. "You owe me."

"For what?"

His golden sword glowed in the candlelight; red rubies sparkled across it's hilt like stars in the night sky, as he pointed it at the men.

But they didn't cower. No, they laughed and gods, was that the wrong move. Their amusement was quickly cut short.

With a swift fluid motion, the mystery man's sword pierced the throat of the old man.

In an instant, the one who tried to kill me ran at him, a warrior's cry escaping his lips. That cry was quickly replaced by gurgling. The golden sword slid through the younger man's body. Blood dripped from his mouth as he dropped to his knees.

He stared up at his killer. His face paled. "You bast—" he started but he was dead before he finished.

The man slowly pulled the sword from him. My captors lifeless body collapsed to the floor, blood pooling around him.

My parents' bodies flashed in my mind; their feet surrounded by similar puddles of red.

The mystery man sheathed his sword and stepped over the dead bodies toward me. My heart quickened.

He was a vision of deadly grace—and he had just saved my life.

I guess that's why I owe him.

I wasn't sure if I should be afraid or thankful, but I clutched a piece of the broken chair regardless. It wouldn't do much against him but at least it was something. I slipped my mask back on, pretending like the situation didn't send chills down my spine. "Are you here to kill me, too?" I raised a brow and tried to sit up even though my head screamed at me.

He reached an open hand to me, but I didn't take it. I stood up as graciously as I could, wiping the dirt off my black pants and navy tunic. My once-braided hair, now a mess of knots, fell over my chest, like white waves in the ocean. I looked up at the man who towered over me; his striking green eyes locked onto mine. I narrowed my gaze. He was probably about my age, early twenties. His jawline was strong with high cheekbones that complemented his sharp brows. Deep brown hair curled over his chiseled face, each strand impeccably trimmed.

"I believe a thank you is in order." His eyes searched my face like mine did his.

"Why help me?" I asked, refusing to give him the upper hand. "You could have let them kill me, went about your business." *Whatever that may be.*

My eyes followed the trim on his collar. The white coat he wore was lined with golden detailing, laced with intricate patterns. A red cloak rested on his shoulders. His clothes were tailored and very clean. I took another look at him and beamed.

This may just be my lucky day.

This man was clean and groomed, meaning he possibly— no, he *definitely*—came from money. And he could possibly have money on him. But I knew better than to let my guard down. I studied him for a few more moments before deciding. *Yes, this will be my lucky day.*

A soft smile crept across my face as I entertained the idea. "Thank you," I let some of the fear I masked slip into my voice, "for saving me."

He nodded, a curl bouncing on his forehead. "Maybe now you can help me?"

"Of course," I said a bit too eagerly. *For a reward, perhaps.*

"Well, you see, I'm looking for a place to stay here in..." his voice trailed off.

"Zandar," I finished for him. Outsiders were uncommon here and an outsider who didn't even know where he was? I raised my chin along with my guard.

"Zandar, yes. Sorry."

"A man of your status," I gestured to his clothes with a nod, "doesn't have a place to stay?"

"Are you judging me?" he asked, raising one of his sharp brows.

I returned the gesture and shrugged. I *was* judging him because it *was* odd. No one travels here, let alone by themselves. If the unforgiving cold wasn't reason enough, the sheer poverty of this town kept most sensible people away.

His hand moved to the hilt of his sword. A golden ring sat on his left pointer finger and *that* would fetch a nice price.

Should I try to kill him? Distract him and grab his sword? He'd made it look so easy; one swift motion and he'd be dead. I could take his things to the closest town. Someone would overlook the fact that it was me—the devil—and buy from me, if only for the right price. I could start a new life...

No, a tiny voice inside my head screamed. My conscience. *You're not a killer, Amara.* It reminded me.

"I'm not a killer," I repeated to myself, reassuring the voice.

The man's face drained of the little color left in his already pale skin.

Did I say that out loud?

"I truly am just looking for a place to stay," he said, knuckles whitening around the hilt of his sword.

I forced a small smile, distracting the inner battle brewing in me. *That isn't me.* "There are some inns, down the road from here."

"For a price, I assume?"

"You can't afford a stay?" I arched a skeptical brow.

"So judgmental." He smirked. "I'm Azral." He flashed his perfectly white teeth, extending his hand, but I could see through his confidence. Deep in his eyes he looked lost, maybe even a little broken. I was no stranger to that feeling.

I stepped back with a smirk, folding my arms.

His eyes twinkled with amusement. "Will I be seeing you in town?" he asked, turning towards the door.

"Not likely," I replied, my tone dripping with disdain. I couldn't risk coming into town again—not after this horrific trip. I had almost lost my life, only to be saved by this stranger. A flicker of gratitude sparked in me, and I couldn't help my growing curiosity.

"Could I offer you dinner?" I cleared my throat, heat creeping across my cheeks. "For saving my life." *It was the least I could do.*

"Dinner?" he mused. "You do owe me; I suppose I could take my payment in food."

I looked down at my dirt-stained clothes, embarrassment flooding my cheeks as I immediately regretted offering now.

"And where will this dinner be?"

I hadn't thought this through at all. My home—if you could even call it that—was no place to bring company, let alone someone who just saved my life. Panic set in as I scrambled to form a plan. "Meet me at the edge of town tomorrow," I said with a steady voice. "There's a clearing, just before the forest."

"Tomorrow it is then." The door swung shut behind him and his footsteps crunched through the snow until they were a whisper on the wind.

Silence settled in the air, my knees hitting the wooden floorboards was the only interruption. My mask faded and the tears of relief I'd held back fell like petals on a dying rose.

Relief that I was alive. My head dropped as I took each sacred breath.

Swallowing the knot in my throat, I steadied myself. I tightened my cloak around me, its worn fabric barely enough to hold back the chill waiting outside. My hand hesitated, trembling for just a moment, before I reached for the book—the reason I had risked everything. My fingers brushed its spine, and with a sharp breath, I pulled it from the shelf.

2

"MY LITTLE STAR," MY FATHER SAID, BEAMING at me as he painted my face delicately. His eyes sparkled like gold in the room's light and I couldn't help but giggle as the brush tickled my skin. He used shades of blue and gold, both vibrant and bold, swirling together in intricate designs that made me look like a fairy.

He finished, brushing my white hair behind my pointed ears and I felt like the most beautiful creature in the world.

"Beautiful," he whispered, reassuring my thoughts. "Just like your mother."

We stepped out of the room and into a hallway adorned with crystal blue and fiery orange ribbons. Servants bustled about, carrying trays of food and drinks. My small hand grasped my father's as we walked, my legs struggling to keep up with his long strides. He noticed my effort and gently lifted me into his arms. I played with the red waves on his head as his magic circled around me, warming my cold body.

He waved his hand and the candles on the walls flashed to life with a bright flame casting flickering shadows across the light blue stone. My mouth dropped in wonder as we approached two enormous glass doors.

"Welcome, Akailo" the silver clad guard said to my father. He swung the doors open, and a blinding light peaked through the room.

I squinted, shielding my eyes with one hand as we stepped into a grand hall filled with music and laughter...

I stumbled, tripping over my feet in the snow.

It was about a two-mile walk back to my cabin from the home I broke into. One I'd traversed many times. The dense forest swallowed me whole; its towering trees formed a dark canopy over me. The faint scent of pine lingered in the air, comforting in the darkness.

But it was in this solitude that my dreams became my favorite company, albeit dangerous company. They pulled me from reality, making me lose track of time as each one played out. They had started after the fire, greeting me each night like a lullaby and I replayed the memory of them whenever I got the chance.

Absentmindedly, I pushed my hair behind my ears, my fingers tracing their round shape. *Not pointy*, I reminded myself. Not magical. Just me.

Each dream felt like a piece of the story I was missing, a story that might explain who I was and where I came from. I was four when Isidore and Lettie found me on the beach, my life up to that point a mystery. And in the dreams, I was always a child in a magical world with a magical family. I assumed this was all a coping mechanism—a sick response to losing everything and everyone. But they were the only things that brought me any joy these days. They gave me something to hope for, something to hold onto, like that magical family existed somewhere if only I could reach them.

The man in my dreams, my magical father…*Nope,* not going there today because thinking about where I came from made me think about Isidore and Lettie. It made me think about the night everything was taken from me.

Someone had set that fire. Someone had impaled their corpses to the frozen ground—

Icy wind slapped my face, breaking me from my spiraling thoughts. The wind howled, as if scolding me for dwelling on it. I gritted my teeth and focused on the present. I had more pressing concerns tonight.

Azral.

I glanced over my shoulder, expecting the shadows to move. They didn't, but my pulse still quickened. Azral's name lingered in my mind like an unspoken promise. Who was he? Where did he come from? Why did he save me? Why, despite everything I knew about trusting strangers, did I feel like I could trust him?

And the final, most pressing question of all: what in the world would we have for dinner?

Food wasn't something I had in abundance. I could barely feed myself, let alone someone else. Gods willing, the traps I set would have something—anything—by tomorrow.

I trudged on until I spotted it: my cabin. A fragile beacon of safety, hidden from everyone who wanted me dead.

I pushed open the creaky door and let out a long sigh. I'd never been so happy to step foot in this tiny place. The whole thing was about the size of my bedroom. There was one very old bed, layered with years of dirt that I'd tried, and failed, to clean. Three windows lined the rickety walls. Two bordered the bed, the glass broken. I'd tried to nail boards to them but the old hammer I found only lasted so long before the top fell off. So, the cold breeze of the never-ending winter crept in.

The only intact window was by the front door, its rusty hinges squeaking every time I opened it. A fireplace sat against the wall to my left, red and brown bricks outlining it. To the right of my bed stood a wooden side table, the only piece of furniture in this place that looked somewhat whole. It held a lantern that lit the small room and my stack of books. I placed my new prize on top.

Beside the books were two silver daggers, their blades glowing faintly in the lantern's light. I didn't know how to use them, but they were better than nothing. *I probably should have brought them with me.*

I removed my cloak—the holes in it didn't do much to block the cold anyway—and tossed it on the small, also broken, chair next to the shattered mirror.

I grabbed a dagger from the side table, adding one more tally to the wooden wall. *Seventy-three days.*

Seventy-three days since everything changed, every*one*, too.

Allen told me it would be safer to stay with him until things passed over. Everyone in town blamed me. They never liked me—my white hair and bloodred eyes were always "unnatural". I was the feared orphan girl, the outcast. It wasn't much of a leap for them to believe I was capable of parricide when it's what they wanted to believe. *But was that enough to crucify me?*

"Witch," the kids would whisper when I was younger.

"Devil," they yelled now.

Their words plagued me, like a dark cloud hanging over my mind. I knew it was wrong; I knew *they* were wrong, but it still ate at me like a sickness and there was no cure.

So, I stayed inside, stayed with Allen. But safety came with a price, and soon enough, his intentions began to shift.

"You know, you are of age to be married," he would tell me after sliding his hand over my thigh. His home was nice. It was warm, there were blankets, fresh water and clean clothes.

Sighing, I pulled myself from the memory and placed the knife back on the table, surveying the tallies. A cold wind swept through the walls and the windows rattled. This cabin was truly dreadful.

But there was no Allen and there were no townspeople.

Kicking off my boots, I tossed some wood on the simmering flames and pulled on the fuzzy red socks I'd stolen. The flames grew larger than ever as I scooted up to the fire, tucking myself into the blanket before it. Even with the gusts of wind blowing through the cabin, the fire roared. Weeks out here and I finally learned to build a decent fire. I laughed to myself and smiled. *I guess I can add hearth-tender to my list of skills.*

Once my fingers had thawed, I crawled into bed, tugging the blanket tighter. I let my thoughts wander back to Azral. *Was he dangerous?* Probably. But so was everything else in my life.

My hand drifted to the thin wound on my neck. I traced the dried blood and shivered, not from the cold but from the memory. I'd almost died today. If it wasn't for him—

My fingers curled deeper into the blanket, and I whispered defiantly, as if daring fate itself, "Tomorrow will be better."

The cold sea breeze brushed against my skin, sending shivers down my spine and extinguishing the flame I'd conjured on my tiny fingertips. Icy waves crashed against rocky cliffs far below, water droplets transforming into snowflakes above me. With my head tilted back, I closed my eyes and laughed as the frosty flakes landed on my tongue.

"You're going to catch a cold out here," my father called from behind me.

"No, I won't," I yelled back, not bothering to turn around.

The air calmed but its icy presence continued to send chills over my small body. I huffed into the air, my warm breath mixing with the cold and turning into a fleeting misty cloud.

"Let's go." My father laughed.

I turned to look at him then; his golden eyes and red hair caught the bright sunlight as he picked me up and held me close. His body radiated heat, magic he used often to keep me warm.

"We can return to Lunhayven in a few weeks, okay?" he said, pinching my pointed ears.

Lunhayven was my favorite this time of year. It was just cold enough to build snow castles without them freezing into ice, so I didn't want to leave now.

Looking back, I spotted my crocheted dragon. The black and red yarn was obvious against the icy frost flowers.

"Papa!" I pointed to my favorite toy.

He chuckled, putting me down and I darted to pick it up. I reached the edge of the cliff, playfully kicking up the snow, laughing, but then my foot slipped and before I knew it, I was falling.

Falling...falling...and...

I gasped, bolting upright in bed. My pounding heart calmed as the cold air seeped through the cracks, sending a chill through me. I squinted, rubbing my sleepy eyes in the early morning sun and wrapped the fur blanket close.

I laid there until the sun reached its peak. I ignored my growling stomach and dry mouth. I couldn't move. I didn't want to move. I replayed the dream over and over, reminiscing in a place where I felt like I belonged, a childhood I was robbed of.

Rage replaced hunger, boiling in my stomach. It was that heat, and the thought that had been circling my mind since yesterday, that finally forced me out of bed.

Today, I would meet with Azral. The man who saved my life.

I shuffled to the dreaded mirror in the corner, pulling my hair into a braid and shivering as the ends grazed my waist. The once-white strands were stained with streaks of gray and brown from not being able to wash it properly. As I flung the braid over my shoulder, I leaned closer to the mirror. My hand slid across the cut on my neck; the scab's reddish tinge almost matched the shade of my irises. When my gaze lifted to meet them, I couldn't help but notice the bags under my eyes. No food, no sleep, no peace of mind—it had taken a toll on my body.

I grabbed my navy tunic from the bed and threw it on. The smell was unpleasant to say the least but it was the only shirt I owned so I'd take the smell over nothing. I slipped on my black boots and leather pants, tacked on my daggers—this time—and tucked myself into the holey cloak.

I looked in the mirror one last time, my shattered image laughing back at me. With a shake of my head, I slung my leather bag over my shoulder and braced against the chilly air.

I headed for the open clearing by the cabin to check my snares. Isidore taught me to hunt but setting a snare was one of the only things I remembered. My hope was short-lived, though, as the first two were empty. I lifted my head to the sky and folded my hands, praying to whoever may be listening. *Please, let there be something. I have an extra mouth to feed tonight.*

Walking to the final snare, a smile crept over my face. There, half-covered in snow, was a hare.

"Thank you," I whispered to whatever god decided to bless me today.

I reset the trap, putting the tiny creature in my bag. It should be enough to feed two. I hope.

I padded back to the cabin, tossing my bag by the door. By the fire, I fumbled with my knife, clumsily cutting and peeling away the skin like I'd seen my dad do. It wasn't perfect, and I winced at the mess, but I managed to get the meat ready and tossed it over the fire. The pelt sat in a crumpled heap nearby—I wasn't sure if I'd ruined it or not. I wiped my hands on my cloak and tried to tidy up, but the smell still hung heavy in the air. My home wasn't the best spot for dinner, and given his clothes, Azral might just run when he saw the place.

My stomach turned, a knot tightening in my gut. Was I nervous because of Azral, because I was going to have dinner with a man—something I'd only ever read about.

I'd spent my entire life as an outsider, the punchline of cruel jokes. Friends? I'd never had any, let alone a boyfriend. The only people I'd ever spent time with were my parents. *What would we even talk about?* This wasn't just uncharted territory—it was a completely foreign concept.

He saved your life, my conscience reminded me. I nodded to myself. Yes, I owed him.

I pushed every thought aside and took a long deep breath, staring at myself in the mirror. I loosened my hair from its messy braid. A cold bucket of melted snow—freshly gathered—waited for me. I dipped my hand in and began to work out the dirt, the rhythmic strokes a soothing counterpoint to my racing thoughts. By the time I finished, I looked more like myself.

"It's just dinner, Mar," I told myself. *It's the least you could do.* I nodded with a confidence I didn't feel.

Without another thought, I threw on my cloak and headed to meet Azral.

3

MY DREAMS DIDN'T ACCOMPANY ME ON THIS walk.

Azral did.

The clearing we met at was silent when I arrived, the snow sparkling under the moonlight. My breath curled into the air as I adjusted my cloak, scanning the shadows for any sign of him.

"Cold night to be out."

I jumped, spinning toward the voice. Azral stood at the edge of the clearing, his dark form blending with the trees. His emerald eyes gleamed.

"It is," I said, trying to keep my voice steady.

He stepped closer, his presence commanding yet oddly comforting. His gaze flicked to my throat, and I caught a glimmer of something—concern? Regret?

"Are you okay?" he asked.

I nodded, my fingers brushing the scab. "Thanks to you."

Azral studied me for a moment before clearing his throat. I turned on my heels and he quickly caught up, towering next to me. He moved with effortless grace, his dark curls bouncing with every stride. Meanwhile, my heart pounded in my chest, my breath misting in the icy air. A bead of sweat formed on my brow despite the cold, and I stumbled, the uneven snow catching my boot.

A hand steadied me—his hand—firm and sure. His touch lingered, and a shiver ran down my spine.

"Thank you," I murmured, my voice small, head down, cheeks burning.

The cabin came into view, familiar and worn, and I exhaled in relief. Back on familiar terrain, I let out the breath I hadn't realized I was holding. I pushed the creaky door open with a cringe and tried not to look for Azral's reaction. Instinctively, I pulled my cloak off and threw it on the chair. I turned to him and watched as he echoed my movements, throwing his cloak, as well. The chair creaked under the added weight and tipped over.

"Oh, I'm sorry." He lurched towards the fallen chair.

I tried not to laugh. "It's okay."

We both reached for the fallen items, our hands meeting once again. Our eyes locked as I looked up. The crisp air, the soft glow of the setting sun, and the rustling of leaves faded into the background.

My stomach fluttered with the unfamiliar feeling, and I cleared my throat and mind, trying to get it to go away.

"Well," I said, lifting the chair and carefully placing the cloaks on it. "Please, have a seat." I gestured towards the fireplace.

Azral hesitated for a moment, his hand hovering over his sword belt, as though unsure whether it was truly safe to part with it. Finally, with a slow, deliberate motion, he removed the belt and leaned the golden weapon against the wall by the door. His movements were calm, but his gaze swept the room, taking in every corner as though assessing it—or me.

His once-pristine clothes were now tattered and dirty, his pants covered in grime and blood stains from the fight the day before.

I watched him closely, my pulse quickening despite my best efforts to seem composed. He didn't seem like the type to steal, but who could say? A flicker of doubt crept into my mind. I took a step back, subtly angling myself between him and my precious books.

I carefully watched as he sat, changing his position a few times on the floor. Once he settled, I plopped down in front of him, overly aware of how unladylike it was. I shifted, trying to make myself more presentable and awkwardly pushed my knees to one side, holding myself up with my hand. *Gods, it was so uncomfortable.*

"So..." I let the word drag on my lips. I should have come up with something to say, questions, facts, anything.

"Care to share how you got yourself in that situation yesterday?"

I coughed to hide my discomfort and mumbled, "There was a book I needed. I tried to sneak in."

"You almost got yourself killed...because of a book?" His sharp brow raised and he tilted his head.

All the men I'd come across in Zandar were rugged, worn. The constant cold was a harsh companion. Azral was too clean, shiny, almost like a dream. He had the stature of a lord from HiVale. A far, far away city I've only ever heard few whispers about. He was undeniably good looking, *very* distracting, and the fact we were alone kept sneaking to the forefront of my mind.

So, I said the first thing on my tongue. "Funny story." I grinned awkwardly, trying to play off the tension. "My parents died."

"Oh, I'm—" His eyes widened, mouth gaping.

"Oh, no!" I stuttered. "Well, they were murdered. There was a fire and blood..." I rolled my eyes like it was nothing. I didn't want to seem like this sad girl, to make him uncomfortable, but I couldn't help my sweaty palms and heavy eyes. Realizing he was waiting for me to continue, I plastered on a pleasant smile. "It was a long time ago."

The lie felt like sand in my mouth.

"I'm so sorry." His eyes were kind, almost understanding.

"Thank you." I nodded. I could be polite. That was normal.

"But why would those men try to kill you?" he questioned.

My lips tightened. "Yes, well, everyone thinks I did it." *Everyone thinks I killed my parents in cold blood.*

He paused, his eyes searching my face. "But you didn't?"

Could he see through my mask, see the hurt lying deep in my soul?

"No." My voice wavered, almost betraying me. I could have cried—gods, I wanted to. But crying felt like surrender, and I couldn't allow myself that. Not here, not right now. "I didn't."

His expression softened. "I know it's not easy," he whispered, his voice barely audible. "Losing someone you love."

His voice trailed off and a shadow fell over his face.

"You lost someone, too?" The words slipped from my lips.

He watched the dancing flames for a few breaths, his features dark with sadness. He nodded and looked back at me, his eyes glassy. "My mother."

My heart dropped into my stomach; it ached for him. "How?" I whispered.

He paused, fiddling with his fingers—his pain. "She was very sick."

I knew my words would mean nothing, could heal nothing. So, I stayed silent, and we sat in our grief for a few quiet moments.

He stared into the fire, the pain in his face was evident as if he was reliving the moment his life changed forever—an expression I knew I'd worn more than once. When he looked back at me, the light returned to his gaze. "You won't be sad forever."

I took a long breath and nodded.

He was right. He *had* to be.

"You have a beautiful home," he said softly, changing the subject.

A laugh ripped from my lips, but I quickly covered my mouth. "I'm sorry," I managed through my laughter, "you think this is beautiful?"

"It may not be the nicest place, but you," he paused, smiling, "you bring a warmth to it the rest of the town doesn't have."

That flutter returned to my stomach and I couldn't help but smile. This time, I didn't try to force it away.

"Thank you." I cleared my throat.

"You don't need to thank me." He took in more of the cabin, not that there was much to look at. He gestured towards the small stack of books by the bed. "So, did you get the sequel?"

A sinister smile broke free and I bit at my bottom lip, trying to hide my joy. "I did."

I looked over to the table. The book I grabbed on the way out of that death trap sat on top.

"My sister has hundreds of books, maybe even thousands," he offered, admiring the small stack.

"Your sister?"

"Yes." He snickered.

My stomach fluttered again and I couldn't help but laugh along with him, his laugh like a melody in my ears. The sound caught me off guard, chipping away at my doubts. Surely someone who spoke so fondly of their sister couldn't be a threat... right?

"She'll read anything she can get her hands on." But his smile quickly faded. "I'm sorry, I—I didn't mean—your family. I didn't mean to brag about my sister like that."

"Just because my family is dead doesn't mean you can't talk about yours," I quipped, trying to lighten the moment.

"I—"

"It's okay, really." I wasn't sure if I was reassuring him or myself.

His brows fell and his eyes narrowed. "Did anyone ever question the accusation that you did it, that you—"

"Murdered my parents? No, it was never questioned." I looked towards the flickering flames and tugged at the ends of my hair. "Hatred flows through the blood of the people in Zandar—it's what keeps them warm at night. The only ones who ever truly loved me were Isidore and Lettie."

His eyes—filled with a mix of sorrow and hope—held mine captive. The tiny voice in my head, once a distant whisper, now echoed with certainty.

Trust him. And I decided to do just that.

I took in a breath, a wave of emotions washed over me. Anger, sadness, determination. The truth felt like a heavy weight being lifted from my chest. His eyes pulled at all the strings of my tortured heart, pulling the hesitation out of me.

"I want to find them," I admitted, to him and to myself. "I want to find the people who killed my family." *And I want to find the parents in my dreams.*

The second half was a truth only for me but saying those words out loud was like reclaiming a part of me—a part that had been stolen.

Keep going, my conscience urged me.

"My parents were taken from me that night, my home burned to ashes and their bodies left for some sick display like they were nothing, *nobody.*" I gritted my teeth, my blood boiling. "I want to find the people who did that to them—to me. I want them to feel that pain." A fire inside me grew, consuming my body and thoughts.

I glanced behind him to where his sword rested. His head followed mine and a knowing glint appeared in his emerald eyes. He understood. He saw my fear, my helplessness, and I remembered the way he cut through the men who tried to kill me with ease.

He could teach me. He could make me strong.

"I need your help," I said, my voice sharp. "Train me."

My heart hammered against my ribs as I studied his face. Had I lost my mind? Asking, no, demanding he become my savior.

I would give him about five seconds before he ran.

But he didn't. And as we sat in the silence, I realized how much I needed him, how much I needed to *do* something about their deaths.

His lips pursed; his fingers tapped against his knee. He looked back at the sword, then me. He leaned forward. "After my mother died," his eyes locked onto mine, "I wanted a fresh start. That pain and that suffering, it's etched in my heart. I would have done anything for a sense of purpose." He inhaled, his chest rising and falling with grief. "She always told me I was given a gift, a talent." He looked back to his sword with a gentle smile. "I think it would be wrong to waste it."

My heart skipped and I couldn't help the hope that bloomed.

"I'll help you with anything you need, Amara."

A wide grin grew on Azral's lips. I giggled, my own grin mirroring his. He was a flicker of light in the darkness, a beacon. My smile grew even wider at the mad thought that crossed my mind. *Maybe he'll even help me find the parents in my dreams.* I pushed the thought aside. *One crazy move at a time, Mar.*

"Should we celebrate?" I reached for the roasting sticks over the fire. The metal skewering the meat was still hot. I wrapped my sleeve around my hand to grab them—

"Careful—" I yelled as Azral's hand came into view, gripping the piping hot stick. "It's hot," I finished but he didn't react.

"It's not too bad," he said, already biting into the meat.

I gaped as he took another bite and another and another. All the while he held the metal that should have seared the skin from his hand. Azral just devoured the food like he hadn't eaten in months. But the muscles popping through his shirt told me otherwise.

"This is amazing," he said around a mouthful.

A nervous laugh escaped my lips. "You don't need to lie." It was possibly the worst food anyone had ever consumed but it kept me alive.

"I'm serious." He said with a piece of meat stuck on his gums. "I haven't had a home cooked meal in..." He looked up, wracking his brain. "I don't remember how long but it's been a very long time."

"Home?" I asked, biting into my own food now that it had cooled. "Where would that be for you?"

He paused, his gaze distant. "I don't think I know anymore. It used to be a place, a feeling. But now...it's just a memory."

A heavy weight settled on my chest. Our losses had left us drifting, like two ships, both searching for a safe harbor.

"So, when do you want to start training?" he asked as he finished his food.

"The sooner the better."

"Tomorrow, then?" His face softened.

I bit my lip, trying to hide the sudden flush creeping across my cheeks. "Tomorrow," I said quickly, a nervous laugh escaping before I could stop it. It was just training. Nothing more. I repeated it in my head to steady myself.

He grinned and a sudden, warmth grew in my stomach. "It's a date."

I blinked, caught off guard by the words. A date? I had read about them in my books—stories of stolen moments and shared glances—but I'd never actually experienced anything like that.

I looked out the window behind him, the moon now high in the sky telling me it was almost time for sleep. My dreams called for me, begging me to return. I stood and wiped the dust from my knees. Azral followed suit, and I couldn't help but blush as he stood so close, his presence filling the small space. His stare pierced me, and the intensity of it made my heart race. I felt like he could see right through me.

"I guess I should be going," he said, distracted.

"No." The word slipped from my lips before I could even think. My cheeks heated. *What am I saying?*

"No." I cleared my throat, trying to sound confident. "You should probably keep a low profile in town, the bodies—" I paused. "They've probably found them by now. It would be safer—" I stuttered. *Gods, I can't believe I'm going to say this.* "It would be safer if you stayed here."

His body went rigid. "I can't impose."

"You saved my life, Azral. The least I can do is give you a safe place to sleep."

He hesitated, his gaze fixed on the floor. Then, a flicker of gratitude passed through his eyes. "Thank you," he muttered.

"Of course." I turned towards my bed but before I could take a step, he gently caught my arm. Time stood still as our eyes met, a silent understanding passing between us. He wouldn't try anything. He wouldn't run. *He* was safe. The world dimmed as he moved his hand away.

My blush deepened. Collecting myself, I kicked off my boots. He sat back in front of the fireplace, pulling his legs to his chest as he stared into the soft glow of the flames. I grabbed the dagger from my boot and placed it under my pillow. As much as I liked him, I didn't know him. *Better safe than sorry.* I slipped into bed and huddled beneath my blanket, silently studying him as he lay on the wooden floor. A part of me wanted to reach out, to bridge the gap between us, but another part, a more cautious part, urged me to keep my distance.

He stared at the ceiling for a long while and I secretly watched him. Watched each and every breath as his chest rose and fell. He turned his head towards my stack of books and gazed up at me. I threw the blanket over my head, cheeks aflame. He laughed, which only made me blush more, and I couldn't help but smile.

"What kind of books do you like?" he asked.

"These days, anything I can get my hands on. Back home—" I stopped, pushed the crippling thought away. "I like to read anything. This one," I stuck a handout from under the blanket and pointed to one of the books, "is about dragons, these mythical creatures who fly through the skies. I also like history books and a bit of...romance."

He grinned. "Have you ever heard the story of Saigus and Melenyz?"

Of course I have. Everyone knew the love story of the Sun and Moon gods—but I liked hearing his voice.

"I'm not familiar." I turned over in bed, leaning my head on my hand to see him.

His expression softened. "Well, surely you know of the Sun God, Saigus, and the Moon Goddess, Melenyz?"

"Of course."

"Well, it's said that he spends his eternal life chasing her, for only one day a year they can be together. Their love spans over centuries, over worlds, each year growing stronger."

I bit my lip, warmth spreading through me. *Was he a romantic, too?* "It's a beautiful story, to be loved like that."

"It's something I dream of one day," he confessed, his grin slipping.

"Me, too," I whispered. I tucked myself further under the blanket, my dagger slipping through my fingers.

"Goodnight, Amara."

"Goodnight, Azral."

4

"SWEETIE, THAT'S TOO HEAVY FOR YOU. MAYBE
when you're a bit older, yeah?" My father cut in as I struggled
to lift the golden sword from the table.

"I want to learn to fight just like you." My tiny voice
echoed in the marble room. I turned to him, white strands of
hair falling in front of my face.

"Why don't we start with something like this?" My father
switched the heavy golden sword for a small wooden blade
from a nearby table. The wooden dagger he handed me was
much easier to hold and I ran around him, playfully slashing
the back of his knee, giggling.

"You're going to be trouble when you're older, aren't you?"

"Teach me, Papa. I'm ready to learn. I want to be strong like you and Mama," I said through breaths as I continued circling him, slashing the air with the wooden dagger.

"One day, sweetie, one day you'll be stronger than all of us."

I almost jumped out of bed from the knock at the door, pulling me from my dream.

"Amara, are you ready?" Azral called. He'd been with me for four months now, and somehow, it felt like he'd been here much longer. Our routine was set in stone—even if I constantly overslept.

"One second!" I yelled, springing out of bed. I threw on my usual tunic and straightened out my pants, grabbing my daggers from the end table and placing them in my belt. I pulled my hair into two braids, not bothering to untangle the knots, and ran out the door.

These past few months had been nothing short of unexpected. I never imagined it could be so easy to connect with someone, especially someone like him. Maybe that's what I needed all along—an outsider, someone who understood loss the way I did. Someone who didn't see me as the town pariah but as something *more*. And it wasn't just our shared pain—it was the way his smile rippled through the room when I would read out loud to him at night, the way my laugh echoed his when we laid in the snow and I taught him how to make snow-fairies.

Gods, that laugh had the power to unravel me completely.

"Hi," I said, my breath heavy from the whirlwind dressing.

"Hi." Azral beamed, his eyes glowing in the morning sun.

His hands were behind his back and I couldn't help my curiosity.

"You got something there?"

He pulled out a flower. Its deep maroon petals graced my fingers as he handed it to me. He'd brought me one almost every day for the past few weeks, and now there were dozens of them in the makeshift vase back inside. They were black dahlias, he told me. I never asked where he got them—by now, I didn't care.

"I spoke with Mic this morning; he may have something for us," Azral said as I stepped back outside.

Mic had knocked on the cabin door a few weeks ago and Azral had thrown me behind him, sword pointed at the stranger. "Who are you? How did you find this place?" Azral's voice had cut through the stillness of the snow.

Mic had raised his arms, fear swirling in his eyes. "I come with helpful information; I hope."

Az was on guard the whole time as he told us of the man he ran into at his tavern. He had been delivering papers when the mystery man drunkenly revealed he was paid handsomely to attack my parents.

Ever since, we'd kept tabs on Mic while he helped us search for where the man might be now.

"Do you think he could have found him?" My heart raced at the thought. *Could he have found my parents' killer?*

But Azral didn't answer, instead, honing in on the anger he knew I felt, sharpening me. "Are you ready?"

I nodded, preparing my daggers.

"Okay, now show me what you've learned." Azral winked. Four months of training had transformed me from a clumsy mess into a fairly skilled fighter, at least with daggers—

swordplay was a different story. We'd started sword training but when I almost chopped his hand off, we thought it best to stick with smaller blades.

Every day, he had me practice landing a hit on him, running these exhausting drills. He insisted we take breaks, but I couldn't. I pushed myself. I needed this. I needed to be strong, to face whoever took my family from me.

"Just like yesterday. Give it your best shot, *Princess*." He winked. He'd recently started using the nickname. When he first said it, over dinner one night, I detested it. I was sitting, very unladylike, with a pile of food in my mouth when I spat, "I'm anything but." But he carried on with it and I no longer minded.

Now, I whirled, spinning into action as I moved on him, my steps measured and deliberate, mindful of where each foot landed in the snow. Circling him, I sliced through the frigid air as he bounded away, gradually getting a better feel for his movements. I needed the element of surprise. He was taller and stronger but I was faster. My speed and small body were my only advantages against him. If I could just find some way to distract him, I could get the upper hand. I moved on him again, each step precise as I ran behind him. Just as I was about to swing low, I paused, watching his feet. He was ready to step to the right. So, I stepped left, stood, and slashed the dagger right over his chest.

What I thought was my victory was short lived. The blade, now level with his chest and my face, sat in his fingertips. Without a scratch, he took a step forward, forcing me into a tree. The bark brushed against my back but that wasn't what sent chills down my spine and flutters to my stomach. Azral looked down and his eyes locked with mine.

"Are you distracted?" he whispered, his voice a soothing contrast to the frantic beat of my heart.

"No," I replied, too quickly, through heavy breaths. *I was definitely distracted.*

He smiled, knowingly, and breathed, his eyes roaming over me. "Does this distract you, Princess?" His free hand traced a very slow path down my side, his fingertips igniting sparks with each delicate touch, the heat between us intensifying.

"No," I managed, slower this time. My eyes never left his.

"Are you sure?" he pressed, his voice carrying the hint of a challenge.

"I'm sure." I swallowed even as I struggled to catch my breath.

He backed away and my heart ached with the distance. "Well, I managed to disarm you," he said, dangling both my daggers like a prize. "But," he dragged out the word, walking back towards me, "you did manage to catch me by surprise."

Each step made my heart beat a little faster. I took a similar step towards him, meeting his challenge. His eyes were soft as he studied me. The back of his hand was warm as he brushed his knuckles against my cheek. I let my face fall into him as he brushed a loose strand of hair behind my ear. "You're ready, Amara," he said, his eyes glued on the little hairs he tucked for me. "Mic will take us tomorrow. He thinks he found the man's home."

A weight lifted from my chest but my heartbeat quickened, so fast I could hear it in my ears. "Are you serious?" My brows furrowed. "You're serious," I breathed.

Az stared back at me, those emerald depths filled with a fear that haunted me.

He was scared. And so was I.

"We're really going to do this?" I asked, my voice barely above a whisper. I searched his face, desperate for answers. What happens next, after we finish this—if we finish this? What does that mean for us? He'd agreed to help me, to train me, but we never talked about what would come after. Would he leave? Go back home?

I hadn't prepared for this—for him. For how much I needed him. Would he leave me when it was all over? Would he want to? I searched his eyes, hoping to find some certainty, but all I found was... uncertainty. A fear I hadn't realized I'd been carrying.

I wanted him. I wanted to tell him all my crazy thoughts, my dreams. I wanted to have every meal with him, every conversation. I wanted it all—with him. But was it too soon? Could I even ask for that, for everything?

His gaze softened, but my heart still raced with the questions I didn't dare ask aloud. "I have to tell you something," I whispered, but before the words could leave my mouth, his hand gently traced my cheek, tilting my face upwards.

His fingers, warm and comforting, tangled in my hair as his lips met mine. The world shifted, and for the first time in what felt like forever, I was whole. Each kiss was a promise, a vow, a declaration. Placing his forehead on mine, his thumb brushed my lips. "We're really going to do this."

The fire glowed stronger than ever tonight, a reflection of what grew inside me.

I placed my daggers on the table with Az's sword, the safety they once brought replaced by him. I unbraided my hair, twirling the white waves in my fingers as I stared at my shattered reflection, which no longer matched what I felt inside.

I crawled into bed, looking at the latest flower he'd given to me in the vase. Az fiddled with the fire, the soft glow highlighting the sharp lines of his face. I couldn't help but admire him—the way his hair had grown longer, his curls brushing the bottom of his ears as he turned toward me. A slow, playful grin spread across my lips.

My heart beat faster with every step he took toward the bed. He stopped at the edge, towering over me, and I could have sworn my heart was going to jump from my chest.

"Az," I whispered. My confidence dwindled.

"Yes, Princess?" He flashed a smile. *Gods, this man was bewitching.*

"Stay here tonight?" I shifted in the bed, leaving an open space for him.

I didn't miss the faint blush that colored his cheeks as he climbed into bed. His body was stiff at first, like he wasn't sure what to do with himself, but I nestled against him without hesitation. Every sound seemed amplified—the rustle of the sheets, the crackle of the fire, the steady rhythm of his breathing.

My head rested against his warm chest, and I let my hand trace slow circles on his stomach. His arm draped over me, and his thumb sketched lazy patterns on my shoulder.

For the first time in what felt like forever, I could breathe.

But the peace was fleeting. My thoughts turned to the man who had taken everything from me—my parents, my home. The anger simmered again, hot and volatile. And under it all was uncertainty. What would I do when I finally found him? Could I become the person I had been accused of being all these years? *A killer?*

"Az," I murmured, my voice barely audible above the crackle of the fire.

"Hm?" His voice was soft, sleepy.

"What... what do you think I should do... when we find him?" I paused, staring at the flower on the bedside table.

His body stiffened slightly beneath me, but his hand never stopped its gentle tracing on my shoulder. "What do you want to do, Amara?"

"I... I don't know." I hesitated, swallowing the lump in my throat. "I've thought about it so many times. Getting my revenge. Killing him, making him suffer for what he did. But would that make me..." *Would that make me like him? Would it make me what everyone already thinks I am?*

"A killer," Az finished for me.

I nodded against his chest, the word heavy on my heart.

Az's hand moved to tilt my chin up so I could meet his burning gaze, but there was no judgment. Only warmth. "Whatever choice you make, I'll stand by you."

I searched his face, desperate to believe him. "And what if I can't decide? What if I don't know what's right?"

"Then we'll figure it out together," he said simply, his voice a steadying anchor.

My conscience, absent for so long, offered me nothing—not even a whisper. All I had to hold onto were Azral's words. And for now, that was enough.

No dreams came to me tonight, the warmth of Azral was all I needed to drift away.

5

IT WAS ALMOST A FULL DAY'S WALK TO MEET
Mic. The sun set as Az spoke with him and I watched from
the shadows of the alley. We were a few towns over, one that
was shockingly worse off than ours. Few people lived here and
the ones that did, well, I couldn't really call it living. Its worn-
out buildings were relics, a land forgotten. The air was heavy
with a mixture of mustiness and decay, rats scurrying through
the streets, their beady eyes glowing as they navigated piles of
garbage.

Az signaled and I ran over to join them. Mic led us
through the shadows. Kicked stones echoed with the crunch
of littered filth beneath our boots as broken windows peered at

us like hollow eyes, their shattered glass reflecting the deterioration.

"He should be in there," Mic whispered, nodding toward the building in front of us. It was a tall apartment, connected to a row of others, but only one window a few floors up was lit by a single candle. Az nodded, shaking Mic's hand before he disappeared into the darkness.

The door creaked open. I cringed as we crept in, cautious of the aged wood floors. Az lifted his hand to the right, signaling me to take the lead up the stairs and down the hall, testing the boards that would be quietest. We entered a larger room and I halted mid-step.

Books were stacked to the ceiling. Tables were laid with maps and notes. Candles flickered, lighting the room as wax dripped onto open pages. And there, right in front of us, was the man Mic had given us.

He was passed out in a chair. Drool ran down his long beard and the bottle of liquor in his hand spilled over. Each drop hitting the floor echoed. Az moved behind me, his hand tracing my hip as he moved behind the chair. I stood before the drunk man, my dagger ready at his throat.

I glanced at the pages on the table next to me. Maps and textbooks were laid out in a craze. There was a map of Zandar, our country. A small red circle was inked on my town. My blood boiled but I was too distracted by the larger map next to it. There in the corner was Zandar, but this map was different than the ones I knew. A large piece of land sat above my own, an ocean separating the two. My eyes narrowed on it, Kaluth, the top read. Azral also studied the maps. His eyes filled with confusion and we shared a look. *What in the world was this?*

Azral looked at the man, the maps, and then me again. A brief glint of gold I'd never seen before flickered in his eyes but before I could question it, he grabbed a bottle from the table and poured the dark liquor over our captive, waking him with a sound one would never believe could come from a grown man.

"What the—?"

"I wouldn't make any sudden movements if I were you and I do appreciate only speaking when asked." I smiled, my facade perfectly in place, as I moved towards him and ran my dagger along his beard, the blade so sharp it sliced off the ends.

The man scanned the room, slowly turning in the wooden chair and spotting Azral behind him. His eyes narrowed. With a nod to me, Azral moved from table to table, reviewing the other maps and documents, leaving me to deal with the drunken fool.

I knew he would be back at my side if I needed him.

I straightened. "What can you tell me about the deaths of Isidore and Lettie?" I hoped my voice came across confident, cruel, even as my insides went watery.

He shrugged. "They were murdered, no?" A bleary grin slipped across his face and my hand tightened on the dagger.

I flashed my teeth and leaned in until our noses were inches apart. His breath smelled of booze and it took everything in me to keep my expression even. "Murdered and left on display. Ring a bell?"

He pondered, his eyes searching my features.

Az always told me I had beautiful but intimidating eyes. He had said my blood-colored pupils were one of a kind and, in this moment, I relished the fact they brought fear to my enemies. So, I let the man look at me, let him take in what he needed before deciding what to say next.

I bared my teeth, a silent warning, and waited. He cleared his throat and finally, he spoke.

"Ah, yes." The man rubbed his liquor-soaked beard. "Yes, I remember them. A pretty price was placed on their heads."

He knows. *This man knows something.*

"Who wanted them killed?" I asked, trying not to show my surprise. Az stiffened in the corner.

He looked at Azral, then back at me. "Not sure." He shrugged. "But you"—he tilted his head—"eyes like the blood moon, hair like snow..." His gaze lingered on me with an intensity that sent shivers down my spine, and not the good kind. I stood frozen, my breath caught in my throat, as he studied me, *recognized* me.

Then, he uttered words that made my heart stop.

"Yes, you're the girl they wanted kept alive."

Time stood still as his words echoed in my mind, each syllable sending a jolt of adrenaline coursing through my veins. *Alive?* The gravity of his words sunk in, the mask I had worn to shield myself crumbled away, leaving me exposed and all too vulnerable. Questions raced in a frantic flurry, each one more urgent than the last. *Why me? What did they want from me? Who are they? Why would they want to kill Isidore and Lettie?*

"Who?" was all I could muster. "Who?" I begged, gripping his filthy shirt.

But he didn't answer. He only laughed, a sinister glint in his eyes. I shoved him back in the chair, circling him like a bear hunting prey. The rage boiled within me, threatening to spill over, and the dagger shook in my hand. He took a swig from his bottle as I stopped behind him.

"Tell me," I pressed against his ear through gritted teeth but, still, he said nothing. I felt Azral move behind me, expecting him to talk me down, comfort me, but his words were ones I never thought I'd hear.

"Kill him," Azral said.

My heart stopped. I turned to look at him but he placed his hand on my shoulder, holding me in place, his touch both comforting and chilling. *Did he say...?*

"Kill him," Azral said again, firmer. His voice was low and cold, a tone I'd never heard from him.

I felt the man shiver in the chair under me as if he was just as surprised. He did as any helpless soul would do and pleaded.

"You're not a killer," the man muttered, like he might convince me.

"How do you know?" I leaned into the game.

Maybe this was Azral's tactic, to scare him into telling us the truth, telling us everything he knows.

I felt Azral move closer, his presence a dark, comforting pressure against my back. His hand brushed my elbow, guiding my blade toward the man's throat.

The cold edge of the steel sent a shiver through me. *Am I a killer?*

"Tell me what you know," I said, my voice low, carrying a hollow promise. "And I won't kill you." The words felt more like a question to myself than a threat.

But he said nothing. A laugh left his lips, a low, mocking sound that clawed at my sanity. It made me angry—no, furious. The kind of anger that burned like wildfire, consuming everything rational in its path. It fueled the darkest parts of me, the parts I tried to keep buried.

My parents had been murdered, ripped from me, and no one had done anything.

This man had stolen my happiness, my family, my peace. And now, he dared to laugh at me?

My hands trembled as the rage coursed through me, white-hot and unrelenting. I stepped closer, feeling the storm building. His laughter wasn't just mockery; it was a reminder of how powerless I had been. How powerless I still was.

My hand steadied. I knew I wasn't thinking straight.

"Any final words?" I breathed, my tone devoid of emotion, my thoughts clouded by rage.

"Good luck, *Amara.*"

Before the weight of the man's words fully registered, my blade sliced through his flesh, crimson rivers flowing down his clothes. Time stood still as I watched the life drain from his body, his words now the only thing echoing in my mind, a haunting melody.

Amara.

His bottle hit the floor. The glass shattered in the frozen room.

A fog clouded my mind like my body had acted on its own, a puppet controlled by anger, rage. Cold dread settled over me. I stood before the man, each tiny piece of shattered glass crunching beneath my boots.

This man, this stranger, knew my name.

And now he's dead.

The room was silent, the only sound was his blood. Each splash hit the ground, an affirmation of my worst nightmare.

Drip, drip, drip.

I didn't know how long I stood there for, over the body of the man I had killed. The part of me that was supposed to feel better, to feel avenged, remained still, unshaken. Was this what revenge was supposed to feel like? *Empty?*

"You're not a killer." His voice played in my mind.

Drip, drip, drip.

The sound of his blood reverberated around us.

"We need to go!" Azral's voice, sharp and urgent, cut through the silence. He moved with a frantic energy, his hands flying as he gathered documents. "Amara!" His words were a blur, his focus solely on securing the papers as if they held the key to our survival.

"Yes?" My voice cracked, looking up from the body that had now fallen from the chair. Tears streamed silently down my face, mingling with the crimson liquid on the floor.

"We need to get out of here."

"Okay," I whispered. "Okay." I looked at my hands. Blood covered them and the dagger I still held. "Okay," I repeated to myself.

I placed the dagger back in my belt and, with shaky hands, wiped the tears from my cheeks. The blood on my fingers was still warm as it smeared across my skin. "Okay."

Baby, a woman's voice whispered through my mind. *Baby, we have to go*, the voice repeated urgently.

"Hello?" I looked around but Azral was the only one here.

"Amara?" His hand clasped my cheek, his eyes filled with concern as they searched mine.

It's too late, a male voice answered and it sounded all too familiar.

My heart sank as visions flooded my mind with the sound of a voice I had come to know only in my dreams. Flames flickered in my head, intensifying with each passing moment. I covered my eyes with one hand while the other pressed against my temples, throbbing with a sharp pain.

Fear coursed through me. Each flash of the vision made my heart beat faster and faster.

"Amara!" Azral's voice was muffled as I dropped to the bloody floor.

Drip, drip, drip.

I tried to reach up to him but another image flashed in my mind: It was a woman with long flowing white hair, pointed ears, and bright blue eyes. She kneeled, flames growing behind her.

Baby, the woman said again, her voice echoing as the pain grew.

Drip, drip, drip.

Azral pulled me tight to his chest. His arms wrapped around my entire head as I leaned against him. I could feel his heartbeat, strong, steady, but fast. *He was scared.*

Visions of the man I had just killed surged through my mind, overlapping with visions of that woman.

"It's going to be okay," Azral whispered, his heart still pounding.

It's going to be okay, the woman whispered only to me.

Azral lifted me in his arms as I drifted in and out of reality, in and out of the visions. Waves of darkness and a heaviness in my head hit me and my last words, before drifting off, made Azral's heart skip.

"Mama?"

6

MY EYES FLUTTERED OPEN TO THE RISING
orange and pink rays filtering through the cracks in the cabin
walls.

Sunrise.

Had the whole day passed?

"Amara." Az's voice pulled me from the haze, and then he
was there, rushing to my side. The wood groaned beneath his
weight as he sat on the edge of the bed, leaning close. His
thumb brushed against my cheek, his eyes wild and frantic.
"Are you okay?"

My head throbbed, my thoughts blurred, trapped
somewhere between now and the memory of my dagger
slicing into flesh. *Drip. Drip. Drip.* I could still hear the blood
pooling on the floor. I blinked, struggling to focus on him.

"What happened?" I looked to my now clean hands, then back to Azral. "I killed him." The words were dry, like I had to remind myself. "You told me too." I blinked, recounting the scene in fragmented flashes.

Az's head fell, and shame washed over his sharp features. When his eyes finally met mine, I saw it—a raw, aching pain that mirrored my own. The sight of him like that made my chest tighten, my anger wavering, breaking apart under the weight of his hurt.

"When he said they wanted you alive, I felt it," his voice was low and desperate. "Danger. Danger for you, for us. Who are *they*, Amara? Who would go so far to hurt you?"

Az flinched, his jaw tightening as he looked away. "I'm sorry, Amara," he whispered, his voice thick with remorse. "It shouldn't have—I thought... I thought it was what you wanted. Knowing that someone responsible for your parents..."

He stopped short when I reached up, my hand trembling as I cupped his cheek. His pain felt like a dagger to my heart. I hated it—hated seeing him like this.

And most importantly, I hated that he wasn't wrong.

"It's okay, I'm okay." I whispered through the lie.

His lips parted as if to argue, but I didn't let him. I silenced his words with a kiss, soft and desperate, as salt from our tears mingled between us. My hands slipped around his trembling frame, clinging to him as if letting go would shatter me completely.

We held each other, two broken souls in a moment too fragile to last.

When he pulled back, his cheeks glistened with tears. "We need to talk about this," he said gently, his voice cracking.

"No," I murmured, shaking my head. "Please, not now. Anything else."

"Amara," he said softly, his tone pleading.

But he didn't press further.

I closed my eyes, leaning into him. I wanted the memory of yesterday to die, to vanish along with the part of me that had died with it. For now, I needed this moment. I needed him.

I felt his jaw clench, the muscles standing out as he fought against whatever he wanted to say.

"What is it?"

He let out the breath he was holding. "You were talking to yourself the whole way home."

The vision came back to me. There were flames, lots of them, and that woman: her white hair and icy blue eyes chilled me to the bone. This vision, this semblance of my dreams, it was different. This was no longer a mere whisper in the night but a harbinger of doom.

It's too late, my dream father had warned through the fire.

Too late for what?

The dreams had never come to me during the day, not like that. Yes, I would replay their memory—but this—this was like a vision. This one, for some reason, was not able to wait until I was asleep. The urgency of it forced me to speak.

"I think I saw my mother." The words escaped in a breath.

"Lettie?"

"No," I whispered. Vulnerability washed over me, mixing with a sense of relief. It was as if a weight had been lifted from my chest, the burden of this secret was finally eased by the simple act of speaking the truth aloud.

Azral's face lit up, eyes widening. He spoke softly, placing his hand on my leg. "Amara, it's okay. You know you can tell me anything."

So, I did. I told him everything— everything about my dreams and the magic that seemed to break through them. I talked for as long as I could, anything to distract me from what just happened.

And he listened. He listened intently, which was something I'd always admired about him. I told him about the man I believed to be my father, his golden eyes, and the magic he used. I told him about the child I believed to be myself, features all the same, the only difference being my ears. And I told him about the woman I believed to be my mother. It was undeniable after seeing her, seeing our similarities.

My voice trailed off. "I know how this all sounds." *Crazy.* "But they've never come to me like that before." The pain still tingled in my temples. "I just have this feeling they're out there somewhere."

He shifted closer, placing his hand on my knee, taking in all the information.

"Are you..." I started but I couldn't finish. *Did he believe me? Did he think I was insane?* I thought I was, why wouldn't he?

He sprung up, his warm hand lifting from my leg, leaving a chill where his touch had been. I hated the emptiness it left behind. My eyes followed him, and when he looked down at me, something flickered in his—a spark of life, of possibility. It was infectious, magnetic. I wanted to know what it was, what had stirred this sudden energy in him. Anything to pull me away from the relentless *drip, drip, drip* that haunted my mind. The sound of blood trickling, the memory of the man I killed—it clung to me like a shadow, cold and unyielding.

Azral beamed, a grin so wide and full of promise that it stole my breath. I couldn't look away.

"Come with me, Princess," he said, holding his hand out to me.

I stared at it, my fingers itching to take it. I needed to know, needed to see what gave him that spark. I craved it—not just the thrill of the unknown, but the relief it promised from the darkness pressing against me.

Without another moment of hesitation, my hand found his.

"Where are we going?" I asked as he put my cloak over my shoulders. He said nothing as we walked out the cabin door, the squeaking hinges the only sound for what felt like ages. "Az?"

We walked hand in hand but this time in the opposite direction of town.

"I want to tell you a story," he said through the whipping winds of the chilly morning.

A story? Is he serious right now? "Okay...?"

"Long ago, there was a crumbling kingdom named Rosetia. The people who lived there were outraged with their king and queen. You see, they had broken a very important rule, an oath they had once made, and the people were not happy with them for it. Towns burned, people fought, it was very ugly."

I stared at his back as he dragged me through the woods, wondering where this was going, where we were going. I pulled my cloak tighter.

"After some time, a lord from a nearby kingdom, Solyrus, came to Rosetia. He brought his family to this new land, seeking peace for its people and his. The people of this new kingdom turned to him, desperate for a just leader, not an oath breaker. So, they rallied behind him, crowning him the new King of Rosetia."

"What happened to the old king and queen?" My curiosity piqued. I did love a good fairytale, even if I couldn't see why it currently mattered.

He paused, then said, "They were exiled; they couldn't stay in Rosetia. Because of them this new king faced many challenges. There were still some people who rallied behind their old queen and they didn't want to see an outsider on the throne. It was only a few but to this day the king protects the castle walls against these rebels. He protects his family, his stepdaughter and his son." Azral stopped walking, his hand pulling on mine, turning me towards him. He placed his other hand on my neck, his thumb brushing my cheek. "Amara," he whispered. His emerald eyes were like a storm, fear and hope fighting each other.

"Az, why are you telling me this?" I asked, placing my hand on his warm cheek. It wasn't normal for him to be so unsure of himself, so erratic.

"That son," he inhaled sharply, "is me."

I gasped. I know I asked for a distraction, but this—
"You're a *prince*?"

His nickname for me seemed all too real now.

"My name is Azral Sallow." Pride filled his voice. "I'm the Prince of Rosetia and heir to the Scarlet Throne."

"Az—" I didn't know what to say.

He continued, "I know you're probably wondering what all this has to do with what you just told me." He leaned his head down, our foreheads barely touching, "Firstly, thank you," he breathed, his hand tightening on my neck. "Thank you for trusting me with that."

He pulled back with a sigh. "The maps we found yesterday, the map of Kaluth."

My body tensed and it felt like chains wrapped around me, forever tying me to that moment. I tried to push the image away. *Drip. Drip. Drip.*

"Hey." Az's voice pulled me back, like he knew I was slipping. "It's going to be okay."

His head fell to mine. I closed my eyes, letting my body fall into his, and wrapped my arms into his chest. He was warm, too warm.

I moved back to look at him. I stared at the man in front of me and time seemed to stand still. The freezing wind bit at my face but I barely flinched, nor did I try to hide my gaping mouth. I took in all his features, trying to make sense of what was in front of me, *who* was in front of me.

His face and body were the same, still utterly gorgeous. But his skin was no longer pale like mine but sun-kissed, like he had been outside for days. His emerald eyes sparkled down on me like always and his curls were still that rich brown but they were shorter now, trimmed at the sides like when I first met him.

And his ears—*gods.*

Just behind those perfect curls, I saw it.

Pointed.

My body trembled and my heart raced. Was *this* a dream? Some sort of sick vision? *I'm definitely losing my mind.*

"Azral?" I whispered hesitantly.

"Princess," he said with the same flirtatious tone that always made my heart skip.

"What is going on?" I pushed back from him, my eyes rapidly searching his face for answers.

He looked hurt at the distance but continued, "I'm not Human, Amara." The trees surrounding us spun. "We call ourselves Fae."

Fae only existed in my books, my dreams.

Uncertainty filled his eyes. "Amara, there's really no other way to say this."

Say it, my conscience begged him. *Say it.*

"The world you described." *Oh my gods.* "It's real. It's all real."

Those words hit me like a heavy storm, flooding my mind.

"How?" Was all I could manage, a simple syllable for such a simple Human. How could there be another world, magic, Fae—"You think it can be true?" The question slipped out. My parents, my lost childhood, could it all be real?

"I don't know," he breathed, hitching, like the answer hurt.

Was I even worthy of such a thing? A family, love?

Drip. Drip. Drip.

Stop it, Mar, I pleaded with myself. Worthy or not, I *had* to know. I had to know why these dreams had come to me, why they manifested into these visions. Each one was a missing piece and I needed to finish the puzzle.

"Take me." A flame kindled in me. "Take me to Kaluth."

Fire lit in Azral's eyes. A mischievous smile played at his lips. "I thought you'd never ask."

I threw myself into his arms, holding on as if he might vanish if I let go. His grip tightened, grounding me.

"Amara," he whispered with a pain in his voice, "this doesn't mean—"

"I know." I cut him off, burying my face in his chest, his heartbeat steady beneath my ear. "I know."

This doesn't mean that my dream parents are real, that I'm not an orphan. It doesn't mean that the answers will fix me. But still, I needed to go.

He pulled back, a playful glint in his eyes. "Turn around, Princess."

I obeyed but what I saw made me freeze. "Oh my—" *gods.*

Two massive horses in the distance caught my attention, both grazing in a snow-covered field of black dahlia flowers. "Az—"

"I've been checking on them every morning," he admitted, stepping closer, his hand brushing mine.

My feet dragged through the snow to the small open field. A sleek, black stallion grazed to the right. Its mane and tail were just as dark as its coat, both shimmering in the sunlight. The one to the left was just as big with a chestnut coat and white hair.

"Did you find them here?" I turned back to Az.

"I brought them with me when I left home. I thought it would be best to keep them hidden, for their safety." He was right. If the people in town got one look at these creatures...I didn't even want to think about it.

"And the flowers." I kneeled in the velvet patch. Picking one up, I twirled it in my fingers. "How can they even grow here?"

"Well," he started, "that's an interesting question." I twisted on my knees to look at him. Looked up and down his now different body, his pointed ears and trimmed hair. I looked back to the flowers, then him, and back again.

"How do you do that?" The question lingered in the air as I stood.

"We Fae have something called martem. It's our magic," he explained. "As an Illion, I can bend perception—craft illusions. When I met you, I changed my appearance to look Human."

"Do all Fae have magic, *martem*?" The word felt foreign on my tongue.

Speaking any of this aloud felt foreign but it felt so right. Every truth he unveiled snapped a piece of the puzzle in place.

"Martem varies between bloodlines. The royal families tend to have a stronger connection to the gods' blessings. Some Fae don't have any, though, and others have very little. The older Fae draw their power directly from the gods; the Sun and the Moon to be exact. Some of us, like me, developed different abilities over time, pulling our magic from other sources."

"Your father," I asked, "can he cast illusions, too?"

Azral laughed. "Gods, no. He has his own set of abilities. Mine...mine come from my mother." His voice softened as his gaze fell, sadness clouding his eyes. "She was incredible. She could turn the entire castle into anything she imagined, anything her heart desired, and everyone would see it. She was a true master."

He let out a small sigh, the weight of his grief pressing into the space between us.

"I'm sorry—" I whispered, my voice trembling.

His eyes lifted to meet mine, and for a moment, I saw the boy he must have been—the boy who had lost so much. "Don't be," he murmured, a faint, wistful smile tugging at his lips.

I reached for his hand, lacing my fingers with his. "She'd be proud of you. You know that, right?"

Azral's grip tightened slightly, and for a moment, he looked like he wanted to say something more. But instead, he simply nodded, the ghost of that smile lingering on his face.

"So, these are all your martem? They're not real?" I looked back at the field. In an instant, the flowers that painted the ground maroon disappeared, replaced by the never-ending snow.

Azral's hand found its way around my chest. His breath behind me, warm against my ear. "They're not real," he whispered.

I turned to face him, and in his eyes, I saw a spark—a growing fire that mirrored my own. "But this is," he whispered, pulling me closer. His lips brushed against mine, soft and deliberate.

He spun me gently, and I giggled. I wrapped my arms around his neck, standing on my toes to hold him closer. But my gaze wandered over his shoulder, back toward Zandar.

It was the only home I'd ever known and yet it was the place where I'd lost everything, the place where everything changed. The memories of all that pain and my guilt weighed on me, but standing here, in Az's arms, I felt the first flicker of something else: hope.

Isidore and Lettie wouldn't have wanted me to stay and suffer. They'd want me to do this, to find the truth.

Could my parents really be out there? Are they looking for me?

My eyes turned back to the snow-covered desolation, the remnants of a life that no longer held anything for me. I pressed my forehead against Azral's. "Let's go."

7

"IT'S ABOUT A DAY'S RIDE, THEN HALF A DAY BY boat to Kaluth," Azral said, walking towards the horses. "For you." He gestured to the black coated horse. "Her name is Mylom."

Her long rich black mane made her look regal. Her eyes were a deep shade of green, similar to Az's with the way they glistened in the sun. She approached me tentatively and I froze. Az nodded and I took a daring step forward. She dipped her head, as if bowing, and I found myself doing the same, a sign of respect I assumed only horses like her gave and wanted in return.

"She's loyal, like you," Az said as he leaned over, grabbing something from the snow.

I rested a hand on her muzzle, her hair silky and smooth. I couldn't look away as her irises flickered to a deep red before returning to their original hue.

I blinked. "Do they all change colors?"

Azral's hand settled on my back and I turned to see him admiring Mylom. "What do you mean?"

"Her eyes. They change colors."

He chuckled softly. "Her eyes have always been that green."

She nuzzled her head into me and I couldn't help but laugh, tripping over my feet.

"Well, she seems to like you." Azral laughed beside me, placing his hand on my lower back. "Hopefully everyone back home is just as welcoming."

Home. This was really happening.

Azral carefully placed golden leather reins around Mylom's face.

"I haven't ridden in years," I shyly admitted.

"We'll take it slow, at first." He flashed a grin, helping me into the saddle. His hand fell around my waist and the other guided my foot into the golden stirrup.

"Riding is a graceful act, Mar," Lettie would always yell at me.

I readjusted multiple times. I was the farthest thing from graceful, even more so now.

Beneath me, Mylom's breaths were steady and sure. Az mounted his own steed, the mare's chestnut and white speckled fur glowing in the sunlight as he trotted towards us.

"Ready?" he asked.

The question was so simple and yet so complicated. Was I ready to leave this place behind, to step into a new world? I took a quick glance back at the life I'd known. And only one thing held me back.

"My book—" I never got to finish that sequel.

I turned back to Az and from under his cloak he pulled out the leather wrapped book. "Don't worry."

My fingers wrapped around the reins. I didn't need to look back anymore; I knew, without a doubt, that there was nothing left for me here.

With that, Az clicked his tongue and the horses moved. Our pace was even, a careful trot across the snow-covered ground.

"You know, you will be a *real* princess now." Azral laughed.

I snorted, covering my mouth with my hand. "Me? Seriously?"

"Seriously," he cooed but the light in his eyes dulled. "There is something I should tell you, before we get there."

Nerves crept through my body. I took a few quick breaths, a futile attempt to calm them.

"When I left home, I wasn't on the best terms with my father." He shook his head, anger darkened his features. "We've been at war for some time."

"How long?"

He cleared his throat. "A little over 20 years."

Gods. That was almost our whole life. "You were just a child when it started?"

"Well, not exactly" he looked at me and drew in a long breath, "the Fae are immortal."

My mind raced. "Az—"

"I'm two hundred and forty-seven years old." He didn't even need me to ask.

"Two hundred and forty-seven?"

"A child compared to some of my family." He laughed and I couldn't help but laugh with him—what else was there to do? The whole concept was absurd to me and yet I knew it was true, deep in my bones.

When he looked back at me, the amusement in his eyes was gone. "It can be dangerous," he began, "a Human in my world..." He shook his head. "I wouldn't be doing this if I thought you'd be in any danger but," he paused, "I need you to know, I'll always protect you, Amara."

"I know," I whispered reaching my hand out to him. I tilted, loosing my balance and quickly pulled my hand away, wrapping it tightly around the reins. "If we're just taking a boat, what stops a Human from entering your world?"

"We call it the Veil," he searched for the words to explain. "It's like a magical wall only Fae can cross."

"But I'll be able to cross?"

"Of course you will; you're with the prince." He winked and clicked his tongue.

The horses flew forward, ending our conversation. My heart raced in sync with Mylom's hoofbeats, a rush of wind whipping through my hair and stinging my cheeks. Mylom's mane danced together with my snow-kissed hair, synchronizing perfectly.

The forest blurred past in a kaleidoscope of colors. A small smile crept on my face as we soared through the snow towards Kaluth, towards my new life.

The horses galloped at full speed until the snow gave way to sand.

Az hadn't told me this was where we'd end up and a wave of nostalgia washed over me as I gazed out at the endless ocean, a vast mix of blue-green that shimmered with the setting sun's reflection.

"It was here," I whispered. "This is where Isidore found me."

The words cut through me like a knife. I could feel Azral's gaze and he knew nothing he could say would make me feel better. Because this was where my story began, a bittersweet memory etched into my soul.

Now, this very beach is where I would leave it all. *How poetic.*

They would want this for me, they would want me to be happy. *Right?* I released a long breath, letting go of that ache in my chest and took in an even deeper one, replenishing my body with the fresh air of my new life.

Mylom slowed as we reached the edge of the beach, her breath steaming from the cold as she pawed at where water met sand. I slid off her, moving to her front to pet her muzzle. Az's hand curled around my waist, turning me towards him. His hand brushed my cheek and he held in a laugh.

"What are you hiding?" I knew that look all too well.

Then, a low rumbling growl shook the ground beneath us. I spun out of Az's grasp and saw—*good gods.*

Two beasts, taller than the tree line, covered the snowy beach. These creatures blocked the setting sun, their wings stretching across the ocean water. Black scales shimmered on one, glowing like the deepest gem. The other was covered in white scales, each one reflecting the pink sunset.

I'd read about these creatures before but that was the only place they existed, in books. Now, two beasts walked forward, each step shaking the earth.

Dragons.

"Mylom," I called out, my hand rising to cover my mouth as the beast slowly made its way towards us. "That thing ate her!" I yelled frantically, searching for the missing horse. Az moved beside me but I couldn't calm my racing heart.

He snorted, a small grin forming on the left side of his mouth. "Come meet your true steed," he gestured towards the dragons.

My jaw dropped. Because it was Mylom I was looking at. Her black fur was replaced with those glittering scales. Every exhale she made released a small flame that danced and flickered around her fierce eyes. She was absolutely breathtaking.

I approached, very, *very* slowly, as Azral left me to greet his dragon. Time seemed to blur and I was transported to another world as I locked eyes with her. It was like deja vu but so much more. She felt so familiar. Her head lowered to the ground, resting on the snowy sand. The flames around her died as she puffed a low breath that sent my hair flying behind me. Her green eyes shifted to that red and her dark pupils narrowed to slits. That red and black pattern flowed through her eyes like a river. Each twist and turn was like the journey of her life.

I reached out my hand, so small compared to the size of her, and placed it on her scales. A surge of something, her power maybe, glowed beneath her. She closed her eyes and leaned into my touch. I pressed against her and rested my head on the scales. Our hearts beat in sync like a rhythm of trust.

"They're beautiful, aren't they?" Azral said, startling me as he came up beside us.

Mylom's eyes shifted back to green and she turned, flames growing around her body again.

"Beautiful is an understatement."

He reached for my hand, kissing the top, "She's just the first of many gifts." He paused with his lips on my palm, flicking his gaze up towards me. "But I don't think you'll be too keen on the next surprise." We walked down the shore, following the dragons, the sand and snow shaking beneath us. "I know I said it would be about a half day's ride by boat." Az paused, hiding that grin of his again. "But as you can see, there are no boats here."

"No." Horror wove through me as I glanced at Mylom's wings.

"It's the only way." His voice was calm but I could see he was amused. "Once we cross through the Veil, it won't be long to the castle. I promise."

My mind raced. *Is he really saying*—"You want me to ride, to *fly,* on her?" I pointed to the dragon.

"It's easy. All you have to do is hang on right here." He moved to Mylom's side, pointing to two horns at the base of her neck. "She won't let you fall."

I believed him, not only because I knew he wouldn't put me in harm's way but also because I trusted Mylom. Delusional? Yes. But either way, I trusted her.

"Just watch me," he called, climbing onto his dragon with ease. But Mylom's size was intimidating. How was I supposed to climb up without hurting her, or hurting myself?

I inhaled, stepping closer to her as she leaned her head down again as she lowered her left wing. As if she was saying, *Hop on.*

I placed my hand on what looked to be her shoulder muscle, and hoisted myself up. She helped me, too, lifting her wing to push me farther up. Her scales were like warm leather as I adjusted myself. I grabbed the small horns Azral had mentioned, trying to push away the fear that clawed through me, and held onto them with the tightest grip I could muster. They were hard and hot, like stones on a fire. I awkwardly adjusted myself on the velvety scales under me.

Next to me, Azral beamed ear to ear as he put his fingers to his lips and whistled.

Without a thought, or even a second to breathe, we shot into the sky. My stomach lurched. Wind deafened me and my heart threatened to beat out of my chest. I closed my eyes, sucking in air, trying to steady my nerves.

When I was finally able to open my eyes, the world stretched out before us. The sea sparkled pink and orange as we flew and the clouds above gave off a cool mist. Mylom's wings beat beneath me and the rush of air was refreshing against my face. I couldn't help the laugh that ripped from my lips. I could feel the freedom now and it was exhilarating.

I'd trapped myself in the past for too long. I was trapped with Allen, trapped in death's claws, trapped with my grief, my thoughts—and I never want to feel that way again.

I looked over to Azral. He was already watching me, his smile radiating through the night sky behind him. Once the sun fully set, the sea below glowed with a thousand tiny stars.

A sudden ringing noise pierced through the roar of the wind. I grabbed my ears, tightening my legs around Mylom as the sound shrieked.

"Az!" I yelled.

The piercing only grew louder and louder. I tucked my head, my elbows now covering my ears. I turned to see Az flying right next to me. He gave me a reassuring nod; Mylom would hold me.

My head grew heavy and I knew what was coming next.

Darkness took over once again and I surrendered to it, placing the weight of my body in Mylom's care.

"Papa, look!" I yelled as my excitement bubbled, pointing to the baby dragons emerging from their eggs. My father's joy was infectious as we stood above the cavern, surrounded by dozens of dragons. We watched in wonder as the newborns wriggled and squirmed, their tiny bodies covered with scales and little wings.

One in particular caught my attention. Its eyes were the same shade as mine and they seemed to lock onto me. There was something pulling me towards the small dragon and I could have sworn she smiled at me.

"This, my love, is a moment you will never forget. Here in the depths of the Silver Mountains, only once every hundred years are dragon eggs hatched." My father's words only added to the magic of the moment.

He lifted me onto his shoulders and I gripped his auburn hair as we continued to watch. His laughter rang out, awakening something inside me...

I woke with a jolt. My eyes slowly adjusted to the bright sun and my body to the softness of the bed beneath me. I spread my arms wide, making a fairy on the soft silky sheets— a feeling I hadn't experienced in months. The comfort was overwhelming, but I stayed alert. I rolled over, tracing my fingers on the golden trim of the ivory bedding. I slowly sat up, my eyes fully adjusted to the light now. And I couldn't believe what I saw.

The room I was in was almost twice the size of my entire cabin. Morning sun shone through floor-to-ceiling windows to the left of me, casting a warm glow on the cream-colored wallpaper and white molding. Bouquets of black dahlia flowers filled every surface in the room: the floor, the bedside tables, even the coffee table—my book next to them. I couldn't help my smile. Some had wilted but most were fresh and vibrant, almost as if they were trying to reassure me that I was safe.

I wrapped myself in the navy robe lain over the edge of the bed, covering the creamy silk nightgown I was dressed in—how I'd come to wear it, I wasn't sure. I pushed off the bed, my bare feet somehow warm on the tiled floor, but paused before the glass doors of the balcony. Beyond them sprawled green hills without a speck of snow, a sight I had only read about, a place I knew only in my head.

I reached for the handle but it was locked. I tried the other handle. Locked. A tinge of fear made my heart skip as I turned and headed for the bedroom door but that, too, was locked.

Trapped.

"Hello!" I shouted, fear clawing its way through me. As if in answer, the door swung open and I stumbled back.

Azral's arm wrapped around my waist, pulling me into him.

"You're awake." Relief was evident in his voice.

"Hi," was all I managed, taking a breath to calm myself. *I'm okay.*

Az gestured towards the couch in the middle of the room. I followed him, my hand wrapped in his, as my heartbeat calmed. The soft purple couch complemented the room. He leaned over to the table before us, pouring me a glass of water.

"The servants changed you into something more comfortable when we got here. I had them design everything how I thought you'd like it," He handed me the glass. "Do you?"

"It's beautiful." I took a sip, wondering. "Can't you just make it appear however you want?"

"True." He laughed. "I only use that when necessary. I find it unfair to mess with what people truly see." His hand caressed my knee, he leaned in, his eyes filled with concern. "How are you feeling?"

"I feel fine, normal?" Though, I wasn't sure what normal meant anymore. How should I feel after crossing a magical border? "Tired?" I questioned even myself.

But the truth was, morning scare aside, I did feel normal. I felt entirely like myself, only with better clothes.

He laughed with a grin that sent butterflies to my stomach. "You slept for almost a week."

"A week! Why didn't you wake me?"

"It's been a while since we had any Humans cross through the Veil, so we weren't sure of what effects it would have on your body. I wanted you to get as much rest as you needed."

How long was a while?

He brushed a strand of hair behind my ear and smiled. His emerald eyes peered into mine, waiting, and it reminded me of Mylom, the way hers had changed.

"I want to see Mylom," I blurted. The dream of the dragons hatching replayed in my mind. *Could that have been her?* "I think she knows who I am."

"Well, of course she does," he replied.

"No, I had another dream," I explained, my voice quivering. "I think I saw her being born and my father, the man in my dreams—" I cleared my throat. "He was there, too."

"Interesting." Az let the word linger, scratching his chin. But he said nothing more and a pang shot through my heart. "Do you want to get some more rest?" He rubbed his thumb under my eyes. *Did I look tired?*

"Az, please. I slept for a week. I think I'll be fine." I placed my hand over his on my face, reassuring. "I'm really okay, I promise."

"Okay," he breathed, nodding. "Okay, then of course, whatever you want to do. We can go now." He smiled reassuringly. "The closet is full but if there's anything you don't like, I'll have a new wardrobe made." He stood, lifting me with him. "Oh, and you won't be needing a cloak."

I looked to the locked balcony, "The doors—"

"For your safety." His tone was authoritative, stern, something I hadn't heard before. "I promise." He planted a soft kiss on my forehead. "I'll let you get ready. I'll be right outside if you need anything."

For my safety. I guess I couldn't really protect myself against whatever magic was here. But I was curious, what could possibly be lurking outside?

I shook off the uneasy feeling and glided across the floors to the massive closet in the corner. Opening the double doors revealed a room in itself. Racks of clothing, in every style and color imaginable, lined the walls. There were shimmering ball gowns, flowy sundresses, tailored tunics, and everything in between. Rows of shoes filled the shelves, ranging from heels to boots to sandals. I couldn't help but run my fingers over all the fabrics. Some were soft, some silky, some beaded, some lacy.

But what caught my attention was the corsets. There was metal and iron, adorned with sparkling gems and lace patterns. Each piece looked like a work of art, carefully crafted with intricate details that added to the beauty of everything in this place. And just like Az had said, there were no cloaks. No clothes for a cold winter's night.

After ogling the beauty of each piece, I picked a gown that felt both new and familiar. The fabric was a deep, rich green, flowing gracefully to the floor with delicate golden embroidery along the hem. The bodice was fitted, accentuating my figure, with a lace-up front that allowed for perfect adjustments. I ran my fingers over the seams, noticing how everything fit me perfectly. It really was all made just for me.

I looked into the full-length mirror—one without cracks or blemishes—and tucked some hair behind my ears, braiding it down my back. A girl I didn't recognize looked back at me. It had been so long since I'd seen my reflection through anything other than a shattered mirror, through the broken image of myself. I think some pieces of me would always be broken, forever stained. But I could see it now: My heart was slowly being put back together.

And it was all thanks to Azral.

"Baby, please sit still. The more you move, the longer this will take," the blue-eyed woman scolded gently, her hands braiding my hair. Her fingers brushed my cheek as a few strands escaped the braid, and I smiled at her cool touch.

We sat in front of the mirror, gazing at our strikingly similar features. She tied a blue ribbon at the end of the braid, placing a soft kiss on my small hand as she stood behind me. Her presence was so comforting, almost surreal.

I jumped. That woman—my mother—was clearer to me than any dream I'd ever had. A lump formed in my throat as I let out the breath I hadn't realized I was holding.

Today, I would see Mylom, see Azral's home—my new home. Then tomorrow, we would search for my parents.

This place, this world, Azral—it was all the proof I needed.

They had to be here.

And if they're not? My conscience stirred, the familiar voice returning with its doubts. I silenced it, pushing the thought away.

Clear-minded I walked toward the door, only to find it still locked. I tried again, frustration creeping in, but before I could attempt another push, the door swung open on its own. Az stood in the hallway, sunlight streaming behind him.

Flashing a grin, he held his arm out to me. "Are you ready for this world, Princess?

8

MY JAW DROPPED AS I FOLLOWED AZ DOWN THE hallway. Gold columns supported the abnormally high ceilings. Cream-colored marble floors stretched beneath us, polished and smooth as our feet moved in harmony. The walls were adorned with intricate red detailing. Delicate patterns intertwined and the gold accents glimmered under the warm sunlight shining through tall windows. Each one was draped with flowing curtains of the purest white. They stood like sentinels along the hallway, inviting only nature's beauty in.

"This castle has been here for thousands of years," Azral explained. "After my father arrived, he restored it to this."

I listened in awe as we reached a wide foyer. A dome-shaped roof loomed over us, covered in stained glass depicting images of the Sun God, Saigus, painted around fields of roses.

Delicate petals unfurled through the room, blending seamlessly with depictions of the royalty on the walls.

Two other hallways stretched before us, leading to what looked like more corridors and stairways and a massive door to the left. The circular foyer was filled with flowers, hanging and planted. Flags were hung, each adorned with what I assumed to be the royal sigil of a golden crown intertwined with thorns and embroidered with red roses.

Two guards stood at each hall entrance and by the main door—all dressed in gold armor with the same sigil embossed on their chest. One of the guards opened the entry as we approached, letting in a breeze that smelled of honey. The warmth of the sun hit my skin and I shivered a little at the intensity. It was nothing like the shivers freezing Zandar air would bring. No, this one was different, something I've only ever felt in my dreams. Closing my eyes, I couldn't help the smile that played at my lips, taking all of it in.

Azral led me down the large stone staircase to the grounds below. The grass was a verdant shade of green and a collage of flowers lined the curved stone path we walked; away from the castle, down the hill, until we reached a large clearing. The stables were directly ahead and I spotted three horses grazing to the right. *Where would one even keep a dragon around here?* But then I spotted her, Mylom, back in her horse form. Her black coat sparkled in the sunlight. She was somehow even more beautiful in Rosetia.

"Do they prefer this form?" I asked, following Az into the gated field.

"I believe so. I could only imagine it's easier for them to move around than the alternative."

We passed through the gate and I took a few steps towards Mylom. She gracefully inclined her head. I reached out and traced my fingers along the contours of her body. Her fiery red eyes locked onto mine as I leaned my head into hers.

A silent connection pulled me into her like it did back on that beach. Was that her in my dream? *Could it even be possible?* Her heartbeat thrumming through my body, matched mine, and I just knew it had to be her.

Tears pricked my eyes because if Mylom was real, then my parents...

"Az." I lifted my head.

"They're all just horses," he said behind me as he searched the field. "No more dragons."

I guess one can only have so many.

"Hey, what's wrong?" He tilted his head.

"I just feel like I know her. I know that sounds crazy..." I shook my head. I couldn't stop the tears now, more of frustration than anything.

"We're going to figure this out, okay?" He lifted my chin to meet his eyes.

"How?" I pleaded, my voice cracking with the weight of everything I couldn't control.

"There's someone who can see your dreams. Interpret them." He looked around as if we weren't already alone. "The dreamweaver."

The who? My eyes widened at the name, curiosity and intrigue overshadowing my worry.

"There's a ball tonight." He nodded. "She'll be there."

"Will you introduce me?" The words spilled out.

He laughed, taking my arm into his. "Of course, Princess."

We strolled back along the winding stone path, the castle looming ahead of us. The massive hill it sat on made it all the more impressive. Its four towers, each of varying heights, pillared upwards from the roof. The central tower—the tallest of them all—boasted the painted glass dome that shimmered and sparkled even from out here. The castle walls were still stunning, if weathered by the centuries, and made from gray stone and glass windows. There was an old beauty to it.

Thousands of years of old beauty, apparently.

The towers were guarded by more soldiers scanning for any sign of danger. Flags with a matching sigil flowed in the calm winds. "The Scarlet Flag," Azral told me, hung high above the main entrance. It was a symbol of pride and honor for his kingdom, his crown.

We approached the main doors. The guards bowed low to Azral before motioning us inside, and it was only then that I realized I had no idea how to prepare for a ball.

"I'll see you soon." Azral kissed my hand before two servants swept me away. He insisted they help me prepare for tonight, and I was honestly thankful he pushed so hard, because I had no idea what I was doing. I sat in my room with them as they braided my hair into loops with golden beads outlining the intricate weaves of white, while the rest of it flowed down my back effortlessly. They lightly dusted makeup on my face, something I hadn't worn in a long time.

Lettie only let me wear it on special occasions when I was young, and the older I got, the less interested I was.

I thought I was more than capable of getting dressed myself, but when they pulled out the gown Az picked for me, well I needed all the help I could get.

I was speechless, utterly captivated by the dress' beauty. It was long and flowing, with a sheer design on the chest and sleeves. The bodice was a pattern of delicate branches and thorns, embellished with red and gold sequins that sparkled in the candlelight of the room. Each thorn and sequin were perfectly placed, creating the image all the way up my collar. It was lighter than I expected as I shimmied into it. Airy and flowy. I took a spin, it fit like a glove.

I almost didn't recognize myself in the mirror.

The dress was stunning, *I* was stunning.

My eyes lingered on the deep red shade of the branches. A pang of unease hit my chest. Was it the tight heels? No, this shade reminded me of something far darker than the fabric dye.

Drip. Drip. Drip.

It was the same color as the one that stained my hands, my soul. A deep crimson shade of blood. Each bead, each delicate stitch, mocked me with memories of the life I stole.

The knock at the door pulled me back to reality. I pushed the lingering image way back in the depths of my mind. I threw on a fake smile as Azral stood there, his eyes widening. The servants left the room quickly, their giggles trailing behind them.

Azral was stunning, as usual. He wore a beautifully tailored tunic with gold detailing throughout, his golden sword sheathed at his side. His dress coat was red, the same shade as some of the branches on my gown. His hair was styled, curls tucked just behind his pointed ears, with a golden crown atop them. Red rubies adorned the points, complementing the sword at his side. With a quirk of his lips, he pulled me toward him.

"You look stunning," he whispered, biting my ear. "I could get used to this."

His touch heated my body, and I couldn't fake my smile now. *So could I.*

"Are you ready, Princess?" He raised a brow, smiling.

"Ready as I'll ever be."

9

THE THRONE ROOM WAS ENORMOUS. COLUMNS and pillars lined the walls. The ceiling rounded above us in an intricate molded pattern with chandeliers that held, what looked like, thousands of candles. Moonlight twinkled in through large windows decorated with hanging roses.

The room was filled with music, laughter, and the clinking of glasses. It was brimming with Fae, all dressed in their finest outfits, adorned with sparkling jewels that glistened in the light. Females twirled around the room in vibrant gowns while some of the males joined in the dance as the music changed to a slower romantic melody. The image was something straight from my books.

Azral led me through the crowd and I held my breath. I wasn't typically a nervous person but this was a lot. I hadn't been around this many people in, well, forever—let alone magical people. We took a few steps, turning heads as we walked arm in arm and *wait*, were they all staring at me? I lowered my head, trying to get one of those braided loops the servants had plaited into my hair to fall over my rounded ears.

Did I stand out, a Human in a crowd of Fae?

Whispers and curious glances followed us as we made our way to the edge of the dance floor. I looked around, finally letting my breath go, because honestly, I was just as fascinated with them. So, I stared right back, stealing whatever glances I could as they moved about. I could almost feel the magic brimming from their very bodies, making the room come alive.

A delicious smell wafted through the air and my stomach practically screamed in response. A male carrying a tray of berries passed us, the colors so vibrant they almost glowed. And then another walked by, carrying more food that smelled so good I couldn't help but close my eyes and breathe it in. It had been months since I'd had anything other than what we would catch in the woods. My eyes followed the trays like a hunter watching its prey.

Azral noticed, smiling, his eyes following my gaze. "Hungry?"

No, I wasn't hungry, I was starving. I nodded, fixed on the food. "Everything smells amazing."

"Whatever you want, it's yours," he said, gesturing towards the massive table against the wall.

An array of colors and textures and smells struck my senses. Trays of gold and silver held dishes of meat, vegetables, and fruits. I tried to remain composed, not wanting to seem like a starving Human girl, but I couldn't resist. I filled a plate with a small amount of meat, cheese, and berries but the first bite of cheese left me reeling. So, I grabbed more, hoping no one was paying me any attention. I shoved a couple more pieces in my mouth, Az's laughter the backdrop to my feast. I couldn't help the moan that left my lips. This food, gods.

His eyes trailed over me as his hand caressed the side of my cheek, brushing loose crumbs away. "There are few things in this world that amaze me; you are at the top of the list." He smiled. "But the beauty of this land never ceases, the food it produces is indescribable."

He turned to the dance floor and we watched the gowns spin and the jewels glow in the candlelight. "Oh gods," Azral murmured and I followed his gaze to see a female running towards us. I quickly put my plate down, wiping any crumbs off my face and chest.

"Is this her?" the female yelled, lurching to a stop just before us, her pale green dress flowing behind her speed. Lilac eyes searched me and I did the same. Her skin carried a golden brown undertone, smooth and glowing under the candlelight that complemented her long deep brown curls. I couldn't help but notice all the jewels on her dress, accentuating her godly figure. She smiled, revealing perfect white teeth, and gasped, "Wow."

I could only assume she was in awe of me, a Human. But I was just as taken back by her Fae beauty.

"Vani, do you have to be so rude?" Az rolled his eyes.

She made an unkind facial gesture at him and corrected, "I'm Sovanni." I looked behind her and her eyes followed mine to the other Fae watching, whispering. "Oh, don't mind them." She playfully pushed my shoulder. "They're probably staring at their rogue prince here." She raised a brow to Azral.

"Leaving without saying a single word to me?" She playfully pouted towards him. Her hand grabbed my hand and she laughed. "How did you even fall for this one? He's utterly terrible."

"Amara, please meet my lovely sister," he said sarcastically. "She's been looking forward to meeting you."

"Half-sister," she corrected with a coy smile.

"It's a pleasure," I replied. "Az mentioned you like reading?" Words began tumbling out of me, my palms became uncomfortably sweaty.

"That's all? He always leaves out the best details." Sovanni smirked. "But enough about me, please. You're far more interesting. How was it crossing the Veil? I heard you slept for a week!"

"Vani," Azral grunted.

"Fine." She frowned towards him. "We'll have more than enough time to get to know each other soon." She pushed her curls behind her ears revealing their Fae point. "Goodbye, brother. Please send her to me soon," she said under her breath. Then she was off, running to the dance floor and grabbing the nearest lone male.

As Sovanni dashed away, Azral let out a deep sigh and rubbed his eyes. "I'm sorry she's—"

"She was lovely," I interrupted, smiling. Sovanni seemed so bold and curious, two traits I liked to think I also had. "But what did she mean—"

"She's the dreamweaver," he whispered, looking around as if everyone had heard. "Not many Fae like to showcase their abilities, the element of surprise can be advantageous in certain situations."

"So, no one knows what anyone is really capable of?"

"Some Fae, like my father, take pride in flaunting their martem and demonstrating how much power they possess. When you have as much as him, there's not much anyone can do to stop you." He moved us through the crowd. "But others, like me, prefer to remain discreet." His gaze drifted towards the man seated on the throne at the front of the room.

"I should introduce you," he said, rubbing his neck.

I nodded, gulping down the nerves that crept up, but I had no reason to refuse. Not only was this the king—I'd never met a lord before, let alone royalty—but he was also Azral's father.

We walked towards the dais. I couldn't get my heart to stop pounding. I was about to meet the king of a world I had only just learned about, dreamed about. *How in the gods' names am I supposed to impress him?* I tried to maintain my composure as Azral led me up the small set of stairs.

The throne before us was enormous. It was crafted entirely from golden vines—thousands of them—woven together forming the grand structure. A deep red dipped their edges, glinting in the soft light, while red rubies were embedded sporadically across the surface. Each gem caught the light and casted tiny flickers of scarlet across the floor.

"Father," Az said, bowing his head and taking a knee. I followed suit, hoping my nerves didn't show. My dress pooled around me as I dropped but curiosity got the best of me and, with my head still down, I lifted my eyes to take just a little peek.

I met the king's gaze head on.

His dark brows lowered. He wore a crown identical to the one on the sigil of the flags, rose-like thorns intertwined with the gold metal and rubies. His hair was brown, too, longer than Azral's and not as curly but there was no doubt this was his father. Their chiseled faces were almost identical but the king's was aged with time and war. His eyes were not soft and kind like Azral's, no, they were like black holes, dark and still. A chill swept through me but I couldn't look away. My stomach lurched into my throat as he smiled.

I quickly dropped my gaze to the ground, catching my breath, shaking the uneasy feeling that threatened to cripple me.

"You must be Amara," the king cleared his throat, standing from his throne and walking closer. The whole room fell silent.

The king cleared his throat as if signaling everyone to get back to the party. They obeyed and the music and laughter grew louder but I could still feel their beady wandering eyes on my back.

He took slow steps towards me, his feet coming to a halt right before my knees. He brushed his fingers against my chin, sending a shiver down my back despite the warmth of the room, and lifted my chin to him. "My son did not do you justice," he said, rubbing his thumb against my chin. "You may stand." He gestured to us, turning back and sitting on his throne.

I didn't even bother fixing the pleats in my gown as Azral held his hand out to me. With sweaty palms, I took his in mine. And I held on for dear life.

"Azral mentioned what you seek here," the king started, taking a sip from his glass. "In private, of course, when he so graciously surprised us with his presence."

I shot Azral a cautionary glance. I didn't think we would be telling the king of my dreams anytime soon.

The king took another long sip of wine. Leaning forward, he gestured for us to move closer. I leaned in with Az. "You believe your parents are here?" he asked, shooting Azral a glare.

"Yes," I whispered, matching his tone.

"She's been having dreams of people, Fae to be exact, who she believes could be them." Azral said low, his voice stern.

I tried not to shoot him another look for revealing so many of my truths.

"And how long have you been having these *dreams*?" The king waved his fingers at the word, a theatrical sarcasm.

I debated lying but I didn't know how much Azral had told him already. This could be a test and I didn't want to fail. "A couple of months."

The king's eyes narrowed but then seemed to soften. "Sovanni will help you," he said. "See to it that they meet tomorrow, son."

"Of course." Az inclined his head.

"We wouldn't want to have to wait for those answers." The king gave me an unnerving grin.

We stepped away from the dais and headed back into the sea of people. I felt eyes burning into my back and I couldn't help but glance over my shoulder.

The king staired at me. He looked like a wolf watching a rabbit, deciding when to make his move.

10

AZRAL MOVED EFFORTLESSLY THROUGH THE crowd of dancing Fae, unfazed by his father. He plucked two glasses of wine from a passing tray and handed one to me with a light *clink* of the crystal.

"That went better than expected," he remarked as he sipped from his own glass.

I raised a brow. *Did we not just have the same tension-filled conversation?*

"What did you tell him?" I asked, sipping my wine. The delicate golden stem was refreshingly cool against my heated fingertips. It gave me something to focus on other than my pounding heart.

"Only that I was ready to come home," he glanced at me, "under the condition you were able to stay." A teasing grin grew on his lips. "My father and I have differing opinions on certain matters but he is still my father." He shrugged, taking another sip from the crystal glass. "He would rather have me here, tending to the duties of an heir, than running wild in the Human realm."

A shiver slid down my spine as the king's gaze weighed on me. I couldn't shake the darkness that radiated from his father. I sipped my wine, swallowing the urge to tell Az, and I focused instead on the flavors of berries dancing on my tongue, each sip intertwining and becoming stronger and more enchanting than the last. Az's mischievous grin widened as he watched me drink.

"Tales have been told of our wine," he started, his voice sounding magical. "It's said to have a stronger eye-opening effect for a Human. It can mimic just a fraction of how Fae see things, how we hear things."

The music grew louder and the laughter of dancers echoed through the room. Fae twirled and spun, their dresses billowing around them like colorful clouds. The hues were so vivid they were almost alive. Az's laugh carried over the magic, a sound I'd fallen in love with over and over, but now, it was more than intoxicating; it made me feel alive. A smile grew on my face. All my worries, that lingering feeling of evil, disappeared as Az pulled me into him.

"Welcome to my world, Amara," he whispered over my mouth, placing a kiss on my lips.

We danced for what felt like hours, my mortal soul struggling to keep up with Az's unending energy. He was brighter than anyone in the room. His immortality gave him a new light. At some point, Sovanni joined us, beaming. Her eyes sparkled with every spin as she and Az taught me dance after dance.

But after one too many glasses of wine, I needed water, immediately. The room was spinning. I excused myself. Azral moved to follow me but Sovanni pulled him away, assuring him I was capable of finding water on my own. I almost objected as I tripped over my feet but, somehow, I safely found my way.

I watched everyone dance, watched Azral laugh and twirl his sister. With every song, they moved in sync. Sovanni's beauty captivated the dance floor. I realized, then, that all those wandering eyes were actually for her.

With water in my stomach, I reached again for wine—*one more couldn't hurt, right?*—but next to my glass was a tiny being. *Is that...?* I leaned closer to the table to see, clear as day, a small Fairy with blue wings and icy skin. Her glittery dress matched her wings. I leaned even closer but she vanished, leaving a trail of blue glitter in her wake. I couldn't help but giggle with disbelief. Of course, they're real.

Are you enjoying yourself? my conscience asked. A hum enveloped my body and I closed my eyes, swaying with the music, wine streaming through my veins.

Until I felt a cool breath behind my ear.

A chill snaked down my spine and I froze.

"Are you enjoying yourself?" my conscience asked from behind me.

Except, it wasn't in my head. No, it was a deep seductive voice whispering in my ear. *How is that possible?* I tried to turn, to put a face to the voice I'd heard too many times, but I was stopped. A cool hand gripped my shoulder, holding me there. The male glided to my side, his nose brushing against the back of my ear, and he inhaled deeply.

Did he just smell *me?*

I frantically scanned the room for Az and Sovanni, my instincts screaming at me to find them, but they were nowhere to be seen.

"*Mar,*" the male purred.

His hand lifted from my shoulder and I whirled on him, almost toppling with my speed.

But there was no one there.

"Are you okay?" Az asked as he grabbed my arm.

I jumped, trying to shake off the lingering fear. "I think I had a little too much wine," I joked.

He scanned the area with furrowed brows. A forced smile played on his lips as he wrapped his arm around me. "Let's get to bed. We have a long day tomorrow with Vani and you'll need the rest."

I nodded, setting the wine glass on the table. I definitely had way too much if I was conjuring my conscience into a being.

I placed my hand in his as we walked out of the throne room. The music stopped almost instantly and the silence was chilling.

Moonbeams danced across the tiles and I walked towards the open balcony doors to get a better look. I placed my hands on the cool marble rail and breathed in the familiar honey scent from earlier but now, a hint of lavender mingled with it, filling my senses with a much-needed calm. The stars were closer than ever, countless diamonds twinkling against the endless backdrop of the night sky.

Azral's arms slipped around me, his warmth pressing against my back. I leaned my head against his chest, exhaling as we took in the night together.

"The stars smile for you, Princess," he whispered against my ear.

I closed my eyes, letting his body wrap around me. Turning, I threaded my fingers through his soft, curly hair. His forehead rested against mine, and for a moment, the world fell away. Our breaths mingled, steady and in sync, a rhythm only we shared.

When I pulled him closer, his lips met mine, soft and warm, igniting a spark that burned through the quiet night.

Az lifted me with ease and placed me on the balcony rail. I giggled as I wrapped my legs around him. Our movements were natural, like we'd done this a thousand times—except we hadn't. But I didn't let that stop me and neither did he. His lips found their way down my neck and I stared at the night sky, taking in the beauty all around me.

"This is not resting," I teased as I considered meeting Sovanni tomorrow.

Az only groaned. With a giggle from me, he carried me towards the bed, his eyes locking with mine. We dropped onto the silk sheets and he pulled me in his arms.

"Amara," he whispered, kissing my ear. "This is forever," he repeated, over and over and over again, a vow for only me.

My chest tightened. Did he feel it too? The unspoken pull that felt like fate itself had woven it? I kissed him back, each one a silent promise, a truth I didn't know how to share yet.

"This is forever."

11

I WOKE TO THE SOFT LIGHT OF MORNING SUN creeping over the hills. Az was next to me and I couldn't help my smile as I thought about last night.

But my thoughts were rudely interrupted by a voice that echoed in my head.

Mar.

I couldn't shake how real my conscience had sounded and there was nothing I could do when the moment replayed over and over. Was it the wine playing tricks on me? My conscience manifesting in some way to get me to stop drinking? I pushed the thought aside as best I could and looked over at Azral sleeping peacefully next to me. I placed a kiss on his forehead before wrapping a robe around my bare body.

Walking to the balcony, I pulled on the handle, locked.

I whirled, my heart leaping out of my chest. But now, Az was right in front of me, distracting me with his own bare skin.

"We have time before we have to meet with Vani." He winked.

My heart steadied, now pounding for an entirely different reason. I headed to the closet, lowering my robe just below my back as my hair brushed against the top of my backside. "Not enough time for me."

Azral ran to me, his arms lifting me from behind. A laugh escaped my lips as he spun me around. He held me close, placing a hundred kisses on my neck before setting me back down. "I'll let you get ready. I'll be back in an hour," he whispered in my ear.

"What's going to happen today?" I hesitated, turning to face him.

"With Vani," he shook his head, "who knows."

He cradled my head, before swiping a robe from the chaise and headed for the door. My eyes trailed to the locked balcony doors, wondering if it was something I should ask about.

A question for later.

I stepped into the bathroom. The marble tiles were cool under my feet. Steam from the large tub in the center of the room wafted up towards me, the heat already making me flinch. Someone's martem had clearly been at work.

I slipped out of my robe and lowered myself into the hot water. The tension in my muscles instantly eased as I washed myself.

But even as I relaxed, that voice crept back into my mind.

Mar.

I tried to steady my thoughts despite the unwelcome repetition; letting the lavender soap calm my mind. When that didn't work, I took one final breath and submerged myself fully, allowing the water to take me.

"Akailo, how are we supposed to help her? To stop them from—this," my mother cried into my father's arms.

I was about to run in, to show them my new stuffed dragon, but stopped when I heard her cries. Instead, I crawled into the room, hiding behind the chair they shared.

"We knew there would be consequences but how are we supposed to protect her when we can't even protect our people?" she cried again.

"I'll fix this," my father promised.

A guard burst through the door, two more following. My mother jumped up, my father following suit.

"What is the meaning of this?" my father yelled.

A loud crash sounded from outside the doors. Screams followed. I jumped up from behind the chair...

I burst out of the tub, gasping for air and coughing up water. I flailed over the side and landed face first on the cold tiles, struggling to catch my breath. *Ow.* I coughed up more water until I was able to breathe in sweet, sweet air—even if my lungs still burned.

Pressing myself up from the floor, I grabbed a towel, wrapping it around myself as I leaned on the porcelain sink and stared deep into my crimson eyes.

That one was so real, so much more vivid than any of the ones I'd had before.

Mar, echoed through my mind. That incessant voice.

With a final glance in the mirror, I turned to get dressed.

I chose black leather pants and boots. There was a comfort in these simple items, some small semblance of my old home. I tugged on a white flowy tunic—its long sleeves left my shoulders bare—and shimmied into a deep violet corset. The silver lace patterns swirled into flowers threaded through the velvety material. My hair was still damp from almost drowning and I let it air dry into loose waves.

Azral arrived, smiling ear to ear in his casually embroidered brown tunic. "Ready?"

"Very."

The plan was to meet Sovanni in a quieter part of the castle. We wound through countless halls and spiraling staircases, the sheer size of the place overwhelming. At last, we reached what felt like the final stretch—a dim, narrow hallway draped in cobwebs. To the left stood a small, weathered wooden door. Azral knocked once before pushing it open and stepping inside.

Sovanni jumped up from a lounge chair as we entered, placing a book on the table next to her. Her dark brown hair curled over the edge of the lounge and hugged her body as she stood with a smile. Her icy blue gown complemented her with a diamond cutout over her stomach.

She practically leaped towards us, wrapping her arms around me and squeezing way too tight. "We must have more parties like that, Az. I had too much fun last night," she said, grinning at me. "Come, I'll show you around." She grabbed my hand.

I couldn't help my wandering eyes. The room was decently sized, a little smaller than mine and dimly lit. But the walls, gods, they were covered in bookshelves—every inch filled like the entire room had swallowed the written world whole. Az had said she had thousands of books; I'd thought he'd been exaggerating. Where there was no more room on the shelves, stacks sat on the floor, piling into a massive hill. Sovanni told me most were about the history of the Fae, Humans, the lands, and martem. Some were for pleasurable reading but she was mainly a scholar, soaking up any history fact she could get her hands on. She went on about her fascination with just about anything and everything.

"I want to learn it all," she said, admiring her own collection of knowledge.

Small windows set into the tops of the walls let in some sunlight but most of the room was lit by candles at even intervals and a crackling fire in the back. The walls were a deep chestnut wood and the floors were covered in layered rugs of all different shapes, designs, and colors. Fabrics laid over rope on the walls separated what looked to be her bed from the rest of the room.

She gestured towards the deep blue chaise she had been resting on and I sat, rubbing my hands along its thick texture.

"Please make yourself at home. What's mine is yours." She smiled.

Sovanni was so kind, maybe too kind, but if Azral trusted her, then so did I. She pulled the wooden chair from her very cluttered desk next to me.

"Az, I think I can take it from here." She nodded towards the door.

"I'll be staying," he shot back. "I won't be in your way," he added, moving to the corner of the room.

"Oh, brother, you know I don't like to work with an audience."

"I'm staying," Azral asserted in a low tone I hadn't heard before.

He folded his arms and leaned against the wall. His facial expression was unreadable in the dim corner but I could see his emerald eyes piercing her.

"Very well." Sovanni sighed, waving a hand before turning back to me. She poured a glass of what looked to be tea, steam escaping from the small cup as she mixed an herb into it on the table next to her.

"So, how much has my brother told you about my martem?" she asked as if magic was something we normally spoke of.

"He called you the dreamweaver but—"

Sovanni let out a howl of laughter. "Oh, gods. I'm sorry." She placed her hand on her chest. "Ahh, I haven't been called that in decades. Brother, you make me sound so terrifying."

She shook her head at him and handed me the cup of tea. Azral ignored her.

"Valerian root opens the mind," Sovanni explained as she nodded to the teacup, "helping to make your dream state more vivid and easier for me to dive into. I've never worked on a Human before so I gave you a smaller dose, to be safe. I wasn't exactly sure what barriers we may need to get through."

"Barriers?"

"Dreams are a tricky thing sometimes. They dwell in our subconscious mind. When we are awake, or conscious, it is harder to get through and see what lies in there. This tea should help open your mind and break through that wall, letting me in," she continued, clearing her throat. "Our dreams, or what's in the subconscious, are just visions that our mind creates most of the time. Whether we create them to fill some void or help us through a difficult time, it all depends. From what Az tells me, you believe these people in your dreams are real?"

"Is it possible?" I blurted. But she didn't answer. "Because I'm Human, you think it's impossible that the Fae I see are my parents?"

She waited a moment before responding. I could see the sympathy in her eyes. "Magic has its limitations." She gestured towards the cup. *I can't be crazy, can I?*

The smell hit my nose as I lifted it to my lips and gods, it was awful. "I'm supposed to *drink* this?" I gagged.

"It's an acquired taste." Sovanni grinned, watching my nose crinkle in disgust.

I tried to smile but I opted to plug my nose as I downed the contents. Warmth and bitterness coated my throat, its dirt-like taste lingering. With a final swig, and an attempt not to gag, I gave her back the cup.

Sovanni rose from her chair and came behind me on the chaise. Placing her warm hands on my cold shoulders, she laid me back. "Open your mind to me, Amara," she whispered.

Her hands moved to my temples. I shut my eyes and took a long breath. The room began to spin, the sounds of the crackling fire fading in and out. I tried to fight it, the feeling of slipping in and out of reality. I hesitated, reluctant to open up, to let someone into my most guarded thoughts. But this was the only way to piece the puzzle together.

Sovanni's voice cut through the spinning. She sounded so far away. "It's okay, Amara. You're safe."

With that reassurance, the room fell quiet and my mind went completely black.

It was like I was standing in a very, *very* dark room. My legs grew shaky and I took a deep breath to calm myself. *Focus, Amara.* I blinked, letting my eyes adjust to the darkness. A familiar hum returned, what I could only assume was her martem at work. It was oddly calming.

I took another deep breath and surveyed my surroundings. An odd light illuminated only where I stood. I turned and turned searching for anything but I couldn't see more than an arm's length in front of me.

Finally, I spotted Sovanni in the distance.

"Hello!" I called, my voice echoing as if I was in a long tunnel but she didn't hear me. I walked towards her, still yelling. The closer I got, I could hear her voice; she was talking to someone, Azral.

I took another calming breath, just hearing his voice, knowing he was still here with me, made my heartbeat steady.

"What do you mean?" His voice was muffled and harsh. My heart sped back up at the tone. *He was scared.*

"There's something else here." Sovanni was muffled, as well, almost like they were speaking underwater. Her hands were in front of her, like she was still holding my temples but my body wasn't there.

"Hello!" I called out to them as fear crawled in.

They bickered back and forth but I couldn't tell what they were fighting about.

Mar.

A chill ran down my spine, my heart threatening to beat out of my chest. I spun around to the sound that came behind me.

There was still only darkness.

"Something's blocking me," Sovanni said.

"Give her more tea."

"It's not my martem." Her voice filled with fear.

And so did my body. I felt my heart actually stop because I knew exactly what she meant.

I wasn't alone.

My mind raced as I spun, looking for a way out, but I froze.

"Mar," the voice said behind me. It was so clear, so close.

I spun around again and there he was.

Standing only inches from me, the male towered over me. His skin was pale, almost glowing in the low light. I looked him over, assessing the looming threat. He wore a black tunic, ruffled and slightly untied. His black pants were loose and he wore no shoes. It was a very odd choice of outfit, unkempt, not one you would usually see an enemy wear. His black hair blended with the darkness around us but it was a bit of a mess, like he was lying in bed. *Did he just wake up?*

But even in his state, he was breathtaking. Every part of him demanded attention and I was like a moth to a flame. I couldn't take my eyes off him. His features were sculpted with a dark precision, each angle adding to his undeniable charm. His eyes had an addicting depth, like an endless midnight sky. Stars sparkled in them with a glow that could trap anyone with a single look.

And he had done just that.

"Do something!" Azral's muffled cry echoed.

I snapped out of the trance, Az's voice pulling me back to reality. The male's eyes were still locked onto mine. Just as I was about to scream, he raised a finger to his lips.

Then he vanished.

Sovanni's hand grabbed my shoulder and I jumped.

"What's going on?" I asked between fast breaths. I looked at her, anger and confusion growing in her features.

"Nothing, my brother is just an idiot," she said through gritted teeth. "Time to go." Her voice was now clear, urgent, as the void of darkness consumed us.

But before it went completely dark, I swore I saw her eyes dart behind me, to *him.*

Gasping, I opened my eyes, the dim candles of the room almost blinding me. Azral hovered above me, spinning with the room. Sovanni shot him a warning look.

"Go," she urged, turning and grabbing a bottle of wine from the table.

Az wrapped his arms around me, lifting me from the chaise and holding me steady as the world spun. Was she okay? *Was I okay?*

"Vani," Azral whispered, his voice laced with compassion.

"Whatever you've got going on, Az, I don't want to be a part of it."

Sovanni spun with the room. She laughed a little, probably at my current state. I watched as she took a long swig from the bottle. Az scooped me into his arms and my head dropped back. Upside down, I swore I saw tears filling her eyes just before my world went black.

A deep voice woke me, erupting through, what felt like, the whole castle. It was familiar, if unwelcome.

"What were you thinking?" the king bellowed.

"We can trust her." Azral snarled in response.

I rolled over in bed to see Erixx towering over Az by the door. His black eyes shot to me and he growled, his face painted with anger.

He grabbed Azral by his curls, dragging him out of the room.

Sovanni flung around the corner into the doorway, startling me as I sat up. "Wouldn't want to be him right now." She laughed moving into the room but her eyes flicked to the door, like the king might come for her next.

"How are you feeling?" She sank onto the edge of the bed.

"What happened?" I rubbed my eyes. Grogginess from whatever drugs were in that tea still tugged at me, the midday sun nearly blinding.

"To you or him?" She laughed. "The king is very private. Az shared a little secret of his with me and well, he's not very fond of me." She shrugged, smiling and flicking her curls over her shoulder like it was no big deal but the light didn't reach her eyes. "We can talk about that later."

"Is Azral okay?" I had to ask. Seeing him like that, it made my heart ache.

"He'll be fine." She grabbed my hand, pulling me from the bed, and I lost my footing. She caught me, smiling. "Come, let's walk off that tea. It's beautiful out today."

Sovanni held my shoulder, straightening my presumably messy hair with her free hand. Her lavender eyes searched my features for a moment, studying me. She let out a low sigh before lacing our arms together, leading us out of the room.

12

WE WALKED ARM IN ARM DOWN THE STONE
path leading to the castle grounds. Mylom grazed by the
nearby stables. She looked up as we walked by, her eyes
locking with mine as she lowered her head.

"She's beautiful, isn't she?" Sovanni beamed, breaking my
trance. Mylom remained fixed on us, almost as if she was
smiling, too.

We walked in silence for a while, the stone path turning
to dirt beneath our feet as we entered a wooded area. The trees
were massive, their branches reaching up towards the sky and
blocking most of the sun. Vines climbed their trunks and
flowers of every color bloomed at their bases. We strolled
deeper into the woods, the sunlight filtering through the

canopy overhead creating a dappled pattern on the forest floor. Leaves rustled gently and in the distance, birds chirped.

"It's breathtaking here, this world," I said.

This place was mesmerizing, nothing like my walks through the cold woods of Zandar. The colors were all so vivid and the weather more than perfect. Sovanni, however, seemed unimpressed. Probably because she had never known the darkness of the Human realm.

She let out a breathy laugh. "This doesn't even compare to what is out there." She pulled her sleeves down her arm as the wind, now cool in the shade of the forest, blew past us. "Kaluth, this world, these lands and its people, they've been woven together in time and history. But the beauty of it all only hides the truth, the tragedies of the past." She sighed, her face serious as she looked at me. "The magic of this world, Amara, is sometimes not worth the loss that it brings."

"You know a lot about it?" I shyly asked. "Kaluth?"

Maybe if she couldn't see anything in my mind, if she couldn't decode my dreams, at least she knew of some people who were possibly, hopefully, searching for a missing child. Maybe she had some birth records stored away in her thousands of books.

"I do." She smiled and a flicker of hope ignited in me. "I know a lot about many worlds but I'm afraid it may take longer than your Human lifetime to learn everything."

My Human lifetime.

I somehow forgot that very crucial detail. I decided not to push my questions, not yet anyway. I wanted to wait for Azral, to find my truth with him.

We came up on a small patch of grass, the trees opening to reveal a crystal-clear stream running through. She led me to the bank and we sat, our feet dangling. Water rushed by as fast as the thoughts in my head. I was lost in them, thinking about Sovanni's words and the idea that this world came at a price.

She must have sensed my unease because she turned to me and placed a reassuring hand on my arm. "Don't worry about what I said, Amara. Focus on the present and what you can learn and experience in this moment," she said with a soft smile. "What questions do you have? The curiosity is just oozing from you, I can tell." She laughed, turning towards me, folding her legs.

I let my legs dangle in the water, the coolness of the stream sent a slight chill through me, even as it gave me the courage to ask, "How old are you?"

Given Az's age, I had no idea the life span Fae could have. The years must be uncountable after so long.

"Three hundred and thirty-two," she replied.

I couldn't help but let out a small gasp. "So, Az is your younger brother?"

"Yes and my half-brother. Right before my mother, Alora—" She paused and I could feel her pain, *Az's pain.* "She had me before she met Erixx. She left me with my aunt to raise me in a small town just west of here, Acrari." She paused again, taking a breath. "Erixx let me come live with them in Solyrus when I was seven, after he killed my father." She shrugged nonchalantly as if that didn't mean a thing. "My mother insisted, but he has always hated me, never trusted me and well, the feeling is mutual. I've only stayed around this long for Az."

Gods, I would hate him, too.

"So, you grew up in Solyrus. Where is that?" I asked, trying to keep the conversation going, because she looked sad, blinking away the small tear in her eye.

She scooted away, grabbing a stick and drawing in the dirt between us.

"There are five territories that make up Kaluth, Rosetia being the largest on the land. That's where we are now." She drew a large jagged oval shape and pointed to the middle. "Solyrus and Lunhayven, they surround Rosetia on the north and south borders."

My heart skipped a beat at the familiar word, *Lunhayven.* She added lines in her circle, separating the territories. Drawing an S in the upper section and an L in the lower. Moving to the right, she drew smaller islands. The makeshift map began to look very similar to the ones Az and I had found.

Drip. Drip. Drip.

I clenched a fist, my nails breaking skin.

"The Isles are here. They're the smallest and most dangerous territory. No one lives there but it's made up of four islands where"—she stopped—"well, that's a longer story for a different time."

She drew another circle on the other side of the islands. "But finally, right here," she looked up, smiling, a twinkle in her eyes, "this is The Ever. There is very, *very* little information about its people and lands. All I know is that someone, *something,* lives there. I've searched for almost two-hundred years and still have no idea what."

The Ever, The Isles. This world was bigger than I imagined and that gave me hope. The possibility of my family being somewhere out there was so much bigger.

"Most people live here in Rosetia." She pointed with her stick. "Lunhayven isn't much of anything after the war. And Erixx rules over both Rosetia and Solyrus now."

"Azral said you've been at war for over twenty years." Merely a fraction of her life. Almost all of mine.

"It's been a long time." She sighed.

I looked back at the map, circling the L with my fingertip. I remembered the frost flowers I held in my dream, the icy cliff. "Is it...snowy there?"

Her eyes shot to me. "How did you know that?" Concern laced her words.

"I think I've been there before, in my dreams." I took a long breath. "What happened to the people who lived there?" I was afraid to ask but I had to know.

"Erixx saw an opportunity to expand his power. He claimed they 'posed a threat to the peace and stability of Kaluth'. Of course, that was all a lie. The real reason was his insatiable thirst for control."

I nodded, a lump forming in my throat. The thought of innocents suffering because of one man's greed made my stomach turn.

"I told you, Amara, the truth of this world is ugly."

"What about The Isles?" I pushed. I didn't want to think anymore of suffering.

"I don't want to send you running, one story at a time, yeah?" She laughed while drawing markings in the ground I didn't recognize.

"Where does the magic come from, martem, Az called it?"

"The gods." She smiled. "It was all pure before. Descendants of the Sun God, were able to wield fire. The Moon Goddess, her descendants wielded water and so on. It's passed down through bloodlines and bonds but over time, bloodlines mixed and the power evolved and grew."

If Azral had power like his mother…"Do you get yours from your father or did your mother have multiple powers?"

Sovanni smirked. "So, Azral did care to share some information with you. "Yes, I got it from my father. My mother always called us danriells—or dreamweavers—but I don't prefer that term. I like to make sure my subjects are willing before taking a deep dive into their subconscious."

"You can do it without them knowing?" Fear laced my question.

"In some cases, yes. But those barriers I mentioned before, the ones that block the subconscious, need to be down. To do that, people are either sleeping or in a deep state of meditation. Most Fae with martem shield themselves before reaching a deep sleep, so it can be tricky."

I tried to piece together the information, not wanting to show my confusion and fear around it. "Azral, he called himself an Illion?"

"Yes," she said sternly. "The illusion master himself." She chuckled to herself.

"He said your mother was much more powerful."

She shook her head. "He doubts himself."

"I'm sorry," I whispered. "She was sick?" I couldn't stop the question from tumbling out, even though I already felt uneasy about it.

Her brows narrowed, her expression hardening. "Sick?" she repeated, her voice sharp, as if the word offended her. "She was killed."

Killed? The air seemed to thicken around me, my chest tightening. Why wouldn't Azral tell me that? I could understand more than anyone a parent being torn away too soon.

Sovanni only shook her head. "Let's go into town. We're already so close to the end of the castle grounds." She stood, dusting off her dress, and reached to help me up.

"What's in town?"

"Wine," she said with a sinister smirk, locking our arms and leading the way.

We stepped out of the forest into a large clearing. The scenery changed, as if a line had been drawn in the ground.

The once-vibrant grass turned to ash, the trees reduced to blackened skeletons. The sweet scent of honey was replaced by the stale smell of smoke and destruction. Sovanni didn't seem shocked by the view, leading us through the ash-covered field towards a small village.

"What happened?" I gasped, taking in the tragedy.

"There was a fire," she sighed, "a really big one."

Stone buildings were scattered throughout the village, their walls marred with soot and debris. People moved about like it was normal. Some carried buckets of water while others hung laundry to dry on clotheslines strung between buildings. A few children sat on broken stoops with wooden bowls, begging for scraps of anything.

We walked the broken path and everyone stared, curiosity on their faces, yet, still, Sovanni smiled at everyone. She was stunning, shining like a beacon in this dark town. I couldn't help but stare, too. Some onlookers bowed their heads as we passed. She made sure to kneel before every lone child, tossing gold coins into their bowls.

We neared a rundown building. A male dressed in soot-covered clothing rushed to the door before we reached it. His hands, rough and covered in ash, held it open for us. We climbed a small staircase to a dimly lit tavern filled with music and laughter.

But the sound died as soon as we walked in. Whispers filled the space, curious eyes peering our way.

The tavern was coated in grime but no one seemed to care. Sovanni didn't seem to care about the whispers, either, taking my hand and leading me towards the bar. We strode past wooden tables and chairs. A fire burned in the hearth to our right. Two males vacated their stools as we neared the bar, gesturing for us to take them. The music resumed its previous volume as we sat but everyone seemed to talk lower, trying not to look our way.

The female bartender turned, glasses in her hands, but as her eyes met mine, they went crashing to the floor.

"Amara?" the female breathed, straightening with her brows raised.

Had they heard about me, the Human girl, this far from the castle?

The female gathered herself, snapping for someone to clean up while she snatched two new glasses and placed them in front of us. Sovanni grabbed the closest bottle, pouring a deep red wine into them. The scent of it hit my nose, stronger than the one at the ball. This berry scent was cleaner and crisper.

"Amara, this is Thysa." Sovanni nodded and took a small sip of her wine.

"Hi," I said shyly. I could feel the eyes on my back as I shifted on the wooden stool. Had they all heard of me?

"Hello." Thysa smiled, pushing back her long black locs, revealing more of her face.

Her skin was a rich mahogany, with a face chiseled in beauty and her grayish green eyes now gleamed at me. Firelight sparkled off the jewels locked between the tiny braids in her hair. Her lips were full, painted in a deep red matching the dress she wore beneath a white apron wrapping perfectly around her body.

"What brings you out this way? Bored of the prince already?" Thysa teasingly grinned.

"I thought I'd sneak her out of that drab castle and give her a little history lesson." Sovanni took another sip.

"Well, Amara, welcome to Raxos, the city of ruins." Thysa lifted the bottle and took a swig.

I lifted my glass and nodded, taking a sip of the rich vintage. Its flavor was much better than the one from the ball and insanely better than anything I'd ever had back home. I felt its effects almost immediately. My senses heightened and the music became clearer. The now-full tavern was louder, the laughs and whispers echoed and the large fire bellowed as its flames grew in rhythm with the music.

I couldn't help but notice the differences between Raxos and the Fae world I had seen at the ball. The tavern was rough around the edges with dirt and ash covering almost everything. But despite the look of it, there was a certain charm. The people were livelier and there was a sense of community the castle didn't have.

"Raxos is the closest town to the castle. I found Thysa soon after I moved here. I wish you could have seen it before, well…" Sovanni trailed off, pulling me from my trance.

"We make do," Thysa reassured her. "But enough of that, tell me about you, *Amara*." She dragged my name out. "As intrigued as you are about us Fae, we are just as fascinated by you."

Sovanni lifted her glass towards me, raising her brow along with it in agreement.

And even though I barely knew them, something told me I could trust them. So, I shared.

We talked for what felt like hours. I told them everything from when I was found as a child to what happened to my parents, then when I met Azral. Thysa had many questions about Human life and Sovanni sat and listened, the scholar in her taking it all in.

They shared stories of their own, tales of their lives and how they met. Thysa was a brewer. She said that the wine we were drinking was made from berries she grew in the nearby forest—better than "that castle piss" as she called it. Sovanni laughed, admitting she snuck in as many bottles of Thysa's brew as she could.

When the room started spinning profusely, I excused myself in an attempt to sober up.

The cold night air hit me like a brick wall when I stepped outside. I drew in a long breath, savoring the chill on my skin and in my lungs. It reminded me of nights back in Zandar and it was oddly comforting. But this place, these people, I could feel it now. Something about it was familiar; something deep inside of me was drawn to it all. The stars twinkled above me and I took one more deep breath before returning.

I made my way to the warmth of the fire. The music had grown louder and people were stumbling, clearly intoxicated. I hoped I looked slightly more together than they did. I put my hands out towards the flames, looking at all the trinkets and glasses on the mantle.

"Hey," I breathed and moved closer to the Fairy sitting next to an empty glass.

She looked like the same one from the ball, her blue glitter glowing in the room. She flew away, leaving her trail of sparkles, right past a male who stood so still in the crowd it made him noticeable.

My heartbeat quickened. I turned to look for Sovanni but she wasn't there. When I turned back, the male was directly in front of me.

I immediately realized he wasn't from Raxos. His all-black clothes were immaculate, nothing like the ones locals wore. I scanned the threat, noting the sword sheathed at his side. Black diamonds on the hilt glowed in the light of the fire. I looked up at him as he towered over me and I met his midnight eyes.

"Still enjoying yourself, I see." He smirked. *That voice.*

This was the voice from the ball, meaning he hadn't been a vision. *And not my conscience?* No, he was definitely real and now right in front of me.

At least I wasn't completely crazy.

But my body, which had just warmed from the fire, grew cold as his eyes bore into mine. "Who are you?" I demanded, my voice trembling slightly.

Before he could answer the tavern door burst open, stopping my racing heart. Chaos ensued as guards swarmed, causing people to gasp and try to run. I glanced from the male blocking my exit to Sovanni behind the bar who looked like the interruption was an inconvenience rather than something to fear. She whispered to Thysa who nodded and vanished through the doors behind her. Sovanni glanced at me and then turned her attention to the male, her brows furrowing.

"Where is she?" Azral's voice boomed as he entered the tavern, his golden sword drawn and pointed at Sovanni.

I whipped my head towards him. *Why is he acting like I was kidnapped?*

The male before me let out a low chuckle and Azral's head snapped in our direction. He marched towards us, pushing aside a drunk Fae in his way; his sword pointed at the mystery male.

In that moment, Azral looked every inch the prince that he was.

The tip of the golden sword pressed against the male's neck but he seemed unfazed. "Are the dramatics truly necessary?" He sneered, raising a brow.

"You have a lot of nerve coming back here." Azral growled through bared teeth.

"I was curious." His gaze drifted to me, lingering as it traveled from my face to my feet and back again, every inch of me subject to his slow, deliberate scrutiny. It wasn't just a look—it was an appraisal. Finally, his eyes snapped back to Azral. "You bring a Human here, especially one as ravenous as that, and expect me not to introduce myself?"

With a swift movement, Azral had the male pinned against the stone fireplace, his sword now flat against his neck. Sovanni rushed to my side, her cold hand slipping into mine.

"You made a huge mistake," Azral growled.

The male raised his arms in surrender, that smirk still painted on his face. "Did I, *Your Highness?*"

"Arrest him!" Az yelled, turning his head towards the golden armored men behind us. I followed his gaze but then Az stumbled into the wall, his sword pressed against nothing but air.

Azral snarled, turning to us with a deadly stillness. My stomach fluttered, and not in a good way. I held Sovanni's hand a bit tighter, my palms ice cold and sweaty. Emerald eyes glowed at us with an anger I'd never seen.

"Let's go," he said to me, then glowered at Sovanni. "I'll deal with you later."

He marched from the tavern and we followed right behind. Each step was like distant thunder, echoing through the silence.

We ducked inside the golden carriage waiting in the crumbling street. Azral sat silent opposite Sovanni and me, our hands still intertwined, laced together with fear. I looked out the window; there wasn't a single star in the sky and the moon was missing. The chill of the night perfectly mirrored the cold tension inside the carriage. Only the sound of rocks beneath the wheels and trotting hooves filled the silence.

I looked back to Azral, trying to read him. *Why is he so angry?* But he didn't look my way, not even a glance. He just glared out the window, frantically tapping a finger on his knee. His golden ring twinkled with each beat.

Sovanni's hand tightened on mine, her grip bone-crushing, as if her very life depended on the connection.

13

WE APPROACHED THE DOORS TO THE CASTLE. The guards that surrounded it before were now gone, replaced by one male whose eyes burned through us. The king.

Azral's hand landed on my shoulder and I couldn't help but jump at the touch. Erixx grabbed Sovanni's arm, her hand slipping out of mine. He dragged her up the stairs and inside the castle door's. Azral's hand lifted and I let out the breath I didn't realize I was holding. He muttered something under his breath as I followed silently behind.

The large doors slammed shut behind us. A gust of a familiar cold wind swept in. I wrapped my arms around my body, shielding myself from the fear that swept through me along with it.

Erixx hauled Sovanni down the left hall and Azral quickly turned to me. "What were you thinking?" he seethed.

"Sovanni, we—" I mumbled, unable to finish my sentence. I wasn't a stranger to fear but I never thought I would feel this way looking at him.

"Why did she take you there?" he demanded.

"We were just out for a walk and she was telling me about your mother." My cheeks warmed and I stuttered, feeling small and helpless.

"She *what?*"

"She wanted to get a drink so we went to see Thysa." The words kept tumbling out.

"What did she tell you?" His voice was calmer but still demanding.

"Just about your mother; where she was from and the other lands." Now didn't seem like a good time to bring up why he didn't tell me the truth about his mom.

Az let out a frustrated sigh and pulled his hand down his face. "What did he say to you?"

"Who is *he?*" I spat, curious about the male who plagued my mind. Frustration grew at all the answers I still didn't have, the pitfalls I kept falling into because Az wouldn't tell me anything.

"What did he say?" Azral repeated, his tone dropping.

"Why are you being like this?" I stepped towards him. "Tell me what's going on, Azral."

He took a long breath, clarity returning to his eyes. He reached for my elbow but I pulled back, eyes narrowing.

"Amara," he whispered. "I'm sorry. I'm so sorry. I just—" He shook his head again. "That person—" Disgust filled his face. His lips curled. "Drayzen," he spat, like the name was poison on his tongue. "He's extremely dangerous."

"Why?" I pressed. "He was here last night and—"

"Last night? He was here?" Azral looked like he might tear the man apart with his bare hands.

"At the ball, I saw him but he didn't say much, he knew my name. And in—"

"Why didn't you tell me someone talked to you last night?"

I held in a snarl. For one, I thought I was just crazy and seeing things. I had been planning to mention what happened when Sovanni entered my mind but there'd been no chance. Now, with his new tone and the way he kept cutting me off, Az was getting on my last nerve.

My arms dropped to my sides. "Who is he?"

Azral cocked his head towards the hall Sovanni had disappeared down. I heard a faint noise but that was all. Azral grunted, cursing under his breath.

"They'll take you back to your room." He gestured to the two guards approaching. "I'll see you in the morning."

With that, he turned, his footsteps echoing in the distance, leaving me in the cold silence.

The heavy door clicked shut behind me, locking as I entered my room. I stared at it defiantly. What was so dangerous that I needed to be locked in? Was it him, Drayzen?

I let out a rough scream that did nothing to take the edge off my anger.

I pulled the thick blanket from the bed and moved to the lit fireplace. Plopping in front of it, I tucked my legs to my chest. I closed my eyes, relishing in the comfort this position brought me. On the floor, in front of a growing fire. It was like home, like Zandar, a feeling I didn't think I would ever miss.

I jumped as the door creaked open. One servant entered carrying a golden tray. She was about my age—or at least the equivalent in Fae years. Hair cascaded down her back, black curls that rivaled the length of my own. Some of those curls fell over her porcelain skin as she set the tray down on the table behind me. I met her plum-colored eyes. Her apron donned the red roses of the castle sigil, complementing the cream dress underneath.

She poured lavender liquid into a small teacup, steam caressing my face as she handed it to me. I inspected the tea sloshing with tiny waves, the porcelain clinking as I set the cup on the saucer. I realized, now, that I was shaking, whether from fear or the cold, I couldn't tell.

My thoughts were clouded, my mind reeling from Azral's behavior towards me, towards his sister, even towards the people in Raxos.

And he was supposed to be their king someday?

"He is easily misunderstood, easily feared, at times," the servant murmured, placing the teapot down. "But you can trust him."

Her words didn't comfort me. This side of him, this wasn't the Azral I knew. Everything up to this moment threatened to swallow me whole. I felt like a child, locked in this room on time-out. I felt lied to, so many details left out, so many things he wouldn't tell me about this place, about him.

I thanked the female with a slight nod anyway. She bowed her head and as she left, the door locked behind her with a soft *click*.

Alone again, one thought snuck to the forefront of my mind.

Drayzen.

Who was he and why in the world did he sound like my conscience? A voice I'd listened to—a voice I trusted. Why did Azral seem to hate him so much? And most importantly, what did he want from me?

I couldn't shake him, especially after seeing him again today. There was no doubt in my mind it was his voice that haunted me. Maybe he was a danriell like Sovanni? Since he was able to get into my head when she did, it was the only thing that made sense. But *why?*

So many questions, too many of them, tired me. The lavender tea only added to my drowsiness. I stood, shedding my clothes and crawling into bed. Silk sheets cooled my anger. I wrapped the blankets tighter, shutting off my brain.

Morning sun cast a warm glow over town, lighting the blooming flowers and the grass fields before it. As we walked, a herd of graceful deer pranced by, their antlers shimmering in the sunlight. I couldn't help but laugh and point at the stunning sight. A deep chuckle echoed behind me and a familiar hand landed on my head.

I turned to see my father, beaming with the smile I knew so well. In one swift motion, he scooped me into his arms and hoisted me onto his shoulders.

The bustling town was filled with lively sounds of residents and merchants. Vibrant carts overflowing with fruits, vegetables, flowers, and jewels lined every street. The chatter and music of a band with flutes and guitars filled the air as we strolled through the crowd. We stopped at a candy merchant. My eyes were glued to all the sweets.

My father surprised me with a small bag and I squealed, unable to contain my excitement as I tasted each raisin. The chocolate flavors burst in my mouth, making me giggle with each bite.

But then chaos erupted. A deafening explosion ripped through the air and flames ignited before us. My father pulled me close, shielding me with his body as we ran for safety. Screams echoed in every direction. As we fled, another explosion rocked the ground.

"Stay with him," he said, signaling a guard to watch me. Tears filled my eyes as he raced off to help.

The guard carried me to a nearby building where residents hid. The room quickly filled with more people, their cries clear over the destruction. The guard placed me in a chair and watched the front door, his hand ready on his hilt.

In the chaos, healers swarmed the injured, their martem desperately trying to mend the burns and wounds from the explosions. My guard removed his gloves, revealing soft white light emanating from his palms. He placed his hands over a badly burned female and the light surrounded her, slowly knitting her wounds. Relief eased her features as the pain faded.

I sat alone in the chair, watching. A woman with kind brown eyes stooped towards me with a glass of water. She kept *her head low as she looked up at me. Her smile was warm, like a cozy blanket, and it softened my fear immediately.*

"It's going to be okay." She placed her smooth mahogany hand on mine, rubbing her thumb in comforting circles. "Your father should be back soon; he will be fine."

I looked up to the female to thank her, just as my mother taught me.

And as I looked up...

I jumped from the bed, my breath catching.

The sheets were damp with sweat and I threw them off before making for the bathroom. After splashing cold water on my face, I gripped the sides of the marble bowl, staring into the mirror.

That town was too familiar. The open field before it, familiar. The fire, that building.

That female.

I splashed water on my face again and again and again. I pinched my skin as hard as I could on my arm, my legs, my hands, just to make sure I was actually awake.

Because these dreams, whatever they were, they were real.

The people in them, real. The events, real.

My parents.

All of it was real.

I was positive because that female, gods, I would recognize her anywhere: It was Thysa.

14

MY THOUGHTS RACED, SWARMING MY MIND AS I paced around the room in a frenzy.

Thysa.

That was her.

Did she recognize me at the bar? Could she know something about my parents? About me?

The endless questions swirled like dense smoke.

I was only sure of one thing. I had to go to Raxos; I had to ask her. And I couldn't wait. No, I'd waited too long for answers and Azral would be no help at the moment.

I scoured the room for any sign of a key. Of course, there was nothing. I pushed against the locked balcony doors, pulling the handles over and over, a cry escaping my lips as I released them. The walls of the room pressed in on me. I needed to get out.

My answers were so close.

A stone vase caught my attention; dying dahlias filled it. A frustrated growl burst from me and I headed for the closet. I dressed in black, throwing on a hooded cloak to hide my white hair in the night. Grabbing as many loose shirts as I could, I tied them together. The makeshift rope was hopefully long enough. I stomped out of the closest and grabbed the vase, tossing the dead flowers.

Standing before the balcony doors, I wrapped my hand in an extra shirt and raised the vase. In Zandar, the cost would have fed me for a month. Now...desperate times and all that.

I clenched my eyes shut as I hurled the vase against the glass. A jolt ricocheted up my arm. I was thrown back, landing hard. The vase bounced off the door, crashing and breaking against the tiles.

"Ugh!" I growled. *What was that?* Some sort of magical barrier? I was truly locked in. Trapped.

For your safety, Azral had said. But right now, I didn't feel safe. Right now, I needed to get to Thysa.

Unwrapping the cloth from my hand, I surveyed the room. There had to be something that could help.

My eyes shot to the window next to the bed. A small twinkle winked outside. I crawled over to it, desperation oozing from me, and I blinked. It was that blue Fairy. Only this time, she had friends. Three Fairies flew in a circle, holding hands. Their blue, red, and yellow glitter created a tiny rainbow. The Fairies glowed in the moonlight and flapped their delicate wings as they danced. I couldn't make them out perfectly but I could see their matching dresses corresponding with the color of their wings.

Three mini dragon-looking creatures appeared, flying around them, also sparkling with matching glitter. They were nothing like Mylom. Each one looked like they could fit in the palm of my hand. One of them flew up to the window lock and blew ice from its mouth. I watched in awe as the lock froze over. The second dragon followed by slamming its razor-sharp tail into the ice, causing the lock to shatter into pieces. The Fairies all giggled and flew away.

I placed my hand on the window and the cool night breeze whispered against my face as it opened. I nudged the frame farther. There was no magic, no barrier. Those Fairies had given me an exit.

I grabbed my makeshift rope and returned to the window, scanning the area below. Luckily, the coast was clear—as much as I could see, anyway. I peered down, estimating the distance between myself and the earth. I counted three windows below me, four stories. The fall would undoubtedly be painful, if not kill me, but it was that or stay here with no answers and no help.

"Okay." I nodded to myself. "You can do this."

I tied the shirt-rope tightly to the bed frame using knots I'd mastered from hunting. With a deep breath, I let my body fall back in the room, trying to place as much weight on it as I could. It held, for now. I tossed the rest of the rope out the window and watched it hang, ending just above the lowest window.

"It's okay." I tried to convince myself. "You'll survive that drop."

Even if it might hurt.

I looked back at my room and nodded. And then I climbed out the window.

Here goes nothing.

I gripped the knots tightly, trying not to look down. I wasn't necessarily afraid of heights but climbing was a whole different story. Sweat slickened my palms. I pushed the fear away, focusing instead on lowering myself one hand at a time. Each window I passed was, thankfully, pitch black. I sighed with relief when I reached the last one. At the end of the rope, I did look down, the ground only a few feet away. The impact still shook my bones as my boots sunk into soft dirt.

Dim moonlight cast a faint glow on the path leading into the woods. I couldn't see any guards but I had a feeling they would see me if I wasn't careful. Pulling my hood low over my head, I moved for the trees.

I realized, now, just how horrible of a plan this was. I had no weapons, no sense of direction, and no way of knowing how long it would take me to wander to town and find Thysa. The only advantage I had was Mylom. If I could make it to the stables, I knew she would help.

I looked back at the castle, my shirt-rope gently swinging in the moonlight. Mylom was a better plan, maybe not the best but better than the original of make-a-run-for-it. She could bring me back, hopefully before sunrise, before Azral came looking for me.

I just had to get to Raxos, to Thysa. The truth couldn't wait.

I walked deeper into the forest, the canopy of trees grew thicker, blocking the moonlight and plunging me into near darkness. It was perfect cover but it also meant I couldn't see a foot in front of me. I tripped over rocks, or maybe that was my own feet, but then those Fairies and their small dragons appeared again. Their tiny glittering bodies provided enough soft shimmering light to see the path and I instinctively followed them.

The trees gave way to an opening and I caught a glimpse of Mylom through the gates. Her maroon eyes glowed in the darkness, locking onto mine. A wide grin spread across my face as I stepped out of the shadows.

Adrenaline rushed as the Fairies and dragons flitted around me like excited children. They flew towards the stables and unlocked the gate Mylom sauntered out of, her black coat sparkling in their light. The Fairies danced, showering her with iridescent glitter. I reached out to pet her muzzle as she met me in the shadows.

"I think we've met before," I said softly, recalling the dream of her birth.

Mylom let out a sigh and nuzzled her head against mine.

"I'll take that as a yes." I laughed. I used a stump to climb onto her bare back, pulling slightly on her mane to steady myself. My breath was calm, my body at peace. I leaned into her, whispering where we needed to go, what I needed to do.

Without hesitation, Mylom trotted towards Raxos. The Fairies and little dragons followed next to us, whispering and giggling amongst themselves. I couldn't make out what they were saying, their voices just as tiny as their bodies. The blue one landed on my shoulder, her pale skin and light blue glitter beamed in the darkness.

"Ow!" I hissed as she pinched the side of my neck and flew away laughing. "What was that for?"

I brushed the sore spot. Her nails were like tiny razors. She flew back to me but before I was able to swat her away,

Mylom came to a sudden stop and so did my heart. The Fairies and dragons stopped, too, all dropping to her head.

"What is it?" I whispered, like any of them could answer. I scanned the darkness but there was nothing, just the rustling of leaves and the sound of the wind.

I slid off, my heart restarting but at twice the pace. I took about two steps, trying to see what could have startled all of us. Mylom's ears twitched. Leaning down, I picked up a large rock, my sweaty hand gripping it like my life depended on it. *Maybe this was a stupid idea.*

A twig snapped behind me. I spun around, my heart pounding in my ears. My rock, raised and ready to strike, suddenly felt inadequate.

"What were you planning to do with that?" a voice behind me said and I whirled. But there was no one there. Something tapped my shoulder and I whirled again, scanning for the threat as I slammed the rock down.

A hooded male grabbed my wrist, his pale hand cool and soft. He glanced at the rock only inches from his face. His features were hidden by his hood but those midnight eyes shot to me, sparkling through the shadows.

Drayzen.

"Drop it," he whispered.

I tightened my grip on the rock pushing against him but his strength was unmatched. "You must think I'm stupid." I gritted my teeth.

He smirked. "You read my mind."

Asshole.

The moon lit a dagger on his belt and an idea formed.

"Drop—" he started.

I released the rock with my left hand, distracting him as my right hand went for the dagger. My fingers brushed the hilt but he was too quick. He grabbed my free wrist, forcing me backwards and pinning both my hands above me against a tree.

Mylom let out a frustrated neigh and Drayzen looked back at her. Her maroon eyes honed in on him and she moved closer.

"She'll be fine," he told her.

Mylom nodded, sauntering off. *Seriously?*

The hum of Drayzen's martem swarmed my senses and the weight of his body pressed against mine, holding me in place against the stupid tree. His grip was firm but not tight. I tried to wriggle free but he tightened his grip. His eyes roamed me, like an animal assessing its prey.

"Let me go," I hissed, squirming. His hood slipped back but I still couldn't see much of him in the dark.

"Traveling alone at night is very dangerous for anyone, but especially *you*." He looked to the ground. "And with a rock as a weapon..." He slowly looked back up and beneath his sharp brows, his eyes pierced me. "What were you thinking?"

My attention shifted to the Fairies now flying around him and the blue one sat on his shoulder, pointing at me and, *ugh,* she was laughing!

"So much for your help." I rolled my eyes at her.

"I see you made friends with the Fairies and the drakai."

"Drakai?" The word spilled from my mouth before I could even try to hide the fact that I knew so little about this world.

"The Fairies' dragons, their companions," he said.

I went cross-eyed as the blue drakai landed on my nose. The blue Fairy flew to me as well and rested on my shoulder, pinching me again. I winced, baring my teeth at her.

Drayzen whistled and they abandoned me, landing on his shoulders. "Don't do anything stupid," he said, releasing me.

The Fairies moved closer to his ear and he leaned his head towards them. *Could he hear them?*

I brushed tree bark from my back but my eyes caught on the blade of the dagger behind Drayzen, lying in the dirt.

He's extremely dangerous, Azral's warning played in my mind.

Drayzen was distracted, he was *laughing* with the Fairies, and if I moved fast enough—

I leapt for the dagger, my hood forced back from my speed. The weight was familiar in my hands and I whirled on Drayzen. Wind caught my unbound hair, blocking my sight. I rolled and swung low for his legs.

But he wasn't there. My hand ripped through nothing but air.

I stood, spinning and then I froze. His body pressed into mine from behind and the cold metal of his sword kissed my throat.

His nose brushed my ear, his breath cool on my neck as he said softly, "I thought we could have a civilized conversation but since you're so intent on fighting me, I guess this will have to do."

I was smart enough to know when to admit defeat. "Fine," I hissed, dropping the dagger and raising my hands. "I surrender." *For now.*

He purred and a chill swept through me.

He removed the sword and I spun to face him but he was already by Mylom, petting her snout. The Fairies sat on her head and she neighed with content. I frowned. *Maybe he's not as dangerous as I thought, if Mylom seems to like him.* Either way, I kept my guard up.

"Don't you prefer her natural form?" Drayzen asked, rubbing her black coat.

"She prefers it this way, it's easier for her to travel," I responded, remembering Azral's answer to a similar question I had.

"Did she tell you that?" He raised a brow, glancing from me back to the dragon.

I stared into Mylom's eyes. *Can you talk, too?*

"Dragons are some of the most magical creatures," he continued, holding his hand out as a drakai landed on him, curling into his palm. "Multiple sources of martem run through them. Shape-shifting, flying, fire-breathing, you name it." The drakai flew from his hand and he placed it back on Mylom's snout, leaning into her. "And you think she prefers to be a horse?" He laughed under his breath, not even looking my way as he shared the information.

"Versi," he said low, his voice coated with a thick accent. Mylom trotted away towards a patch of grass, the Fairies with her.

"So, you're running away?" He brushed his hands together, facing me.

"No," I replied sharply.

"You escape in the middle of the night but you're not running away?" His brow rose.

"I didn't escape. I'm not a prisoner." I crossed my arms. "Why are you out here and who even are you?"

"I asked you first." A devilish grin painted his lips.

Moonlight broke through the trees as the wind blew and I was finally able to get a good look at him. The blue-black of his hair shimmered in the light. It was straight and slicked back, the ends tucked just around his ears. His non-Fae ears. *Human?* It couldn't be, not with his strength and speed. His midnight eyes met mine again. I couldn't help but get lost in them, like pools of the night sky, twinkling with a thousand stars.

Everyone in this world was beautiful but Drayzen, he was something else entirely.

"You're not Fae?" I asked, ignoring the flutter in my stomach.

He moved so quickly I didn't even notice, didn't even see him. In an instant, his mischievous smirk was too close and his deep eyes were bright. I took a step back but I was too curious.

"How do you do that? Is that your martem?"

He hummed. "So many questions, yet mine remain unanswered." *Gods, he's arrogant.*

"I just needed some air," I stated firmly, appeasing him.

"Going to Raxos in the middle of the night?" He looked me up and down, his lips curving slightly. "The prince doesn't please you enough?"

I shot him a killing glare, was he really insinuating...? *Ugh.* He laughed as I cleared my throat.

"I was going to see a friend," I replied, tightening my already crossed arms. "And how did you even know that's where I was going?"

"Thysa's only ever in one place," he said. Shock coursed through me but I kept my face even.

"You know her?"

He shrugged his shoulders. "I know everyone."

"How do you know Azral?" I asked, a little too quickly.

His voice dripped with sarcasm. "Old friends."

"Why were you at the ball the other night?" *Slow down, one question at a time Mar.*

"I wanted to see the beautiful Human everyone talked about," he said, smirking as the shadow of the moon covered where he stood. "And the rumors were true," he whispered on the back of my neck.

I whirled around, pushing against his toned chest. His body didn't move an inch. The power and strength of the Fae were still new to me but if he wasn't Fae, how was he this strong, this fast?

His smug look vanished. "Why are you out here?"

"I already told you," I hissed back, feeling a chill run down my spine.

"I find it hard to believe Azral would have let you leave in the middle of the night on your own. So, why did you sneak out?"

"What are you, his spy?" I snapped.

He let out a low laugh and gods, the flutter in my stomach was infuriating. "No, I am not his spy."

"Then who are you?" I crossed my arms again, taking a breath of the cold night air to cool my insides.

"You already know my name. Why do you need me to tell you?"

"How do you know that?" I couldn't hide the shock in my voice.

"And you didn't tell him about me until today, or Sovanni?" He clicked his tongue. "Why is that?"

How does he know all of this?

My brows furrowed, searching his face for any clues. "How did you get in my head? Are you a danriell like Sovanni?"

He looked over me, like some sort of prize. He took a step forward and I took a step back. There was a hum in the air, his martem, I assumed. It was like a magnetic force, annoyingly drawing me closer no matter how many times I moved back. His piercing eyes sent shivers over my body, igniting a fire in me I struggled to contain. He flashed another smirk, a silent challenge passing between us. My heart pounded louder and louder. The sound echoed in my ears like a drumbeat. Nerves coursed through me, making it hard to breathe as I struggled to steady myself against the onslaught of emotions raging inside me.

I took one last step back and my world tilted. My foot caught on a rock and I went toppling backwards. Just as I braced myself for impact, his cool hands wrapped around my waist.

He lifted me up and I stumbled into his chest. I knew he was tall—I was reminded each time we met—but this close to him, I had to strain my neck to see his face. Silver swirled through his eyes and the hum pulled me in. My hand grazed his chest but then he was gone, a respectable distance. The shift left me shivering.

His eyes returned to their normal hue. "Drayzen," he said softly with a tone I hadn't heard before. "My name is Drayzen. It was nice to officially meet you, Mar." His stupid grin was back on full display.

The moon hid behind a cloud, shadowing us in the night, and as quickly as he had appeared, he melted into the shadows.

I stood, alone in the night, grappling with too many emotions that threatened to consume me.

I let out a long sigh, turning to Mylom behind me. I pulled myself over her, the weight of whatever just happened settled in the pit of my stomach like a stone. *Go back*, my conscience begged me. I looked around for Drayzen but the woods were empty.

I peered through the trees, the direction I thought Raxos was in, but I didn't know for sure. I'd wasted enough time with Drayzen that I wouldn't make it there and back before sunrise anyway. Besides, what would I have done if I'd found Thysa and she had the answers to my questions? How would I even tell Azral I left? *How would he react?*

Each gallop back to the castle felt like a lifetime with my tangled mess of emotions. Drayzen's words replayed incessantly in my mind. *It was nice to officially meet you,* Mar.

The sound of my name on his lips felt like a promise, a secret whispered between us in the night.

15

THERE WERE STILL NO GUARDS THAT I COULD see as I scaled back up the castle on my makeshift rope. The place wasn't well guarded for being at war but that worked in my favor.

I paced restlessly in my room, the cool night breeze easing the heat building inside me. The drakai perched outside my cracked window, their eyes watchful as the Fairies flitted around the room, giggling as they filled the tub with steamy water and frolicked in the bubbles.

"What was I thinking?"

Drayzen had been right about that, at least. Going out alone? I clearly wasn't thinking, blinded by my search for answers. For my family.

The blue Fairy fluttered to me, bubbles clinging to her tiny body as she tapped my nose, grinning impishly. I wiped away the bubble she left with a sigh.

I had to find Thysa somehow but with the reaction to Sovanni's and my previous departure, the chances of leaving were slim. Would Azral even take me? He didn't seem particularly fond of Thysa or leaving the castle in general. But if I told him about my vision, he would have to understand, right?

And if he doesn't? my conscience asked, Drayzen's voice asked. *Would* he *help me?*

"Gods," I seethed, tripping over the broken vase. The Fairies swarmed as I kneeled to clean up the mess. A piece sliced my palm and blood dripped onto the floor. The blue Fairy landed on my wrist, bouncing up and down and pointing to the wound. "Yeah, I know." I sighed and made my way to the bathroom to wash it off.

The yellow Fairy, apparently strong, lifted the bucket of water and poured. My blood dripped in the sink.

Drip. Drip. Drip.

"Not now," I begged myself.

I wrapped a towel around my hand and tied it to my wrist. The cut wasn't too deep, so it would be fine as it was.

The red and blue Fairies had already collected most of the broken vase and placed it on the shirts. I wrapped the pieces into the makeshift rope and hid it away deep in the closet. This place was filled to the brim with clothes, so I doubt anyone would find it in the back corner, just in case I ever needed to use it again.

I fell back onto the bed and let out a long sigh. Emotions, too many to name, ate at me. Anger made me flush, anger at

Azral for the way he treated me, the way he treated his sister. Confusion fogged my brain.

Each day here, I felt like I was getting closer to finding my truth but each night left me with more questions than the last. A persistent fear gnawed at me. Fear of the unknown, fear of the king. Then guilt made my stomach turn. I'd replayed the voice, Drayzen's voice, too many times.

It threatened everything I knew, everything I cared about. It sang like a soothing melody in my mind, putting me to sleep.

Mar.

The morning sun streamed through the windows. I felt the familiar warmth of a body next to me and snuggled in closer. My hand traced across the toned stomach as I nuzzled my head against an arm.

"Good morning," rasped the male beside me and I looked up to see Azral smiling back at me. His sharp features glowed in the sunlight as he placed a kiss on my forehead.

"Good morning," I said, my voice still croaky with fatigue. But my heart skipped and my gaze darted towards the now-closed window. I scanned the room but saw no sign of the Fairies.

"Are you okay?" Azral asked, sitting up.

"Yeah," I glanced at his shirtless chest, "did you sleep here?"

"Yeah, I"—he stumbled on similar words—"Is that okay?"

"No, *yes*, I'm sorry. I just forgot where I was, I guess."

When did he get here?

He leaned closer to me, placing his hand on mine. I quickly pulled away, remembering the cut under it. Where was the bandage?

"Is everything okay?" He moved closer.

"Is that bacon?" I turned, trying to change the subject. Because everything wasn't okay.

The Fairies were missing, the window was now mysteriously shut, and my hand...I looked at it. The cut was still there but the cloth wrapped around it was missing. I scanned the room for any sign of my little adventure but there was nothing. Instead, I spotted a tray of breakfast foods on the table by the chaise. I made for it, practically drooling.

Azral let out a low laugh and gracefully rose, following me to the table. "I had them bring breakfast so we could spend the morning together."

His hand rested on my lower back. I tried not to flinch at his touch, the feeling so foreign now. *Did he think everything was okay between us?* Placing his hand on my hip, he pulled me in closer.

"It's lovely." I stopped him with a hand to his chest, pulling away. Pastries, meats, and fruits filled the table and the smell, gods, it was amazing. But I wouldn't let it distract me. "Let me just wash up real quick." I turned to the bathroom, hoping he didn't sense my growing tension.

Alone, I lifted my hand for a better look. The cut was still very much there but at least the bleeding had stopped. How was I going to hide this? Maybe I could say I fell while out with Sovanni, or tripped? I needed an excuse because "smashing a vase against the magic doors to escape," well, I didn't think that would sit very well.

After brushing my hair and teeth, I felt more confident. I walked back into the main room to find Az standing by the balcony doors, looking at...*gods, help me.*

"Did you break something?"

"I..." All the excuses I'd thought up disappeared and I stood there. "I was..." My eyes widened as his eyes filled with fear? Anger? I couldn't tell and my pulse began to race.

"You cut yourself?" He moved to me, grabbing my hand.

"It's not as bad as it looks." I said, trying to downplay the injury.

"I'll call for a medic right away. Stay here." He kissed the cut before leaving.

I sank onto the chaise, inspecting the floor by the door. *How did he know?* I didn't see any glass and the doors weren't damaged thanks to that stupid barrier.

But then I saw it, the tiniest shard under the edge of the table. How did he see that so quickly?

The door *clicked* open.

"She should be here shortly." He kissed the top of my head as he sat next to me.

"It's really no issue; it doesn't even hurt." I assured him even though it burned.

"Why didn't you tell me? Why didn't you call for help?" He brushed the side of my cheek with his thumb.

I looked away, hopefully seeming embarrassed, but I just didn't want him to see the lie in my eyes. "It was late. I didn't want to bother anyone and like I said, it was really nothing."

"What happened?" he persisted.

"I woke up from a dream and I was grabbing a glass of water and, well, I guess I was tired and I dropped it. I just cut myself picking up the pieces."

"Have they been worse?" he asked, his concern now evident.

My dreams. I knew this was the time to tell him, tell him what I'd been seeing and everything that happened. But I didn't.

I wasn't sure if it was my anger towards him but something inside me screamed not to tell him, about Thysa, about Drayzen.

My conscience, *his* voice screamed at me not to tell him. I hesitated but it was a voice I'd come to know, a voice I trusted. And it hadn't steered me wrong yet.

"No, I was just tired. I'm fine though, I promise." I gave him a reassuring smile even as guilt wove through me.

I reached for a plate. The smell of the food filled my nose as I leaned closer. Fresh bacon was stacked high on a porcelain dish next to warm croissants and a tray of berries. I filled my plate with more than enough food, leaning back.

Azral watched me cautiously; his eyes narrowed. He reached for a glass of orange juice and took a sip.

"You're not going to eat?" I asked, my mouth full.

"I want to take you somewhere today." A hint of shame clouded his eyes as he looked at me shyly. And that look hurt. I didn't want to be angry with him, I didn't *want* to fight. "If you're up to it, of course." A small smile grew on his face.

I couldn't help but mirror it, my hand reaching for his. This was the Azral I knew.

"Of course."

Before we could continue our conversation, there was a knock at the door. The medic strolled in, her blonde pin-straight hair was cut just above her shoulders. She inspected my wrist, and applied a clear ointment to prevent scarring and pain. That was a handy little salve I would have loved to have all the times I'd cut myself while hunting in Zandar. She wrapped my hand in a cloth and handed me a small bottle of the ointment. Bowing, she left the room.

Az's fingers ran the length of my hair. He flashed a grin and planted a soft kiss on my forehead as he got up. "I'm going to change. I'll meet you back here soon."

"Where are we going?" I asked, watching as he opened the door to the hall.

"Wear something for riding. We'll need to get Mylom before we go."

He winked, closing the door behind him, its lock latching.

I leaned against the back of the chaise, a smile spreading across my face. "Mylom."

16

AZ AND I STRODE DOWN THE MAIN CORRIDOR
of the castle. I took note of the increased number of guards
stationed along the halls. The servant who brought me tea last
night waited for us, her dark curls trailing over her porcelain
skin as she bowed her head. With a graceful movement, she
extended a crimson cloak adorned with the royal sigil
beautifully embroidered on the back. Each golden thorn was
stitched perfectly around the red gems. Az turned to me and
then back to the maid, a smile spreading across his face as he
tilted his head.

"Thank you," he said, taking the fabric from her.

With one final bow, she scurried away, leaving Azral to
place the cloak over my white tunic.

"For you," he whispered, his breath warm in my ear.

"It's beautiful." The lightweight cloak fell over my shoulders.

"Only the best for my *princess*," he said with a wink, pulling my loose hair over the back of it. His hand brushed against the nape of my neck and I couldn't help the flutter the touch sent through me. No matter how mad I was at him, I couldn't deny his pull.

He turned me towards him, my hands finding their rightful place on his chest. "My beautiful princess." His thumb brushed over my bottom lip. I breathed, leaning into his touch.

I missed him, missed us, missed this. Everything had changed so quickly but in this moment, the world faded. The worries that plagued my mind drifted away and all I could feel was him.

We made our way hand in hand to the stables. Rays of morning sun spread over my cool skin—mornings were always cooler. But nothing compared to the cold of Zandar. The ground and flowers were covered with a dewy mist. I spotted Mylom, carelessly grazing in the field as we walked through the stable gates. Her now-green eyes gazed up at me and Azral. She snorted, trotting towards us with an attitude. *Maybe she was mad about our little trip last night.*

I groomed her, brushing back her dark coat while Azral saddled his horse, then Mylom. I almost mentioned that I didn't need a saddle, recalling my previous ride, but I caught myself before I said anything foolish. *Would Drayzen tell Azral what I did?* Something inside made me think not, that he'd keep our little secret.

We rode through the forest. The sun lifted the mist and shone through the trees, warming the earth. I drew back my hood to let the breeze caress my face. The calming scent of pine filled my nostrils and my clammy palms dried with each inhale.

"Where are we going?" I asked over the click of hooves at an even pace.

"Vani and I used to come here a lot," he replied, riding next to me.

Sovanni. "Is she okay?" I blurted, the image of Erixx dragging her away flashing through my mind.

"She's fine." Azral looked away from me. "I'm sorry she put you in that situation."

Situation? "She didn't put me in any sort of situation," I snapped, my anger slowly returning. "I wanted to go with her. We were...having fun."

"She never should have taken you off castle grounds," he said, his tone harsh.

"It wasn't dangerous. We were just—"

"Nothing seems dangerous until it is," he interrupted.

Anger surged through me. *Why was he being like this?* "I'm not a child, I can take care of myself."

"Not against him." His words were dry, almost emotionless.

"Drayzen?" His name on my lips felt like a crime.

He didn't seem like a threat. A little arrogant, yes, but he hadn't done anything to hurt me or even seemed like he wanted to, after I surrendered my rock...and then the dagger. If anything, I was more of a threat to him.

"He's not like us. He will do anything to get close to the crown, to take whatever he can, whatever he wants."

"Not like us?" I kept my tone light, pretended not to have suspicions about that interesting fact. "What is he?" I asked, hoping not to seem too anxious for an answer.

"He's Denazin." Azral adjusted himself on his horse and swept curls off his face. "He's a monster, a devil."

The words sliced through me, sharp and unrelenting. *A devil.* That's what the townspeople called me, because I was different. He didn't seem to notice, though, too distracted by his anger.

"Denazin?" I said through gritted teeth. "What does that mean?"

"He's immortal like us but he doesn't get his martem from the same source."

"From Saigus and Melenyz?"

"I see Sovanni got you up to speed." He nodded slowly, pursing his lips. "That's good," he breathed but his tone was unconvincing. "No, his power doesn't come from them." He trailed off and stiffened. "You've heard of Autyr?"

"The God of Death?"

Azral scoffed at the seemingly absurd concept, disgust evident on his face.

I'd heard of the gods briefly when I was small. Everyone believed that Saigus and Melenyz, the Sun and Moon gods, were responsible for the passing of our days. Their tragic love story was also very well-known, one Azral had previously shared with me.

I also knew of the Goddess of Life, Nyrah. Her blessings brought joy to everyone. Then Autyr, the God of Death. Some people prayed to him for a peaceful afterlife for the departed but most cursed him for taking those they loved.

What kind of powers could the God of Death give?

"So, he's not Fae?" I asked, trying to wrap my brain around it all.

"No, and he's the only one of his kind," Azral replied.

"How did he become one then?"

"Some say that he was Fae once and his parents were killed when he was very young. He traveled to the Isles, where the gods live."

The Isles. Sovanni had mentioned them briefly. She did *not* mention the gods living there.

"Only the Goddess of Life can bring someone back but she wouldn't answer him. Only one god did. The God of Death promised to return their lives. But Autyr betrayed him, turning him into what he is now."

"He was hurt, his parents—" I could feel the pain he must have felt, how he must have pleaded, ready to do anything to bring them back. I would do anything to find mine, to be able to see Isidore and Lettie again.

"He's a monster, Amara. You know what powers Autyr granted him?" He shook his head, rubbing his chin. "He *feeds* off people. Feeds off the Fae."

"What—?" Words escaped me.

"He feeds off of our blood, Human blood, whatever he can get his hands on." Azral's brows furrowed and his voice lowered. "My blood, *our* blood. That's what keeps him alive."

"How do you know all this?" I asked, still trying to process everything.

"I've had the privilege of getting to know him for some time." A sinister smile played at his lips before turning to me with a seriousness. "He's an abomination to the balance of life, the balance of martem."

Everything these days seemed hard to wrap my head around but one thought was persistent.

"It must be lonely," I caught myself saying out loud.

Azral's cold eyes snapped to me, his jaw tightening. "*Lonely?*" he repeated, his voice thick.

"Losing your parents, being the only one of your kind." I could relate in too many ways.

"He's filled that void with the hundreds he's slaughtered."

My stomach turned. "Do you think that's why he was so interested in me?" *To feed from me?*

Azral looked back to the road ahead. "I'm sure of it. He likes to play with his prey and I believe the unknown of it all, of you, is what's lured him in."

If that's what he wanted, why didn't he take advantage last night? It would have been the perfect opportunity and yet here I was, unharmed.

I shook off the growing unease of the conversation, changing the subject. "So, Sovanni, she's really okay? Can I see her later? I want to apologize if I got her in any trouble—"

"You did nothing wrong." he snapped softly. "She should have known better." He shook his head. "I'm sorry, I—."

Our horses halted. He reached his hand out to mine. "Amara, if anything happened to you, if that monster got what he wanted, I wouldn't be able to live with myself."

"Azral, I'm okay." I leaned over to soothe him. "I'm okay."

He smiled, the light returning to his eyes. He squeezed my hand with a reassuring grip. I followed his gaze to the opening canopy of trees ahead of us.

A large waterfall cascaded into a clear blue lake, gushing over the rocks and creating a pool below. The flowers surrounding the pool were shades of yellow and purple with daisies dominating the scenery. I could smell the sweetness of the blooms as the breeze kissed my skin.

Azral dismounted and lifted a hand to help me. He stood tall before me, his tanned skin glowing in the sunlight and his eyes sparkled as they met mine.

"This is beautiful," I breathed in awe.

"Not as beautiful as you," he said, nipping my ear. I bit my lip, playfully pushing against his chest and walked past him, right up to the crystal-clear pool. Kneeling, I dipped my fingers into the sparkling water.

Azral approached me from behind, placing a kiss on my head, his fingers laced between my hair. I looked back at him as he undressed and I shamefully watched. His white shirt hit the dirt and my eyes, wide with anticipation, followed his every move. With a graceful dive, he disappeared under the water's surface, sending ripples across the pond.

I hesitated, a warmth creeping across my cheeks, but I followed his lead, carefully removing my cloak and hanging it on a nearby branch. Then, one by one, I shed my clothes, my stomach fluttering. I stepped into the cool water. I couldn't help but steal a glance at Azral who watched me with an intensity that made my heart race.

"Your beauty never ceases to amaze me, Amara." They were words I'd heard before and words I wouldn't mind hearing forever. As soon as I was fully in the water, he pulled me close.

The cool water caressed my skin and the touch of our bodies sent chills down my spine. He noticed and pulled me closer, kissing the side of my ear, which only caused more chills.

"Follow me," he said, swimming towards the falling water.

The sound of it hitting the pond intensified and the mist surrounding us didn't help my vision. Azral mouthed something before diving under. The wave of water hit my back as I followed behind him. I broke the surface, Azral's body behind me.

"Look," he whispered against my ear.

I wiped the water from my eyes and gasped. The dimly lit space was filled with a soft glow, rays of sunlight filtering through small cracks in the top of the cavern, casting dancing patterns of light on the water and the walls. Vines and flowers growing up the sides of the cave were so vibrant they almost glowed in the dim light. The scent of rose and jasmine drifted through the air, mixing with the cool water of the pool. That, combined with Azral's honey scented skin created an intoxicating smell that filled all my senses.

We swam deeper into the cavern. The sound of the water hitting the surface behind us became softer, almost like a distant melody, and the mist added an ominous beauty. The water was crystal clear, which allowed me to see the bottom where small fish darted back and forth and little plants swayed in a gentle current. Shimmering crystals also covered the walls of the cave. They reflected the soft light in such a way I just knew no one would ever be able to replicate.

"This is—" I started but trailed off. Because words couldn't fully describe the beauty of it all. Azral was behind me again, his chin resting on my shoulder.

"I love coming here, to clear my head," he said, his voice barely above a whisper. "And to apologize." As he spoke, he kissed my shoulder and turned my body towards him. "Amara, I have no excuse for the way I treated you yesterday." His eyes were glassy, a storm of guilt and longing. "I only want you to be safe and when—" His voice cracked, vulnerability breaking through. "I just can't let anything happen to you." He leaned his forehead against mine, a single tear escaping.

My heart twisted. How could I stay mad at him when his pain mirrored my own? I would act the same way, if I thought he was in danger. I would tear worlds apart to save him. I leaned closer, letting the pull between us erase the remnants of the fight.

"I forgive you, Az." I whispered, my lips brushing his as I spoke.

His gaze wandered over me, not with possession but with reverence, as though I were the only thing keeping him tethered to this world. His hand rose, tracing the curve of my cheek with a touch so gentle it felt like a prayer.

"I love you, Amara," he confessed, his words a breathless release. "I've loved you from the moment I saw you. I knew then—I *knew*—that I would do anything for you, follow you anywhere, like the sun does the moon. Through time, through space, if the gods willed it. If it meant I could have just one more day with you."

His fingers brushed my face, and I leaned into it, my own hand finding the back of his neck. I met his gaze, and it was then I realized I've felt this for a while. The words I was too afraid to say before.

"I love you, Azral," I whispered, my declaration hanging. I, too, would follow him anywhere, any life, any realm, any existence. "Azral Sallow, you will have my heart forever."

He didn't respond with words, but his lips found mine, and in that kiss, I felt everything—his love, his fear, his devotion, his *promise*.

The main hall of the castle was brimming with activity. Guards were stationed at every cream-colored pillar, their gold armor refracting the thousands of colors from the stained-glass dome above.

Azral and I walked hand in hand, staff darting about with food and drinks.

"What are they preparing for?" I asked, watching the mayhem unfold. Could it be another ball? It had only been two days since the last.

"My father is preparing dinner for us," he replied, running his fingers through my still damp hair. "Let's get cleaned up." We started to turn down the hall to the right but my attention snagged when I saw—*oh, gods.*

Sovanni.

She stumbled through the hall. Her arm hung limply at her side and her face was covered in dried tears, bruises, and cuts.

I ran for her but Azral grabbed my arm and the force of it swung me around. I fought against his hold but it was no use.

"What are you doing?" I seethed, pulling against him.

"Let her be," he whispered in a deadly tone. "It will only be worse if she knows you've seen her like this." He pulled me into him, away from prying eyes.

"What do you mean *worse*?" I demanded, frantically trying to look back.

What happened to her? Had Erixx done that? *Did Azral know?* Anger exploded inside me like a thousand tiny volcanoes, the fiery rage all-consuming.

"Just let her go, Amara. We'll see her soon." He pulled me back, lifting me over his shoulder as I continued to fight. He carried me down the hall like a child and I couldn't help but look back at her.

I met her eyes across the crowded room. One single tear fell down her bloodied cheek. She turned away and didn't look back.

17

WE SAT AT A LONG RECTANGULAR TABLE IN THE throne room. The center was draped in an elegant white cloth trimmed with sparkling gold. Chandeliers hung above, their flames flickering with a fiery intensity that seemed to mirror the storm brewing within me. The table was set with pristine silverware, crystal glasses, and delicate plates adorned with floral patterns. Golden candles lined the center, unlit, their presence more decorative than practical.

The chairs were grand, gilded with high backs and plush red cushions, but the one at the head of the table stood out—a massive throne-like seat encrusted with red gems, clearly reserved for the king.

When we had arrived in our room earlier, Azral left without a word. The servants arrived not long after, though, to help me get ready. They said Erixx wanted to have an official meeting with me, to get to know me better.

"Get to *know* me?" I asked them as they helped me into a white gown with red lacy accents on the sleeves and skirt.

The fabric was soft to the touch and it flowed down my body, hugging my curves in all the right places. I had them leave my hair untouched, not bothering to style it.

Azral returned just as I'd started pacing the room, his silent entrance catching me off guard. He was dressed in a white coat with matching red detailing. The sight made my stomach twist, the deliberate coordination feeling like a mockery. He reached for my hand and I let him lead me in silence, my cold hand limp in his grasp.

Now, seated at the table, the air between us was stifling. Sovanni sat across from us, wine glass in hand. My leg bounced, the only outlet for my growing frustration. It had only been a few hours since I saw her and her once-bruised face was now almost fully mended thanks to the incredible healing abilities of the Fae. But the deep cut under her left eye lingered, telling me that whatever happened to her was bad enough to outlast even magic.

Why had he done this to her? I had no interest in getting to know a king who would treat anyone this way, let alone his family, blood or not. Sovanni mentioned that she was not very fond of her step-father. That she had stayed for Azral's sake. Was he just as cruel to him? Even so, why didn't Azral stand up for her? The questions wouldn't stop piling on but one thing did: *She should have known better.*

Azral's words sounded in my mind and I shook off my unease at the thought of what he actually meant. Because if he knew this was happening—

He placed a hand on my restless knee, distracting me from my spiral. I swatted it away without bothering to look at him.

The large doors swung open and Azral and Sovanni rose to their feet in perfect unison. I stumbled a few breaths behind, not used to the formalities and not caring for them at this moment.

The staff lining the room all bowed low as the king made his entrance.

The now lit candles cast a warm glow on his tousled brown hair. He moved with a predatory grace, each step deliberate and purposeful. The flames on the table flickered to life as he passed, casting eerie shadows that danced across the linen. I couldn't help but feel intimidated by him, his power. Was this his way of showing it?

My eyes drifted to the crown sitting proudly atop his head. Would Azral wear that crown one day? Something told me that Erixx wouldn't easily relinquish the title.

The power, the respect, the fear that came with it. He relished it.

He approached the table and I followed Azral and Sovanni's lead, bowing my head in respect. I couldn't help but steal another glance. And like he somehow knew, I immediately met his piercing eyes. A sinister smile graced his lips before I looked back to the ground. I gulped down the fear creeping up my throat.

He took his seat at the head of the table and we all followed. Staff swarmed around, placing food and drinks around us. The tension that filled the room remained, stagnant in the air as we ate in silence.

Sovanni reached for the bottle of wine after we finished. She took a long swig. "May I be excused?"

Erixx didn't even look her way, his gaze solely fixed on me. "Don't be rude, Sovanni." He smiled cynically. The look was pure evil. "Tonight, we are all here to honor our beloved guest."

The unease in the room seemed to grow. How it was possible to get even more uncomfortable in here I had no idea but it did just that.

"Are you enjoying your stay?" the king asked.

I swallowed hard, meeting his stare. "Yes."

He let out a low growl and turned to Azral. "And my son," he asked, raising a brow, "you love him?"

"Father," Azral cut in, but Erixx silenced him with a gesture.

I looked at Azral and anger pooled in my gut. I remembered the words we only just said to each other, the promise we made. But as mad at him as I was, I couldn't lie. "I do," I said, my voice steady. "I love him."

Erixx's eyes narrowed as he leaned back in his chair. "These dreams," he said cynically waving his hands. "What makes you think they are real?"

"I just—I have a feeling."

"A feeling." Erixx laughed like my words were a joke. "Humans never cease to amaze me." He took a sip from his glass.

With a sip of water to quell the growing anger inside me, I attempted to stay calm and explain myself. "I understand your skepticism but I can assure you, they *are* real."

Erixx leaned back in his chair. "And why is that? What makes you so *sure* of their existence and that this isn't just some fairytale you concocted?"

"She's—" Sovanni started, but Erixx cut her off with a sharp look. Her head immediately dipped as her knuckles whitened around the neck of the bottle.

"You'll have your turn." He raised a hand to her. "I'm speaking with *Amara* now," he said coldly, sarcasm coating my name. "The Fae are not unknown in the Human realm. You could have heard a story when you were young, no?"

I tried to gather my thoughts, thinking back to the visions of my parents. The ones I'd had since I'd arrived in Kaluth, of Mylom and Thysa. "Like I said, I am positive they're real."

And I knew. In my heart, I knew it was true. This world was somehow where I belonged. *It had to be.*

Erixx shot a curious glare at Azral before raising an eyebrow. He took another sip from his glass, his eyes quickly glaring back to mine. "Your assurances mean nothing to me. Sovanni will do another dive, find out more information. Then we can determine who is right, *you,*" he raised his glass towards me, "or me." He grinned, wide and crazed as he lifted the wine to his lips.

I looked at Sovanni and she took another swig from the bottle. She quickly blinked and quietly said, "We can do it tomorrow."

"Tonight," Erixx demanded. "It will be done tonight."

"Father, she's clearly not in the best condition." Azral gestured towards Sovanni's near-empty bottle.

"Son, you are a fool if you think she has not consumed more wine than *that* and been able to use her martem," Erixx retorted sharply. "I'm sure Amara is more than ready for her answers?"

His words made my body shiver. *Was I ready?*

"He's right, I can do it." Sovanni laughed bitterly, taking another swig from the bottle as Erixx shot her a withering glare.

At least he acknowledged her now, in his own rude way. His piercing gaze lingered on me before he stormed out of the room, the candles blowing out with him.

Azral turned to me, concern etched on his face as he reached for my hand. "Are you okay?"

"I'm fine." I pulled my hand away.

"Amara," he begged, his hand caressing my cheek. I turned my head at his touch. "Please, can we talk about this?"

"Did you know?" I seethed. "Did you know he did *that* to her?" My eyes shot to Sovanni as she stumbled out of the hall behind us.

"He is the king," was all he said, shaking his head. Like he didn't like that very important fact. He took a breath, the light in his eyes disappearing. "I told you she should have known better than to bring you there or even go there herself. Raxos is in enemy territory."

"How are they enemies? They were so kind and Thysa—"

"Just because someone seems kind doesn't mean they haven't betrayed the crown in some way. And by going there, that's what Vani did." He turned away from me. "What happened to her was a light punishment. She should be grateful it wasn't worse. Luckily, she heals quickly, so she'll be fine by tomorrow."

"A *light* punishment?" I rasped. "If she were Human, she would be bruised for weeks, would probably have broken bones." Anger oozed out of me.

"But she is *not* Human," he said, his voice cold, facing me.

"And if I were to betray the crown?" I pushed. "Would you see to it that I receive a *light* punishment."

"Amara, stop." He pushed back, his eyes welling. My bones ached at that look in his eyes. He was upset, but gods, so was I.

"I should go wash up." It was all I could manage without crumbling to pieces. I pushed by him, walking silently back to my room. Alone.

A guard opened the door, accompanied by the now all-too-familiar *click* as it closed behind me. I shed the dress that matched Azral's coat, pulling on a comforting pair of black pants and a navy tunic.

I hastily paced in the room. A stabbing thought crossed my mind, sending a knife through my heart. Had that ever happened to Azral? Did Erixx treat them so badly that it was normal?

I shook my head, shook off the sinking feeling that threatened to consume me. Even so, how could he let that happen to his sister? *Would he let it happen to me?*

Almost all the black dahlia flowers painting the room were now dead. I laughed at the irony, depicting how I felt on the inside. I grabbed one, plopping onto the soft bed and hanging upside down.

I love you, Amara. His words were a declaration. *I love you.*

A promise and a betrayal.

I rolled over, picking at the velvety petals one by one. "He loves me." The petal floated to the floor. "He loves me not."

Each petal fell, one by one, drop by drop.

Drip. Drip. Drip.

"He loves me—"

The door clicked open and my eyes shot to it. Azral, upside down, stood in the doorway. His eyes were glassy and swollen as he watched me. His voice was low. "Vani is ready for us."

We walked through the halls, silently making our way to Sovanni's room. I wondered if Az wanted to say something but I didn't care. I didn't want to hear anything he had to say right now.

A guard opened her creaky door, Azral gesturing for me to go first. Sovanni sat on the chair in the center of the room, grinding the same herbs she had before. Erixx leaned against the opposite wall with his arms crossed, his crown shining in the dim light. Azral joined him while I took my spot on the chaise. Sovanni handed me the cup of tea, which I drank without comment this time. The air in the room seemed a bit too heavy for jokes.

I drank every last disgusting sip and placed the cup on the table beside me. Sovanni stood behind me as I laid down; her empty eyes fixed on mine.

"Azral will go in with you," Erixx demanded from the corner. My head lolled to the side, looking at him, but the herbs were kicking in. My vision blurred.

Azral and Sovanni, just as shocked, did the same.

"Father—"

"No," Sovanni shouted, cutting Azral off. "There's no telling what bringing someone else in could do to her mind."

"Are you refusing an order?" Erixx moved closer; his face twisted in anger.

I tensed and Azral's eyes shot to me. They were filled with defiance and he took a step towards his father. It made me hopeful, that even during our fights, he wouldn't let anything happen to me. Before he could make his stand, Sovanni spoke.

"I am," she replied, her voice firm. "Do whatever you want to me but I will *not* take that risk."

Azral whispered something in Erixx's ear and the king grunted. "Fine." He waved his hand in frustration before moving back to lean against the wall.

Sovanni turned to me, brushing my hair behind my ears and placing her hands on my temples. "Do you remember how this works?" she asked, her voice soft.

I nodded. My heart was racing but I gave in to the tonic. I took only one last look at Azral. He nodded with approval and I closed my eyes.

I turned to see Sovanni's hands hovering over my imaginary body at the edge of the abyss. It hit me that this was my subconscious mind and it was completely black. *Was that normal?* I made a mental note to ask her about it when I was awake.

I could tell she was speaking to Azral and Erixx but her voice was muffled again. I couldn't make out their words but Sovanni's raging features spoke volumes. What was she seeing in my mind? I moved closer to her, calling out her name, but she didn't answer.

Then I heard his voice behind me, clear as day. "Mar."

I turned and Drayzen's midnight eyes met mine. "What are you doing here? How—"

"There's not enough time to explain," he blurted.

"Not enough time?" My brows furrowed. "Just get out of my head, leave me alone. Azral told me what you want anyway."

"Oh, did he now?" he crooned.

"You want to *feed* from me." I crossed my arms. Could he feed from me in my own mind? It seemed unlikely but I took a cautious step back.

Drayzen only laughed and moved closer. "If that's what I wanted, why haven't I done it already?" He raised a knowing brow, taking another step towards me.

He looked behind me at Sovanni, still fighting with the Fae males.

"You need to listen to me. Listen very closely," Drayzen said, his voice low and urgent.

"Why should I listen—?"

"You will if you want to find out the truth—"

"What are you doing here?" Sovanni's voice cut him off, clear as day next to me. She stood with me, wrapping her arm over my shoulders.

"Calm down, Thysa sent me."

Sovanni and I tensed at the mention of her friend.

"She needs to get out of here, Vani," Drayzen pressed. He used Sovanni's nickname as if they were friends. It couldn't mean much though, given that he always called me Mar and didn't seem to care much for formalities.

"How are you even here?" she asked.

At least someone was as confused as me.

"Oh, come on. Someone as smart as you can't figure it out?" Drayzen asked, smirking and sending a wink her way.

I couldn't tell what her face filled with, confusion, realization, shock?

"Would anyone care to tell me what is going on?" I finally cut in.

"We don't have much time," Sovanni said, looking back to, well, nothing. But I could hear Azral and Erixx's muffled shouts coming through. "They can't hear us here." She nodded to Drayzen.

"What's going on?" I demanded. They spoke like I wasn't even there.

"Can you get her out of the castle?" Drayzen asked Sovanni urgently.

Get me out? What are they talking about? My head snapped back and forth between them, following the conversation.

"I can tomorrow but we'll need a distraction," she replied. I opened my mouth to speak but Drayzen was faster.

"I can do that." He raised a brow, a feral grin on his face.

"Azral..." Sovanni trailed off.

"Forget him," Drayzen growled. "He lost his chance at redemption years ago, you know that."

What happened years okay? The question gnawed at me but all I could do was listen.

Sovanni sighed and turned to me, putting her hands on my shoulders. "Amara, if you care about finding the truth, if you value your life, you *will not* tell him what happened here. Tell him you saw nothing; tell him it didn't work. You need to trust me, do you understand?"

"Why? What is going on!?" I cried. I didn't have time to process.

"Tomorrow night, then?" Drayzen asked Sovanni.

"Yes. We need to go, now." And with that, Sovanni vanished and I felt myself drifting awake.

Drayzen's smirk dissolved and his brows dropped, replaced with a concerning glare right before he disappeared too.

I shot up from the chaise, gasping for air as the dim lights overhead blinded me.

"Easy, easy," Azral said as he grabbed my shoulders.

"What was that?" Erixx growled. "You weren't supposed to go alone!"

He pushed Sovanni down onto the chair beside me. My head spun, the dizziness already threatening to take over. I tried turning to her, searching for any answers. Her gaze locked on mine as Erixx screamed at her. His words were a howling echo in the blur of the room. But one thing was clear, everything in her lavender eyes pleaded with me to listen to what she'd said.

"Hey, what happened?" Azral asked, his thumb turning my chin towards him. His eyes frantically searched mine. They were filled with concern and tears threatened to break free as he rapidly blinked.

"I don't..." I trailed off. The fog of the drugs did not help while I was still struggling to make sense of everything that had just happened, what Sovanni had said.

If you value your life...

I looked back at her, her silence pleading with me.

"Azral!" the king roared in a tone that shattered the glass cup next to me.

I flinched and looked back at Az. His glassy eyes flashed with a golden tint, something I'd seen before.

Drip. Drip. Drip.

I decided at that moment to tell him.

"I didn't see anything."

18

I FELL INTO THE DARKNESS OF MY MIND AS I
passed out in Azral's arms. I called into the emptiness, hoping
for any response.

I was only met with a distant voice echoing my name,
barely audible. "Mar."

The voice grew louder with every repetition. I spun to find
Drayzen behind me, his gaze piercing through the dark. I
instinctively took a step back.

"What is this?" I demanded, my quivering voice betraying
me.

"You need to listen closely, Mar," Drayzen replied in a
stern tone meant for a child. I didn't let my annoyance get the
best of me, though, because this tone was new, not the light
one he used with me.

"How are you here?"

He sighed, his eyes deepening on me as he took his next steps. "You need to listen to me, *now*."

"I don't know who you think you are," I retorted, holding my ground.

"Listen," he hissed, grabbing my chin with a force that made me flinch but not in a hurtful way, more in surprise from his speed. Silver swirls danced in his eyes as he lowered his head to me.

"Tomorrow," he commanded, his voice like liquid. His thumb lightly brushed against my chin. His fingers were cool and I could feel a hum of martem seeping from them.

His voice echoed over and over like a mantra. It was hypnotic the way it washed over me, a tingling sensation snaking through my mind. I tried to resist the feeling but I gave in. I repeated his words over and over. "Tomorrow."

"Do not tell him what we talked about, what you saw." Those words echoed, too, a command I couldn't resist.

"I won't say anything," I replied automatically.

His hand left my chin, an emptiness inside me accompanying the feeling.

"Tomorrow," he repeated softly, a hint of sadness lacing the word, before finally releasing me from the mental hold. "You'll know when." A smirk played at the corner of his lips, "I'll see you soon, Mar."

And just like that, he was gone, leaving me alone in the darkness. His words still echoed through me, his voice repeating softly.

Tomorrow.

I cracked open my eyes, squinting at the glow of moonlight filtering into the cream and violet bedroom. My head fell to the left, heavy with the weight of everything that had happened. Glitter trailed by the window and I couldn't stop my body from slumping out of bed, crawling to the Fairies on the other side of the glass.

Their little arms waved at me while the three drakai fluttered around them, playfully bumping into one another. I placed my hand on the window, reaching for them, but they darted away.

"What are you doing?" asked a groggy voice behind me. *Azral.*

I whipped around on my knees, almost toppling from the speed. "Azral," I said, hoping he hadn't seen the Fairies. *How did I not notice him lying there?*

"Are you okay?" he asked, sitting up, moving to the edge of the bed, closer to me. "What are you doing down there?"

"I was—" I turned to the window. The Fairies were gone and the glitter trail had vanished. *Good.* "I just woke up and I thought I saw something."

"Saw what?" he pestered, his voice growing serious.

I looked back to the empty window. "It was nothing, just a moth," I assured him, sitting back on the bed, next to him.

"You should be sleeping." He tucked a strand of hair behind my ear.

"I wasn't tired."

"Amara," he said dryly.

I looked at him now, really looked. That golden tint was still present in his eyes. I pulled back but his brows lowered with my movement.

"Vani said the herbs she gave you would have you asleep for much longer than this." He was too concerned, his eyes searching mine for a hidden answer.

"Is she okay?" I blurted, the image of Erixx screaming at her replaced any thought or fear I had.

"She's gone," Azral said with a sigh.

My heart stopped at his words, fear seeping through my veins. "What?"

"She's going back to Acrari. She said she didn't want to stay here with my father anymore."

"To her aunt?" It didn't make sense, why would she leave now? After everything she just said, asked of me? *Tomorrow.*

"Yes," Azral said, moving closer to me. "What else has she told you?"

"She told me about your mother." Pain radiated through his now fully emerald eyes. But I pushed anyway. "Why didn't you tell me she was killed?"

He was quiet for a moment. "It's not important. What's important is that you're okay. What happened in there?"

"I feel fine." And I did. Annoyed, mostly at the piling lies. Confused. But I was fine, maybe a little off balance but I recovered quickly.

"You don't look fine."

"Neither do you," I snapped back.

He looked stressed, bags painted his under eyes and wrinkles lined the corners. His hair was a mess and I could see the dried tears on his cheeks and that made my heart ache. I was mad, no, I was pissed at him, scared at that look in his eyes—one I never wanted to see again. But nothing could compete with the pain I felt watching him hurting.

"Please. Tell me what happened," he begged. His eyes filled with, well, nothing. He met my gaze dead on with a blank stare. *Is this his way of hiding that he's hurting, putting on some illusion?*

Tears welled in his eyes again but in an instant, they disappeared. And gods, that stung. The male I loved was hurting, hiding. I pushed and moved closer to him, placing my hand on his cheek and rubbing my thumb over his warm skin. He looked at me again. The life in his eyes was still gone, eerily reminding me of the king.

He looked down, removing my hand and pressing a kiss to my palm. When his eyes met mine again, they shimmered with glassy emotion, only to cloud over a moment later. This had to be his power—this constant push and pull, this subtle game of vulnerability and control. It was like his true feelings surged to the surface, raw and unfiltered, before vanishing behind a carefully crafted mask. Was he trying to show me that he was strong, like his father? Strong like a future king, someone who could bear the weight of a kingdom while keeping his heart hidden behind layers of armor?

I wiped a welling tear from his face as I kissed his lips. "Azral," I whispered. "You don't need to hide from me."

"But you hide from *me*." His voice broke, a tear escaping as he pulled back.

"I—" My mouth dropped.

I tried to collect myself. This was *Azral*, the one I trusted, the one I loved. This mess with his father, it was bringing us down, like he was trying to sabotage us. But I wouldn't let that wicked male win. He had hurt Sovanni and he'd most likely hurt Azral. I could see it in his eyes, that deep pain clawing at him to be let free. I wanted him to open up to me, I wanted to open up to him, to tell him everything.

But I couldn't.

I literally could not say the words. A tingling feeling swept over my mind and I heard Drayzen's voice over and over.

Do not tell him what we talked about, what you saw.

"I don't remember anything," I uttered, the words tumbling out without my control. It was like he had robbed me of my voice. "I—"

That unsettling sensation compelled me to keep silent, as if my own mind was held captive.

What had Drayzen done to me? *A monster,* Azral had called him. Maybe he was right because only a monster could make me feel this way, strip me of my free will.

"Did Vani say anything before she left?" I finally managed, battling against the invisible restraints.

"She did." He sighed, placing his hand on my knee.

"Well, what was it?" How could she just leave after everything that had happened? And without even saying goodbye?

"Amara." He moved in closer. "She told us that she was able to see your dreams."

My heart almost stopped until the confusion took over and it sped up again.

"What do you mean? What did she say she saw?"

"I'm so sorry." His head dropped, shaking. "When you told me about your dreams, I thought that bringing you here was the right thing to do. I knew how important it was to you, to find whatever family you may have had left—"

"What are you saying?" I pleaded, tears blurred my vision.

But I could see it in his face. I knew what he was about to say.

"No," I whispered, the realization echoing in my own voice.

The realization that Sovanni was able to see my dreams and Az was here telling me about it. He wasn't here telling me how we were going to go find my dream parents. Vani wasn't here telling me how she was able to find some clue about where they might be. No, Azral was telling me she saw them and found nothing. Found that they were just dreams, delusions of a crazy girl. Breaking free from his grasp, I stood, pacing to the other side of the room. "*No.*"

He followed me, reaching out and taking hold of my hand. "I'm sorry," he murmured, pulling me towards him.

I yanked my hand away. "No!" I shouted, my voice growing louder as I tugged at the locked handles.

The doors were a cruel barrier that trapped me within this dreadful reality. I tugged harder, my screams accompanied by tears. Slamming my fists against the unyielding glass, I continued to cry out, "No! Let me out! Please!"

"Amara." His arms wrapped around my body.

I growled, breaking free from his hold. My hands bounced off the magical barrier, each strike echoing my desperation.

"No!" I cried again and again. My voice broke with each syllable.

It was like losing my parents all over again. Isidore and Lettie, their bodies, the sick display plagued my mind. Flames engulfed the image, my dream parents now burned beside them along with the last shred of hope I had.

This couldn't be happening.

I gasped for air. My body heaved with cries and deep breaths. Azral's arms wrapped around me again but this time I couldn't break free. I collapsed to the floor, sobbing uncontrollably. He held me there, brushing my hair as I cried.

Am I really just crazy? I couldn't believe it, I wouldn't—

"I need you to say it," I finally choked out, my voice broken. "I need to hear the words."

My cries drowned out everything around us. Only his voice, the truth, was louder than my breaking heart.

He gently brushed my hair back, cradling me in his arms, as he whispered, "Your dreams, they're just that—dreams. And you, Amara, you're just Human."

19

I LAID ON THE COLD TILE OF MY ROOM, MY body heavy and unresponsive. The hours slipped away unnoticed. I looked at my reflection in the glass doors. Warm rays of late afternoon sun filtered through, casting a glow on my tear-stained face, revealing the redness of my eyes and the swollen contours of my grief-stricken skin.

Azral stayed with me through the night. From the chaise where he sat, he tried getting me to have lunch after I'd ignored breakfast. But I still refused.

"You have to eat something," he begged.

A knock sounded from the door but I didn't bother turning to look. I could faintly hear Azral rise to answer it, his movements a muted symphony in the stillness of my despair. My eyes remained fixed on the world beyond the glass.

Trapped.

I realized now that's what I was. Something I swore I'd never be again.

He said this was for my safety, keeping me in here, locked away.

Trapped.

The word echoed in my mind, a relentless mantra that defined my shattered reality.

I was confined to this room, confined to this Human body that had now revealed itself to be my only truth. And that truth shattered everything I'd clung to for so long. Everything I believed—every conviction that fueled me—now laid in ruins, crumbling like sandcastles swept away by a merciless tide.

I didn't know who I was anymore. I didn't know what I was fighting for, *searching* for.

Azral's plea carried through the air as he spoke in hushed conversation with whoever was at the door. "I'm not leaving her like this," he growled.

I slowly turned my head. His eyes met mine but he looked away, like I was one of the many wilted flowers in the room, too broken to look at, dead after such a short life.

I rolled over. Azral's whispers stopped as I spoke. "Behold world," my voice was scratchy, "the crazy girl who clung to her dreams as if they were reality."

No wonder Erixx was so short with me: He recognized my ridiculous fantasy. To believe in the possibility of such a thing, a *Human* being anything other than just that, was ridiculous. The belief was a survival mechanism, a desperate lifeline thrown to a girl drowning in sorrow.

The realization settled on me like a gentle caress, mingling with the acrid taste of the bitter truth.

"Hey."

Azral's voice reached my ears. He leaned down, his warm hand cupping my cheek. Servants stood behind him, waiting for instructions. With them was the girl who gave me the beautiful cloak earlier and helped me with tea the other night, her cheerful expression unfortunately doing nothing to make me feel anything.

"They're going to get a bath started for you, alright?" He nodded and they moved into the bathroom. "I have some things to handle but I will be back as soon as I can. I promise."

He helped me up, practically dragging me to the bed where he sat me down. It was more comfortable than the floor.

"I love you, Amara." He kissed my forehead before disappearing out the door.

The lock *clicked.*

Servants bustled about. The symphony of water bubbling in the tub filled the hushed atmosphere accompanied by the sweet fragrance of jasmine soap.

The kind servant approached, unafraid of my emotionless state. Her black curls cascaded down her back as she held her hand out to me. Her plum eyes were warm. "Let's get you some fresh air."

"I can't. I'm trapped."

"You are not trapped," she insisted, wrapping her arm under mine and lifting me up. "Your safety is all that matters to anyone." She tugged me towards the balcony. Her hand settled on the door handle.

"It won't open," I protested but she merely smiled and pressed down on the handle, causing it to obediently *click* open. My gasp was loud in the quiet room. "How?"

"Like I said, you are not trapped." She motioned her arm outward. *Maybe I'm losing my mind more than I thought.*

A rush of warmth wrapped around me as the amber light of the fading sun caressed my skin. I closed my eyes, savoring the fragrance of sweet honey and relishing the gentle touch of sunlight. I held the cool marble handle of the balcony as fresh air consumed me.

"We only want you to be safe," she whispered, her words barely registering in the intoxicating hold of freedom.

"Thank you..." I whispered, embarrassed. How did I not even know her name?

"Analise." She beamed.

"Thank you, Analise." I bowed my head. I peeked up at the balcony doors and looked back to her. "How did you get it to open?"

"Everyone has their own little tricks around here," she replied playfully. "Now, please, let's get you cleaned up while the water is still warm."

With one last breath of fresh air, we moved back into the room, the balcony door closing behind me.

I eased myself into the lukewarm water with a sigh. I couldn't help but smile as I dragged my hands through the bubbles, remembering the Fairies that had danced in them just the other night. I submerged myself further, allowing the water's soothing embrace to ease my embarrassment.

"So stupid," I muttered to myself before ducking under the surface.

I had spent the whole day wallowing on the floor in front of Azral. My cheeks heated, even under water. I wondered what Sovanni thought of all this. Maybe that was why she left, because she couldn't bear to tell me I was wrong, that my elaborate imaginary life was nothing more than a product of my sad, deluded mind.

Emerging, I blinked away the soap and water clinging to my lashes only to find Analise by the door, her laughter filling the room. She moved to sit behind me, extending her hands to gently massage my scalp.

"Let me help," she offered softly. "I'm sorry, for all that has happened."

"You have nothing to apologize for," I snapped. "I should be the one saying sorry. It's my fault anyway. Wasting everyone's time—"

She let out a long sigh. Silence lapsed around us but it wasn't uncomfortable. I couldn't help but think of Lettie as Analise's fingers worked at my scalp. Lettie would comb through each strand, ensuring all the dirt was gone so the color would shine.

"It's good to be different," she always told me as I hid under a hood on my way out of the house. She would pull it down, pull my hair out for everyone to see. *Gods, I miss her.*

Analise finished and handed me a robe as I rose from the deep tub. The scent of a fresh spread of food permeated the room even before she opened the doors. My room now glowed with flickering candlelight, warding against the darkness. *How long was I in the bath?*

"Thank you for everything, Analise." I nodded to her.

She only bowed her head. "Please eat something. You will need the energy," she urged, knocking gently on the bedroom door before it was opened from the hall.

I settled onto the chaise in soft robe. The table was filled with cheeses, breads, and fruits, while savory meats tempted from the other end. While it smelled amazing, I didn't want to eat. I was about to stand when—*was that...?* I reached for the tiny balls of chocolate, grabbing one and inspecting it. I popped a chocolate covered raisin in my mouth, holding in a moan against the sweet and salty combo. I looked back to the door and smiled. Analise must have had something to do with finding my favorite snack. *But how did she know?*

I filled up on the sweets, slowly making my way to the other foods on the table. The more I ate, the more I realized how hungry I'd truly been and I whispered my thanks to the female for knowing what I needed. I picked at the small feast, attempting to satiate both my hunger and the void in my heart.

A loud crash brought me out of the food tunnel and I jumped. My bread dropped to the floor. I hurried to the windows but my movement halted as the main door swung open.

Azral rushed in. He looked disheveled and his breath was labored.

"What happened?" I gasped.

"You need to stay here." He placed his hands on my shoulders. "There are rebels, hundreds, outside the castle walls," he panted, his words filled with urgency.

"What?" I gasped, placing my hands on his chest to brush off the dirt that clung to his shirt.

"I have to go but I need you to stay here. No matter what happens, Amara, stay *here.*"

"Why can't I come with you?" My heart raced.

"It's too dangerous. I have to fight." He took a quick breath. "Take these." He handed me two daggers, silver blades with gold detailing along the hilt. The blades glowed with red roses and gems. They weren't very suitable for defense but they were beautiful nonetheless—and better than nothing.

"What if they get in? What about everyone else? What about Analise?"

"Who?"

"The servant, who helped me—" I stumbled on my words as I watched the confusion continue to grow on his face.

"I'm sure she'll be fine. They know what to do if we're breached." His hand moved behind my neck, placing a kiss on my forehead, and my hands rose to his cheeks. "I love you." He pressed his lips against mine briefly before disappearing through the door, which promptly locked behind him.

Restlessness consumed me as time dragged on. The moon moved through the sky, casting its silvery glow. Then came the sounds of war. I watched from the windows, a symphony of screams and bursts of magical light pierced the night. My heart raced, my palms relentlessly sweaty. Was Azral okay? Was I going to be okay? He said the servants had a plan if we were breached. I circled the room. What about me?

How did they get through the castle walls anyway? Guards were swarming like flies just yesterday. How many of these rebels could there be? I let out a frustrated sigh and resumed my pacing but out of the corner of my eye, I caught sight of them again, the Fairies.

I rushed to the balcony and watched as they frantically flew around the handle. "It's locked," I yelled through the glass. I moved my hand to show them and I fell forward, through the opening door. *How in the world...?* Had Analise left this open?

They laughed as I tripped, their delicate forms darting around as the three drakai soared through the opening.

"What are you all doing here?" I asked as if I could even hear their responses.

The two Fairies flitted into the closet accompanied by the drakai, while the blue one gracefully landed on my shoulder. Without warning, she jabbed me in the neck again.

"Ow!" I yelped, shooing her away. Her mischievous expression seemed to revel in my discomfort and she joined the others.

If we survived this, I was going to have a serious conversation with her.

The sounds of battle flooded the room, amplified by the open door. I shivered in the cool night breeze. The iron tang of blood, so much blood, filled the air.

The Fairies flew out from the closet carrying my makeshift rope. They dropped it in front me.

"No," I murmured, shaking my head. "Az told me to stay here."

But then it struck me, the words *he* had uttered earlier. *Tomorrow. You'll know when.*

Was this what Drayzen meant? Had he known this was going to happen?

The Fairies proceeded to secure the shirt-rope to the edge of the balcony, their strength surprising as I tugged on it, finding it securely fastened.

"I can't," I reiterated, though curiosity gnawed at me.

And of course, Drayzen's words urged me to take up this offer.

Tomorrow.

The dream I had of Mylom flashed through my mind, then my parents, the cliff I sat on in Lunhayven—a place I'd never heard about, not until I came to this world.

...then Azral's words. *You're just Human.*

As if something was controlling my mind, another remembrance of a dream came hurtling through, pushing those words. It was my dream of Thysa.

Doubt twisted through me. Could I *not* be crazy? Could Sovanni's power not be as good as they thought and she couldn't see the truth? Or worse—could Azral be lying to me? But why?

My heart rebelled against the thought, but my mind couldn't help circling back to the possibility. He'd lied before. But he'd also saved me, stood by me, fought for me, loved me... didn't he?

Come find out, my conscience challenged me. Drayzen challenged me.

"Fine." *I accept.*

I changed into something more suitable. All in black, the fabric was lightweight yet durable, allowing me to blend seamlessly into the shadows. I secured a fitted leather vest around my torso. It was crafted with meticulous detail, like everything in the closet. I opted for a pair of sleek black pants, the pockets and leather straps perfect for my new daggers. I quickly braided my hair and pulled up the black hood.

Before the mirror, I couldn't help but feel a surge of confidence. This was the Amara I needed. A *survivor.*

"You can do this, Mar," I told my reflection. "You are not crazy." *You can't be.*

I went back to the balcony and grabbed the shirt-rope, nodding at the Fairies as their glitter guided me through the darkness. The agonized screams of the wounded and the stench of blood and death took over all my senses, providing a grim backdrop for my descent.

20

DISTANT CRIES KEPT MY ADRENALINE RACING.
Luckily, all the guards seemed to be distracted with the battle
as there were none in sight. The climb was much easier this
time. It wasn't a skill I'd imagined I'd learn but I would take
what I could get.

I leapt from the end of the rope, my boots thudding softly
as they landed on the cool dirt. The Fairies fluttered around
me. Their faint glimmer was barely visible in the dim
moonlight. I huddled against the stone wall, though it wasn't
like anyone would hear me over the slashing swords. With my
arm brushing against rough stone, I crept, moving in the
opposite direction of the ongoing battle.

I couldn't fight my way out of this one but I just needed
to make it to Mylom.

I took cover behind what appeared to be a dense bush as a figure ran from the agonizing screams. The male's hand clutched his neck. He whimpered and crumpled to the ground. I approached slowly, still surveying my surroundings in the darkness. When I got closer, the Fairies emitted a subtle glow, revealing the arrow piercing the male's throat.

There was a *whoosh*. I threw myself to the ground beside the body, gently cupping the Fairies in my hand.

Archers. My heart ratcheted.

The cries grew louder, accompanied by a growing pile of lifeless bodies scattering the open field before the castle. I looked at the body next to me. His eyes, cold and dead, stared up at me. Fear still weaved between his pupils.

"I'm sorry," I whispered, tenderly closing his vacant eyes before stepping back towards the safety of the castle wall.

But before I knew it, I was falling, and *fast*. My foot caught and I found myself hurtling backwards, plummeting towards the ground with alarming speed. I braced myself and landed on my back with an unceremonious *thud*.

I turned to see what caused my fall. Another body, an arrow piercing his heart—the one I narrowly dodged.

Back on my feet, I followed the Fairies with a shiver. They flew farther out, lighting the path ahead of me, and I dove into another bush. My heart was so loud in my ears, dulling the *clang* of metal on metal. Moonlight, once again, burst through the clouds. I peered over the foliage. I was almost at the edge of the woods. If I could just find an opening...

My eyes darted in all directions, taking in the chaos. Soldiers clashed, bodies fell. Arrows cut through the air, striking down anyone who dared to flee. I recognized the golden armor of the king's guard but the attackers wore tattered clothes, leaving themselves completely vulnerable. There was no doubt the guards were winning but the attackers weren't going down easily.

There was a small gap between fighters to my right. If I kept low enough, they might not notice me.

Then, amidst the chaos—Azral.

His emerald eyes shimmered in the moonlight, even across the battlefield, as he carved his way through Fae after Fae. Blood coated his face and hair, matting it against his pointed ears.

The clouds pulled back farther and I gasped.

The castle. It was no longer the beauty I'd come to know, no longer the unspoiled building that had held up over decades of fighting. Its walls were in ruins, pockmarked with gaping holes. The once-pristine stone bricks were marred by soot, the hue now an ominous black. Uncut vines reclaimed the fortress as they snaked over the decaying walls.

This damage...There was no way it could have happened in one night.

Azral's words surfaced. He'd said that his mother's power was strong enough to manipulate the castle's appearance; he'd said he was nowhere near that strong. *But this?*

I stumbled backwards.

My eyes widened as a shattered window caught my attention—a dimly lit room. Candles flickered, casting eerie shadows on its run-down surroundings. The room was uninhabitable. Cobwebs clung to the walls while dust cloaked the furniture.

Oh, my gods.

My heart skipped a beat, or maybe even two, when I looked at the other castle rooms, all the broken windows.

All in the same state as the first.

There was no way Azral could be out there, draining his energy fighting, and have the power to make the castle appear so desolate.

But if this wasn't an illusion—

I couldn't believe it, didn't *want* to believe it.

Another lie, my conscience warned.

That could only mean the castle I was looking at right now, *this* was reality.

Confusion and anger clawed at me as I shook my head. How could Azral have lied about something so big? I turned back to the battle, to Azral, and froze as I met his stare, his eyes already locked on me.

Suffocating fear consumed me, as if a dense fog had descended on my very being. It gripped my heart in a vice-like hold, squeezing and constricting until each beat felt like a desperate struggle for air. This emotion, this feeling, I had never once experienced it in the presence of those eyes.

But I knew the feeling all too well.

And those eyes, the deadly stare they held, were not of the male I loved.

They belonged to someone, or something, else entirely.

Azral's sword sliced through the air, finding its mark with brutal precision, as he took down the male who charged at him. With a swift kick, he sent the body flying. He never once broke his gaze on mine. Azral moved through the field of dead bodies effortlessly, a macabre dance of death. Wiping the blood from his blade on his arm, he sheathed it and closed the distance between us.

I couldn't move.

The fear that gripped me was more than physical. It was fear of the person he was becoming, someone I barely recognized. This person, this creature, was a stranger. The Azral I loved was kind and gentle. The Azral I loved fought for me, cared for me. He made me laugh when the past crept in at night, made me smile every time he brought me a dahlia flower. He me want to fight, to *live*.

That Azral died when we left Zandar. Rosetia had brought out the worst in him and I'd excused his outbursts, his dark moods and behavior. But as I looked at him, I saw the darkness deep inside, a darkness that plagued the image of the male I loved.

I felt my heart cracking with every step he took.

The Fairies flitted around me. Their persistent nudges were a desperate plea for action but I couldn't tear my eyes away from Azral's. I was trapped in their haunting emptiness.

The blue Fairy darted forwards, piercing my neck with her tiny sting and jolting me out of my fear-induced coma.

Drayzen's voice echoed throughout my mind. *Run, Mar.*

And I did.

I stumbled, my legs carrying me in haphazard strides. I reached for my daggers but my hands were trembling so badly I dropped them both. I didn't even look back, running as fast as I could, the path now littered with fallen and the moans of the wounded.

When my breaths heaved and my lungs ached, I glanced for Azral, only to find him clashing swords with an attacker.

"Thank you," I gasped to the poor souls who delayed him, if only for a moment.

Mylom galloped out of the forest and I nearly sank to my knees. She came to an abrupt stop and I threw myself over her.

"Sorry," I whispered, out of breath, as I pulled my body up with her mane. But she didn't react. The moment my left leg met her side, she was off. With a thunderous gallop, we raced through the woods, straight for Raxos.

I glanced over my shoulder, my stomach sinking as Azral sprinted for the stables. He must have seen Mylom. Which means he wouldn't be far behind and I had no doubt he knew exactly where I was headed.

Where else could I go? Sovanni and Drayzen had spoken about getting me "out" but what had that meant? She was gone now, anyway. I took a few deep breaths, steadying my heart rate. Whatever their plan was, I had no other choice but to put my trust in him.

Drayzen.

Relief washed over me and I couldn't help but release a long sigh when we reached the ashen clearing before Raxos. I had to find Thysa quickly, find out if she knew anything about this plan Sovanni and Drayzen had. I frantically checked behind me—still no sign of Azral. Mylom raced through the town. Curious onlookers stared, their whispers trailing us as we headed deeper into Raxos.

"Thank you," I whispered to Mylom when we reached the tavern. The Fairies and drakai perched on her head, braiding her long mane as I slipped from her back. I smiled at them, a fleeting feeling of safety.

That feeling shattered as a strong arm encircled my waist and a hand covered my mouth, forcefully pulling me back into the darkness of the alley. I tried to squirm free but his strength was overpowering.

"Stay quiet," Drayzen whispered behind me, holding me against him.

My head shot to the street as two guards in golden armor galloped by. Drayzen's grip loosened but he didn't let me go. I sank my teeth into his hand with all my strength. He only chuckled.

"Now isn't the best time for that, *little kitten.*"

I grunted, kicking back against his legs, hands clawing at his arm. With a small laugh, he released me.

"What the—?" I seethed.

But before I could finish my sentence, I found myself pinned against the bricks behind me. One arm lightly pressed against my chest and his free hand covered my mouth. His midnight eyes bore into mine but for the first time, he looked genuinely afraid.

"You have a problem with listening, don't you?" he hissed.

"Hey!" A female voice pierced the air from the end of the alley. *Thysa.*

I strained to turn, still partially trapped in Drayzen's grasp, and caught a glimpse of her standing in the moonlight. She merely grunted and retreated into the building. I glanced back at Drayzen, a smirk playing at his lips.

Before I could move, he lifted me. Dark shadows swirled around us, enveloping our bodies in darkness. My eyes widened but before I could even blink, we were inside, with Thysa.

I stumbled out of his grip, dizzy at whatever just happened.

"What was that?" I gasped.

My eyes darted between the two of them in the dimly lit room. It looked like a small office; one large wooden desk sat in the center of the room, two chairs in front and one larger one behind it. Papers, melted candles, and a few bottles of wine were scattered across the surface.

Drayzen grinned. "One of my many useful tricks."

"What is going on?" I demanded.

"Where's Sovanni? Did you see her before you left?" Thysa's brows narrowed, the concern evident in her words.

"She went back to Acrari."

Thysa's eyes welled and she covered her mouth, sinking into the chair behind the worn wooden desk. Drayzen took the seat in front of it, rubbing his hand over his face. He muttered a curse.

"What? What is it?" Fear swirled as I tried to piece things together but there was so much they hadn't told me.

"Acrari is no longer a city." Thysa's tone was pained. "It fell years ago when Erixx—"

I frowned. If Acrari didn't exist... *What did they do to Vani?*

"Did they follow you here?" Thysa asked with tears in her eyes.

"Yes," I whispered.

She turned to Drayzen. "We have to go back for Vani."

"Right now, that's not an option."

"It's always an option—"

A scream echoed from the other side of the door that led into the tavern. I flinched.

Drayzen quickly stood. "We need to go, *now.*"

"I'm not going." Thysa stood tall, resolute.

More screams came from beyond the door and Thysa hastily threw a cloak over herself, heading towards the back door.

"I'm taking Mylom," she started and I opened my mouth to protest. "I won't just leave her. Try not to do anything stupid," she spat at Drayzen before disappearing into the night.

"Wait!" But Thysa was gone. I whirled on Drayzen. "Care to share what's going?"

Answers, apparently, weren't something he was good at. He turned, his expression unreadable, and stalked towards me, each step deliberate. He flashed that infuriating smirk and my irritation burned, along with a flutter I didn't want to name.

The door to the office swung open but Drayzen didn't even glance back at the figure in the doorway. He just vanished.

Leaving me to face Azral alone.

My eyes locked onto the lifeless depths of his.

Azral moved for a chair, flinging it across the room. It smashed into pieces against the wall. I trembled, betraying the mask I tried to slip on. No, I couldn't even pretend anymore. Pure terror seized me as he moved. He slid his arm across the desk, a warrior's cry escaping his lips as he threw papers and bottles to the floor, glass shattering.

He crept around the desk, his eyes low and cold, fixed on me like a predator. I stumbled back, one step, then another, the space between us widening but never feeling like enough. My heart pounded so fiercely it drowned out everything else.

Tears streamed freely, unchecked, carving burning trails down my face, their salt stinging my lips.

"Where is he?" Azral roared. "I know he's here!"

"Please," I choked out.

Azral stopped mid-step, and for a moment, I saw it—the familiar light returning to his eyes, confusion replacing fury. He looked around the room as though seeing it for the first time. Then his gaze locked on me, wide and vulnerable, his lips trembling.

"Amara—" he cried, his voice breaking as he dropped to his knees. "I'm sorry, I—" He crawled toward me, his hand reaching out, trembling.

I took another step back and I felt a body behind me. But this time, I didn't jump. Drayzen's hand fell on my shoulder.

Azral's jaw slackened, and his eyes widened as he shook his head.

I just stared at him, at the prince who had lied and schemed, at the male who had promised me a better life, promised me forever.

The cracks deepened, threatening to shatter me entirely, but I swallowed the sob rising in my throat and lifted my chin. My pain burned into something sharper, colder. I wouldn't let myself be broken. Not by him. Not by anyone.

I was no one's pawn.

I placed my hand over Drayzen's defiantly, his martem humming through the connection.

"No time for games now, Mar," he whispered, his voice cool in my ear.

Without looking back, we disappeared into the shadows.

21

DRAYZEN'S ARM FELL AROUND MY STOMACH, lifting me as gusts of wind smacked my body from all directions. Slowly, I opened my eyes, greeted not by the empty void of my mind but a different kind of darkness. We were in motion, moving through unseen currents. The whirlwind lasted for only a couple of seconds before my feet landed on the cold ground.

"We should be safe here," Drayzen said, his arm sliding away from me.

I whirled, swiping at my burning eyes, unsure if it was from my dried tears or the wind of whatever we just went through. Midnight eyes met my gaze, swirling with rivers of concern and rage. They glowed with a fire I hadn't seen before.

"Are you okay?" he breathed.

I didn't know how to answer but before I could even try, salty ocean air caressed my skin, steadying me. The rhythmic crashing of waves against a distant cliff filled the air. I turned to the familiar sound, déjà vu washing over me. The snow-covered cliffside glowed as each wave hurtled against it, turning to tiny snowflakes. Snow crunched beneath my foot. Another step, *crunch*. My breath mingled with the cold as I made for the field of ice flowers along the cliff's edge.

"I've been here before." The words escaped before I could fully process them. This place...this was the cliff from my dreams. "I—"

You're just Human. Azral's words rang in my head. His *lies* because this was proof; it had to be. Proof that I wasn't crazy, proof that Azral—the male I loved—was lying to me.

I wanted to fall, to drop to my knees and let the snow catch me. I wanted to crumble, to cry, to scream and beg for answers. But one thought kept me standing.

"Why did you bring me here?" I said in a tone I didn't even recognize, turning back to Drayzen. "How did you know to bring me *here*, to this very spot?"

He looked me over, no longer bearing his mysterious facade. No, now he looked hurt, in pain, maybe even a little confused. His brows lowered, head tilted as he said, "Come on, we need to get inside, in case anyone is watching this area."

He nodded towards the large castle on a higher cliff.

I followed his gaze, cracks and crevices marred the broken castle. Glimpses of fallen stones and shattered glass pillars poked through the cracks. Moss and ivy clung to the crumbling surface, as if it was seeking refuge from the chilly night. The decay was perched near the edge of the cliff and it overlooked waves cresting a snowy beach. The cliffside was eroded by the ceaseless lashing of waves and winds, its jagged edges mirroring the castle's fragmented state.

"Why did you bring me here?"

He turned towards the castle and whispered low enough I almost didn't pick it up over the wind. "I think you know why."

I froze but not from the cold. My mind reeled, questions, thousands of them flew through my head. The answers, what I thought I knew, could it all have been a *lie*? But why would Azral lie to me? Why would everyone? If they were all so bent on getting me "out", getting me away from Azral, why not just tell me what was going on?

"Hey!" I yelled at Drayzen's back. Determination coursed through my veins. "Hey!" I yelled again, catching up to him. "Why did you bring me here? *How* did you?"

"How did I do *this*?" He smirked and in an instant, he was behind me again. His cool words brushed against the back of my ear as he whispered, "Or how did I do this?"

I spun around but he had already vanished. I looked, turning in useless circles until I spotted him halfway up the cliffside. That infuriating smirk was still etched on his face.

"Why should I go anywhere with you?" I yelled through the cold air.

He appeared in front of me. His hands brushed my shoulders as he turned me to face the castle. "We're meeting Vani and Thysa. Now, come on."

Vani. "Is she okay?"

Drayzen's hands pushed me forwards and up the cliffside. "She's fine. And we need to get out of the open."

We climbed snowy stairs in silence, my mind buzzing. I restrained myself as long as I could but my legs were so tired. I couldn't resist the urge to speak, curiosity gnawing at me.

"If you can teleport wherever you please, why are we walking up this stupid cliff?" I managed to say between gasps for air.

"I'm tired," he replied curtly. "And I don't teleport."

"Then what do you do?"

I glanced back at him, almost tripping. He apparated in front of me and his cool hand caught mine, steadying me. I felt anything but steady as our eyes met. His black hair danced over his sharp brows in the wind. That flutter returned to my stomach. Time stood still once again, frozen like the ice surrounding us. But it melted, picking up speed as heat spread through me. Drayzen only smirked before whirling away.

We walked the rest of the cliffside in silence. I tried to steady my mind and body as each wrestled with my emotions. I brushed my hand against the snowy rocks, pressing cool ice onto my heated cheeks.

By the time we reached the top, I was heaving breaths. My hands fell to my knees as I gasped—and tried to pretend I wasn't utterly exhausted. The fallen castle, battered by time and what I could only assume had been war, still possessed a deadly beauty under the moonlight. I took a haunting step forward. This castle, this cliffside...

I stooped to the flowers growing underfoot. Each one was made of ice, their petals sparkling in the moonlight. I moved my hand under a stem and the petals melted from the heat of my hand as I picked it up.

I felt Drayzen move next to me. His footsteps were silent but I could feel the hum of his martem as he approached.

"Are we in Lunhayven?" I whispered.

"Yes," he answered, his voice low.

My dream father had taken me from this place. In it, I was a child playing with a crocheted dragon. *Mylom.* I turned my gaze back to the crumbling castle. "There's no one left here, is there?"

Drayzen didn't answer; this time, he didn't have to. I stood with a deep breath, wiping wet fingers on my pants. How could this be possible?

I kept my questions to myself as we stepped inside. Moonlight filtered through shattered windows and gaps in the decaying walls and roof. Through the veil of falling snow, through the cracks, glass windows shimmered, their surfaces frosted over with delicate ice crystals. Intricate patterns of light and shadow danced on the decaying floors etched with blood stains, each pattern scattered across the hall where remnants of broken furniture and charred debris lay.

Goosebumps painted my arms.

"You should get some rest." Drayzen's voice sent another chill through me.

"Rest?" I almost laughed. "How do you expect me to rest here—after everything that just happened? And with *you*?"

"You don't even know me," he growled, stepping closer.

"Exactly." I crossed my arms. "Who even are you? Why don't you tell me what's going on and then maybe I can *rest*." I curled my fingers around the word and took a challenging step forwards. *Drayzen,* the mystery male. Granted, he had saved me from Azral's rage-induced state, but *why*? What was this secret plan him, Vani, and Thysa had?

"What do you know that you aren't telling me?" My brows furrowed. "What are you all planning?"

"So many questions, Mar," he whispered behind me, his breath grazing my neck.

I hissed in frustration, partly with him and partly at the way my cheeks heated. I spun, pushing against his chest. "I said: Stop. Doing. That!"

"I am not the enemy here. And you need rest—we both do. We have a long way to travel." He gave me a final, tired, look and walked away.

"Travel? Where exactly are we going?"

"Somewhere else. Don't you worry, little kitten." That smirk was the last thing I saw as he disappeared into the shadows.

"Hello!" I yelled but there was no answer.

I paced around the room. Most of the furniture was broken or burned but I was able to find a relatively intact couch. Brushing off the accumulated dust and snow, the remnants of countless years past, I took a seat and pulled my legs close to my chest. My chin rested on my knee, fingers brushing against each other as I rocked in place. I closed my eyes but my body went rigid. Azral appeared in my mind but it wasn't the Azral I loved. No, this male tore through that office, wood crashing against the wall. I tried to open my eyes, to get as far away from the memory as possible, but I was trapped. Azral's rage-filled eyes locked onto me and held me there.

Still frozen, my parents greeted me next, their bodies left on display, the puddles of blood under them. Then, my mind snapped to a different puddle of blood, a wooden floor, a broken bottle.

Drip. Drip. Drip.

"Stop!" I cried.

My eyes flew open. I clenched my hands, running them anxiously through my hair, pressing against my aching head.

One last thought intruded on my already racing mind, *Drayzen.*

Had he known this whole time? Was this plan of his and Vani's to get me away from Azral?

"He lost his chance at redemption years ago," Drayzen had said to Vani.

Thoughts swirled and clashed in my mind like the relentless waves outside. Endless questions, endless theories, but no *real* answers.

A crash from the far corner of the room broke my spiraling thoughts. My legs snapped to the ground but darkness engulfed that area, untouched by the moonlight's gentle glow. Another *thud* and I shot up from the couch. The hairs on the back of my neck stood.

Before I could move, Drayzen appeared in front of me. His cool hand covered the tiny scream I let out; his other hand gently rested on the back of my head.

"Stay here," he whispered before disappearing.

But I inched closer to the source of the sound, my footsteps light. The metallic scrape of a sword unsheathing reached my ears and I ran. My heart beat rapidly as I crouched behind a broken column, trembling. How I wished I still had those daggers. Another *thud* echoed through the air, followed by the clatter of a sword hitting stone.

Peeking around the column, moonlight glowed over a body sprawled on the cold stone, clad in golden armor. The rose sigil shone and I froze. My eyes slowly traced the blood trail on his armor straight up to the soldier's neck that was...torn open, crimson liquid spilling from him. Two more soldiers entered through the broken wall behind the body, both cursing at the sight.

"They're here," one whispered.

I ducked behind the safety of the column. My breath grew more and more rapid.

Drayzen appeared before me. One hand muffled my scream while the other hung at his side drenched in blood. He pressed a finger to his lips, red smearing. And those teeth...*how did I not notice before?* Two fangs brushed his blood-stained lips.

It was true, then: Drayzen was Denazin.

For the first time since leaving Azral, I began to worry I made the wrong choice.

Tears welled in my eyes as I met his once-midnight blue gaze. But now they were transformed. Trails of silver slithered through his irises, brimming with something I'd never seen. I squirmed, desperate to break free from his grip, but he growled, whispering, "Stop."

His command imprisoned me.

The words reverberated through my mind, penetrating every fiber of my being. *Stop, stop, stop, stop...*His voice was sultry, almost hypnotizing, as it locked me in place. The moonlight disappeared behind a cloud as he vanished. His final command whispered through the darkness. *Stay here.*

And all I could do was obey.

I was frozen in place and not from the fear of what lurked behind me but because I had no other choice. Snarls and thuds echoed through the darkness. Two more bodies fell to the floor as Drayzen reappeared before me.

"Okay." His voice was gentle now. The silver glow disappeared from his irises, replaced by a sadness I couldn't quite place. He brushed a stray piece of hair behind my ear, his bloody fingers turning the white strand red. "I'm sorry I had to do that."

The weight of his words, his command, lifted from my body. I took a gasping breath. I slowly, *very* slowly, peered around the column to see the other two guards now-lifeless bodies, blood pooling around their necks. I turned back to the Denazin before me, the *demon* made by the God of Death.

Drayzen quickly wiped his blood-stained lips on the sleeve of his shirt. "I'm sorry you had to see that." His voice was genuine, laced with concern.

"You—" But I didn't know what else to say.

"We need to get out of here. More guards are coming," he said as if I wouldn't question it, as if I would just willingly follow him.

"Who are you?" I yelled. I pushed him away with a grunt and he let me. He fell back, taking a little step. "Who are you?" I cried again.

"I need you to be quiet because more guards are coming and we need to get out of here," he said gently.

"I'm not going anywhere with you until you tell me what is going on." I was tired, so tired of the secrets, the lies, the games.

He tilted his head back, staring at the open ceiling, and took a deep breath. "Please, don't make me do this, Mar." He sighed, scrubbing his face.

"No—" I almost yelled. But at the very moment I parted my lips, a familiar feeling washed over me, hypnotizing me again. My voice had been silenced.

Our eyes locked again; a mix of sadness and regret filled his. With a heavy sigh, he pressed his hand against the nape of my neck, a touch that sent a warmth down my back.

"I'm sorry." His words echoed before the darkness swallowed me whole.

22

BITING GUSTS OF COLD WIND GREETED ME. I squinted through the morning sun. It was fierce and unyielding as it pierced through my eyelids, forcing me to cover them. But as soon as I lifted my hand, I lost balance and grabbed for the cool hard surface I was sitting on. I squinted, looking for anything. My hand returned to the solid surface beneath me. The texture was warm, rough; it reminded me of...scales.

I ran my fingers over the surface, confirming my suspicion. I was on Mylom's back. *Flying.* Wind whipped through my hair, an echoing calm in my ears as I felt us dip and weave through the sky. A hint of cool lavender swept through my senses and I breathed in the calming sensation.

But a voice, unmistakable, broke that calm as it sounded in my ear. It was close enough for his every breath to tickle the nape of my neck. I felt him now, his arms wrapped securely around my waist, stabilizing my position.

Drayzen.

My cheeks heated no matter how much I protested the feeling. I rolled my eyes at myself. This was seriously *not* the time.

"You're awake." His voice sounded over the wind, that snarky tone traveling with it.

Even without seeing his face, I could picture the self-assured smirk. Every one of my instincts urged me to hit back with a cutting remark but I swallowed my words and took a moment to compose myself.

"Just in time to see the sunrise," he purred.

Now, I rolled my eyes at him but I couldn't fight a smile. My sight finally adjusted and the view was incredible. The sky transformed into a canvas of vibrant hues with streaks of fiery orange, soft pink, and purples.

Drayzen shifted behind me, careful about where his hand laid on my stomach. I looked at his other arm, rigidly in place on Mylom's horn, as if touching me was a sin.

Did Mylom really trust him? Did she know him? This Denazin, could we possibly be similar? Outcasts and orphans in our own ways? I lifted my hands from Mylom's horns, tracing my fingers along her scales. *Can I trust him?*

It wasn't like I could run away, unless I wanted to jump to my death. But even then, I couldn't help but think Drayzen would save me.

"Where are we?" I managed to croak through the wind.

"In the sky." His response was laced with an irritating nonchalance. "I'm taking you home."

"No." My body went rigid. *Home. Zandar.* No matter what happened here, going back there was not an option. "No, I can't—"

"Sorry, *my* home," Drayzen clarified.

I wasn't sure which was worse. His home could only mean one place: We were going to The Isles—The God of Death's Island.

As if reading my mind, he said, "Did Sovanni mention it to you?"

I gulped down my rising fear. "She did but she said it was a long story."

I recalled our vague conversation about the islands. Azral had only given me so much information, too.

"It is and unfortunately, we don't have time for it now," he replied curtly, shifting behind me. His body brushed against mine and I couldn't fight that warmth that spread through me again.

"And what are we going to do at *your* home?" I asked. "Am I your prisoner now?"

He laughed again, brushing off my question.

"We're almost there, Mar."

"Stop calling me that," I snapped. "We're not friends."

"You can call me Drayz if it makes you feel better." I could practically feel the tug on his lips.

My heart skipped and I couldn't tell if it was because of him or Mylom as she dipped straight down. I grabbed Drayzen's arm, clinging to him for support with one hand, the other on Mylom's horn. I couldn't scream; gods, that would be so embarrassing. So, I clung, my eyes shut, the terror intensifying as we hurtled downwards. My stomach flew into my chest, then dropped back down as Mylom came to a glide.

"You can open your eyes now," Drayzen whispered.

I peeled one eye open, my gaze immediately met with another breathtaking sight.

"Gods," I breathed.

Before us were the four islands Sovanni had mentioned. The farthest island had thousands of trees and a white sandy beach painting its surface. The area glowed with what looked like the light of a thousand suns. This, I imagined, could only belong to Saigus. It sat above an isle of similar size and layout but this one was shadowed in darkness. A single light shone at its center, the soft glow of what could only be Melenyz.

Under them, was an island larger than the rest. This one was filled with a glittering forest, almost like the Fairies. This one had to belong to Nyrah because the final island, the one we were flying straight towards, belonged to none other than the God of Death. A house sat by the sandy beach where dark waves crashed against the shore. Its waters, painted a deep black, surrounded Drayzen's home.

His hand gently glided up my back, the touch oddly comforting, and found its place on the back of my neck.

"Sorry about this," he said, his voice soft. "Again."

And just like that, the beauty before me transformed into a hazy blur. *For gods' sake.*

I blacked out just before my body fell into his.

I sat up on a small bed, my eyes scanning the room in disbelief. This *really* had to stop happening.

I was in a modest space, the room furnished only with the essentials—a bed and a small bathing area. Flickering candlelight cast dancing shadows on the walls but something seemed off. I searched the room, my gaze darting in every direction. There wasn't a single window.

I stood, moving to the door, my hand wrapping around the handle. But as I pulled, a sinking feeling took over—the door was locked.

The walls seemed to close in around me. Each inhalation grew faster and shallower. *No.* I turned, spinning as the walls pressed. *No.* I was trapped, again. A prisoner in this world.

"No!" I yelled, my knees cracking against the wooden floor.

My vision blurred as my eyes snapped to the open door. Drayzen came crashing in, panic etched in his ungodly features.

Rage eclipsed my fear. "What is this? What's going on!?" I yelled.

"It was for your safety—"

"My *safety*?" I snapped, tears betraying me. "That's what Azral told me!"

Drayzen's eyes widened. He was, for once, seemingly speechless and I couldn't understand why.

"Amara, I—" he stumbled. "It's not what I meant. I—"

"Gods, you're going to frighten her to death." Thysa's voice sang from the other side of the door.

She entered, her presence commanding. The golden silk two-piece she wore highlighted her features perfectly. She sidled up to Drayzen. Her skepticism of him was evident with each calculated step she took.

"Why don't you just tell her already?" she muttered with frustration.

"Stop," Drayzen interrupted sharply.

"Tell me what?"

More secrets, more lies.

"If you don't, I will," Thysa declared. "She needs to know."

"Back off," Drayzen growled, turning to her, his fangs gliding on his bottom lip.

How did I not notice them before?

"Is Vani okay, is she—?"

"She will be. She's resting right now," Thysa interjected.

A small sigh of relief escaped my lips as I nodded.

Drayzen turned to face me. I recoiled instinctively. I couldn't help the small gasp escape my lips as he moved closer to me, his brows furrowed with intensity.

"Do you trust me?" he pleaded.

Do I trust him? The question of the day, apparently. Could I truly trust anyone completely? I trusted Azral and look where that got me. I blinked away the tears that echoed his memory and pushed back.

"Give me one reason why I should trust you after practically kidnapping me?"

"I *saved* you, this—" Drayzen laughed, rubbing his face. He looked deranged, as if he couldn't keep his mask on anymore. He took a breath. "I did *not* kidnap you."

"Knocking me out and locking me in this room, that doesn't sound like kidnapping to you?"

Thysa balked. "You knocked her out?"

"Twice." I crossed my arms.

"I wouldn't trust you either." She laughed. Thysa waved a dismissive hand, urging him to proceed. "Just get this over with."

"I can't do it all at once," He growled at her, taking a step closer to me.

But now there was nowhere for me to go. My back was pressed against the wall behind me. Fear surged through my chest and tears came rushing back.

"What are you going to do?" My voice quivered though I tried to still it.

"I need you to trust me," he whispered, no begged.

His eyes searched my face as a cool hand met my cheek. He brushed the back of his finger across my skin, my fallen tear sliding along with it. Each move, each look, was deliberate and slow, like he was studying my face. His brows lowered, his eyes frenzied as they searched mine. The hum of his martem wrapped around me like a warm blanket.

Please, Mar. My conscience begged. *Drayzen.*

Gravity pulled me in and I felt myself nodding, the words falling from my lips.

"I trust you."

His other hand slowly moved to the other side of my head, brushing hair behind the opposite ear. His thumbs pressed into my temples, my head gently hitting the wall behind me.

"I'm sorry," he whispered and I swore I saw a hint of hurt in his eyes. It wasn't long, though, as excruciating pain shot through me.

The ache corroded my mind, tearing through what felt like layers of my consciousness. I couldn't help the scream I let out, this feeling, it was like my mind was being ripped apart.

Flashes of disjointed images flickered before my closed eyes. I screamed louder, my hands desperately grasping at his, and my body sagged, his grip on my mind the only thing keeping me upright.

"I'm sorry," he whispered again as he dove deeper, tugging at more layers.

This, *this* was his martem, his twisted form of magic. I could feel it coiling and dancing in me as more fragmented images assaulted my senses. I saw them now, my dream parents, their faces fleeting as they raced through my mind, their presence hauntingly distant.

Then, in an instant, I wasn't in the small room anymore. I wasn't standing with Drayzen, the hum of his martem no longer keeping me sane.

No, I found myself standing in a larger room. The cream columns and tiled floor stretched before me. I looked up from the cold tiles, the golden chair adorned with dripping vines and red rubies sat on the dais before me.

Erixx's empty eyes bore into mine from his place on the throne.

23

I WOKE UP ON A COLD FLOOR, TREMBLING. THE taste of salt and iron lingered on my lips. I glanced down to see my hands smeared with crimson. But they were so small, a child's hands. The long white sleeves I wore were drenched in red, the skirt billowing in the red puddle I sat in.

"Do it." Erixx's deep voice reverberated through the room.

I looked back at him; his body was also drenched in blood. Slowly, he rose, stalking closer to me. I scanned the area. The once-lively throne room was now stained with dead bodies. They were scattered across the floor, cut down and empty. Only a select few guards remained by the king's side as he moved.

A warm hand landed on my skin, causing me to jerk my head towards the familiar touch.

Azral.

He stood behind me, firmly gripping my shoulder as he kneeled. His emerald eyes met mine with their golden glint and I jumped, hands shaking.

This was the Azral I saw on the battlefield, the Azral I saw in that room. And it was someone else entirely. He grabbed the hair at my nape, yanking my head back. The last time I'd been in this position, it was Azral who saved me.

Who would save me now?

My eyes snapped open to find Drayzen. His features rippled with pain. I fought back my tears but they welled, traitorous as they stained my cheeks.

"I'm sorry," he whispered.

And I swore I saw a tear fall down his own cheek before I was thrown back into the vision. Pain surged through me as his martem pushed deeper. I shut my eyes tightly, bracing myself.

I was back in the throne room but this time, I viewed the scene from the perspective of a guard by Erixx.

Azral's golden armor glowed in the candlelight, revealing spots of blood across his chest and arms. I watched helplessly as he grasped the head of the small child.

The child's mind I was just in.

Her body was covered in blood, her white hair fell in waves down her back as he pulled it, eliciting a yelp from her. He tilted her head back, his dagger dancing around her neck.

"Don't kill her," Erixx commanded from beside me.

"I won't." Azral laughed, his dagger now hovering near her pointed ears.

And then the realization hit me like a wave crashing on Lunhayven's rocky cliffside.

That child was *me*.

It was *me* that Azral held that way; it was my bloodied and broken body. I couldn't have been older than four or five.

Four.

That's when Isidore found me.

Agonizing screams echoed through my mind as I witnessed the scene unfold. Tears burned the eyes of the body I was in as Azral brought the dagger to the child's delicate pointed ears, *my* ears; a twisted smile on his lips.

With a swift motion, he sliced off the tips.

The child screamed—I screamed, at least I tried to. The mind I watched from only stood, unable to move, unable to help in this memory that did not belong to me. Pain radiated through the child momentarily, then she fell into unconsciousness.

Erixx approached Azral and the child with a female in tow. Her hands were bound by chains as she kneeled beside them. The woman was small and frail, her matted golden hair cascaded to her waist. She gently placed her hands over the child's, *my*, severed ears. A soft white light emanated from her touch. The bleeding stopped and my ears began to mend.

Leaving no trace of the wound.

The woman laid shaky hands over my heart. She closed her eyes, uttering words I couldn't comprehend, but they carried a weight of power. Another light, different from the one that healed the child, enveloped them both. But this light, something about it was harsher, darker. The candles throughout the throne room flicked and the chandeliers shook. The guard looked around. Our hand inched towards the hilt of the sword at our side.

The woman stopped her incantation and the light swiftly dissipated as she rose from the floor. Turning to face Erixx, she bowed her head, the clinking of her chained hands resonating in the silence.

"It is done," she said, raising her gaze to meet him and I saw her tears fall freely.

A wicked smile curled on Erixx's lips, sending shivers through my mind and down the spine of the guard. The king adjusted the crown on his head and slowly turned to Azral.

Azral mirrored the sinister smile and addressed him. "May I?" Sarcasm dripped from his lips.

Erixx smiled in approval and walked away, reclaiming his seat on the throne. The guard shifted—even he was uneasy about whatever was happening. We looked back to Azral. He was a stranger in this light and as his attention shifted back to the female, that wicked grin still painted his face. With a swift motion, he unsheathed his sword. The rubies embedded in the hilt glimmered with an intense glow, bathing the whole room in red.

The female dropped to her knees, the chains on her wrists colliding with tile. Her voice trembled with desperation, "Please, I am loyal, this was not—"

But her plea was cut short. Azral's sword met her neck in one swift blow, sending her head rolling. More blood splattered his armor and drenched the child, drenched *me*, as the body of the female crumpled to the cold floor.

Agonizing pain seared through my mind and I felt myself being forcefully torn away from the vision. I let out another piercing scream, hurtling through the darkness within my own head. Flashes of images raced past me, fragments of the past, pieces of a puzzle I hadn't been able to put together. It was as if I were being propelled through a chaotic selection of memories. The pain was overwhelming but slowly, I regained awareness of my physical body. I clutched my throbbing head, meeting Drayzen's hands lingering on my temples.

I forced my eyes open. Those deep midnight eyes were the only thing I could see, pulling me into their calming darkness. I slowly blinked and the room materialized around us. I tasted salt and I parted my lips, desperate to release a cry, a scream, anything.

But nothing came out.

I collapsed to the floor. Drayzen fell with me, his hands still hovering around my temples, gently brushing away strands of hair that covered my eyes, tucking them behind my ear.

My ears.

I reached up with trembling hands and touched them, feeling their familiar rounded shape. I opened my mouth again but only silence greeted my futile attempts. I was hollow, empty, as if my very essence had been drained. The haunting images replayed in my head, over and over and over. My cold fingers stayed on my ears, blocking out any sound, blocking out the truth.

The truth that *Azral* did this to me. He lied to me, he mutilated me, he betrayed me. He told me he loved me. Was this the type of love I was worthy of, betrayal? Was the way he gasped for breath as we laughed real? How it felt when he held me at night, when the cold was unbearable? The way he looked at me when he told me I was his? *Was any of it real?*

My tear-filled eyes locked with Drayzen's.

Did he know? Did they all know? Sovanni, Thysa...

Did they all know I was *Fae*?

"I'm sorry," Drayzen whispered, breaking the suffocating silence. "I never wanted you to find out like this, this..." His voice trailed off, the weight of his words hanging in the air.

"What was that?" I cried but I already knew. My hands slid down to rest on my trembling knees.

"You know what that was," he replied dryly, rising to his feet and holding a hand to help me.

But I slapped it away. "Did everyone know?" I hissed. "Did everyone know this whole time?"

Drayzen's voice was barely a whisper. "I'm sorry."

I could hear the anguish in his tone, it sent a pang to my chest. But I was too angry to care, too angry to examine the reaction I had to his pain. Because they all *knew*, they all knew what Azral did to me. They knew and they let me *be* with him.

I shot to my feet. "Why? Why keep this from me? What sort of sick game are you—?"

"It was too risky to tell you the truth." Drayzen slid his arrogant facade on and emotion disappeared from his voice, like he was reading from a book, like he was afraid to show how he truly felt. "We needed him to get you here, to get you across the Veil."

"Why wait this long to do whatever you just did? Why wait this long to tell me?"

"I couldn't risk them finding out about my martem," he explained, his gaze meeting mine. "They only know what I want them to know."

I sank back on the wall, the wood pulling against my shirt. I shook my head, straining blankly at the near-empty room. The memories continued to flicker in my mind.

"I need to know everything," I declared, my gaze fixed on him. "Why did this happen? Why keep me there for so long? How did I even *get* there?" I couldn't help the questions pouring out of my mouth. There were too many, each one threatening to consume me.

Drayzen ran a hand through his dark hair, pushing back stray strands. He joined me on the floor with his back against the side of the bed. He took a breath, then said, "You needed to get close to Azral, to trust him enough to come here with him."

Those words echoed in my mind. *Trust him.*

I'd heard them before; I'd heard that exact voice before, the voice I'd listened to on one too many occasions. The voice that led me here, to this very moment.

"It was *you*?" I breathed. "I thought you were my conscience."

My eyes widened. I was speechless. *How did he manage to get in my head, especially from so far away?* It was him all those times I'd questioned myself, him urging me to open up, to trust, to feel.

It had been Drayzen all along.

"I had to. I—" he paused, "there was no other way of getting you through the Veil. The guards that watch it would have been alerted immediately and it would have all been for nothing. You had to come through with him, on *their* agenda, their timeline."

Did they know it was me Azral brought back to Kaluth? Could they all see what I was so blind to?

"When did everyone find out it was me?" The girl he'd mutilated.

"No one was sure. Sovanni had her suspicions. I think she knew earlier than she let on but she still believes there's something left in him, some shred of humanity. After her first dive, she couldn't deny it anymore." He took a breath, searching my face. "Thysa knew as soon as she saw you."

Thysa had been shocked when she met me; she'd used my name. But everyone was shocked. The townspeople, the other Fae at the ball. They watched me like I was an anomaly, weary and curious eyes followed me everywhere I went. My heart sank further, fighting to stay afloat with the weight of his words, the truth. I was a pawn in whatever game this was, manipulated by everyone I had trusted.

And Drayzen was no exception.

"When did *you* know?"

He took a deep breath, his fingers twiddling together in his lap. *Was he nervous?* He looked up through his fallen hair, a shadow cast over his eyes.

"I've known you for quite some time, Mar," he whispered, his voice betraying his facade. He looked back down but before I could push further, he said, "The war started twenty-four years ago, when *you* were born."

When I was born...

"Your parents were set to rule both major Fae kingdoms, Lunhayven and Solyrus."

My parents.

"Akailo, your father, was born in Solyrus. While your mother, Cyra, was from Lunhayven. Akailo had just been crowned the King of Rosetia and was tasked with finding a queen."

"My mother," I whispered. "Cyra." Her name sounded so right. These were my *Fae* parents.

"Your father was supposed to marry someone of the same power. It was forbidden for two major powers to cross bloodlines. No one wanted it, the creation of something they could have never even imagined, a power derived from two gods." He smirked and looked up at me. "But your parents instantly fell in love and decided they weren't going to let old rules determine their lives. The counsel for both courts objected to their joining but since Akailo was already king, he overruled them all." Drayzen cleared his throat. "The fear that came from what they did, what they made—"

"*Me?*"

"You." Drayzen met my gaze. "The first of your kind."

My eyes widened and I fell back against the wall. I shook my head, mouth opening, but no words came out. My hand pressed against the cool floor, holding me up as the room spun. My eyes met Drayzen's again and they steadied me as he continued.

"Erixx was always hungry for power, infamous for his insatiable desires. He was a measly lord back in his day but when your parents married, the kingdom was outraged. People rallied behind him and his cause to reclaim The Scarlet Throne for Solyrus. Then, you were born and it only gave them more cause for war. All the people in Lunhayven and many in Rosetia supported your family. But Erixx's influence spread like wildfire, fueled by the fear of the unknown, by what you may be capable of. Your parents..." He paused.

I knew what came next. I think I'd always known, deep down. I always hoped they would be out there somewhere looking for me. Isidore and Lettie always told me they were, told me that one day I would meet them. I never believed them, not until my dreams started. I thought maybe, just maybe, they were right. Maybe these magical parents were out there, looking for their lost daughter, searching worlds and lands to find me. Maybe those were just lies I needed to tell myself. Some purpose to keep going. But I knew the truth.

"They're dead, aren't they?" Drayzen didn't need to say anything. I could see the truth on his face. "I need some air," I breathed, rising to my feet and storming towards the door.

"Mar—"

He stumbled to his feet to follow me but I was too quick. I reached for the doorknob and to my surprise, and relief, it swung open. I tried to navigate through the long hallway. The dim candlelight lit the corridor, leading me towards what looked to be a front door. I pushed and it opened but I was blinded by the morning sun.

I squinted through it, a tear escaping as I tried to shield my eyes. In the distance, beyond the hills, was the sparkling beach I'd seen flying in—where the black waters merged with soft sand.

Then I spotted her. *Mylom.*

Her black scales glowed as she laid by the water. The distant crash of waves reached my ears from the ocean. I moved for her and then I was sprinting.

"Mylom—" The cry escaped my lips.

Her eyes were no longer that fake shade of emerald. Now, they glowed with fiery intensity, something like an understanding coursing between the two of us. She never showed this side around Azral, always masking her true self.

She only showed this side around one other person. *Drayzen.* Had she been trying to tell me this whole time?

I threw myself onto her scales, my hand resting on her nose, and she exhaled. Warm steam wrapped around me as I sank into the sand beside her. Her body curled protectively around mine, the heat pushing back against the chill of the breeze off the water. Before us, the ocean stretched endlessly, black waves crashing against the shore's stark white edge. The sand beneath me was cool, my fingers tracing through it as I inhaled the salty air mingled with the sweet scent of lavender.

For a fleeting moment, the hollowness in my heart disappeared. She lowered her head over me and I let myself crumble.

24

I MUST HAVE FALLEN ASLEEP BECAUSE WHEN I opened my eyes, all I could see was the night sky painted with thousands of stars. They reflected off the inky ocean, endless waves mirroring their patterns. I took a long, much-needed breath that mingled with the cool night air.

"It's beautiful." Drayzen's voice broke the silence from behind me.

I pulled my knees to my chest, not bothering to turn. Silence lapsed. Mylom wrapped her wing around us both. I didn't want to know but I had to know, and so I asked, "How?" It was all I whispered through a shaky voice. But I knew he would understand. *How did my parents die?*

Drayzen's voice dropped to a low somber tone, his words like a dagger. "*He* killed them."

Silence filled the air, allowing the harsh reality to settle. I didn't have to ask who "he" was. *He* was the person I'd trusted over everything—the person I gave my heart to. He was the one who brought me here and told me he'd help me *find* my parents.

But he was the one to draw the blade.

Azral.

The truth crushed me, like bricks weighed on my chest. My breaths grew heavy, rapid, but they were thick, like I couldn't catch the next one. Drayzen sat next to me. Through glassy eyes, I watched him cautiously place a hand on my knee, his martem humming as it overtook the consuming feeling. I breathed deep, shaking.

We sat like that for a few moments. My breath steadied with the waves and his magic.

"Thank you," I whispered, almost embarrassed by my feelings. I didn't want to be so vulnerable in front of him. I never wanted to be this vulnerable in front of anyone ever again. To trust someone again...it seemed like an impossible task.

I brushed stray strands of hair behind my ear, my hand lingering a bit too long. I didn't feel any scar. I'd never seen one and I was sure Lettie would have said something after all the times she brushed my hair.

Drayzen looked at me, his midnight eyes complemented by the night sky. He looked at my hand and I dropped it.

"They used a healer," he said to the ocean, his voice thick with anger. But I knew it wasn't towards me. No, we now shared a common enemy. "She healed you so it wouldn't leave a scar. So you would never figure out what you are, *who* you are."

He took a long breath. "She took your martem."

The cool breeze of the night brushed against my face. I sat there for a while, letting his words sink in. *My martem.* Some power I once had. A power no one else had, a power everyone feared.

A power they *stole* from me.

I looked at Drayzen trying to calm the anger pooling in my gut. His pale skin glowed in the moonlight and the stars reflected off his black hair. I couldn't help the tingle in my toes but the feeling was quickly replaced by a flicker of realization.

"How did you show me what was happening? Were you there?"

He shook his head.

"You pulled me away, put me into someone else's mind." I tilted my head, leaning into him. "Was it because I passed out?"

His fingers swirled in the sand as he looked back at the water. "I didn't want you to relive that pain. The memories, they can be lifelike."

One final question loomed at the forefront of my mind. If I had power, but now it was gone—

"What does that make me?"

Fae or Human?

Drayzen took a moment, letting the sand fall through his fingertips. "My power shouldn't work on humans but it has on you all these years, so..."

"All these *years*?" I interrupted. The floodgates of questions reopened. How long had he been this silent presence in my mind?

Mar, his voice whispered through the dark depths. How much did he really know about me?

"I came to Rosetia about four years ago to investigate the war. I'm not from here, so I was curious what all the fuss was about." He shrugged. "I'm from Menasai." The word fell from his lips with that thick accent I had only heard him use one other time, when he was talking to Mylom. He looked at me, his usual smirk back on full display. "You may know it as The Ever."

My mind spun. Sovanni told me she'd been searching for any bit of information about it, did she know her answers were right here?

A smile danced in his eyes. "No one knows anything about it and we like to keep it that way."

I couldn't help but linger on that word, *we*. "There are more of you?" *Denazin.*

His head tilted. "Like I said Mar, they only know what I want them to know."

"How—?"

"Before I came here, we got word of what happened in Lunhayven." He picked up more sand. "The guards called it Death's Coldest Night. The people who lived there—they were all slaughtered." His tone dropped to a deadly low. "I heard what had happened to you and to your people, the plans Erixx had set in motion for your crown." He shook his head, disgust marring his features. "I couldn't just stand by and let it happen any longer."

But the realization hit me like a thunderbolt. *My people, my crown.*

If my parents were royalty, king and queen..."Wait, are you saying—?"

His eyes met mine, that infuriating smirk on full blast. "You are the daughter of Akailo and Cyra Raine, the true King and Queen of Rosetia."

No.

That wasn't possible.

"Andrasteia Amara Raine"—*No.*—"you are the true heir to the Scarlet Throne."

25

MY WORLD SHATTERED INTO THOUSANDS OF fragments. The sand beneath me felt like it was dragging me down but pulling me nowhere. Truth consumed me. The words echoed in my ears, bouncing off the walls of my mind. Each syllable was an unbearable weight.

And it was too much to carry.

This truth of my life unraveled the dissonant threads of my existence, leaving me gasping for air, clinging to anything that could keep me from spiraling. Time stood still, the air thick with my disbelief, and all I could breathe in was the truth.

The true heir to The Scarlet Throne.

Then, as if I was struck by lightning, the mirage of my past crashed to the forefront of my mind.

Azral.

My dreams.

I swiped away the tendrils of fear before they drowned me.

"One of your loyal guards slipped a note when they took you to Zandar, a paper with your name on it. I guess only part of it made the trip." Drayzen sounded a million miles away, then the words came crashing back.

Andrasteia Amara Raine.

"You're lying." I wanted it to be a cruel joke.

But I knew it wasn't.

This was the truth I searched for but it was so much more than what I asked, more than I ever wanted. I wanted to find my birth parents, to find a family after mine was ripped away.

By *him.*

"I'm sorry—"

"Why not just kill me, too? Why let me live?"

"When Erixx took your power, there was one caveat: You couldn't die. If you did, then your power would go along with you. So, they sent you to Zandar." Drayzen sounded like he would crush them for what they'd done. "They thought you would suffer there, alone and unwanted. I don't think they were expecting you to find your parents."

My eyes shot to his.

"But eventually they had their way with them, too."

Crash. Another wave of truth hit me, an unstoppable force shattering the barriers of my thoughts. My parents. Their slaughter. The fire. It was *them.*

It was Azral.

The few pieces of my heart that had remained unscathed now crumbled. My breath skipped and my hand fell to my chest.

"But—" The words caught. I couldn't move. If he did this, if he knew—"Why would he help me?" My throat burned. "Why bring me here, so close to the truth?"

Drayzen sneered, tossing a pile of sand towards the inky sea. "He's sick, they all are. It's just a game for him, toying with you, making you think you had a chance, a *choice.*"

Drayzen shook his head.

Azral trained me. He helped me look for answers about who killed my parents. And that whole time, the one I was searching for was right next to me.

He loves me not. The final petal fell in my mind.

Crash.

The images that crossed my mind threatened to send me over the edge.

Drip. Drip. Drip.

My heart beat with each drop of blood, remembering the man I killed, the man he told me to kill.

I was a puppet in his twisted show.

And the rules of his game were finally being read.

The man I killed, the maps he had, he knew of this place—and I could bet that wasn't the only thing he knew. No, before I took his life he spoke one word. One name.

My name. I bet he knew who Azral was, too.

Crash.

The realization hit me like a punch to the gut—because my name. *How could I have been so stupid?*

"I never told Azral my name. When we met, I never told him. He just knew it and I didn't even realize." I shook my head and I couldn't help but laugh. A small chuckle that turned into a wicked roar. *How did I not see?*

Drayzen said something low beside me and I almost didn't hear it. But I did. And those words made me freeze. "What did you say?"

"I know," he whispered.

He took a long breath and looked out at the water, his arms falling over his knees. "I wasn't able to cross the Veil, not without them knowing." He paused, his head tilted slightly towards me, his face shadowed by dark hair. "But I had my own way of reaching you. It took a while but once Azral crossed, I was able to make the connection."

He looked at me and the world stood still. "That's when I started sending the memories to you."

It was as if the ocean held its breath, the stars left no shimmer, the wind forgot its path. It was another truth I couldn't carry, another burden crushing me.

"All your dreams, the memories—"

"It was you?" My tears fell, unable to contain themselves any longer. "This whole time?"

Our eyes locked and I caught a fleeting glimpse of shame in his. As if he thought himself an unwelcome guest in the sanctuary of my mind. But did he even know what those dreams meant to me? How much I relied on them when the weight of my reality was too much?

"They were always watching, waiting to see if you would remember, if some glimmer of your power would come back. But eventually they grew bored and irritated with your happiness. He sent Azral there to—"

"Kill them." I cut him off. "Azral killed Isidore and Lettie." The truth was like a knife through my tortured heart.

"They were going to leave you there alone but then the fire..." Drayzen paused.

Crash.

The last wave settled across the shore.

"Amara, you started that fire."

26

I STARTED THE FIRE? "HOW?"

"I'm not exactly sure. I think being close to another Fae might have sparked something." He turned to me. "Have you felt any different since that night?"

It was all too much to process. "My power started the fire?"

"Do you ever feel it?"

That familiar hum wrapped around me again, a warm embrace in the cool night. I nodded, meeting his eyes. "Yes. I mean, I think so." I tried to piece together an explanation. "There's this hum. I always thought it was others' martem but..." I paused. It sounded crazy because it was crazy. But I had to ask. "Do you think it could be mine?"

"It could be," Drayzen said to the waves. "Once Azral saw what you could do, he stayed. He wanted to see how much your power grew, how much of it you still had left."

"Why?"

"Erixx kept your power the first time. So, this time, he'd keep it for himself."

That was all he'd seen when he looked at me. I was a pawn, a vessel he could use. I couldn't stop my tears. My breaths came short to the point of hyperventilation. It was as if I was drowning in the sea of truths, each revelation filling at my lungs.

"How do you know all of this?" I dared to ask.

"I have my ways," he replied cryptically. His familiar smirk returned but there was a hollowness to it. "I got close to some of the guards there, some who were friends with Azral."

"How?" I was weary of the question. The last time I saw him close with guards, he was ripping their throats out with his teeth.

"Compulsion. One of my many tricks." Pain seeped through his mask.

"Compulsion?"

"It's sort of like mind control."

"You've used it on me before." I couldn't help remembering the feeling, the way his words echoed in my mind when I tried to say one thing and nothing came out.

Shame clouded his features. He looked away, lowering his head. "I don't like to use it but yes, I had to intervene."

"How does it work?" I leaned towards him.

"It's like diving into someone's mind, similar to what Vani can do but much easier for me. I make a connection and place whatever thoughts or commands I want."

"So, you commanded them to tell you all this? How did you know they weren't lying?"

"I could see each of their memories, each conversation they had with Azral and Erixx."

Just like he saw each of my memories.

I nestled closer to Mylom, her warm scales pressed against my back. My gaze drifted to the starry sky, each breath I took was slow and deliberate. The tranquility seemed almost foreign, a fragile veneer over the truth simmering beneath. The truth that I was the one who started that fire. My hidden power dwelling deep within me—a power that Azral wanted to take.

Mylom adjusted her wing as she nuzzled her head deeper into the sand. I focused on her eyes—those maroon orbs that held secrets beyond my grasp. Whenever Azral had gotten close to her, they were a vivid green, a warning, but around Drayzen, they matched mine.

"Why does she keep this side of her hidden from him?" Nausea churned at the thought of saying his name.

"Dragons are the most loyal creatures in this world. When they're born, they're bonded with a Fae."

"Me," I whispered, recalling the dream of her birth.

"Yes." I felt Drayzen shift beside me. "When Erixx took over the castle, they killed all the dragons and Fae that wouldn't give up their bond, leaving only two. I think Mylom knew, somehow, you would be back and you would need her."

Shame laced my next question. "What am I now?"

His head fell to the side, facing me as his eyes searched my face. "Do you really need me to say it?"

"Yes," I breathed. I needed to hear it out loud, needed confirmation that *this*, this is my truth.

"You're Fae, Amara."

I'm not Human. I wasn't sure if being Fae was more surprising or the way my name sounded on his lips. Either way, I shivered. His head fell back against Mylom. I watched as each little strand of hair laid against his forehead. He looked at me and that smirk reappeared, a fang pressing into his bottom lip.

I cleared my throat, shifting in the sand. "Why doesn't it affect Humans, your martem?"

"Every power has its weaknesses. Fortunately, we don't have many but Humans are off limits." He winked.

"And this power, all the Denazin possess it?" I pressed, hoping he wouldn't notice the heat spreading across my cheeks. I didn't think my mind could handle another truth but the look on his face told me that was what he had.

He smirked and turned his gaze back to the sky, a mischievous glint in his eyes. "Like I said, no one knows about Menasai, The Ever. Only a few of us have crossed the sea over thousands of years. No one's ever come close enough to let the Fae discover our existence." A small laugh escaped his lips. "Until me. I had to create a story to avoid raising suspicion about where I was from."

"You told them the God of Death created you?" It seemed like a questionable cover story but if one wanted people to be afraid of them, it was definitely an option.

"Well, that part actually is true," he replied, his jaw tightening. "Autyr did create the Denazin, just like Saigus and Melenyz created the Fae."

I let his words settle. Pieces of this world that I never knew existed were finally falling into place, but it still wasn't enough.

I sat up and crossed my legs. Determination guided me towards Drayzen. Sand ran through his fingers as he sat silently.

"Show me everything," I commanded. "Everything about the Fae about me—"

His hand froze, sand stilling. Concern etched across his features. He straightened, looking back at the ocean. Waves crashing against the shore was the only sound. But I needed to know. I needed to unlock my lost memories.

"It will take time," he said to the water.

"I can handle it, all of them." Conviction fueled my words. "I don't want to wait any longer."

"The way you want this to happen," his eyes bore into mine, his jaw clenched and his gaze hardened, "would be what finally breaks you. And I won't be the one to do that."

A thousand questions swirled inside me. Was he able to see everything—every memory, every thought? Or was there a limit to what he could access? Was this why he hesitated—to get closer, to understand me first?

Anger coursed through my veins. Mylom felt it, too, and she shifted uneasily. But I wasn't angry with Drayzen. No, I was angry at the lies, the deceit, the unfathomable betrayal. It all boiled within me, leaving only one all-consuming thought in my mind.

Azral had truly taken everything from me—my parents, my power, my trust, my heart.

Every last bit I'd had to give, he'd taken it all.

"I want it all back," I whispered to the sand. When I looked up, Drayzen was watching me, searching my face, maybe even reading my mind as that little smirk finally found its way back to his lips.

Drayzen rose, extending a hand towards me. This time, I didn't swat him away. My fingers slipped into his palm and I shivered at the connection that hummed between us. He had been my savior. Time and time again, he had pulled me from the darkness of my mind. Now, he lifted me towards revenge, towards salvation.

Beside us, Mylom stirred, rising to her feet and exhaling a breath before leaping into the air. The wind swirled around us, crackling with her power.

A spark ignited in me. Whether it was my martem or the part of myself that felt like it had been missing, I wasn't sure.

"I want it all back," I repeated. "My memories, my power, my throne. I want to take everything from them, I want to take everything from *him*. I want them to suffer like they made me suffer. I want them to feel the pain I felt, taste their own blood on their lips as they scream. I want them to curse my name as they beg for mercy."

Drayzen's voice dipped to a sultry purr. "And what name is that?"

I straightened to my full height. "Andrasteia Amara Raine, the Scarlet Heir."

Something coiled around my fingertips, an indescribable heat mixed with the chilling cold of a dreaded night in Zandar. Tendrils of dark shadows spilled from Drayzen's fingertips, encircling us in a cloud of power. Mylom roared and shot to the sky, leaving a trail of fire in her wake. Something burned inside us, an indescribable power, and it was a force to be reckoned with.

27

I DIDN'T KNOW WHAT WOULD COME NEXT—
only that it wasn't over. Revenge burned in my chest and an
icy fire singed my fingertips. I would face Azral. I would make
him pay for everything he stole from me, for every scar he left
on my life. How I'd do it, I didn't know yet, but I wasn't alone.

Drayzen's power settled and he made for the shore.
Glancing over his shoulder, he called out, "Well, what are you
waiting for?"

He moved steadily up the hill, his steps sure, as if the
weight of the night hadn't touched him. Watching him, I felt
a flicker of hope, because I knew he would help me.

I jogged to catch up with him, taking in my surroundings
now with a clear head. The land was mostly open fields with a

sparse scattering of trees and grass. Fields of gray spider-like flowers stretched out for miles. Perched on top of a small hill was the largest tree, standing proud above the rest. Willows' weeping guarded a two-story home built beneath. It was massive with branches that hung low, like a mournful sculpture, its tears falling endlessly.

Intertwined in its leaves was a soft glitter that cast a subtle glow on the home. The two-story cottage was something straight from the books I read. Warm candles burned from the inside as wisps of smoke rose from the chimney, carried away by the gentle breeze. The stone and wood structure was painted with moss and those hauntingly beautiful spider flowers.

I continued to scan my surroundings but there was nothing more—at least as far as I could see.

"This is where you're from?" I questioned as I observed the seemingly empty place. "Menasai?" *He said there were other Denazin, so where are they?*

Our footsteps carried us towards the home and he didn't stop as he looked at me. "Menasai is much more than this," he said, a knowing smile playing on his lips. "This is just Autyr's island."

The God of Death.

I'd prayed to him many times, questioned his intentions and why he took my parents from me so soon. Now that I was standing on this land, *his* land, I almost fell and worshiped the soil. I wanted to apologize for the many times I'd cursed him. Because I knew, now, it was not the work of a god—it was the work of someone else entirely.

"Menasai is a bit farther from here." We walked side by side as he continued, "All of the land here is blocked by a barrier created by Saigus and Melenyz, so no one could bother them. They wanted peace; at least, that's what they claimed." Drayzen shrugged, rolling his eyes. "After so many years, the two grew bored and they began to grant one wish to any Fae able to cross their border. But it was more like their own personal death trap."

"And this barrier, we were able to cross without any issue?" It seemed almost too easy, just a dragon's ride away apparently.

"We did. I have no issue getting through it." He smirked.

"The same rules don't apply for Denazin?" I questioned.

"Autyr plays his own games. He never intended for his creations to mingle with Fae. So, we can come and go as we please."

I frowned. I wonder what the god would think of us now, think of me, a Fae on his land.

"But I'm Fae, so how—?"

Drayzen looked up as if he was still trying to figure out the answer himself. "I think it was your absence of power. The barrier didn't detect you."

I looked down. My hands no longer tingled with icy fire. A fleeting moment of power, just like when I burned my house down. My heartbeat quickened and I shoved that feeling deep down. That fear, the guilt of what *I* did. *Not now, Amara. Do not crumble now.*

Drayzen continued, pulling me back. "They call it The Fading. Any Fae who tries to cross it is stripped of their power." *I guess I didn't have much to take.* "If they survived the journey, they'd be granted one wish, whatever their heart desired."

"Has anyone ever crossed?"

"Only one, centuries ago."

I halted, my feet catching in the grass. Drayzen stopped in front of me, slowly turning.

"Well, what did they ask for?"

Drayzen smirked, his fang tugging at his bottom lip. "Death."

"Why?"

A flicker of pain flashed through his eyes as his tone lowered. "Immortality can be cruel."

He turned, continuing in silence towards the house. His words left a sinking feeling in my stomach.

"So, you can cross because you're not Fae?" The pieces started to click together.

"Ah, catching on, are we?" He winked at me with a glimmer of amusement.

"What are we doing here then? I thought you said you were taking me to your home?"

"This has been my home ever since I left Menasai," he confessed. "Traveling between both lands just takes too long."

Between Rosetia and The Ever, the Fae and Denazin lands.

The weight of his words settled and suddenly, it dawned on me. "You haven't returned home since..." He said he left Menasai four years ago.

"It's not as long as you think," he replied, his usual snark gone.

I matched his pace, stealing a glance at the flicker of sadness painted on his face. My heart ached as I asked, "But you've been alone? All this time?"

He didn't answer as we neared the cabin door and before Drayzen could even touch the knob, the door swung open. A female flew out, long wavy black hair streaming behind her in the wind of her speed. She flung her arms around Drayzen and he returned the embrace, lifting her off the ground and twirling her in the air. *Maybe he hadn't been alone this whole time?*

Laughter spilled from her plump lips, a radiant smile lighting up her fair complexion. Her deadly jaw line and sharp brows were chiseled to perfection. Her eyes were a captivating blend of turquoise and familiar midnight hues that sparkled as she released Drayzen. She leaned up, planting a kiss on his cheek.

A pang of something shot through me as my stomach hardened. I'd never felt this way before and Drayzen, of all people, was a stranger. A godsdamned gorgeous stranger but a stranger, nonetheless. He may know more than I wanted about who I was but I didn't know him, not enough to feel this way. I clenched my jaw, trying to quell my rising frustration.

"Stop it, Mar," I scolded myself in my head.

My cheeks quickly heated as they both looked at me. *I really have to stop doing that.*

"Already bickering, you two?" a male voice called from inside the house, saving me from having to explain my outburst.

Drayzen pulled away from the female, snarling as he hastily wiped the mark from his cheek. In response, she threw a punch at him with full force. The impact sent him stumbling sideways.

I bit down on my knuckle to stifle a laugh, but it still bubbled out.

The female adjusted her black sleeves with precision, crossing her arms and letting out a sharp, annoyed grunt. She redirected her attention to the male emerging from the doorway.

He, too, had black hair. His was longer, cut just below his own sharp chin. The strands waved around his ears as he pushed the excess back. His piercing eyes lowered on Drayzen with a similar turquoise shade. Chiseled and defined, his stubble only enhanced his strong jawline. His complexion mirrored the other Denazin's pale skin and his body had a warrior's build with muscles that rippled under black sleeves. He slowly approached Drayzen, towering at the same height with a smile revealing fangs.

"Brother," the male rasped and Drayzen's smile widened, exposing his own fangs. It was a smile I had yet to see, genuine, not like his usual smirk.

I could tell it was rare and that only made me want to see more of it.

The two Denazin embraced, holding each other for a moment before pulling away. Drayzen cupped his brother's face with both hands, as if savoring the sight.

"It's been too long." The male grasped Drayzen's shoulders.

So, he was *alone.*

The female grunted again, impatiently shoving the two apart. Their connection broke but the male wrapped his arm around her neck, drawing her head beneath his shoulder. She pushed against him and then vanished, only to reappear in front of him in the blink of an eye. With a swift strike to his gut, he doubled over.

"Cheater," he gritted through clenched teeth, clutching his stomach.

She shrugged nonchalantly and brushed her hands as she turned back to a laughing Drayzen.

"I see someone's been practicing." Drayzen smirked at her.

My stomach heated but the feeling was quickly washed away with relief as she said, "One day I'll catch up to you, brother." She smiled, a wide grin, a bit crazy with all her teeth on full display. Her own two fangs were visible.

Denazin. Both of them were Denazin. I couldn't help but smile at the reunion but my joy was quickly replaced by an overwhelming guilt. Drayzen had a family, a family he left to help *me.*

The female's eyes met mine and I blinked away the burn.

"Is this her?" she asked.

"Amara," Drayzen turned to me, "this is Violet."

Violet's expression brightened as he said my name and she dashed towards me, pulling me into a tight hug. I stood, frozen, unsure of how to react. Why was she *hugging* me? Eyes wide, I looked over her shoulder to Drayzen.

"Vi—" he called.

And then I was free as she stepped back with that eerily big smile. "It's so nice to finally meet you."

To finally meet me. Did everyone know who I was?

Everyone except me, apparently.

"It certainly is," the other male chimed in, approaching. "Cade."

He stretched out a hand to me. I set my hand in his and he clasped it firmly. His grip was strong but I had a feeling it wasn't his full strength.

"How long have you been here?" Drayzen asked.

Cade's voice was deep and velvety. "We just arrived. We left as soon as we got your message."

Drayzen nodded. "Let's get inside. There's a lot to discuss."

"Oh, there certainly is," Cade muttered, shooting Drayzen a glare.

And that look was one I didn't want to be on the receiving end of.

I settled into the living room of the cottage. It was a small space off to the side of the foyer, dimly lit with silver sconces on the walls and a crackling fireplace. The smell of citrus mingled with burning wood as I sank into the deep red couch. Two matching chairs faced the round table in the center of the room. It was oddly homey, which I was not expecting given that we were on the God of Death's island—and that it was Drayzen's home. It was something I'd missed in my panicked state earlier.

Drayzen sat on the chair to the left, that infuriating smirk meeting my wandering eyes. He was, apparently, full of surprises. I looked away as my stomach fluttered, trying to distract the confusing feeling. My eyes dropped to my pants and I scratched at the dirt staining them. It had only been a day since I'd changed and bathed but I felt disgusting.

Violet grabbed a pitcher from the table, poured a glass of water, and handed it to me with a nod. I smiled as she took the seat next to me. Cade stood in the corner of the room, his arms crossed as he leaned against the wall, his sharp gaze fixed on me.

Silence swept the room. The only sounds were the crackling of the fireplace and the rhythmic tapping of Drayzen's fingers on the armrest. I glanced at Violet. That persistent smile was wide. I gave her a small smile back, quickly looking back down to my pants.

"Care to join us?" Drayzen's voice shattered the silence.

I shot my head up, following his gaze to the open door. Thysa entered and, without hesitation, I rose.

"Sovanni," I uttered, my voice trembling as she trailed behind Thysa.

I froze. I didn't even look down as Violet took the glass from my hand. A rush of emotions surged through me. Relief at seeing a familiar face, joy that she was unharmed, but also anger, betrayal, confusion, and now, fear. Fear that Azral would be right behind her.

"Amara—" Sovanni said softly. Her lavender eyes turned glassy and she dropped to her knees in the doorway. "Please, forgive me." She bowed, her long curls falling over her face. Thysa mirrored the action, though she remained on one knee.

"Please, forgive us." Sovanni reached for Thysa's hand. Their fingers intertwined and Thysa lowered to Sovanni's level, braids now mingling with curls on the wooden floor.

"I—" My gaze darted towards Drayzen, seeking any sort of help. I had no idea what to do, what to say. *What are they doing?*

"You are their queen," he answered my thoughts.

Queen.

It still didn't seem real, didn't fully register. I didn't think any of this truly had.

"Please, you don't need to do that," I almost begged. But they remained, unmoving, their bodies frozen. I looked at Drayzen again. He only raised a brow.

"Um, you can stand, please." It came out more like a question than a command.

Fortunately, they rose. Sovanni wiped at the tears on her cheeks.

"I'm so sorry," she wept. "I'm so sorry—" Thysa reached out to her, arms wrapping around Sovanni. "As soon as I found out, I wanted to tell you. I was scared—"

"I understand," I interjected. And I did.

Because at that moment, everything became clear. I could see the fear on her face. Even Thysa's strong demeanor broke as Vani wept. But it wasn't me they were scared for; they feared what would happen to them, what would happen if they defied Erixx, *Azral.*

This lie, wasn't only for my protection. It was to protect themselves and so many other lives.

Because it was him. All of it was *him.*

I skirted the couch, my body fighting against my mind as I approached the Fae. I was afraid, hurt by the fresh wounds of the lies, but I had to be understanding, towards them at least. Towards my people. I would not rule in fear like the ones who currently sat on my throne.

Sovanni looked to me and I could see the healing bruises across her skin. *What did they do to her?* Without any further hesitation, I threw my arms around her. She held me with equal tightness, an understanding passing between us.

I pulled back. "Please, join us." I motioned into the room.

She nodded and sniffed through tears. Thysa followed as they stood opposite the wall Cade occupied. His posture shifted, his relaxed demeanor replaced with heightened vigilance.

I retook my seat on the couch and watched as Thysa and Cade locked in a stare-down, both protective of their own. Thysa's arm wrapped around a still-weeping Vani. The tension cut the room and I realized how abnormal this was for them. They were strangers, enemies even. Two peoples who had never met, one unaware of the other's existence entirely.

This would be *so* fun.

Drayzen slouched in his chair, running a hand lazily through his dark hair. "It's been a day, so let's cut to the chase," he declared. "I think we all know what needs to be done."

They all nodded in agreement. Violet's eerie smile finally faded.

"Everyone but me," I shot back at him.

"Are you sure it will work?" Violet asked. "Would they really grant her one?"

"It's our only option," Drayzen replied.

"Once again, I have no idea—" Violet's words replayed in my mind. Then Drayzen's tale of The Fading: the wish the gods would grant a Fae for crossing.

Drayzen's infuriating grin resurfaced.

"No," I breathed.

His smirk widened. "You have to meet the gods."

28

"MEET THE GODS?" THE IDEA SOUNDED INSANE.
insane. It *was* absolutely insane. "Both of them?"

"Whoever decides to show first," Drayzen purred.

"It's not as crazy as it sounds," Violet chimed in.

Oh, but it really was. Drayzen had just told me that only one person had ever done it. I looked at Vani and Thysa. "How did you two cross?"

Vani sniffled, wiping her nose. "When we came over on Mylom, the feeling was almost instant. As soon as The Isles came into sight, I could feel this overwhelming weight, like it was pulling me down. My martem drained the closer we got."

Thysa chimed in, "It was like my breath was being sucked away but as soon as we landed here, the feeling lifted."

"You can thank Autyr later," Drayzen mouthed.

Was he allowing them to be here, on his island, unharmed?

"Since we already made it through the hardest part, it should be smooth sailing the rest of the way." Drayzen shrugged. "You two obviously won't be coming." He looked to the Fae females, then back to Violet and Cade.

"We can help." Vani insisted.

Violet straightened. "The only reason you made it this far is because of the interference of another god. Without Autyr, you would both be dead—no special wish for you unfortunately.

Vani whispered something to Thysa and whatever it was made Drayzen smirk, dragging his tongue across his fang.

I hated not being able to hear as well as them, hated not knowing everything he did. Hated the feeling that brewed inside me as his midnight irises narrowed on them. And most of all, I hated how attractive that was.

"These things have no effect on us," Cade said in response to whatever Vani had whispered, flashing his fangs at the Fae.

Gods.

Thysa looked ready to object but Sovanni pulled her back—it wasn't a fight she could win.

"We have a boat," Violet continued. "We can't shift to the islands but it should take less than a day's ride, if the winds are in our favor."

The room fell silent again. Drayzen's tapping finger was the only sound as thoughts reeled in my mind. The answers I wanted were so close, just a boat ride away apparently, and I knew exactly what I would ask. Knew exactly what I *wanted.*

My power, my throne, and most importantly, revenge.

My voice dropped to a chilling tone that frightened even me. "When do we leave?"

Drayzen's head snapped to me, his mask fading for only a second as his jaw clenched. But his small smirk returned as his head lowered.

"Shouldn't you rest?" Vani pleaded. "You've been through—"

"So much?" I finished. "Yes, I have been through so much." Anger boiled inside me. "And that's exactly why *rest* is the last thing I want. I don't want to wait around to see what Azral's next move is; I want my power back, now."

Violet's hands clenched. "You need to be extremely specific in your wording. Whoever you speak with—"

"Are we simply assuming this will work?" Thysa interrupted. "That they will just give her power back so easily?" She crossed her arms and moved closer to the chair where Drayzen sat. I noticed Cade stepping away from the wall, inching towards her.

Thysa stared at Drayzen, a deathly glimmer in her eyes. "And we're just supposed to trust you with our queen?" Her words were laced with contempt.

Cade disappeared into the shadows, reappearing right in front of her, teeth bared. "Watch your tone. Like you were even able to protect her—"

"Easy," Drayzen cut in, lifting his hand.

But his eyes never left mine.

Tension swelled, the air thick with charged martem. I shifted on the couch, unsure whose power swirled around me.

Sovanni grasped Thysa's arm, pulling her back to their wall and whispering something to her. Thysa straightened. Her gaze fixed firmly on Cade standing his ground.

"I've done nothing to betray your trust," Drayzen finally said.

"Vani told me how you got into Amara's mind, *without* permission. How can we trust you if you're capable of something like that?" Thysa fired back.

Drayzen directed a half-grin at Sovanni. "Was it truly unwelcome, though? Maybe I'm not the one you should be questioning."

My cheeks heated, and I realized I wouldn't know what to say if they asked. I still didn't even understand his silent presence in my mind—*all this time.*

Confusion passed over her face as she turned to Sovanni, only to be met with a seething glare.

"Regardless of whether you think it was welcome or not, going into someone's mind without them knowing is unacceptable," Sovanni said.

Drayzen waved his hand dismissively.

Thysa was right, though. *Could* he be trusted? Could any of them be trusted? They'd all lied to me, either for my, supposed, well-being or theirs. They let me believe everything Azral told me. They let me fall in love with him, let me stay in that gods-forsaken home with him, let him *touch* me.

I brushed off the thought quickly, I didn't want to think about that right now, not in this room with all of them, with Drayzen.

I straightened. What we needed right now was action and sitting here arguing wouldn't get us anywhere. So, I stood like the queen I was. "We will leave tomorrow," I commanded.

Drayzen raised a brow with amusement. "That's the attitude I was looking for."

Thysa huffed, rolling her eyes in annoyance as she stormed out of the room.

"Sorry, she—" But Sovanni was gone before she finished.

"You'll train with Cade for the night," Drayzen declared.

"Train?" I raised a brow.

"You won't become an expert overnight but basic training to protect yourself is always useful." Drayzen rose from his seat, closing the distance between us.

I didn't back down, instead getting almost uncomfortably close to him, pressuring him to fold. I looked up from where my eyes met his chest and that midnight gaze pierced through me. My heart gave a precarious *thump.*

I broke eye contact first.

He stepped back, giving me just enough space to move towards the door. I paused in the opening, facing Drayzen and Cade. Cade was visibly bigger but I doubted Drayzen was lacking in strength. They stood tall next to each other, both utterly captivating. I felt my cheeks warm and I quickly cleared my throat.

"What, exactly, am I protecting myself against?" I asked, straightening.

Drayzen only let out a small laugh. "You're about to find out."

Cade stepped forward, his rigid demeanor intimidating, and I leaped aside, letting him pass. "Keep up!" he yelled as he pushed through the front door.

"You don't want to get on his bad side." Drayzen winked.

29

I FOLLOWED CADE AS HE LED THE WAY DOWN to the beach, my gaze drifting to the large imprints left in the sand by Mylom's claws. *Where did she go?*

"Are you ready?" Cade asked as he sat, sand rustling, his voice deep and devoid of emotion.

I noted the absence of weapons. My gaze fell to the single sword sheathed at his side. "What are we training with?"

"Our *minds*, now sit," he replied curtly.

I didn't think it was possible for anyone to be as snarky as Drayzen; apparently, I just had to meet his brother.

Cade pulled me down and I shimmied into the sand, crossing my legs. He scooted closer and closer until our knees touched.

"Ever heard of personal space?" I inched back.

But he persisted, closing the gap between us.

Did the Denazin know nothing of social cues?

"Your back will hurt if you have to reach too far." He placed his hands firmly on the tops of my knees to stop me from moving again. I tilted my head down, studying the black wings inked on his large hands.

I peered up through fallen strands of hair. He looked uncomfortable and I couldn't help but tease him. I placed my hands on his knees and met his turquoise gaze.

"Close enough?" I purred.

He fought the small smile that tried to break free. His voice dipped again, low and calculated. "I see why Drayz likes you."

I recoiled, pulling back at his words.

"You won't be able to distract me, Amara. Drayzen likes to play his games but I like to make sure everyone stays sane."

"Might be a little too late for that," I whispered, crossing my arms.

He examined my features before looking towards the water. I followed his line of sight and watched the mingling of the sea, the blue and black hues. The *crash* of waves against the shore filled the air.

"The mind has to be strong, fortified when facing anyone but especially the Denazin," he finally said. His eyes fixed on me, now.

"And will we be facing a lot of Denazin on our trip?"

"No." He shook his head, shrugging. "Like Drayzen said, the hardest part is already over. It should be a fairly simple process getting to the island."

"So, why are we doing this then?" Why were we "training my mind", whatever that meant.

"It's what he wants."

Drayzen.

"So why isn't *he* down here? Why do you answer to him?" I pressed. "Surely, your efforts can be better used in physical training." I nodded to his arms.

"Physical strength will only get you so far. What you can do with your mind, your martem, that all starts here." He tapped his finger to his temple.

My martem. I hadn't even thought of how I would use it, how I would learn to wield such a power when it returned to me. "Even if I were to get my full power back," vulnerability threaded my words, "I don't know how to start—"

A faint glimmer of empathy danced in Cade's eyes. "Remember," he said gently, "you are the first of your kind. Whether you learned it as a child or now, this was never going to be easy."

The first of my kind. My very being, a ripple in the fabric of existence.

"Okay," I whispered and nodded. "Okay, I'm ready."

"First, we will start with fortifying your mind."

"Against Denazin?" I had to ask.

"Against anyone who may possess the ability to reach in. But yes, mainly Denazin."

"Why does Drayzen want me to know this?"

"We have the ability to access your mind, your memories. Depending on who you come across, those memories can become your downfall—the weakness they exploit to break you," Cade continued.

My memories were a recurring topic lately. Everyone seemed to know more about me then, well, me. *How long will Drayzen wait to let me see them all?*

"Most Denazin cannot access that part of your mind without physical contact. However—"

"Some don't need the contact," I finished, already knowing that answer. Drayzen seemed to be one of them.

He nodded. "There's also the matter of compulsion that you need to be aware of. Unfortunately, there's no way around it for you, now."

The feeling resurfaced in my mind, Drayzen's words echoing like the command never left. That sense of my mind being overridden as my will was stripped away completely.

I hated that feeling with every fiber of my being.

"Once we train more, we'll practice building a wall around that part of your mind. And once you're stronger, you may be able to block out the compulsion. But for now, it's better to know of the ability than be caught off guard."

"Right." I tried to absorb all the information, even though it still felt hopelessly overwhelming.

"I want you to open your mind to me now, so I can demonstrate," he said and extended his hands towards me.

"Open my mind?"

His hands remained still, waiting for me to take them. "Take my hands and think of a happy memory."

I took a deep breath and placed my hands in his. His skin was cold and calloused, the hands of someone who had been in many battles.

How old could he be, how many battles could he have fought? *How old were any of the Denazin?*

Cade's body was rough, rigid, like jagged cliffs. His aura filled the silence and his presence demanded respect. He was disciplined but there was a rawness simmering below the surface. But most importantly—didn't seem like the type of person who enjoyed answering silly questions.

I closed my eyes, deciding not to ask the millions looming in my mind. I allowed my thoughts to wander, searching for a happy memory as instructed.

I immediately went back to my childhood. It was my tenth birthday. I had taken my seat at the head of the table. Isidore stepped into the dining room, a dusting of snow and changing autumn leaves covered his cloak. Lettie lectured him on being late and I laughed as he picked up my mother, covering her in snow. *They loved each other so much.* They turned to me and my father ran, picking me up in his snowy arms.

"Stop." Cade's voice broke my tranquility and I opened my eyes. There was a darkness in his gaze, now as deep blue swirled in his irises. "That joy, that memory, I want you to *feel* it. Picture it over and over." His voice was hypnotizing. I felt his words take hold, compelling me.

The sensation of joy was overwhelming. A smile stretched across my face as the vision of my parents replayed, over and over, just as he'd said.

"Stop," Cade commanded once more and his eyes shifted back to their turquoise hue. His voice retreated from my mind, the image of the memory faded, and the euphoria slowly dissipated. "Do you see how this could be a significant weakness?"

"But it felt...nice." It wasn't anything like Drayzen's intrusions.

"Think of the worst thing that has ever happened to you, your most agonizing memory, and how it made you feel."

I hesitated. There were too many painful ones to choose from. The list seemed endless. A shiver of realization rolled down my spine. "Gods."

The mere thought of reliving the worst moments, over and over again, being compelled to endure that terror of a memory.

What kind of person would you become after something like that?

"This is why we begin training the mind right away," he explained. "It'll take time but the sooner we start, the better the chances of shutting out someone who means harm."

I placed my hands back in his and nodded. But I couldn't help wondering why Cade's power wasn't as strong as Drayzen's. He obviously needed physical contact to get into my mind.

How strong was Drayzen? And how much power did it take to be able to reach me all the way in Zandar?

"Now, I want you to clear your head. Don't think of anything except your subconscious, that place Sovanni took you."

"The black hole in my mind?" I questioned.

"Exactly." He nodded. "Take me there."

I was nervous, letting him in, but I pushed aside the feeling and focused, allowing in only the black stillness.

It wasn't easy. I was constantly distracted by little sounds around me. The wind whipped by my ears and I couldn't help but crack an eye open. I was met with a deadly glare from Cade. I quickly shut my eye and tried to focus. He didn't seem like one I should disappoint. I took a deep breath and let the crashing waves in the distance provide a soothing backdrop. Eventually, I formed in the darkness.

My surroundings fell silent as I stood in the void. Cade appeared behind me with a faint smile as he settled onto the nonexistent ground. He gestured for me to join him and I took a seat, mirroring our position on the beach.

"That didn't take too long," he commented as I settled in. "You're a natural."

"Thank you?" I replied, unsure if it was a compliment or simply an observation.

"Do you hear anything?" he asked.

I closed my eyes, focusing on the sounds around us. "The waves are crashing. The wind is blowing by, maybe a bird, too."

"Good," he breathed. "Now, focus only on your mind. Try to step away from your body, step away from us. Focus on this space."

I took a calming breath and tried to do just that: focus on my mind. I peeked another eye open but this time Cade didn't look as disappointed.

"It's okay, we can practice that later. This place," he gestured to the darkness surrounding us, "is where Denazin come before completely diving into the part of your brain that holds your memories, think of it as a waiting room." He scanned the area. "For now, we will sit. I want you to become familiar with being here, to feel comfortable in it."

I looked around the space then back to Cade. "Comfortable, here?"

All I felt here was a weariness, a loneliness that tugged at my broken heart. Was this what it was supposed to feel like, what I was supposed to find comfort in?

"Just close your eyes and try to relax," he said, setting the example by closing his own and stilling his body. His chest rose and fell with each deliberate breath.

I followed his lead, allowing the sensation of nothingness to wash over me.

And it was oddly comforting.

Time stretched on as we sat there. I couldn't help but glance at Cade every so often, trying to gauge his state, only to be met with a death glare each time.

"Close them," he commanded.

"How much longer?" I didn't miss the whine in my tone.

Cade sighed and shook his head. He vanished, causing me to jump in the darkness.

I squinted against the sudden intrusion of moonlight. We were back on the beach and I could feel Cade's calloused hands around mine. The familiar sound of crashing waves welcomed me. We must have been practicing for a few hours because the tide had rolled in and the moon was now low in the sky.

"Try to block me out." Cade's grip tightened on my hands.

"How am I supposed to do that?" A hint of frustration limned my voice. "All you've really taught me is how to breathe and, fun fact, I already knew how to do that."

His grip tightened further, his brows furrowing. "There's only so much I can tell you. This, you'll need to experience for yourself. Just try to feel me, like I'm knocking on the door to your home, but don't let me in."

Feel him? I sighed, rolling my eyes. "Fine."

"Now, think of a memory."

I closed my eyes and gripped his hands. My mind raced, desperately trying to conjure up a memory that wasn't too embarrassing or personal as I knew there was no way I would be able to block him out.

I tensed and my stomach fluttered at the only thing I could think of. *Drayzen.*

It was that night in the woods when he had found me running for Raxos. I couldn't stop the thought pushing through my mind, no matter how much I willed it away. The way his body pressed against mine, pinning me firmly to the rough bark of the tree, our breath mingling in the cold air. The way his hood slipped just enough for little black hairs to fall over his forehead, framing those midnight eyes.

Anything else, please.

This was the last thing I wanted Cade to see because I could feel him, like a soft whisper on the walls of my mind. I squinted at him nervously. His eyes were closed but a small smirk tugged at the corner of his lips. I yanked my hands away from his and stood, brushing the sand off my pants.

"This is stupid." Embarrassment laced every word.

Cade rose to his feet, as well. "We'll try again tomorrow, without any interruptions," he said, a hint of disappointment in his voice.

"Interruptions?"

His gaze shifted towards the house and I turned to see Drayzen walk out the front door, wearing that infuriatingly smug smirk of his. Irritation burned within me.

"Don't mess with my lessons, brother," Cade chided.

Drayzen shrugged. "I don't know what you're talking about." He raised his hands in surrender.

I glared at him, shaking my head. *He* put that memory at the front of my mind. I grunted, crossing my arms.

Drayzen only laughed, throwing his arm over Cade as they spoke in hushed tones, walking into the house together. I followed but I froze at the threshold as a deep horror sank into my bones. Drayzen, sensing my shift, looked back. His eyes were no longer playful, instead, filled with an understanding that chilled me.

Because Drayzen, this infuriatingly arrogant male, had the ability to see *all* of my memories. I wasn't sure before how much he knew, how much he had seen of my past, but with that look, I finally knew: He had seen everything, every laugh that left me
doubling over, every cry that left me numb, every ounce of pain I held onto.

I was like an open book to him and he had read every page.

30

WE ALL SAT AROUND THE LONG DINING TABLE in silence. I found myself next to Violet, whose wide smile never seemed to fade as she watched my every move. Thysa and Sovanni sat together at the opposite end of the table. Vani looked better, the bruises on her face lighter. I wanted to talk to her about what happened with Azral, what they *did* to her. But I couldn't, not yet. Just the thought of it brought acid to my throat.

Cade took the seat across from Violet and I, his expression still void of emotion as he absentmindedly pushed his food around his plate. To my left, Drayzen occupied the head of the table, observing. But there was no plate in front of him. *Is he not hungry?*

Violet, on the other hand, greedily devoured every bite on her plate.

I glanced down at my own meal, the fish and fruits before me looked far from appetizing. Maybe that was why Cade was toying with his instead of eating. Sovanni had admitted earlier that her culinary skills were lacking but no one had refused when she offered to cook.

I made a mental note not to make that mistake again.

"Eat," Drayzen commanded, his eyes fixed on me.

"You're not eating," I retorted.

"Yes, I am." A fang peeked out from behind his lips as he lifted his glass. The thick red liquid swirled in the crystal glass as he brought it to his mouth, taking a sip and winking at me. Blood. He was drinking blood from a *cup*.

It was then I noticed Cade and Violet also had glasses with the same liquid. Cade, dropping his fork with a clatter, pushed his plate away and took a long swig.

"Do you not eat regular food?" I asked, confused, then, as to why Violet was stuffing her face with—gods, it couldn't even be called food.

"We do," Drayzen replied, taking another sip. "But it's not necessary."

"And this is not regular food," Cade chimed in, his tone dry.

Thysa hissed at him from the end of the table and Sovanni's cheeks flushed with embarrassment.

"I think it's amazing," Violet mumbled around a mouthful, some of it spilling onto her plate.

"Disgusting," Cade whispered under his breath, shaking his head at her.

She responded with a dirty look and continued shoveling the food down.

Thysa whispered to Sovanni and a small smile grew across her warm face.

Violet's gaze shifted to them. "Me too," she agreed.

Thysa grunted and shot Violet a less-than-friendly look.

"Thank you," Sovanni replied, glaring at Thysa before starting to eat.

"You could hear them?" I finally asked.

"We have excellent hearing," Drayzen sarcastically remarked, his smirk still firmly in place.

So, he could hear the Fairies that night.

"The Fairies can be cruel; it's best you couldn't hear them." Drayzen swirled the liquid in his glass.

"Get out of my head!" I sneered.

"The Fairies?" Sovanni questioned. "They're real?"

Drayzen nodded but before she could press further, Cade interjected. "Stay out of my student's head, Drayz."

"Relax, I wasn't in her head," Drayzen dismissed.

I glared. "Then how did you know what I was thinking?"

He simply shrugged and took a sip from his glass. "Just a lucky guess."

Cade's brows furrowed while Violet burst into laughter, spraying bits of food in the process.

"Interesting," Sovanni commented.

"Very," Violet added, changing the subject. "Drayzen tells me you have an interest in history."

"Yes." Sovanni cleared her throat.

"I would love to tell you more about us," Violet beamed, wiping her face with a napkin and pushing her empty plate away.

"Vi," Cade rasped, shooting her a death glare. "You can't—"

"Oh, it doesn't matter now. All the Fae will find out who we are soon enough." Violet shrugged. "Might as well start with someone who will genuinely appreciate listening."

"I would be honored," Sovanni said quickly, lowering her head in respect even as eagerness oozed from her.

Thysa, on the other hand, scoffed and crossed her arms. She and Cade had one thing in common: their hatred towards each other. Cade mirrored Thysa and shifted his gaze to Drayzen, who, for once, remained silent.

I looked back at my plate. The fishy scent hit my nose and as much as I didn't like it, I couldn't stop myself from eating every last piece. It had been a day since I'd eaten and I was starving.

Drayzen and Cade took the initiative to clear dirty plates from the table when we were done. Drayzen returned from the kitchen with two glasses. He set one in front of me, returning to his seat at the head of the table. Cade took his seat with a similar amber colored liquid in his glass.

"Whiskey," Drayzen remarked, pointing to the drink he handed me. "It won't make you vulnerable like the Fae wine," he growled through gritted teeth. He directed a death glare at Sovanni and Thysa.

If I wasn't supposed to be on Cade's bad side, I didn't even want to think about Drayzen's.

The atmosphere shifted as those words left his lips. Violet's smile vanished and she squirmed in her chair. Cade took another swig, finishing his drink, and leaned back. Thysa and Sovanni watched Drayzen but even Thysa tensed under his gaze.

A sudden chill swept through the room and Violet sighed, shaking her head. "Is this really necessary?" she asked and in an instant, the temperature dropped even further. Icy coldness seeped into my fingers and Sovanni's expression turned to terror. Thysa tried not to react but her eyes betrayed her.

And then it hit me—*this* was Drayzen's martem. The Denazin were descendants created by Autyr and this feeling, this bone-chilling cold, it was death itself.

I turned to look at Drayzen who seemed unaffected as power surged from him. Silver swirled in his midnight irises and tendrils of dark shadows coiled around his fingertips clasped around the glass.

"Drayzen." Violet cursed. "Stop this. You know they did everything to help—"

"Getting her drunk? Letting her wander around? You said you'd watch her—"

Drayzen held Sovanni's gaze with unwavering rage as the coldness in the room gradually lifted. When he looked at me, I watched the darkness dissolve from his fingers like dissipating mist and the midnight blue return to his eyes.

He looked back to Sovanni. "I apologize for my...outburst. It's been a long day."

"It's been a long day for all of us," I reminded him.

Drayzen wasn't one to cower but he did shift in his seat as I tossed a heavy glare his way.

Cade's gaze snapped to Thysa as she sprang from the table, slamming her hands on the wood. Sovanni tugged at her arm but Thysa ignored her. "Remember, *Drayzen*, we don't answer to you."

"Watch your tone," Cade growled, rising.

"No, you don't," Drayzen replied calmly. "You answer to *her*." He looked at me and my heart stopped. "And you are on our land, in our home. Don't the Fae teach any manners?" He smirked and I didn't miss the fury simmering in Thysa's eyes. "I don't think I need to remind you, again, how much more powerful we are." He gestured towards Cade and Violet. Violet only sighed, shaking her head subtly, while Cade grinned smugly.

"I believe what my brother is trying to say," Violet interjected, "is that we all need to get some *rest*." She shot a death glare at the males. "We are all tired, angry, hurt even. No need to take it out on each other."

Thysa finally relented, sinking back into her seat. "You're right," she whispered.

I was finally able to sip from the glass as the tension in the room eased. The amber whiskey carried a delicate scent of caramel, with a wood and chocolate aftertaste. I'd never had whiskey before but it was surprisingly more appealing than Fae wine. It didn't leave me feeling hazy. It warmed me, calming my nerves.

Drayzen took the final swig from his glass and rose. He turned his gaze to me. "Vi will show you where you can stay. You'll need all the rest you can get."

Violet stood, gripped my hand, and guided me out of the dining room. Her familiar smile reappeared. Just as we reached the hallway, Drayzen called, "We leave at sunrise."

31

MY ROOM WAS VERY SPACIOUS BUT IT HOSTED only the essential pieces. A large bed made up with black sheets and a matching quilt. There was a long table positioned by the wall-length window, a modest dresser along the opposite wall, and a collection of books stacked on the nightstand. Dark wooden floorboards and walls absorbed much of the light but sconces beat back the deepest shadows. Though, it was the soft glow of the moon brightening most of the room through the wall-window overlooking the willow tree.

Violet guided me towards the adjoining bathroom decorated in polished marble and mirrors. Towels were neatly stacked on a nearby table and a bar of soap rested on the shelf beside the tub—the generous-sized tub currently filling itself.

My jaw dropped. "How?" I gasped.

Violet's smile widened as I looked at her. "One of my little tricks," she remarked with a wink and steam began to waft through the air as the water continued to rise. "I'll leave some clothes out for you," she said before exiting the room.

"Thank you," I called after her.

She smiled, more genuine than usual, and shut the door behind her.

I undressed, relishing in the warmth of the steam on my bare skin as it rose from the tub. I tossed my, very dirty, clothes into a pile by the sink and looked in the mirror.

Gods, I looked *dreadful.* Grime covered my face and my hair resembled a chaotic mass of knots, braids, and tangles only partially tamed by being shoved behind my ears. With my fingers, I combed through the tangled mess on my head, as well as the knot of lies inside it.

The quiet pressed in on me, amplifying every thing inside my mind. I was finally alone with my thoughts, and I wasn't sure if that was a blessing or a curse. I leaned over the marble to inspect my ears. I pushed each one to the side, examining every inch of skin, but there were no visible scars.

The memory echoed in my mind—of what Azral did to me. What he *took* from me. A weight built behind my eyes, threatening to spill, but I fought to blink them away. I tried to come up with anything else before that memory consumed me but my mind caught on a worse truth. The truth that my dreams, the parents I searched for, *were* real. But I would never meet them. I would never see how they loved each other like Isidore and Lettie had. I would never be able to ask them their favorite book, their favorite song. I would never *know* them. *Akailo and Cyra.* It had been the final piece in my puzzle and it shattered everything left in me.

I ran for the bucket in the corner, hurling myself over it as my dinner came spewing out. Vomit mixed with salty tears as the images dominated my mind—images of the fire, both my parents, me, and *him.* They all fought for attention.

I wiped my tears away and moved to the mirror. Washing my mouth out with clean water, I examined every inch of the girl who looked back at me. She was scarred, broken, manipulated, deceived. *Stupid, naive, worthless.*

"No." I shook away the intrusion.

I snatched a towel from the nearby bench and draped it over the mirror. I couldn't look for one more second, disgusted at what I saw, what I truly was. Instead, I lowered myself into the almost-too-hot water. It made my skin tingle but I pushed past the burning and dipped my head under the water, letting it engulf me. Shame washed over my body, trapping me in its despair.

The room rippled as I stared from beneath the surface. But then my heart skipped. Above, the face of a male clarified. His brown curls fell over his forehead and he smirked as I shot out of the water, gasping for air. My eyes shot around the room.

Water splashed on the floor as I gripped the sides of the porcelain. But I was alone. *Crazy.* My pounding heart settled and I grabbed the bar of soap from the shelf to scrub. I scrubbed away the dirt. Scrubbed away the lies, the betrayal. I scrubbed and scrubbed. I needed to rid myself of Azral—the scent of him, the memory of him, all of him. My eyes burned with tears and I scrubbed harder as they flowed.

I was numb by the time the water cooled, the only thing alerting me to how much time had passed. I looked at the once-full bar of soap now dwindled to a sliver in my hands. I slowly rose, dripping the only sound as I mindlessly grabbed a towel. I left a tiny piece of me behind in that bath water.

On the bed was a black tunic and pants, neatly folded, accompanied by a note with the word "tomorrow" in elegant script. Next to them was a delicate nightgown. I lifted the paltry fabric and decided almost immediately to find something more comfortable. Turning towards the dresser, I searched for anything remotely better, settling on a loose-fitting gray short-sleeve shirt. The fabric was gentle against my skin and I slipped it on along with the undergarments Violet had left. The shirt nearly swallowed me whole as it fell to my thighs, hitting just above my knees but it was infinitely better than that lacy handkerchief.

I glided across the smooth silk sheets on the bed. Pulling the wool comforter tight, I snuggled into the plump pillows. The bed was massive and I felt like a cat as I curled into the fabrics.

If someone had asked me a year ago, I would have told them I hated sleeping in any bed but my own. But after being at Allen's, my cabin in Zandar, and then *his* bed...Well, this one was by far the best. Something about it pulled me in. Maybe it was the dark sheets or the lavender scent but it lulled me to a calm I very much needed.

I was physically and mentally exhausted. I'd had no time to really process everything that's happened. But I didn't think there would ever be enough time, not even in my immortal life.

My mind darted in every direction, a torrent of countless thoughts overwhelming me from getting my power back, to meeting the gods.

There would never be enough time to process that.

Would the gods even answer me? Would they see me as nothing less than a human since I had so little power? Would they know who I was, who my parents were? Did they know what was happening in their realm, what Erixx did, what Azral did?

One thought lingered at the core of it all, pulling me from the spiral, and that was Drayzen.

He'd seen my life story, all my tears, all my pain, sifted through them like the pages of a book, selectively choosing the chapters to read to me. Choosing what I would feel, what I would relive.

And he relived them all with me. He felt the pain I felt in those moments as he let my memories unfold. He felt the gut-wrenching shatter of my parents' death. He felt the crack when I killed that man. And he felt the final break when I learned the truth.

He had been with me, a silent presence, saving me from myself this entire time.

Did he even know how much those memories meant to me? The flickering flames of hope they ignited?

Did he know how they saved me?

How *he* saved me?

I could see his stupid smirk now as I closed my eyes and I vowed to myself then, I would never give him the satisfaction of knowing.

My eyes fluttered open. The soft glow of the moon spilled into the room, casting gentle shadows across the space. The ambiance was dim as most of the sconces on the wall had gone out. My eye caught on the figure standing by the dresser and I jumped up.

Drayzen spun on his heels and his eyes met mine.

"What are you doing?" I pushed, my heart pounding as I instinctively wrapped the blanket around my bare legs. Thank the gods I wasn't wearing that lacy nightgown.

"I was getting—"

My heart pounded faster but not because of my shock. No, my eyes cleared from blurry fatigue and I saw Drayzen fully, standing with his bare chest and low-slung pants. The moonlight cast a lethal glow on his sculpted skin. My heart sank as I looked closer at the scars and burns that marred his body. Each one told their own hauntingly beautiful story.

"Could you put on some clothes?" I cleared my throat, hoping he didn't notice me staring.

"You're wearing them," he quipped, his voice filled with amusement.

I froze. This was his shirt and this—I looked around again. "Is this *your* room?"

He nodded and grabbed a shirt from the dresser. I didn't look away—I couldn't—as he pulled it on. The contours of his chest rippled. His eyes dropped to mine as he ran his fingers lazily through his tousled hair.

"Why am I staying in your room?" I choked out, desperately trying to distract myself.

"This was the only one unoccupied."

My head titled. "Where are *you* sleeping?"

"I'm not."

My brows furrowed. "You have to."

A small smile painted his face in the moonlight. "Get some more sleep." He shut the drawer and headed for the door.

I looked at the massive bed and the small space I took up. Before I could even think, the word slipped from my lips. "Stay."

Drayzen stopped in his tracks. He looked down, his face covered in shadow. "That's okay."

"You need to sleep," I urged.

"I'll sleep on the couch."

The couch had been comfortable but not enough for a good night's rest, especially not compared to his bed. "Stay," I commanded.

He slowly turned, his eyes piercing through the shadows. He was hesitant and cleared his throat before he said, "If you insist."

"I do." I nodded, making space for him.

He crawled into the bed awkwardly, keeping a safe distance from me. On his back, he kept his hands glued to his sides as he stared at the ceiling. I mimicked his position but I couldn't help my eyes drifting over to him.

"You should really try to get some more sleep, Mar." His words laced with a familiar tenderness. "We still have a couple of hours before we need to leave."

My nickname, so effortlessly spoken, tugged at the shattered pieces of my heart.

He shifted, turning his head to me. I tried to look away, pulling the blanket over my head to hide my embarrassment but he shot up. I jumped at his speed. He grabbed my arm from under the blanket and jerked it towards him.

"Hey!" I exclaimed, sitting up and trying to pull my arm back.

"What happened?" His eyes filled with genuine concern as he inspected my skin.

I looked down and my heart sank. The skin was broken, dried blood forming over the rash. *How did I not notice?*

"Tell me." he demanded.

"It's nothing." I pulled again but his grip didn't waver.

"What happened?" he repeated, turning my arm in all sorts of directions checking for any other signs of a wound.

"How did you know?" I tried changing the subject, tugging on my arm but getting nowhere.

"I could smell your blood," he said in an unfamiliar tone.

Seeing he wasn't about to let it go, my shoulders drooped and I whispered, "I was dirty."

I flinched as he reached out, his hand gently cradling my chin, guiding my head upwards to meet his gaze. His cool thumb grazed the probably still-swollen skin under my eyes. Concern etched across his features but they softened as he took in the entirety of my face.

"I was washing up." *Washing away the past.* "I didn't realize how rough the soap was."

It wasn't an outright lie but it certainly wasn't the full truth.

"You did this to yourself?" he asked, his voice gentle yet firm, concern evident.

I pulled away from him and turned in the bed, tucking myself far under the blanket. A stinging pain lingered on my arms and I realized how it burned where skin brushed fabric. Drayzen stayed seated, his eyes fixed on me, observing my every move.

With a long sigh, I flopped on my back, my gaze trailing to the ceiling. I knew he could see what happened if he wanted to. He could dive into my mind and watch how I scrubbed until the bar was nothing. How I vomited when I thought of the truth. How I *saw* myself. He could see it all if he wanted, every part of me.

"I'll be fine." I sighed.

I watched him from the corner of my eye as he laid back down, maintaining a cautious distance. Resting his arms behind his head, he mirrored my gaze towards the ceiling. The silence swelled.

"I can heal it for you," he said, almost too fast. "Your arm, if it bothers you." He glanced at me and I met his gaze, curiosity flickering.

"How?"

"My blood," he stated matter-of-factly.

His *blood?* "How?" I repeated. The possibility seemed crazy but so did everything else in Kaluth.

"Our blood is able to heal wounds. I've never given any to a Fae, so I'm not entirely certain if it will work on you," he explained. "But it can't hurt to try."

A Fae. *Not Human.*

"You drink each other's blood then?" It made sense, I supposed. Where else would they feed from?

"We feed from each other, yes." He nodded.

"But you've drank from Fae before?" I asked, remembering Azral's words and what I'd seen in Lunhayven.

"Fae blood is...unappetizing," Drayzen uttered.

"Does it bother you, then?" I looked at the rash on my arm. "My blood, its scent."

"No," he responded, a little too quickly.

Was he trying to make me feel better after he described me as unappetizing?

"If you don't want to—"

"How much would I need?"

"Not much." His jaw tensed. *Is he nervous?*

Silence grew around us. I looked back at my arm; it wasn't bad, nowhere close to needing any healing, but I couldn't rest my curiosity.

"Okay," I whispered.

"It can be...overwhelming," he warned, concern flickering through his eyes.

"Overwhelming?" I echoed, raising a brow. Up to this point, everything had been overwhelming. While the fact that I was about to drink blood didn't help, it wasn't the most difficult thing to digest.

He nodded, his eyes darting around in search of my thoughts.

"I'm ready," I lied.

He brought his wrist to his mouth. I watched his fangs puncture the delicate skin, drawing forth crimson liquid. Two distinct holes appeared and then he extended his wrist to me. The blood trickled down his arm as I took his hand in mine. That hum returned and I assumed it was his martem trying to calm my racing heart. It worked, whatever it was.

I took a breath as my fingers brushed against his skin. He was cooler than I anticipated, icy, almost. I could feel the calluses and roughness around his fingers. And the question I was too afraid to ask Cade lingered in my mind.

"How old are you?" I blurted, my eyes still glued to his wrist.

"Much older than the Fae," he said, his voice tinged with anticipation. "It's really just a number at this point."

I looked at him but I couldn't read his expression. "Nothing is going to shock me more than the fact that I'm about to drink blood, so just spit it out."

"Eight hundred and thirty-two."

I didn't let the shock of that number take effect on me. Instead, I used it as fuel, as encouragement. I pulled his wrist closer. His blood dripped on wool but he seemed unbothered, his eyes fixed only on me. Guided by my own will, curiosity, and something else, I pulled his arm up.

I met his eyes through my lashes and he nodded.

My lips met his wrist, and I drank.

Cool blood spilled down my throat. Its taste was initially metallic but the more I drank, the more the flavors unfolded and bloomed. It was like raindrops gently dancing on my tongue followed by a woodsy essence similar to the whiskey or a burning fire. Lavender and pine scents filled my nose, intertwining with the sensations coursing through my body. Unconsciously, my free hand grabbed his arm, pulling him closer as my head nestled on his chest.

He shifted and pulled me against him. His free hand found its way to my hair. I closed my eyes, surrendering myself completely to the experience, to him.

With each sip, a fire ignited deep inside me. I pushed closer, unable to control my movement. I couldn't stop the stirring that grew. I tried to push it away but my body was consumed by it. I gave in to it, our bodies pressed against each other, no, I pressed against him, melding us in an intoxicating unity.

The feeling of his touch, each one of his delicate fingers caressing my face and threading through my hair, sent chills through me, electrifying *all* of me. He leaned his head against mine. His fast breaths teased my ear and ignited another pleasurable shudder.

"That's enough," he whispered, his voice like a bitter antidote.

But I didn't listen.

I drew his wrist deeper into my mouth, my teeth gently sinking around it, craving more of him. I couldn't get close enough. It was a euphoria that surged through me.

And I didn't want it to stop.

"Mar." His voice was more commanding. "That's enough."

Terror took over as a quiet fear lingered in the back of my mind, a fear that this may never be enough. I shoved his wrist away and scooted back on the sheets, my cheeks warming. I cleared my throat one too many times as I examined my arm. The blood-stained rash was gone, my dignity along with it.

"Thank you," I mumbled, avoiding his eyes. I threw myself under the blankets.

He slowly laid back down, maintaining a new distance between us. "It's normal," he said after what felt like the longest silence ever.

"What is?" I asked, hoping he was referring to anything other than what I'd just felt.

"You don't need to be embarrassed," was all he said and that was all I needed to shrivel into a ball of mortification.

Gods, strike me down, *please.*

"Get some sleep, Mar."

I obediently closed my eyes, attempting to quiet my racing thoughts, and allowed sleep to claim me, even as the echoes of what just happened played over and over again.

32

I CAUTIOUSLY TURNED, LEANING MY HEAD ON my arm as I watched Drayzen sleep. He was still on his back, his hands glued to his side. His chest rose and fell with every slow breath. His hair was tousled with strands falling over his forehead. He looked so at peace.

My stomach turned as the events of last night flooded my mind. *It's normal,* he had said. Was it normal to still taste him on my lips, to want more?

I crawled out from the bed, careful not to wake him, and made for the bathroom. I focused on getting ready. Black tunic, pants, brush hair—the mirror was still covered by a towel, and I had no intention of moving it—braid hair. When I felt seemly again, I opened the door.

A bare chest glowed in the morning light. Lavender and pine kissed my nose as I dragged my gaze up...up...and met Drayzen's head on.

His voice was groggy as he said, "Good morning."

"Good morning." I cleared my throat, hoping the telltale warmth in my cheeks wasn't too noticeable.

"Vi has breakfast ready. Make sure you eat before we leave."

"Of course," I replied hastily, stepping aside to let him past.

I turned, instantly finding the towel still draped over the mirror. *Oh no.* Dread ripped through me; I didn't want to explain, for him to know that shame. But he didn't ask and he left the towel where it was.

I should have looked away, but I couldn't. Not as I noticed the scars that painted a story, one I desperately needed to know. He picked at the buttons on his pants but stopped mid-pull and his eyes met mine through fallen hair. Drayzen raised a single brow as his signature smirk bloomed.

I'd never moved so quickly as I ran from the bedroom. *Gods, it just got worse by the second.* Out of breath, I found Violet waiting for me in the kitchen. Her unusually wide smile greeted me, along with the scent of breakfast cooking. She also wore all black and her hair was pulled into two braids laying over her chest. Small waves framed her face, cascading over her perfect skin.

She handed me a plate filled with crispy bacon and perfectly cooked eggs. It was glorious after the torture of Vani's dinner last night.

"I'm so glad the clothes fit," she said, taking a seat at the table beside me. "It's easier to go unnoticed in the shadows when we wear black."

"In the shadows?"

"When we shift, it's easier not to be seen," she clarified. But the explanation didn't help.

"Shift?" I repeated, my mind racing back to Drayzen's teleportation ability. *Is that what it was?*

"Shadow shifting," she began around a mouthful of food. "We can only travel a certain distance. We'll be able to shift to the boat offshore and leave from there."

"Oh." *Shadow shifting.*

Cade joined us and of course, he, too, was dressed in all black. He settled across from me with his own plate of food. The dark of his clothes made his tattoo stand out more. I followed my gaze up his arm only to be met by his concerned eyes. He squinted, searching my face.

"What?" I questioned, feeling a bit self-conscious.

"You were hurt?" he asked.

I nearly choked on a piece of bacon, quickly spitting it out. *How does he know?* "I—"

"She just had a little fall," Drayzen interjected from behind me. He took his seat next to me, his own plate in hand. My head snapped towards him and I felt the blood drain from my face. "She's okay now."

I looked back to Cade who seemed unconvinced as he began eating.

Sovanni and Thysa entered the kitchen hand in hand. Their beauty commanded the attention of the three of us.

"Good morning!" Violet yelled through a mouthful.

"Good morning." Sovanni smiled, but her features filled with a fear I recognized.

"What's wrong?" I set my fork down.

"They're going back to Rosetia." Drayzen's voice was low and calculated.

I almost choked again. "What?" I glared at him.

"It wasn't my idea." He shook his head.

I whirled on the Fae. They wore similar clothes to us, ready for their own battle, apparently. "Why?" I breathed. "Why are you going back?"

"We'll be okay." Vani nodded, a newfound hope glowing in her eyes. "We need to check on Raxos. The people there—"

Thysa's head dropped, her braids falling over her face. Vani's free arm moved across her chest and held Thysa's close.

"They'll find you. Az—" I couldn't even get his name out without bile singeing my throat.

"Mylom will take us to the outskirts of town. We'll be back here before you all, most likely."

I wasn't convinced. "But The Fading, your power?" *Would it hurt, crossing back and forth like this?*

"I'll be okay." Vani smiled, lighting up the room.

"Thysa—" I begged.

"I don't have any power to lose," she said under her breath.

Her words struck me then—Thysa had no power. Sovanni mentioned that some Fae lacked martem but I wasn't sure how common it was; everyone I knew possessed something.

"We'll be okay," Thysa said now, her missing smile finally returning.

They joined us at the table, plates in their hands. To my surprise, Drayzen also ate and I couldn't help but ask, "So, you *do* eat regular food?"

"Only when Vi cooks," he replied, that rare genuine smile cracking. I turned to Violet who paid him no mind as she shoveled bacon into her mouth.

Before we left, Violet handed me a weapons belt and garter. The black leather accessories were sleek and smooth as I fastened them on.

"Drayzen wanted me to give you these," she said, handing me two daggers.

The black-gray blade was cool against my skin as I turned it over in my palms. The metalwork on them was beautiful, sleek and dark. A detailed snake design wrapped around the hilts, the vipers' eyes filled with a glowing black diamond. I slid them into place on my belt and thigh. The feeling was familiar, missed. I leveled Violet with an animalistic smirk and she returned the gesture with her wide smile.

"Ready?" Drayzen asked Violet as he and Cade walked up behind us. She nodded in agreement.

The four of us stood in our black leathers. I couldn't help but notice that we looked like a pretty badass team.

Violet's fingers intertwined with mine. Her touch, like Drayzen's and Cade's, was cool but unlike theirs, hers lacked the calluses of a warrior.

"I'll meet you there," Cade declared as he stepped into the shadow cast by the house and vanished. It was still shocking to me, even though I'd seen Drayzen do it so many times. Now, I had a word for it: shadow shifting.

My jaw dropped and Violet chuckled. "Yeah, I still think it's pretty cool, too."

Drayzen's hand slipped into my free one and I recoiled. Not because I was afraid of him, no, I was afraid of myself. Afraid of the flush that warmed my cheeks as I stared at our laced fingers.

"Are you ready?" he asked, as if it was a simple question. Was I ready to meet a god? To ask them to return my power to me? I didn't think I'd ever be ready for such a task.

But I was ready for one thing. One thing that's fueled me since the beginning.

Revenge.

"I'm ready."

Violet slipped her free hand into Drayzen's, their eyes locking as she nodded. I barely saw his wink before the clouds obstructed the sun and shrouded us in shadows.

Before I knew it, we were nothing more than a black mist. I could still feel their hands in mine but it was as if we were mere ethereal beings. My stomach lurched. I closed my eyes and felt the wind all around us, transporting our bodies through time and space. *It would never not be cool.*

The wind calmed and my feet met a hard surface. I slowly cracked one eye open as Drayzen's and Violet's hands released mine. We were on a ship, a massive one at that. Black flags hung from the sails with intricate silver bat-like wings embroidered on the fabric. I squinted, making out a snake encircling the wings, eating its own tail. *Was this the sigil of the Denazin?*

I looked around the ship, my eyes finally adjusting to the sunlight. We were on the upper deck and I counted about thirty or so sailors kneeling on the lower deck. Their heads were bowed, nearly touching the wood, and they all fisted one hand on the ground while the other rested over their hearts.

"Who are they bowing to?" I asked, my heart quickening at the possibility.

"You *are* a queen," Drayzen replied swiftly.

"But I'm not *their* queen," I said through gritted teeth.

"It's a sign of respect," he explained, glancing at them before nodding to Cade who issued orders to the sailors. They scurried around the ship in response. "We'll be leaving soon. The water shouldn't be as rough once we get through the Black Sea."

He extended his arm, leading me to the rail of the ship. My hands trailed along the wood as I leaned over. The water was completely black with only white-capped waves providing contrast as they crashed against the ship's side.

"We should reach Melenyz's Island by nightfall."

I nodded, entranced by the ocean. *Nightfall.* So close and yet so far away.

"Amara."

"Yes," I replied as I stared into the water.

Drayzen's hand fell to my elbow and I turned to face him. "When you meet them, you need to be very specific with your words."

"Violet mentioned it—"

"She did," he cut me off, "but you have one shot at this. They will try to twist what you ask. You need to be precise."

"How do you know, if only one person ever made it to them?" And that person was dead now.

"Autyr." Drayzen smirked.

"You talk to him?" I should have been more shocked but after everything, this seemed the most normal.

"Only on special occasions." He shrugged. "Just really take some time to think about what you're going to ask."

I nodded. I'd briefly considered it but "give me my power back" seemed like a pretty simple command.

"For now, Cade will show you the basics of swordplay," he said, placing his hands on the rail beside me.

"So, I'll be doing some actual training?" I tried to hide my enthusiasm.

"Meditation *is* actual training," Cade interjected from behind us. "I told you not to underestimate the power of the mind."

"I'll find you all in a little while," Drayzen said, nodding towards Cade. "Violet will join you, too. She could certainly use the practice."

Violet grumbled, shoving him playfully. "Meet me later and I'll show you just how much practice I've gotten over the last few years."

Guilt coursed through my veins at the reminder that he'd left his home, his family, all to help me.

"I can't wait," Drayzen yelled back and flashed his signature smirk.

"Let's go," Cade commanded and we trailed him to the lower deck of the ship.

33

THE HUSHED WHISPERS OF THE SAILORS
barely reached my ears. They all cast respectful nods in Cade's
direction as we hurried past. We stopped at the most open
area of the deck, a chest in the center. A dazzling array of
daggers, swords, and throwing stars were carelessly tossed
inside, like someone had stuffed in as much as they could
before a dangerous journey. The various shades of silver and
black sparkled as the sun rose.

All the hilts on the swords and daggers had a similar
snake to the ones Violet had given me but my eye caught one
in particular. Beside the engraved snakes were bat-like wings
similar to the sigil on the flags, silver and smoky tones

covering them. It was breathtaking. I reached for it but before I could touch it, Cade's hand firmly clasped mine.

"Not that one." He took the weapon. "This one's mine." He secured it on his belt, eliciting a less-than-pleased expression from me.

I turned my attention back to the chest and went for the throwing stars instead. Each one was embossed with a black diamond at its center. The razor-sharp edges sang against my fingertips. "Interesting," I whispered, envisioning hurling one into Azral's eyes. *That* brought a small smile to my face.

"Ah, throwing stars?" Cade said, plucking the star from my hand. "Not exactly practical in a real fight. Let's start with something more reliable."

My smile disappeared. I turned back to the chest again, opting for a modest sword that comfortably fastened to my belt. Violet grabbed her weapons and, together, we faced Cade.

"So, Amara, you've never used a sword before?" he asked.

"One time—" The words caught in my throat as memories resurfaced, memories of *him*. I almost wished I'd cut Azral's hand off, now. I pushed back the wicked thought. No matter how much I wanted Azral to hurt, the thought of him at all was crippling.

Cade nodded as he unsheathed his sword. The metal clanged through the wind and the black diamonds gleamed under the sun's rays as he raised it. The tattoo on his hand glowed; silver tendrils outlined the ink. I looked back to the flags, then to his hand. The same symbol painted both. His head lowered and his jaw clenched under his stubble. Those turquoise eyes pierced through us as he pointed the sword straight at Violet.

I turned to see the mischievous grin crest her face. Unsheathing her own sword, she met his challenge. "Watch and learn, Amara."

And in the blink of an eye, she vanished. Cade swiftly followed, dissolving into the shadows. They seamlessly shifted in and out of the darkness, occasionally colliding with each other. The clashing of their swords accompanied Violet's infectious laughter.

The sun emerged from behind the clouds and just as quickly, they reappeared. Cade was still, his breath steady as his sword pointed at Violet's neck. She breathed heavily, raising her hands in surrender. I swore I saw a smile on his face but it died as my legs buckled with the rock of the ship. Both turned their attention to me as I clutched the nearby mast. The flags above fluttered and swiveled while crew members ran around, shouting orders to one another.

Violet laughed, playfully brushing aside Cade's sword with her hand. She skipped over to me, unfazed by the rocking. "Have you ever been on a ship before?"

"No," I replied, releasing the mast. I straightened. The gentle rocking of the ship made my insides wobble with each crash of the waves.

"You'll get used to it. Just try not to think about it," Violet said.

I've ridden a dragon. Could this really be that much worse?

"Did you watch?" Her wide smile returned.

"What I could." I wasn't sure how much they'd actually expected me to see as they popped in and out of the shadows.

"Watching is not as fun as doing," Cade said from behind us. "Take out your sword." He looked towards my hip.

I cautiously unsheathed the metal, feeling its weight settle into my grip. Daggers were my safe space. I liked to be quick, precise, and the sword was just so big and clunky. I held the blade awkwardly.

"How does it feel?" Cade asked.

"It's...heavy," I admitted, slowly swinging the sword side to side. "I'd rather use my daggers or maybe those throwing stars." I glanced back into the chest.

"No daggers, you already know how to use them." His tone left no room for negotiation. "And no throwing stars."

"Let her use the stars," a voice sounded from behind us. Drayzen glided across the ship's deck as the wind tousled his hair. His black attire hugged his frame and his midnight eyes met mine. "I could use a good laugh."

A good laugh? The sting of embarrassment morphed into burning rage. I may not be a warrior like him but I wasn't helpless.

Losing this stupid sword would be a relief for me and luckily, I knew just how to play this game. "Cade is right. I should go through basic training first," I retorted sarcastically. "It will give you more time to practice. Then maybe, you would actually stand a chance against me." I smirked, raising a challenging brow.

I stood absolutely no chance against him, against any of them. I wasn't that naive. But if this was what I needed to get my hands on those stars, then so be it. Men always answered a challenge, Human, Fae, or Denazin.

Violet was practically buzzing. Her hand slapped over her mouth in an attempt to contain her laugh.

Drayzen's grin widened, revealing both his fangs. It was one of those rare smiles but this time, it was almost animalistic. So, I mirrored him.

I looked to Cade, he was unamused, his deadly glare fixed on me. "If you manage to hit him with one, you can use them."

Violet clapped and grabbed the stars from the chest. She closed the lid and sat on top, handing them to me. I shot her one of her trademark grins, something stirring within me.

The cool touch of dark metal met my palms. They were light and nimble, a far cry from the weight of that clunky sword. I turned and directed my attention back to the Denazin males. Cade leaned against the wooden mast, his muscles straining against his shirt as he crossed his arms.

Drayzen stalked to the center of the deck. "Ready whenever you are." He winked.

I looked back at the stars. *Five chances.* What were the odds that I could get at least one of them to land? I didn't have high hopes for myself. I looked back up at Drayzen. Little waves of black hair blew across his forehead, his lavender scent snaking through the air. I was distracted by the sudden image of the way he'd brushed my hair from my face last night.

I grunted. "Get out of my head!"

But he only raised his hands. *Had that not been him?* I grunted again, this time at myself.

Then, I moved.

I was fast but Drayzen was undeniably faster as he slipped through the shadows. *Cheater.* I sprinted across the deck towards him but every time I got close, he shifted away. This lasted for some time and my hands tiredly fell to my knees. I tried to catch my breath, peering up at him through my lashes.

He shifted back into the light, leaning against the mast next to Cade, picking at his nails.

I growled, grinding my teeth. I looked around the deck and sprinted away from him. The ship rocked under me but this time, I was ready for it. I leaped onto the balcony of the upper deck. Violet and Cade watched me, curiosity etched on their faces as I observed, attempting to track Drayzen's movements. Sunlight and shadows danced over the deck while he effortlessly weaved between them.

My eyes darted back and forth, hunting him down like an animal in the woods. With a cry, I hurled a star. He froze. It grazed the mast to his left. He winked and disappeared once more.

I wasted another star, missing again. *Gods, this was impossible.*

I jumped from the balcony, landing on all fours, and scanned the open area, the sky above, strategizing. I needed to get into the sunlight. I studied the ship. Then, it clicked. Most of the deck was obscured by shadows from the sails but right behind Cade was the bow. The wood stretched over the sea and that would be my opening—because there were no shadows.

It would be risky to get over there, considering how rocky my steps had been. Every time a wave crashed, my knees buckled and threatened to send me sprawling on the deck. But the bowsprit was my only shot at victory. Taking a deep breath, I shut out the fear and sprinted past Cade and Violet. They exchanged confused looks as they turned and followed me.

Fear was far from me as I leaped onto the bowsprit. That was, until a wave rocked the ship and I had no choice but to cling to the wood. The ocean raged far below. I gave myself one breath, two, before pushing to my feet. *Maybe this wasn't the smartest idea.*

Drayzen apparated from the final line of shadows, gracefully stepping into the sunlight. Radiant rays cast an ethereal glow on him while his midnight eyes shimmered with a touch of silver.

I couldn't help but smirk. I had him right where I wanted him.

With a swift movement, I sent my dagger hurtling towards him. He effortlessly caught the blade just before it hit his face. He glanced at it, twirling it around his finger.

But that was exactly what I expected him to do and I launched the fourth throwing star.

He didn't even glance up as his free hand snatched the weapon mid-air. "Is that the best you can do?"

In an instant, the sunlight vanished and the clatter of blades echoed as they fell to the deck. Before I could blink, Drayzen stood before me. The sun just broke through the betraying cloud. I bared my teeth at him and retreated a step. He moved, too, closing the distance between us. With every step he took, I took a step back.

Until there was nothing beneath my foot but air.

Drayzen gripped my arm before I fell straight into the crashing waves below. He held me there for a second but I didn't let the fear of the fall sink in. I reached for the final star.

It was missing.

Drayzen raised his free hand. The black diamond glimmered as he twirled it.

He hoisted me back up, our bodies colliding. His chest was hard against mine as he pulled me in, his hand wrapping around my waist. He leaned down, his words were cool in my ear. "You'll have to be quicker than that, little kitten."

Memories of the night before flooded my mind—how close we had been, how close we were now. *Was he toying with me or was this my own treacherous mind?*

He pulled away and my heart slowed to a normal pace. My stomach rippled but I couldn't place the feeling.

Drayzen jumped back onto the deck and I followed. But I was much more careful as I stepped off. Violet looked mildly disappointed. *Had she actually believed I would beat him?* Cade remained where he stood. He didn't say anything as he held out the sword to me and I knew exactly what that meant.

I trained tirelessly with Cade as he patiently taught me the fundamentals of sword fighting, guiding me through the basic techniques. I was no master at the art, constantly tripping over myself from the shifting boat. It was a miracle I hadn't accidentally stabbed anyone.

"Can we please take a break," I begged after a few hours, hands heavy on my knees.

"No." His voice was always low, always commanding.

"You said we already made it past the hard part of the journey. Can't we do this another day?"

"No," was all he answered every time.

Even if someone attacked the ship presently, I would still much rather use my daggers. But he insisted on training until the sun dipped below the horizon. Violet stayed throughout our session, honing her already impressive skills.

Drayzen, however, was not with us. Once our little game ended, he left for the ship's main quarters, cryptically mentioning a discussion he needed to have with the captain.

By the time night fell, my bones and muscles were screaming at me for rest. I was exhausted.

Violet led me below deck. The area was much bigger than I imagined. Six doors lined the long wooden hallway she pointed down.

"This one is yours." She smiled as she opened the first door to the left. I peeked my head into the dark room. I couldn't see much more than the wan light emanating from the port window on the opposite wall.

"I'll see you soon," she said, closing the door behind me.

As the door clicked, a light flicked low. The room was small but I was used to that. The bed took up most of the space. Its gray and black sheets added to the dark glow of the room. There were two empty tables beside the bed, a small chair under the circular window, and an open door to the right, which led to an equally small bathroom.

My feet ached but the first thing I did was find a loose towel and toss it over the mirror. A bucket of steamy water sat beside the sink and I quickly washed up before collapsing onto the bed. It was nowhere near as comfortable as Drayzen's and I shuddered at the thought.

Still, as I laid there, it wasn't the anticipation of meeting a god in a matter of hours that lingered in my mind. It wasn't the realization that this world was now my reality—a world where I was a queen, a world where my enemies ruled in my place.

No, my thoughts centered solely on the male who had saved me—Drayzen.

I couldn't help but wonder what his eyes looked like as they drifted off to a sweet slumber. How his hair would be messy in the early morning. I couldn't help but wonder if he felt alone. *Because I did.*

Right before I fell asleep, I could have sworn that the scent of lavender and pine kissed my senses.

34

CALM WAFTED OVER ME AS I WOKE TO THE scent of vanilla and lilies. Violet was crouched next to me, her turquoise eyes wide with anticipation.

"We're here," she whispered.

I rolled over to find the sea coated in darkness beyond the small window. Moonlight no longer graced the room and candles burned low as she hauled me up. I threw on the same black attire from the day before and met everyone on the top deck.

Drayzen and Cade spoke with the crew, their voices sailing through the quiet night. I yawned, walking towards the rail of the ship. Sailors scurried past me, yelling to one another as the ship slowed to a halt. The movement surprised me and I stumbled, grabbing for the rail as I looked over it. A small island sat just beside us. Unlike the God of Death's, this one was painted with a forest that looked like it spanned for miles. The now-blue ocean water was unusually still, save for the ripples under the boat.

Violet's hand fell into mine. A larger hand landed on my shoulder. Before I could look back at Drayzen, the shadows engulfed us.

I faltered as my feet hit soft sand. Drayzen's arm steadied me and as I looked up to him, my eyes caught a different beauty. The starry night blanketed the sky above us. I looked around, tracing the constellations but something was missing. *Where's the moon?* In its absence, realization settled: We were standing on the island of the Moon Goddess, Melenyz.

I kneeled, gathering a handful of the deep blue sand that covered the shore. It slipped through my fingers, soft and cool, each tiny grain glistening faintly in the starlight.

Cade eventually joined us. The four of us stood there, all clad in our black leathers, blending into the night. The equally dark sand stretched only so far, giving way to the dense forest looming before us. Oak trees towered high above a mix of others. Heart-shaped leaves twisted in the cool wind, carrying a sweet caramel scent.

"So, we're just going to walk in there?" I questioned looking into the never-ending forest. "How will we find her?" *How do we find a god?*

"She'll show up when she wants," Drayzen said.

And I remembered now, he'd done this before—spoken with a god. The thought sent shivers through me. "And if she doesn't?"

"We'll just go to the next one." Drayzen smirked.

Right. Because I wasn't only Fae, but a Fae descended from both gods. *One of a kind.*

I pushed away the fear of the unknown, took a deep breath and nodded. "Let's go then."

Violet and I trailed quietly behind Drayzen and Cade as we moved deeper into the forest. It was kind of strange that there were no guards but I supposed that was what The Fading was for. If someone made it this far, they'd already won.

The air grew cooler with each step and the thick trees above us blocked out all the starlight. I could barely see my hand before my face. I grabbed Violet's arm, following her steps to keep my footing.

"Are you nervous?" She whispered.

I nodded. It was obvious though, my hands sweating around her.

"Have you ever spoken with one before?" I asked her quietly. "A god?"

"Only in my prayers," she replied. "He's the only one I know who ever has." She nodded to Drayzen, his back to us.

A chill snaked down my spine. To think I would be one of only two people she knew, out of the countless individuals she has surely known over her gods-only-knew-how-long life... *Was I even worthy of such an honor?*

Drayzen's voice made my heart drop to my stomach. "She's here."

The forest opened up into a clearing and as one, the four of us turned our gazes to the sky. The stars still twinkled but what was above the clearing—

"An eclipse," Violet gasped, her mouth open as she stared at the celestial phenomenon. Even Drayzen and Cade were wide eyed.

"A lunar eclipse," Cade breathed.

Violet looked like she might fall to her knees on the spot. "Does that mean—?"

"Saigus and Melenyz are both here," Drayzen finished.

My jaw dropped. I was about to meet not one god, but two.

"This makes things a bit easier, yeah?" Drayzen's chipper tone didn't match my own feelings.

As if things were easy to begin with.

No, this made things insane, impossible, absurd. There weren't enough words to describe the fact that I was about to meet *two* gods.

I looked at Drayzen, peeling my eyes from the ember lit moon. His usual smug smirk was absent, replaced with compassion. He faced me and lowered his head. "What are you going to say?"

I took a breath. "Give me my power back."

"Good." He nodded but concern limned his features.

The clearing was vast and eerily empty. Cade took the lead through the meadow as we all followed. But as soon as I crossed over the boundary of the forest, my heart sank.

A hazy veil of gray smoke surrounded the clearing and what looked to be guards appeared, blocking any exit in. Half of them donned silver armor while the other half wore golden. The only thing visible on the soldiers were piercing eyes— glowing in similar shades of gold and silver. They stood sentinel, observing our every move, and the forest seemed to vanish behind them. Cade and Violet unsheathed their swords, prompting the soldiers to mirror the action. The clearing filled with the resounding *shing* of metal.

I stood frozen by Drayzen's side but he just calmly raised a hand. Violet lowered her sword but Cade remained steadfast, as did the unwavering soldiers. Drayzen casually slipped his hands into his pockets, his signature smirk slowly forming on his face. It didn't annoy me this time. At least someone wasn't freaking out.

My gaze followed his towards the far end of the clearing. Two figures emerged. The one on the left was covered in a blinding glow like the sun. And to their right stood a shorter one, covered in a white glow similar to that of the full moon.

In front of me stood the gods Isidore would pray to when the freezing winters showed no sign of warmth. Lettie would pray for the moon's guidance and protection when I was bullied relentlessly. They were once just something I believed in, stories I was told as a child.

But here they were.

I sank to my knees before Saigus and Melenyz. Cade and Violet gracefully lowered themselves to one knee, heads bowed with respect, mirroring a more graceful position on the ground. I glanced to my right only to find Drayzen standing.

What was he doing?

Like a child, I tugged at the hem of his pants, silently urging him to kneel.

Drayzen let out a laugh—an *actual* laugh. I turned to Violet. She only rolled her eyes and stood awkwardly, extending a hand to help me.

"He doesn't kneel to anyone, not even Autyr," she whispered.

Was he so arrogant he couldn't even show respect to the god who created him?

"Remember to choose your words carefully," Violet said, her smile now a comforting sight.

"*Very* carefully." Drayzen commanded in my ear, urging me on.

"Give me my power back," I repeated quietly, my very own mantra. I nodded again and again. *I can do this.* "I can do this."

I took a small step only to come to an abrupt halt as the courage I'd built disappeared in an instant. A flash of white light blinded me and I found myself transported across the clearing. I stumbled as my feet touched ground and I spun to see Drayzen holding back Cade. His approving nod shone through the amber fog they disappeared into.

I spun again, heart racing. My eyes widened at the gods before me.

"*Andrasteia Amara Raine, first and only daughter of Akailo and Cyra, descendant of both Sun and Moon.*" They spoke in unison, their voices intertwining, one deep and sultry, the other light and whimsical. "*Once lost but now returned to us.*"

35

STANDING BEFORE THE TWO GODS, I TOOK IN their features as the light around them dissipated. Saigus, with his commanding presence, stood tall and his deep tan glowed around him. His eyes were a mesmerizing golden hue. A mane of burnt red hair adorned his head, like Akailo's. A combination of curls and waves cascaded down his back and around a golden crown. The crown itself looked to be made from actual rays of sun, blinding and beautiful. He wore a deep red tunic, a shade nearly as dark as Mylom's irises. The fabric clung to his body, hinting at a well-toned physique beneath.

Melenyz, too, was breathtaking. Her skin, similar to my own pale complexion, beamed in the amber eclipse. Her eyes were an icy shade of shimmering blue. Her long hair was gracefully braided past her midsection in a rope of snowy white, just like mine and Cyra's. A flowing gown of white and silver hugged her chest and skimmed just below her midriff as the skirt split into two, accentuating her legs. What appeared to be actual stars laced the hem and twisted up her body to her knees. She wore no crown but it didn't matter; her presence exuded her status.

Apart from their un-shocking good looks, Saigus and Melenyz appeared surprisingly ordinary. Their ears, unlike the points of the Fae, were rounded like Human or Denazin.

Melenyz's words broke my trance, her calm voice enchanting. "Our first and last creation,"

"To what do we owe this pleasure?" Saigus finished for her.

I blinked. First and *last* creation*? What did that even mean?* I was tempted to look back, to see if Drayzen was somehow still there, but then Saigus laughed deeply.

"They cannot hear us," he assured me with a hint of cynicism.

Could the gods read minds like the Denazin? I stood tall, trying desperately to fortify my mind as Cade had taught me. I tried to feel their presence but it was no use.

"To what do we owe this pleasure?" Saigus asked again.

Gathering myself, I took another deep breath and spoke with the authority of a queen. "Give me my power back." But my voice betrayed me as the last word quivered. I may be a queen but they were my gods. No one ruled them.

Melenyz's smile washed over me but it did little to soothe my nerves.

Saigus, on the other hand, responded with a dry tone, "We cannot return something we do not possess."

My brows furrowed and my jaw clenched. I couldn't hide my annoyance as I said, "You're a god—"

"And?"

I tried not to glance around the clearing, like the answer might be hiding just beyond the trees. "You owe me my favor. I made it across The Fading, made it all the way here."

"Ah yes, the challenge of crossing The Fading. A task many died trying. But *you*," he leaned down to my height, "you had too much help, too much interference from a god who should not meddle in our business." I blanched. *I hadn't asked for Autyr's help and yet...* "Did you think it would be so easy?"

Saigus sneered and that look in his eyes—that hatred and anger. I pulled back, trying to calm my racing heart.

Melenyz stepped forward, placing a hand on his arm. "As you are a child of *both* of us," she chided. "We will compromise and grant you two questions that we may answer."

"So, what will they be?" Saigus asked impatiently.

Two questions? I couldn't afford to ask a vague one; I needed precise information. I needed to be careful. My mind reeled. *We cannot return something we do not possess,* Saigus had said. I knew that Erixx had it but was it inside him or did he keep it on him like a prized possession? And how in the world did I get it back *into* me?

"Where exactly is my power?"

Melenyz stepped forward, an eagerness in her gait. "You, Amara, were a creation we had never anticipated, one we had sought to prevent for centuries. A creation we knew would become the center of a corrupt power struggle. And indeed, you did just that." Her voice carried a weight. She paused, then gently clasped my hands in hers. I flinched as her cool silky skin made contact but then I could feel her, in the corners of my mind. I didn't try to block her out. I took a calming breath, letting the goddess enter the sacred space, suddenly thankful for Cade's training.

A vivid image flashed in my mind—Erixx.

I stood, silently observing the vision she projected. The false king walked through what seemed to be his chambers. A worn bed sat in the middle of the space with a mess of golden sheets on top. He looked disheveled, his brown hair a mess, and his white tunic was torn.

I almost asked what it was she was showing me but stopped myself, remembering the warning to choose my words carefully. I didn't want them to mistake such a trivial question as my second.

So, I watched in silence, fixated on the unfolding image. Erixx approached a towering mirror in the bedroom. Leaning down, he gingerly lifted the scarlet crown. The rubies' were different from the last time I'd seen them as he placed it on his head. He shivered at the touch, the golden circlet shaking. The vibrant red hue of the gems dulled to an inky black but with a simple snap of his fingers, the shuddering ceased and the rubies resumed their crimson glow.

That crown—*my* crown. I saw it now. That was where my power was being kept, trapped, just like I had been in that castle, stuck in a constant struggle to break free.

I let out the breath I was holding. Physically and metaphorically, I needed to reclaim my crown, to take back the power that rightfully belonged to me. *The power they stole from me.*

"Understood," I whispered. I refused to dwell on the seemingly insurmountable odds of wresting the crown from Erixx. That was a problem to deal with later.

"Good," she said, withdrawing her hand from mine.

I looked to Saigus, confusion lingering on his face. *Could he see the answer she gave me?* His eyes snapped to mine, his head tilting. "And your second question?"

A myriad of questions fought for attention in my mind but I pushed aside the swarm until one floated to the surface.

"How do I reclaim my power?" The words came out a little too fast.

Melenyz let out a low sigh, the icy swirls in her eyes dissipating as her gaze focused on Saigus.

He smirked and his voice took on a cruel tone. "You need to reunite with your soul."

Huh?

"How do I reclaim my power?" I asked again with a brow raised. Was I not clear enough? Did he not understand? "How do I get it to me?"

"You need to reunite with your soul," was all he said again.

"My soul?" It was a riddle, a new piece to my puzzle.

"Well, my purpose here is done," Saigus shrugged.

Melenyz nodded in agreement and he gracefully retreated.

He stopped, looking back over his shoulder. "Andrasteia," he uttered. Then he was gone, dissipating into the bright light permeating the clearing.

The sun's rays pierced through the sky. I shielded my eyes, temporarily blinded. When I moved my hand, soft moonlight painted the land. Only Melenyz stood before me.

She caressed my face tenderly. The absence of her smile was cold and she gazed deeply into my eyes. I could only watch as she examined my features, her touch carrying a bittersweet finality.

"Goodbye, Amara," she whispered.

And then she vanished, too.

The mist in the clearing evaporated and the knights dissolved into thin air. I turned my attention to where Drayzen, Cade, and Violet reappeared and trudged over to them.

You need to reunite with your soul...

Saigus' words repeated in my mind.

"Well," Violet stretched the word into multiple syllables, "how did it go?"

Cade, still holding his sword, seemed more content with the knights gone but he remained on guard. I looked at Drayzen; he studied me in silence, his expression unreadable.

But then Violet couldn't contain herself and I was barraged with questions. "What did they say? What were they like? Were they nice? Did they—?"

"Vi." Drayzen scanned the clearing. "We need to go."

The sound of armor clashing echoed through the trees.

"Now," Drayzen growled, grabbing my hand as we shifted.

We landed hard on the beach. Violet and Cade materialized beside us, both struggling for air. Violet doubled over, clutching her knees, her face pale and strained.

"Something's wrong," she gasped, her voice trembling. "Our martem—it's blocked. I can't feel it."

Cade staggered upright, breathing heavily but recovering faster than her. His sword hung loosely at his side.

Drayzen, unshaken, turned sharply towards the forest. The clank of armor grew louder and gold shimmered through the leaves.

"What's going on?" I panicked. My question was met with silence, everyone too focused, too uncertain.

Drayzen's grip tightened around my hand, urgency flashing in his eyes. "I'll take Mar first and come back for you two," he said quickly, his voice a mix of command and desperation.

Everything in me screamed that this was wrong, that I wasn't worth it. Violet was still gasping, her chest heaving as she fought to steady herself. "Take her first," I pleaded, yanking my hand free from his.

His gaze split frantically between me and Violet and the approaching knights. They marched closer. We didn't have long before they'd reach us.

"Go!" I yelled, moving closer to Cade who seemed to be gathering his bearings.

"We'll be fine." Cade nudged Violet towards him.

"I'll be right back," he promised, his midnight eyes locked onto mine. I nodded as he placed a hand on Violet's back right before they apparated.

I turned back to the forest, my hand instinctively reaching for the dagger on my thigh. Cade stood beside me, sword at the ready, and his tattoo glowed, only faintly.

"Did you piss someone off back there?" he rasped.

"I—"

Cade pushed me behind him and launched himself at the onslaught. His martem may have been dampened but his sheer strength was a sight to behold. Finding the gaps in their armor, he sliced through knight after knight, his sword finding one enemy while his dagger struck the next.

Something whizzed by me. A sharp pain sliced across my arm. Glancing down, I saw the tear in my sleeve, the gash on my skin, and I watched as my blood fell in the dark sand at my feet. I looked back up.

Cade was already before the knight with the arrows. One swift motion severed the golden-helmeted head from his body.

Corpses of golden knights littered the earth. Cade—who was about thirty feet away from me last time I checked—was suddenly in front of me, grabbing my arm. His breath came in ragged gasps, whether from utilizing his martem or from killing, I couldn't tell.

He twisted my arm left and right to inspect the cut in the moonlight.

"It's fine," I said, even as blood continued to find its way to the sand. Maybe it wasn't fine but it wouldn't kill me. I pressed a hand over the wound, hoping to stop the bleeding, but my mask betrayed as I cringed under the pressure.

"It's fine, Cade," I repeated.

His typically emotionless eyes now held a glimmer of confusion as he stared into mine. "You fed from him?" he whispered, as if we were the only people around.

I froze. *How—?* Before I could ask, Drayzen grabbed me and within seconds, we were off the island.

36

THE SHIP WAS ALREADY MOVING AS WE
shifted onto the deck. Drayzen led us to the captain's quarters.
Maps spread across tables and scattered seating gave the whole
place a chaotic feel. At the edge of the room, overlooking a
large window, stood a sizeable wooden desk. Soft light from
various sconces and candles lit the room.

Violet was collapsed on a black couch across from the
window. Cade pulled up a similar chair beside her, falling into
the cushion. My attention shot to Drayzen. He seemed
unaffected as he grabbed three glasses from a sideboard loaded
with an assortment of decanters.

A drink did sound needed but liquor was not what he
poured. He brought his wrist to his mouth, baring his fangs as

he bit into his skin. The scent of him, that mix of lavender and pine, filled the room and, oddly, brought relief to my ever-anxious mind. His blood filled the glasses, the last one containing a lesser amount.

He handed the nearly full glasses to Violet and Cade—Violet desperately chugging hers before Cade even touched his. Cade took small sips, his curious eyes burning through me. But Drayzen stepped between us.

"Sit." He gestured to the couch where Violet had made space.

I obeyed, wincing slightly as she pulled my arm closer. She ran her finger over the gash, studying the blood with a confusion similar to Cade's. But she didn't question me about it. Instead, she offered a genuine smile—not one of her wide ones but one that washed relief over my nerves.

She turned to Drayzen and took the glass from his hand. "For you," she said softly.

"I'm fine, really," I reassured them. Memories flooded of how I had reacted the last time I'd had his blood. And that was the last thing I wanted in front of them.

My head snapped to Drayzen but he only nodded, taking a seat across from us. "Drink," he insisted.

You'll be okay. His voice echoed through my mind as his eyes met mine. His voice—it was a reminder of all the times I'd listened to him, before I even knew what was happening.

So, I did what I always had and trusted it. I took the glass from Violet, its clear surface swirling with only a few drops of the blood. Raising it to my lips, I inhaled before taking a sip.

My eyes never strayed from Drayzen's as I drank. Familiar raindrops danced on my tongue and the cool liquid glided down my throat. Warmth swept through my body, quickly erasing any lingering pain in my arm. Within seconds, the wound had disappeared completely.

The room faded into darkness until it was just the two of us. Drayzen leaned in, studying me. His thumb brushed my bottom lip, wiping that last drop of blood. His martem weaved around me, the now familiar hum soothing my racing heart. His gaze dipped lower, tracing the path of my healed wound before lingering on me.

"Good," he whispered.

Cade cleared his throat. I slammed back to reality, back to the candlelit quarters, and shifted free from Drayzen's gentle grasp. He settled back in his seat, clearing his throat. I bit my cheek to hide my grin.

Focus, Mar. I placed the glass on the table beside me, pushing it as far as it could go.

Drayzen's cool demeanor painted his face as he lowered his head, meeting my eyes through a raised brow. "So, what went wrong?"

I sat up at the question. "How do you know something went wrong?"

Drayzen stood and walked to the liquor, pouring himself a glass.

"I was very clear." But I still replayed the scene in my mind, wondering if I could have made a mistake.

I could feel Drayzen's snarky remark brewing but he just shrugged and took a sip of his whiskey. "What?" he purred.

"Nothing you wanted to add?" I bit back.

He lifted a hand.

"Show us," Cade chimed in. "Show us what happened."

"Oh, yes!" Violet jumped, her wide smile growing.

"How?" I was still struggling to comprehend how their power worked.

"Just take our hands, we'll do the rest," Cade answered. "Just as we practiced."

I nodded. I leaned in as Cade extended his hand, placing my own in his grasp. Violet's smile faded as she took my other hand. I glanced at Drayzen leaning back in his chair, leg crossed.

"Go ahead," he said, nodding in my direction, as if I needed his approval. *Maybe a small part of me did.*

I closed my eyes and conjured the memory, transporting us all to the open expanse of woods we'd just fled from. The memory felt so real. I could feel their martem swirling around my mind, each detail meticulously examined. They pulled apart every piece of the scene, replaying certain parts.

I opened my eyes when I felt their power withdraw and Cade pulled his hand away. I turned to Violet, who still held mine. Her turquoise irises glowed as she whispered, "Thank you, for allowing me in."

My heart skipped at the sincerity. I nodded, smiling as I settled back into my place on the couch.

We were silent for a long moment.

"Did you lose it?" Violet asked. "Your soul?"

You need to reunite with your soul.

I huffed a defeated breath and shrugged. "Apparently."

"So, now what?" Cade asked, defeat heavy in his voice.

"Please don't tell me we actually have to go there," Violet interjected, making a gagging noise.

I didn't have to ask where she meant. *There.* I shivered. The place I once called home. The place where my fate was stripped from me. The place where my enemy lurked behind its walls. *Rosetia.*

Cade cursed, standing and making his way to the liquor. He poured himself a generous tumbler of whiskey and tossed it back before refilling it and returning to his seat.

Violet groaned as she sank further into the couch, crossing her arms. "Great."

I turned to Drayzen who watched me with his usual impassive expression, no emotion evident in the face of the terrible news.

"Her power is definitely in that crown," Violet said to Drayzen, shaking her head. "Can't you just shift in and grab it?"

I knew it couldn't be that easy. My eyes met his piercing gaze as he rested his chin in his hand.

"You got in before," I said. "How did you do it?"

Cade shot a daring look at Drayzen but he seemed unbothered. "They weren't expecting me." He smirked.

"Sovanni said they were in the process of putting new wards up, anyway. No one can get in that place without their approval." Cade cursed as he sat back in the chair, taking a long sip from his glass.

"Unless we take down the ward." Violet's tone was surprisingly chipper. "Wherever it is."

"Yeah, and how are we supposed to do that? Just stroll in and ask them nicely?" Cade shot back.

Cade was right, *we* couldn't just walk in. But they'd allow one person in, to trap in their twisted games.

I straightened. "I—"

"No." Drayzen stiffened.

I ignored how he knew what I'd been about to say. "I can do it." And in that moment, I knew it was true. I *could* do it. I would, to get my power back.

"No."

"They have no idea what happened to me. All they know is that you were there and then I vanished."

"No." Drayzen set his glass down with a loud clang.

"Yes," I seethed. "You don't know what I'm–"

"I know *exactly* what you're capable of, what you've been through," he snarled. "But this–" he shook his head.

I shivered, pushing the threatening realization aside. I needed to do this. "I'll tell him you held me captive, that I was your prisoner and I managed to escape. I can *do* this. If I can just get in that room—"

"No," Drayzen growled.

"Drayz," Cade said, straightening in his seat. "She has a point."

"There are other ways." His voice dipped to a deadly low. "We have an army, do we not?"

"Autyr would never allow it," Cade snapped. "Let alone the countless lives—"

"No one is dying for me," I hissed.

The room chilled and shadows danced around Drayzen's fingertips as he tightened his grip on the armrests. His eyes locked onto Cade's, a warning.

"I can do it." I wouldn't let him decide this for me. "It's not like they can kill me."

"There are fates worse than death," he shot back, too quickly.

The silence deepened, the temperature turning frigid.

The smokey tendrils from Drayzen's fingers pulled back and the room warmed. He took a breath, then a sip. "It's not up for discussion," he declared as a flicker of pain wove through his irises.

"I'm going," I said.

Drayzen shot to his feet, his movement almost too quick for me to see. "You are *not.*"

"Gods." Cade sighed, finishing his drink.

I straightened to my full height. "I want to help, I *can* help. This is the best plan and you know it."

"What will you say when he questions why you ran, when you saw the truth?" Drayzen's voice dropped.

"I'll tell him I was scared. But once I saw what you were capable of, I did everything I could to escape."

A small breath puffed from his lips and he ran his tongue over his fang. I gulped down that incessant feeling in my stomach and peered up at him through lowered lashes.

"And what will you say when he catches you in your lies? When he finds you snooping around or when he realizes he's the one being played? What will you do when he tries to touch—?"

"He won't," I seethed. I did not want him to finish that sentence, did not want that thought to poison my courage. "He won't."

In an instant, Drayzen was before me. Shadows swirled around us as he towered over me, a hint of silver dancing in his eyes. We stared each other down, both stubbornly waiting for the other to break.

But I would not break, I would not back down.

"I have a friend who may be able to help find out where the ward is. If she can help me—"

"A friend?" Drayzen sneered.

I was exaggerating, remembering the servant who helped me bathe and gave me fresh air when I so desperately needed it. I thought she may have even left that door open for me. Would she help me again?

"Yes." I stood tall.

"And who is this friend you think will risk their life for you?"

"Her name is Analise."

Drayzen's head tilted, contemplating my crazy request. Violet leaned forward in her seat.

"Fine," he growled. His brows furrowed. "You have three days."

"Two weeks. Give me two weeks. It'll be too suspicious if I go back and immediately start asking questions."

Our breaths mingled as he watched me. "Is this really what you want?"

No. Of course it wasn't what I wanted. I didn't want to go back there, didn't want to pretend that Drayzen was this devil who captured me, didn't want to pretend that I missed Azral. I didn't want to pretend that I was helpless, that I needed his protection. But it was the best option, the only option to keep everyone else safe.

"It's what I have to do."

Drayzen's eyes narrowed. "One week."

I stuck out my hand. Drayzen glanced at it, like it was some kind of trick, but then his fingers wrapped around mine.

"One week." I nodded.

37

I MADE MY WAY BACK TO MY TINY ROOM ON
the ship. The door shut behind me and I leaned against it,
releasing a breath. I dragged my tired feet towards the
bathroom. Placing one hand on the solid sink, I used the
other to pull the towel covering the mirror. The bags under
my eyes were prominent. They sagged with a sadness I was
afraid would never be tamed.

I pulled my hair from the braid and let the waves fall over
me. Like my own personal blanket, I wrapped my face in the
strands and stared into my reflection. The slit on my sleeve
peeked through the curtain of hair. I pulled it down,
examining the once-wounded skin, now perfectly healed.

The taste of blood clung to my lips, seeping through me and stirring too many emotions to untangle. My gaze drifted to the dimly lit room, landing on the empty bed. A thought slipped in before I could stop it—where was Drayzen staying tonight?

But I couldn't let my mind linger there. I needed to reclaim a sense of control, to feel like I wasn't being swept away by everything unraveling around me. That meant going back. It meant facing him again.

Azral.

I needed to look him in the eye, to peel back every lie he had told me. I needed the truth.

I needed closure.

I fell into bed, the wooden boards creaking. I rolled over, tangled in my own hair, as I reached for the small paper on the side table. It was sitting on a stack of books, all crinkled with ripped edges like someone had written on it one too many times.

A distraction for you, I hope, the note read.

Warmth bloomed. I could only assume who the books were from—though I didn't know how she'd delivered them.

Sifting through the tomes, I saw a book on the history of Menasai, The Ever. There was one about the Fae—my people—and the final was titled *The Sapphire Shadow*. Judging from the back matter, it was a sultry love story. Now, *that* was definitely more my speed.

I was interested to learn about the history of this world, of the Denazin and the Fae, but I needed a distraction. Really, I just wanted to read a love story.

I plopped back onto the bed, tossing the two history books aside for later, and dug in. I was so fascinated, I didn't know how much time had passed when a knock on my door pulled me back. It creaked open and, to my surprise, Violet stepped in.

"Hi," I said, placing the book on the bed and sitting up.

She stayed in the doorway.

"You can come in." I smiled.

She was across the room in a second. My book flew into the air as she jumped on the bed in front of me. "Oh, good. I mean, thank you. Sorry, I couldn't sleep." Her signature smile glowed in the candlelight.

"It's okay, I couldn't either."

"*Sapphire Shadow*, that will definitely keep you up." She laughed, winking.

My cheeks flushed because I knew exactly what she meant.

"Did you not care for the history books?" She nodded to the others.

"No, I just—"

"I'd be more than happy to tell you," she interrupted, a bit eager. "Unless you wanted to get some sleep." She looked down to the bed and my mouth dropped open.

A silver tray appeared out of thin air, along with a teapot, two cups, and a bowl of tiny chocolates a moment later. I examined the candy, then looked at her, wide-eyed, but she only laughed.

No, I definitely wouldn't be able to sleep, now.

She filled a cup and handed it my way. "How?"

I popped a candy into my mouth and sweet chocolate exploded over my tastebuds with a salty caramel aftertaste. *Chocolate covered raisins.* I almost asked how she knew they were my favorite but decided against it.

She poured herself a glass as I shoveled the treat into my mouth and she started her story. "Denazins' abilities range greatly. Most of us just have strength, longer life span, and the ability to compel but some of us have a little extra." She smirked, like those things weren't already enough. "Cade has strength that only Drayz can rival, pulling martem from gods-only-know-where." *Could it be that tattoo that glowed on his hand?*

"My power," she continued. "I honestly have no idea where it comes from. I've never met another Denazin with this ability. Conjuration, that's what I call it. I just visualize something I've held before and poof, there it is."

I couldn't help but ask, "And Drayzen?"

"Drayzen is—" She paused. "He's just different," she said blankly.

It didn't surprise me though, that someone so close to him also didn't understand him. My eyes remained locked on the items that she'd conjured.

"I'm still honing my skills, though. Some of us excel in different areas, like Drayzen and Cade. They've both been incredible shifters from a young age. I'm still a work in progress."

"How old are you?" The question slipped out before I could stop myself but she didn't seem to mind.

"I'm two-hundred and thirty-four."

I hesitated. "And Cade?"

She sipped her tea. "Cade and Drayzen are only a year apart, Cade being older.

That made Cade eight-hundred and thirty-three. The number was so large I couldn't even fathom living that long.

Although, being Fae, I supposed I would make it somewhat close.

"Age loses its significance after a while." She shrugged.

"And you're all siblings?"

"By choice, yes." Her smile slowly faded. "Drayzen and Cade crossed paths when they were about sixteen. Cade," she paused, dropping her head, "he was orphaned. He and Drayzen met when they joined the King's Guard."

My chest tightened with familiarity, losing parents...

Violet conjured some bread, the golden loaf appearing on the tray. She stuffed her face and continued, "They've been inseparable ever since, climbing the ranks of the Guard together. They were trouble-makers though." Some bread fell from her mouth. "When they were younger, Drayz got caught using compulsion for money; Cade was the lookout. But Drayzen's always been stronger than anyone else in that field, in most fields, honestly."

It felt almost invasive, learning about their past from someone else, especially Drayzen's. "How did you meet them?" I asked, changing the topic.

She took another sip of tea and let out a breath. "Ages ago, Autyr decided to whip up the first Denazin recipe. It all started with a beautiful Human woman ready to meet her death. But Autyr stopped that. He fed her some of his blood and then he killed her."

"Oh—"

"Don't worry, she woke up. It's all part of the recipe. She became the first Denazin. The first Turned"

"Turned?"

She nodded. "I'm not sure if Autyr had a crystal-clear idea of what he was doing but gods can be a bit impulsive, you know, creating stuff on a whim." She nudged me, as I was a member of that special club.

"Fast forward a bit, this new Turned Denazin went a bit mad and started turning Humans. The ones that were turned eventually had kids. So, now we have the Turned and the Born. And so, Menasai was made."

"The Ever," I muttered under my breath.

"Correct."

"I thought Humans were off-limits?" Drayzen's words floated through my mind.

"They are now but back then, it wasn't like that. Autyr realized Denazin were a bit greedy for Human goodies—blood and lives and whatnot. So, Nyrah had to step in. She put her foot down on the Denazin hopping into the Human realm."

The Goddess of Life.

"But that didn't solve everything. Some Denazin still managed to sneak over, feeding on Humans and turning them before anyone could intervene. And the ones who were Turned? Well, they got a one-way ticket to Menasai. Then, they were left to navigate their new immortality."

"I can't even imagine—" I frowned. Being torn away from everything you knew? At least I didn't have any memories left from when it happened to me.

"So, the Turned and the Born, they aren't exactly friends. Most Borns have this superiority complex. To this day, the two fight. Starting wars, killing whomever they want. It never ends." She sighed.

It was even crueler now, to be thrown into a new world as an underdog.

"That's how I crossed paths with Drayzen and Cade."

"They were Turned?"

"I was."

Her words hit me. She had been Human?

"I was sixteen when…" She stopped, taking a breath. "Drayzen and Cade took me in, made me part of their family. I owe them more than I can ever repay."

Gods, we were all more alike than I ever could have ever imagined.

"But the dead need to stay dead. There was too much of an imbalance in the world and Nyrah—she had enough. A law was set in place, no more Turned. I was the last one."

The last of her kind.

"Learning to control my power's still a work in progress, even after all this time. Shifting doesn't come naturally to all Denazin. It's mainly the Borns who get that perk. But I'm practicing," she said, brushing over her pain.

"Did it hurt?" I asked quietly. *Dying, turning.*

Violet sat there for a moment and I'd never heard her so quiet. It brought an eerie stillness to the room.

"There's a reason why it's forbidden."

"I'm sorry," I breathed.

It was all I could give her, all I could say. Her past and Cade's, from being orphaned to forcibly uprooted from a life, we shared an understanding, an invisible string between us all.

"No need for apologies, Amara."

After a weighted silence, I couldn't help but ask, "Do you ever…miss being Human?"

There was a pause, like maybe no one had asked her before. Her expression was unreadable. "No," she finally said, her smile returning. "If I'd stayed Human, I wouldn't have met them, or you."

I mirrored her grin. "Mar. Please, call me Mar."

"Mar." She bit her cheek.

"So, Fae, were they created before Denazin?" I asked.

She leaned back. "Oh no, Denazin came first. But after Nyrah went through the hassle of keeping them out of the human realm, she had to let Saigus and Melenyz whip up their Fae to even the score. It was a friendly warning to Autyr to keep Denazin in check."

"I never learned much about her." *The Goddess of Life.*

"She's quite the enigma. I don't even know that much. But I *do* know that without her, the world would be a mess of war. She keeps the other gods in their places, only allowing them to interfere so much. Without her, without life, none of us would be here."

Nyrah, queen of all gods.

"Saigus made his Fae first, jumping at the opportunity to rule over more than just Humans. Originally, Melenyz wanted no part of it but she couldn't stand Saigus and figured he'd get drunk on power, so she cooked up her own batch."

"Them I know," I said, remembering the stories of the lovers, their eternal dance across the skies. "The sun forever chasing the moon, cursed to only spend one day a year together."

Violet laughed, shaking her head and placing her hand on her chest. "Oh, it's quite the opposite. If anything, Melenyz is always running from him."

They hadn't exactly been harmonious with each other when I met them.

She grew quiet, which was odd for her. She tapped her finger against the porcelain and looked up to me through her thick lashes.

"What is it?"

"Do *you* miss it...believing you were Human?"

Her question seemed impossible. I didn't miss the town or the people. I didn't miss the way I was stared at like an outsider. But I did miss the silence of the snowy forest. I oddly missed how the cold night air swept through the cracks of the broken cabin windows. I missed when Isidore would bring home a bouquet of flowers for Lettie, how her eyes lit up when he would walk through the front door. I missed my parents; I missed the way they loved me.

But that was all gone now.

"No, I don't miss it."

Violet paused. "Do you miss who you were before all of...this?"

That answer was simpler. "No."

"Why?"

I couldn't help the grim smirk that tugged on my lips. "She was easier to fool."

38

WE MADE IT BACK TO AUTYR'S ISLAND AND JUST the thought of being on Death's doorstep still sent shivers down my spine.

Thysa and Sovanni arrived on Mylom simultaneously. I ran over to the dragon, her eyes lowered on me. She playfully nudged me and I fell back in the field of spider flowers. She dropped down next to me, her sheer size making the earth rumble. She nudged me again and I was like a child, rolling around in the grass, a laugh ripping from my lips.

But with my head tilted back, I noticed Drayzen, his expression serious, and I leaped to my feet. With one step, Mylom was already next to him. Her head bumped him and—though he tried not to move—he stumbled. A small laugh bubbled from me. Mylom took to the sky, a gust of fiery wind in her wake. I moved back to the group and Sovanni searched our, now, uninjured bodies.

"Thank the gods," she muttered.

"Literally." Violet chuckled.

Inside, I kept my eye on Drayzen as he disappeared into the living room, returning with the entire bottle of whiskey. He said nothing as he took a long swig, slumping into his seat at the head of the dining table.

"So, how did it go?" Sovanni asked eagerly.

I didn't answer, though; no one did as we waited for Drayzen. He lifted the bottle, raising an eyebrow in invitation. Cade made for the table first. Drayzen passed the whiskey along. When it seemed like he wasn't going to bite anyone's head off, the rest of us took our seats, the bottle making its rounds.

"It was an utter failure," Violet huffed. "Were you able to get anyone out of Raxos?"

Vani and Thysa exchanged a glance; defeat painted both their faces. "It was an utter failure," they said in unison.

"Wonderful." Drayzen growled next to me, his fingers tapping on the armrest.

Thysa took a sip and passed the bottle to him. At least they could both relate in their irritation.

"They're holding everyone in Raxos for questioning," she said through gritted teeth. "Even the children. They think they know something, know where *you* are."

She looked at me and I clenched my fists under the table. It was me they wanted and everyone was suffering because of it. Her words were only fuel to my desperation. I *had* to go back, had to do something to help.

To help my people.

"Any news on the wards?" Cade asked, his voice low.

Vani shook her head. "No, but there's still time to—"

"There's not enough time," I interrupted.

"We can go back, look again."

"You won't be going back." My voice dipped lower than Cade's. My fingers tingled with the icy flame of what little martem I embodied. "I will."

"What?" Sovanni pressed against the table, straightening. "Are you crazy?"

"Maybe," I said in my mind. But by the look on everyone's faces, that one may have slipped.

"I need to get the crown," I said. "That's where they're keeping my power."

"Erixx's crown?" Thysa frowned.

Sovanni gasped, shaking her head. "Gods, I should have known. I could have—"

"This isn't your fault," I urged. "You did everything you could."

"I should have known," she whispered again, lowering her head. "Amara, I'm sor—"

"Don't." I raised my hand. "You don't need to apologize."

"I do." She pushed past her teary eyes. "Azral"—she shook her head—"he's been off for a long time."

"That's one way to put it." Drayzen muttered, taking a swig.

"When he left for Zandar, I thought he was just being stubborn. He was always fighting with Erixx about something. But then, when he came back and he told me he'd fallen in love, I saw a different side of him, someone I hadn't seen for a long time." She paused, mourning her brother.

"Then he told me your name—" Disbelief colored her eyes. "Rosetia thought you died along with your parents. Nobody knew they sent you to—" She wiped a tear from her cheek. "I couldn't believe it, didn't want to believe my brother could do something so cruel, so twisted. But when I dove into your mind and I saw your dreams, your parents." She paused. "He told me his secret then but he threatened Thysa. I couldn't risk it."

That day flashed in my mind, when Erixx screamed at Azral, dragged him out of the room. That was the secret he'd shared with her.

My truth.

"I'm going to make this right." I swore to her, to everyone.

"So, what's your plan? Just walk right up to the castle doors?" Thysa laughed. "And say what, you were a prisoner?"

The Denazin and I exchanged a look. That *was* the plan. Although, it did sound a little silly coming from someone else.

"I can do this," I reassured them, reassured myself. All I needed to do was find out how to bring down the wards.

I turned to Drayzen, already aware of his scrutiny. He shook his head and let out a sigh. "You don't even look like a prisoner."

Thysa laughed again. "Azral may be a fool but he considers Drayzen to be the devil himself. If you show up without a scratch, he won't believe for a second that you were held against your will."

There was that word again. *Devil.* I shared a look with Drayzen, one only we understood.

I knew that simply walking into the castle unharmed wouldn't be convincing. We had to make it look like I had been a captive of something truly evil. And unfortunately, I knew what had to happen next. Drayzen's eyes held me captive as swirls of silver danced in his midnight irises but there was a softening to them.

His fingers incessantly tapped on the table. "One week," he reminded me. "Don't go snooping around for the crown. Find this friend, see if she has any answers about the wards."

"And what happens after one week?" Thysa questioned.

It was a valid question; one I hadn't yet posed and I didn't want to think about. There was a chance I wouldn't be coming back.

That will never happen, Drayzen's voice echoed in my mind. That faint hum caressed my cheek as I looked to him. I nodded.

Violet stood from the table and Cade followed.

"When will you go?" Vani asked.

I looked at her and Thysa. "You said they're holding children for questioning?"

They both nodded.

"Now." My gaze shifted back to Drayzen. "I'm willing to do whatever needs to be done."

Violet's cool hand brushed loose hair off my neck. Her fingers traced my skin. "I'm sorry," she whispered behind me.

A searing ache struck the back of my head, Drayzen's pain-stricken eyes were the last thing I saw as I plunged into darkness.

39

THE DARKNESS SEEMED TO BE ONE OF THE only constants in my life. I stood in the now-comforting void, scanning my surroundings. My heart skipped a beat when I turned and saw Drayzen.

Shadows flowed around him with each delicate step he took towards me. I flinched but not because of him. I pressed my hand against the shooting ache coursing through my head. I squinted, struggling to focus as his body blurred in front of me.

Then, I was falling. But in a blink, he was beside me. His arm wrapped around me, holding me up.

"I'm sorry," he whispered. Pain rippled through his eyes and I moved my free hand to his forehead, pushing back the black hairs spilling over.

We stayed like that for what felt like forever. And gods, I never wanted it to end.

But sadly, it did. He lifted me back to my feet. His eyes never left mine, though, as he said, "Once you're back, I'll make sure you have no scars from this."

Meaning he would give me his blood. And that thought brought a faint smile to my lips. I didn't care if he saw it anymore, especially because the ache spreading through my body was too much to hide that one good feeling.

His thumb brushed my neck. I shivered but not from pain. No, his touch was electrifying, igniting something deep within me.

"Violet bit you but didn't take any blood. Just to make it look real." His thumb lingered and I watched his eyes dance around the area, inspecting the wound. "Sovanni is letting us search through her memories. If we find anything about the wards...Well, you'll know." He smirked but the light was missing from his eyes.

"And if I find anything?"

"You know where to find me."

And I did. I knew exactly where he would be. It's where he'd been this whole time.

I was never alone in this world, never alone when I'd cried myself to sleep in Zandar, never alone through all the cold nights I thought I might freeze to death.

I was never alone because he had always been right here with me.

My eyes welled but before I could thank him, he disappeared.

Wake up, Mar.

I squinted open to cream-colored walls illuminated by the setting sun. Blinking, I found that I was in my room—or rather, *his* room. Confusion lingered but there was no denying I was in the castle.

My castle.

I grunted and my body screamed as I sat up slowly. My vision was still blurred from the lingering pain in my head.

What had Violet done to me? I made a mental note to never get on her bad side.

I scanned the room; everything appeared the same from my stay—Azral's martem clearly at work considering the state of the place the night I left. The few days that passed since I'd been here felt like years, an eternity. My stomach turned as I thought about it, all the lies, the betrayal.

And now I was back. I brushed away the numbing thoughts.

Focus, Mar. I took a deep calming breath, just as Cade taught me. But as I inhaled, I jumped when the main door swung open.

Hastily grabbing the blanket, I pulled it up over my black leathers. My heart skipped as I looked at the male standing in the doorway. His chiseled features were glowing in the sun and his emerald eyes met mine. I caught a glimpse of the lifelessness from before but it dissipated, replaced by the illusion I'd once loved, the one I'd foolishly believed.

"You're awake," Azral stated, his tone dry and his emotions unreadable.

"What happened?" I asked. And that question might be the only honest thing to come out of my mouth for the foreseeable future because I really had no idea how I got here.

"He did a number on you." Azral's gaze narrowed as he surveyed me.

I reached for my neck, dried blood cracking away under my fingers. "Drayzen," I whispered, hiding my smile.

"Do you remember anything?" he asked.

I shook my head. Hopefully, I could just play dumb and get through this torture.

"Guards found you by the stables," he continued, retrieving a folded piece of paper from his pocket. I fought the urge to flinch at his every movement.

"With this note," mockingly, he read the words scrawled on the paper aloud, *"you can have your Human pet back. She tastes just as bad as you."*

Human. That very important word was written there as a reminder to me. Azral didn't know how much I truly knew and I needed to play that to my advantage.

His sharp gaze lingered on me from the doorway but he didn't approach.

I used my rising fear as courage, embracing it as I spoke. My voice cracked, real tears threatening to escape. "I'm sorry," I cried but not for him. "I'm sorry I left."

Azral had known he was the one I ran from and it was an admission I needed to make, an apology for willingly abandoning him, disobeying him. "I was confused. I was scared and I—"

"Why didn't you listen to me?" His voice was low. He stalked into the room, the door locking behind him.

My heart pounded as he towered at the edge of the bed. I attempted to slow its rapid rhythm, hoping he couldn't hear the unsettling beat. I slowed my breath and managed to quickly calm myself.

"I thought I could help," I replied, voice steadier than before. "But now I know. I'm not afraid."

He shifted. "Afraid of what?"

"I'm not afraid of you," I declared, though it was only partially true. Pushing to my knees, I met his gaze at eye level. "I'm not afraid of the secrets you keep to protect me." The next words pained what was left of my heart. "I was scared, yes. I was scared when I saw the castle, when I saw *you*. But I wasn't scared *of* you, I wasn't scared of who you were trying to hide from me. I was just scared of losing you." I held his hands gently in mine.

"Losing me?"

"Yes," I assured him. "I saw what the enemy was capable of, the toll this war has taken on you, your home. I was afraid I would lose you. And I've already lost so much." The lie flowed effortlessly from my tongue. "I ran to protect myself because I can't handle another heartbreak."

My final lie left a venomous taste on my tongue. "I love you, Azral."

He placed his hand on my cheek and I couldn't help but flinch at his touch. Thankfully, I had a persistent pain in my head to blame this time.

"Ow," I whispered.

"I'm sorry." His gaze fell to the bite mark on my neck.

He tilted my chin upward and I kept myself still. His eyes locked with mine. I stared into them, refusing to be tricked by the illusion. This facade was one I would never fall for again.

"Let's get you cleaned up," he said softly, pressing a kiss to my forehead.

I walked with him into the bathroom. The tub filled from nowhere. Steam billowed from its surface, caressing the room with its warmth. Martem was no longer a surprise to me but it was still impressive what one could do with it.

Something I was eager to start learning for myself.

"Thank you," I whispered, stopping him in the doorway.

"Let me help you, Amara. You're too hurt," he rasped, pushing past me and retrieving a wooden stool to place behind the tub.

Once again, I focused on controlling my breathing. Fear crept back in as I approached the bath, standing over the steam and the fragrance of the lavender soap. I soaked in the scent of it, Drayzen's scent. A faint smile tugged at my lips.

I turned to Azral with my newfound courage. "It's not you, it's just—I just need some time, that's all."

Azral's eyes searched mine and after a moment he nodded. "Of course. I'll wait right out here."

I watched as he moved for the chaise. Once he was out of sight, I shed my clothes and climbed into the tub one aching limb at a time. I hissed as the warm water stung the wound on my neck.

"Are you okay?" Azral called urgently from the room.

"Yes." I seethed. "The bite, it just hurt that's all," I called, trying to play off the pain.

"I'll have a healer look over you once you're done."

Images of the healer he killed flashed through my mind— the blood that spilled around her lifeless body.

Drip. Drip. Drip.

Another numbing image assaulted my mind. "I don't think I want one," I yelled back a little too harsh. No healers, no bloody reminders.

Drayzen would heal me in one week, maybe less if I was successful. I could handle a little pain until then.

I sighed softly, leaning forwards. I scrubbed my body but the more I cleaned, the dirtier I felt. I didn't over scrub this time though, just accepted the feeling.

After I was as clean as I could get, I wrapped myself in a towel. But I'd only put one foot on the cool title when the other slipped in the water.

Before I could fall, Azral was next to me, his arm wrapped around me. I panicked thinking of any excuse to get away from his grasp.

"Maybe I will see that healer," I said, moving away from him as I grabbed my head with my free hand.

"There's something I want to show you first but we can go right after."

I offered a soft smile. "I'll get changed then." I left the bathroom, seeking refuge in the huge closet.

This was going to be harder than I thought.

40

I OPTED FOR A THIN RED GOWN. GOLD METAL detailing hung over my bare arms, intertwining with the embedded detail around my bodice. The fabric billowed from my waist. If I was going to play the dutiful princess, I may as well look the part.

I turned to the mirror. The dress imitated the color in my eyes as I leaned in, pushing some hair behind my ear. Two tiny holes painted the side of my neck. My fingers grazed over the indents.

"Ready?" Azral called. I nodded and we headed for the door.

I couldn't help but gasp at the state of the corridors. The once-bright cream marble tiles and tall pillars now were in ruins. The walls had turned a shade of gray with chunks of stone missing from them. The floor was scattered with dirt, shattered tile, and streaks of dried blood. Moss grew between the cracks, indicating just how long it had been in this state.

"I kept the illusion in your room, to make you feel more at ease," he explained, noticing my shock.

"Of course," I replied, nodding, still taking in everything around me. "Is it safe here?" I asked hopefully not sounding too disgusted. But I was generally curious, why stay in these ruins?

"It is. It may not look fortified but giving up the castle would be like giving up the battle. Giving up our home." *My home.* "The wards protecting this place are stronger than any we've ever had. After the last breach, we won't risk anything."

My eyes shot to his. "Wards?" I questioned, forcing my voice to stay even despite the need for answers. But he only nodded.

He guided me through the dimly lit halls where guards stood every few feet. They lined the walls, watchful and vigilant. *Not a good sign for me.* I followed Azral out a small door behind the castle. The full moon was high as we walked to the edge of the forest. The moonlight lit up...*gods.*

A massive field of black dahlia flowers cascaded over the grounds, bathing the hillside in deep maroon petals.

"Az," I breathed. I leaned down, my body throbbing as I picked up a velvety flower. I twirled it in my fingers. I knew this was his martem and as much as I hated it, it was beautiful.

"I grew these, for you." His words pulled me from my trance.

"This isn't an illusion?"

"No." His eyes met mine. Those eyes, filled with pain, remorse. I couldn't help the pang in my heart as he looked at me like that.

"I wanted them to be real. I was going to show you, before you…" He stumbled on his words, stopping himself.

Before I ran.

I dropped to my knees in the field of flowers, trembling and numb all at once. I couldn't hold back the rivulet of tears descending my cheeks. My mask slipped away as I felt my heart ripped out of me, left to wither in this very spot. Because it took me until now to realize I was in mourning, grieving the loss of the Azral I knew, the male I loved. He died the moment I learned the truth, the moment I saw what he did to both of my parents, what he did to me.

"I missed you, Amara." His mummy whispered beside me.

I screamed inside but no one heard. Screamed for the loss of our memories, our love, because for a short while, it *was* real—for me. I dropped my head, tears pooling on maroon petals, but they mocked me. They hid whether or not they were real—if any of this was.

His warm hand lifted me up. He looked like Azral, sounded like Azral, felt like Azral. He wiped a tear from my cheek, his thumb lingering on the spot.

No. I know the truth. I saw the truth.

I took a deep breath, sniffing the tears away and placing my hand on his chest.

Action.

"I missed you too, Az."

We sat there for a moment, both trying to decipher what was true and what wasn't.

"Let's get you to the healer."

The shattered doors had a haunting creak to them as guards opened them towards us, leading us into the throne room. What I saw now was completely different from what I remembered. The once-golden and red flowers painting the walls were gone, cream columns broken and crumbling. The air was heavy with the scent of blood. Fresh stains marked the broken stones leading to the steps of the dais.

My attention was drawn to two guards dragging a male figure by his arms out a side door. *Was he from Raxos?*

I quickly looked away, refusing to let the swelling anger consume me. I clenched my fists. I had a purpose here and I would not let my emotions jeopardize it.

Find a weakness in the wards—hopefully, before Drayzen—destroy the wards, take the crown. Then, get as far away as possible while we figured out where my missing soul was.

"Father," Azral said, his hands gently caressing my lower back. I swallowed, turning my attention to the throne. It was the only remaining piece of the once-magnificent room that maintained its pristine state. I had a feeling it wasn't part of Azral's illusion, though. Something told me they'd want me to see it in all its glory.

My throne.

So close, yet so far away.

My eyes lifted, meeting Erixx's piercing gaze. He bore into me but I was more interested in the gold circlet resting on his brow.

My crown.

The embedded rubies burned with deadly fire. My fingers tingled, pulling me towards it.

My power.

I folded my hands behind my back, restraining the silent pull.

"I am delighted to see that you have returned to us, alive," Erixx said. A sinister grin formed on his lips. Fury pulsated through me as Azral kneeled.

I had to kneel to him?

This was a test. The first of many, I presumed. I stood there, seemingly frozen in time, my gaze locked with his. I would not kneel, not for him—the false king.

But I had to do something.

"Ow." I reached for the sore spot on my head, my knees buckling in the process.

"She needs a healer." Azral's whole posture seemed to urge his father.

Guess it worked.

Erixx waved his hand and a female emerged from behind the dais, flanked by two guards.

My palms grew sweaty at the eerily familiar sight. But before I could panic, I caught sight of her black curls that cascaded over her rosy-colored gown. She smiled at me, her porcelain skin beaming in the moonlight. *Analise.*

A smile crept onto my lips as she knelt beside us. I relaxed as she placed her hands on my head and the sore spot on my neck.

"Losing as much blood as I assume you did, being with him," she said in a low tone, her voice calm yet firm as she placed her hand on mine, "you must be so tired."

Her words were a warning, a reminder: If they were to believe I was held captive by a demon, I would have lost a significant amount of blood.

I nodded and a soft white light flickered at the corner of my vision. The pain in my head subsided, gradually dissipating until it vanished completely. The bite on my neck was no longer sore and immediate relief washed over me.

"She will need rest," Analise stated, directing her attention to Azral.

"Thank you," I whispered to her. *For everything.*

She nodded and stood while the two guards escorted her out of the throne room. Azral helped me to my feet and I purposely let my balance falter to feign exhaustion.

"She needs rest, father," Azral repeated. His arm was heavy around my waist.

"Of course." Erixx's voice dripped with sarcasm, his gaze still locked on me. "Join me for breakfast tomorrow, Amara," he sneered, "to celebrate your *homecoming.*"

Truth laced his words, poison intertwined.

"I would be honored," I replied, my voice dipping perhaps a bit too much.

He let out a low chuckle that spread through the air like poison.

I rolled my eyes, changing into the silk nightgown laid out for me as Azral spoke quietly with the guard behind the now-locked door.

"You do need rest," he said as he entered the room, taking a seat on the bed beside me.

"I know," I replied, sliding beneath the silky sheets. I pulled the blankets over my bare legs.

He tucked under the sheets beside me. His body, once a source of comfort, now felt foreign. "Are you okay?" he asked, noticing my subtle shift away from him.

"Yeah, yes," I said. "I just..."

"Do you want to talk about it?" His tone almost convinced me of genuine concern.

I shook my head but then a thought occurred. "Will *he* be able to get to me here?" *Maybe I could get some more information about these wards.*

"No," Azral responded. Avoiding eye contact, he chuckled softly. "Next time he tries, and he *will,* I won't let him get away again."

"Again?" My brows furrowed.

"We've captured him before, held him here for years." He laughed bitterly, empty eyes flickering. "That's when I learned so much about him."

"How many years?" I asked, perhaps a bit too eagerly.

"Not long enough."

My mind flashed to Drayzen's body. The scars and burns that painted his torso. I didn't think it was possible to be angrier, more disgusted, than I already was but for this—Azral would pay the ultimate price.

"You let him go?" I seethed, even though that seemed highly improbable.

"One of the guards got too suspicious. Curiosity about whatever abomination we kept below." He shook his head. "We ran tests on him, draining his blood, giving him more, only to drain him all over. He just wouldn't die." He shrugged, like torture was something he enacted regularly.

"We drained him for a whole year once. The guards thought he wouldn't be able to move after so long. But they got too close and he tore them to shreds. He was gone before the bodies were cold."

I looked at Azral. His eyes were filled with rage. But not at what he did, no, he was mad because he lost.

My rage threatened everything I came for. I no longer cared about my power, my throne. I didn't care if they burned this place to the ground. My heart pounded out of my chest as I looked at the true devil: Azral.

The look on his face was the final nail in his coffin.

He would die for this.

Azral's face quickly faded to concern, probably hearing my pounding heart. "Hey, you're safe. You don't need to worry." He leaned closer to me.

I wasn't safe here. And neither was he.

I cleared my throat, simmering my rage. At least he thought I was scared and not angry.

"I should get some sleep." I sank further into the sheets. "Are you staying?" I asked, expecting the worst.

"Of course," he replied softly. He tucked himself closer to me. I froze as his arm fell over my waist. "I'll never leave your side again."

Great.

I didn't move as Azral slept beside me. I just patiently waited for his breath to steady. Gently, I shifted away from him and closed my eyes. I took long deep breaths, focusing on each one. I allowed myself to descend into the darkness of my mind, the sacred place where I felt completely safe.

"Cade would be proud," Drayzen purred.

I didn't need to look at him to know he was smirking but I couldn't help myself. I turned on my heels, watching each step he took towards me.

"Would he?" I raised a skeptical eyebrow. "I find that hard to believe, considering I was clearly unsuccessful in blocking *you* out."

"Is that what you were trying to do, little kitten?" He raised a brow in challenge, his midnight eyes sending a chill down my back. I bit my cheek.

But Drayzen was right; I had been thinking about him. He sank to the ground. His tunic was untied, revealing a small scar across his chest. I flinched at the thought of what Azral had done.

"I think I prefer you in my shirts rather than that." He gestured at my silk nightgown.

"For once, I agree with you." I sat in front of him, my knees awkwardly folding to the side.

"Well, since you're well-dressed, I assume you were able to convince him of your wanted return?"

"I was," I said. "He wasn't very fond of the note you left."

"Mmm, yes, such a bore." He rolled his eyes. "He doesn't know how to have any fun."

We sat there for a short moment and his smirk fell. "Are you okay?" His tone was serious, searching for any signs of pain in my eyes.

"I'm fine," I replied, looking away.

"Show me," he softly demanded.

And I knew what he meant. So, I closed my eyes, letting the events of the day unfold. My stomach twisted into knots when I was once again sitting in the field of dahlia flowers. I wished I could hide those moments from him. Just as he probably wished he could hide things from me. The last conversation with Azral replayed and Drayzen shifted beside me.

I opened my eyes and met the pain lingering behind his. My gaze fell to the scar he wasn't trying to hide.

"How long?" I whispered. He didn't need to ask what I meant.

"About three years." His voice carried a smoothness, an edge worn down after too much use.

The timeline unfolded in my head. He'd spent four years away from home, and the majority of that time he'd been in a cell—captive, mutilated, tested...drained.

And it was all because of me.

"Drayzen—" His name fell from my lips, each haunting syllable a strain on my heart.

"Don't." His voice was tired. "Don't," he repeated, this time with a heavy sigh.

"I never thanked you—" for all the nights he secretly spent with me.

But he interrupted again, "You don't need to thank me for anything."

How could I not? How could he not know what he did for me, what his silent presence meant?

I couldn't bear the silence anymore. "Why not just compel them to let you go?" The question seemed silly and I knew there must be a logical answer but I wanted to keep talking.

"My compulsion doesn't work on all Fae. I tried over the years, tested it on different guards. I think the stronger Fae, the ones with more martem, build a similar barrier in their mind to block out power affecting it."

Drayzen's fingers tapped agitatedly on his knee. A familiar hum wrapped around me and I reached out with it, placing my phantom hand on his restless nerves.

He looked up, shock etched across his features. I was a little shocked, too, at whatever this was. But I didn't care, I draped the humming sense over him and one of those rare smiles painted his face.

An unspoken force pulled me towards him through the darkness. I could feel his breath on my nose; the cool piney scent coursed through me. I almost leaned in but stopped as he spoke.

"You should rest."

A pang shot through my heart. I pulled away, cheeks flushing, and cleared my throat. He seemed unaffected by the moment and that only made my chest hurt even more. But he was right, sleep was something my body desperately craved.

"I can't," I admitted, knowing I wouldn't get any rest, not with Azral in the bed next to me.

"Sleep here," Drayzen offered.

"How?"

"Does it matter?" he countered, that smirk was back.

I bit my lip, a question burning in my throat. "Will you stay?"

My heart stopped because, in an instant, he was gone. *Gods, I am so stupid.* Embarrassment flooded me but before I could completely spiral, that lavender and pine scent wrapped around me. I laid back but not onto the dark ground. Instead, my head met toned muscle and I looked up.

Drayzen looked down at me, my head now resting in his lap. A hint of something twinkled in his eye. "I'll always stay with you."

I quickly looked away, that smirk and those strands of hair falling over his face threatened any sense of self-respect I had. My heart pounded; I couldn't even try to hide it. I needed some other distraction.

"How did you get out?" *How did you escape the castle?*

"Sovanni. She would visit me often, trying to learn whatever she could about me."

"That's how Azral knew so much?"

He nodded. "I didn't tell her anything useful, mostly stories I thought they would be more willing to believe."

Azral had said Drayzen was the first of his kind, which wasn't true because of the story Violet told me about the Denazin. But I wondered if some of the things he told them were true.

"So, your parents?"

He paused, searching my eyes before looking up. "They're alive."

My heart warmed. He had already been through so much and to know his parents were waiting for his return...I couldn't help but smile.

"Good," I whispered.

"When Azral went to Zandar, that's when she let me go."

"And that's why he was so mad when he saw you in Raxos?"

His nose twitched. "The prince doesn't like losing his toys."

I took a breath, attempting to quell the fear that grew with his words. "I don't know if I can last a whole week here, being near him—"

"I know." Drayzen stroked a hand over my hair. "Vi is still searching through whatever Sovanni might remember but she may have found something. Cade is investigating it as we speak."

Perfect. Hopefully, whatever he found would be what we needed to break the wards. Especially since Azral wouldn't stop trailing me like a puppy. I didn't think I'd be able to get to Analise without company and that only mattered if she even knew anything.

"And when they're down, you'll come for me?" I asked, quickly adding, "You, Violet, and Cade."

"As soon as they're down," he promised.

I nodded, a sense of relief washing over me. "I have to see him tomorrow—Erixx. He'll make me kneel."

"If we don't find something before then—"

"I know," I replied. If I didn't pass this test, death would be a mercy.

I turned over, nuzzling into Drayzen's leg. I was too tired and too scared to second guess the movement. His hand fell to my arm, tracing circles over my bare skin. Each stroke was like a lullaby, quietly singing me to sleep.

41

"WAKE UP, MAR." DRAYZEN'S SMOOTH VOICE CUT through the haze, cool and composed. I opened my eyes, greeted by darkness.

"Vi may have found something," he said, his tone carrying a glimmer of hope.

"Really?" My eyes shot open as I sat up.

"I have to go check, but Mar," he paused, extending a hand to me, "please, don't do anything stupid while I'm gone."

I knew what he meant. I needed to set aside my pride just this once.

"Go have your breakfast, play this final game." He lifted my chin, his eyes worried.

I nodded, the lump in my throat keeping me from saying anything. He pressed his thumb down and nodded, vanishing into the shadows.

My hands trembled in his absence. The darkness of my mind was vast, empty, and I realized now without Drayzen, this place wasn't as comforting as I once thought. I shivered at the thought of Azral, who was surely still lying next to me, the thought of Erixx, and the thought of what would happen if I didn't kneel. What would they do to me? What would they do to my people, the ones suffering in Raxos?

"Not now," I scolded myself, my mind threatening to drown me. "You will not fall apart. You will not let them see you crumble." I placed my hands on my head, as if cementing the mantra there.

I tamped down my fear, my mask falling in place as I opened my eyes.

The morning sun was blinding as I blinked fully awake. The light off the cream-colored walls was almost too bright. I felt the unwelcome weight of Azral's arm draped across me and fought the urge to push him away. Thankfully, he was still sleeping. *He was always a heavy sleeper.*

My head fell to the side and I spotted the window I once escaped from. The Fairies danced into view, their shimmering glitter leaving trails. Barely breathing, I slid off the bed towards the window, kneeling and pressing my hand against the warm glass. It glowed with the presence of martem—martem meant to keep the window shut. I pulled back at the unwelcome feeling. It was smart of Azral to assume I might try to escape again but it was unfortunate for me.

Sighing, I watched the Fairies and drakai as they continued their dance. At least they were happy.

"What are you doing?"

I jumped. Azral stood across the bed.

"I can see the flowers from here," I replied with a smile. It was a quick lie but a good one and I prayed he was too groggy to see the faint trail of glitter they left behind.

His eyebrow raised but thankfully, he asked nothing more about it. "Ready for breakfast?"

Nope. "Yes." I forced a smile. "I'm starving."

"You must be," he replied. "Let's get ready. He'll be waiting for us."

I opted for comfortable clothing, praying to the gods that whatever Violet found was the answer we needed as I slipped into the black pants and maroon tunic. The shade made my eyes stand out and I reveled at the feeling.

Azral led me down the hall littered with guards and as we entered the throne room, my attention sharpened. My gaze flitted around the room full of people. Their tattered clothes told me all I needed to know: These were the people from Raxos. But what were they all doing here?

A round table in the center of the crowd was set for three, adorned with an array of pastries and breakfast meats. Erixx was already sitting at the table with a smug look. The crown glistened, calling out to me again.

Stop, I silently urged it. And as if it could hear me, it did just that.

I quickly took my seat and filled my plate, feigning the starved captive. Azral bowed slightly to Erixx, the king shooting me a deadly glare.

"Oh, sorry," I muttered. "I'm starving." I ducked my head in Erixx's direction.

His smile was tainted with disdain. I ignored it, continuing to fill my plate. Maybe if I just kept eating, I wouldn't have to talk.

The two of them remained silent as I devoured the food, occasionally exchanging glances. But after what felt like hours and no time at all, my stomach was screaming at me to stop. I was honestly surprised they let me eat for so long. As soon as I set my fork down, the room filled with clattering metal. Guards, at least forty, filled the space between the people of Raxos.

That is definitely not good.

"So, Amara," Erixx said, pushing his own plate aside. "Are you feeling better?"

"Much." I smiled, biting my cheek.

The king's smile turned dangerous, challenging. "I'm delighted to hear that you've found such comfort in *my* home. I'm also glad to see that you've found so much comfort in my son, as well, that you returned to us."

I plastered a smile on my face, glancing at Azral. "Very much," I lied.

To my right, a small child tripped clashing with the metal armor of a guard. He quickly pulled his sword out and I almost jumped out of my seat—right before Erixx's hand flew into the air. I took a breath as the guard lowered his sword. The child crawled back into the whispering crowd. The people were all scared, faces streaked with dirt, blood and tears.

"Do you remember anything that happened during your absence?" Erixx asked, his voice oozing with skepticism.

"I don't remember much," I said, looking back at him. "All I know is that he was displeased with me, with my blood," I added, hoping that was compelling.

"Typical," Azral spat, crossing his arms in frustration. "I'm surprised he didn't tear you apart like—"

"Enough." Erixx interrupted. "Why should my son trust you? Why should *I* trust you?" he questioned. "How can I be sure your mind hasn't been poisoned by the devil's lies?"

I held back a laugh at the irony of his words. I took a deep breath and picked up the tea pot in front of me. I tarried, wasting away the minutes by slowly filling the porcelain. The lavender cooled my senses as I took a long sip.

I looked up and smiled. "He saved my life. He helped me find my truth, helped me see who I really am."

I looked at Erixx, then back to Azral, then to the teacup. My next words were chosen *very* carefully, knowing that I would not be the only one to hear them come my salvation.

So, I did not lie as I spoke. "I would never do anything to betray *him*."

"You would do anything for my son, yes?" Erixx's voice deepened as his brows furrowed.

"Anything." My mask slipped back on.

"My son is the future King of Rosetia, heir to the Scarlet Throne," he continued. "How can I give my blessing to a mere Human if you cannot even kneel before me, the reigning king?"

The guards around us drew their swords as the crowd shifted uneasily. He was going to make me do it.

I held Erixx's piercing gaze. A grin split his face as he rose. The scraping sound of the chair against the stone floor echoed in the room. He turned, slowly moving towards the throne. Azral stood, his napkin falling from his lap. He stooped to pick it up and, while they were both distracted, I snatched a knife from the table.

Erixx's feet echoed on the steps of the dais. A nervous cry slipped through those gathered. He turned, taking my crown off his head. He polished the rubies, *taunting* me.

The act was too deliberate.

He knows.

He shot me another wicked grin and straightened the crown back on his head.

"Kneel before your king." His deep voice echoed, not only in the room but at something deep inside of me.

I stood, my chair falling backwards. The guards began to close in. Azral advanced towards me. With every step he took, my heart *thumped* a corresponding beat. I clenched my fists as he came to stand behind me.

"Kneel before your king," Erixx roared, lit by fiery determination. Literal flames danced in his eyes. Orange whispered around his fingers and all the candles and sconces in the room burned brighter.

My heart pounded on but it wasn't because I was afraid. No, an uncontrollable rage boiled within me. I would not show an ounce of respect for the one who betrayed my parents.

I would not bow to my usurper.

Erixx's power grew, flames boiling from his hands.

My power responded to its lost counterpart as my fingers tingled with that icy flame. Because those were *my* flames. That was *my* crown. *My* throne.

And it was *my* people that gasped from the corners of the room as I took a single, defiant step forward, my voice cutting through the chaos like a dagger.

"I am Andrasteia Amara Raine, daughter of Akailo and Cyra Raine. Child of both the Sun and Moon; first of my kind."

My words dropped like a death sentence.

"I am the Scarlet Heir and I will bow to no one."

Before I could even process what I declared, my head was yanked back. Azral gripped my hair, dragging me across the tile and shoving me into the unforgiving wall. My forehead collided with stone, shaking my skull, and I blinked away stars.

But I would rather die than let this traitor have my power. I pulled the table knife from my sleeve, placing it against my throat.

"Stop!" Erixx roared.

I seethed as Azral ripped the knife away, a small sliver of blood trickling down my skin. His hand wrapped around my neck, pushing me back against the wall. I clawed at his arm but his grip only tightened as my feet lifted off the ground.

"Stupid little girl," he cursed. I kept clawing, tearing at his skin as he squeezed the breath from me. His grip tightened and he lifted me higher, higher, higher.

My vision blurred as life was choked from me. *Maybe I will get to meet my parents.*

"Don't kill her!" Erixx bellowed from the dais.

Azral's eyes were wholly black now, reveling in the life he was slowly draining from me. His grip tightened even more. I couldn't see past the throbbing in my head and my arms gave out, dropping to my side.

"Stop!" Erixx screamed. "You cannot kill her!"

His grip finally loosened. Stone scraped against my back as he lowered me to eye level. I gasped at the harsh breaths aching in my lungs.

He leaned closer to me, his breath warm in my ear as he whispered, "Look around you."

I obeyed through watery eyes. Screams ripped through the crowd and the guards pushed them back as some tried to find a way out.

"All of this—the people, the castle, the throne. How could you think you'd ever be worthy of so much?"

He pulled back, his nose grazing my cheek. I flinched away.

His free hand wiped a fallen tear. "Who could ever love someone as pathetic as you."

I looked back at him, that golden hint of evil flicked in his eyes, and I knew Drayzen had been right: Death would surely be better than this.

"Not even a god can save you now."

Before I could accept my fate, a voice echoed in my mind. *They're down.*

I choked out a laugh as a familiar hum encircled me. My voice dropped to a deadly chill, matching the now freezing temperature of the room, and I narrowed my eyes on him.

"You're right. No god can save me."

Azral tilted his head. But before he could question it, shadows gathered around his hand on my throat. "What the—?"

The guards surrounding the crowd were ensnared by darkness. Cade darted through the people, shifting in and out of the shadows. The sound of his sword slicing through the air was the only indication of his movements. Each guard's head rolled off simultaneously, their bodies dropping to the ground like dominos. People ran from the room, their screams echoing down the hallway with Cade's sword.

More guards surrounded Erixx as he drew his own sword and stood. They formed a small circle around him but not small enough. Behind him, Violet's long black braids materialized as she snatched the crown from his head.

"I'll take that," she winked. A guard sliced through air as she apparated.

Erixx released a furious roar as he tried to push through his guard. "Kill her!" he growled. "Kill her now!"

But Azral didn't listen. I landed on hard ground as tendrils of shadow tightened around his arm. He reached for them with his free hand but they were beyond his control. They swarmed around him and he took a step back, clawing at his own chest.

"What is this!?" he bellowed, fear evident in his voice.

I watched as Drayzen appeared behind Azral, leaning in. "You're going to regret that."

Azral whirled but Drayzen was already gone. He spun again, growling as he looked down at us. Drayzen's arm encircled me and we shifted out of the castle.

42

LUNHAYVEN'S ICY WIND STUNG MY FACE, burning the fresh cut on my neck as the shadows around us dissipated to a snowy field. Drayzen's thumb brushed against the wound, his hand falling to the back of my neck. He lingered like I might just evaporate if he let go.

"Hey." I struggled to find my voice after almost being choked to death but I managed to rasp, "I'm okay." The tremor in my words betrayed me. I placed my hand over his wrist and stared into his eyes, the silver tendrils in them swirled in a frenzied rage.

Drayzen jerked his head back. Violet emerged from the clouded shadows, Cade at her heels. The snow-kissed field was their stage as she carried the crown, its rubies a fiery dance of crimson. A warm smile graced her lips. "I believe this belongs to you."

The world stilled around us and the glow of the crown intensified the closer she came.

My crown called for me, my power fighting to break free.

How could you think you'd ever be worthy of so much? Azral's taunt repeated in my mind. It was a question I'd thought of one too many times. Was I worthy of this, worthy of family, of love?

I looked up at Drayzen, trying to quell the flutter he caused in me. My eyes fell to a beaming Violet and then over to a concerned Cade. The three of them stood before me, their support unwavering. They believed in me, fought for me.

I was worthy of them, my *new* family. I was worthy of love—I looked back to Drayzen, nodding.

I was worthy of my title.

I reached for the crown, my trapped power fighting to break out. It was heavy in my hands, the weight of my destiny settling over me, forever altering my fate.

"Well, put it on," Violet urged with her signature smile. Drayzen shot her a daring glare but she only stuck her tongue out at him. I glanced at Cade, his intense gaze fixed on me, his usual blank expression betraying nothing of what he might be thinking.

Saigus' riddle rolled into my head. *You need to reunite with your soul.*

Was this it? Could this be the missing piece of my soul— the key to unlocking my power? A spark of hope flickered inside me. Maybe this was it. Maybe my prophecy wasn't as set in stone as I thought.

Time and space slowed as I lifted the metal to my head. The three Denazin tracked my movement as it settled on my hair. And it fit perfectly.

That familiar hum wrapped around me, warming me in the chill of the snowy night. I waited for one breath, two. Could it be my martem? My power calling out to me?

"Do you feel anything?" Drayzen asked.

"Just this hum but it's nothing I haven't felt before."

Violet looked to a stiff Drayzen.

"What is it?" I pressed.

"All that matters is that we got it back. We'll find a way to get your power out," Drayzen assured me. I narrowed on him but before I could question him, a gust of wind swept over us.

Mylom soared above the snowy trees. Her shimmering scales glistened in the sun and her fiery eyes locked onto me.

She landed, engulfing us in a gust of snow.

"We'll meet you two back at The Isles once we get everyone out." Cade nodded.

"Where are you guys going?" I frowned.

"Thysa and Sovanni are helping to free Raxos. We're going to make sure things go smoothly," Violet said, her smile not as comforting as it should be. I did not like the idea of splitting up but I nodded.

"Be careful, brother," Drayzen said to Cade, pulling him in. They clasped forearms. Then, Drayzen placed his hand on Violet's cheek but she shoved him away.

"*You* be careful." She leveled her gaze on him. "Please." She looked at me then, concern etched in her eyes. Cade's hand fell on her shoulder and they shifted.

I looked at Drayzen, unable to read his face as he watched his family disappear.

"Why aren't we going with them?" I begged. "We can help—"

"They'll be okay," he said to the spot where they'd just been. "We need to get out of here. They'll have an army searching for you."

I knew he was right but gods, I wanted to help. I needed them to be okay but we needed to be okay, too.

Nodding, I mounted Mylom. Drayzen took his place behind me. His body cautiously pressed against mine as I tried to steady my racing heart. He placed his hand on the scales next to my leg but I took an encouraging breath, pushing down my nerves as I grabbed his hand and wrapped it around my stomach. His touch sent a flurry of emotions through me but I only smiled, embracing him.

Without warning, Mylom shot us into the sky. Drayzen leaned forward into me, holding us both on her horn.

"It looks good on you," he whispered in my ear.

"Thank you," I whispered. I knew he would hear me.

We flew for some time, The Isles slowly coming into view through the clear sky. The distinct meeting point of the blue and the black sea crashed against each other. My eyes fell to the small assemblage of land just before the four islands. What looked to be small pockets of sand and dirt scattered the ocean between Rosetia and The Isles. I hadn't seen it on our last flight over but it was clear now. It was The Fading, the place that stripped any Fae's power and, eventually, their life.

Would it affect me now that I wore my crown?

"When is the—" Blood splattered my cheek. The lavender scent hit me immediately, Drayzen's blood.

"Dammit!" he cursed. I turned to find an arrow sticking right through his shoulder, narrowly missing my cheek.

Something *whizzed* past us and Drayzen threw his body over me. He seethed as a cool liquid dripped down my back. He buckled, struck by another arrow, and there was nothing I could do under his weight.

"Drayzen!" I shouted but I was quickly cut off as my stomach flipped when Mylom bellowed with fury, descending rapidly through the sky. I could only watch as she labored through every flap of her wings, arrows piercing her scales.

Drayzen growled. "They must have known we would come this way."

I peered out under Drayzen's arm, trying to get my bearings. Autyr's island was so close. I searched the sky and cursed. There wasn't a cloud in sight. No shadows to aid us in a quick escape.

That is, until darkness formed from above. I grabbed onto Drayzen's hand, ready for him to shift us away, but he didn't. And I followed his gaze up to the dragon spearing right for us. The shadow disappeared, replaced by a beam of fire. Drayzen crashed against me as Mylom dropped straight down. With a cry, she wrenched her wings wide just above a clearing and threw us off her back onto the gravel. I grabbed my crown, tumbling with Drayzen as his arms stayed locked around me. We skidded to a halt, his body cushioning my landing. Heat rushed to my cheeks as I scrambled off him, looking back to Mylom.

She was already back in the sky and the other dragon followed her as she led it away. The field we landed in was empty, only dirt and rocks painted its barren surface, but three ships lined the shores, golden soldiers marching off. About fifty of them were on the island already, their leader out front.

Deadly emerald eyes sparkled, even across the distance, as Azral threw his bow and arrows to the ground.

My hands shook as I watched Drayzen wrench the arrow from his back, then his shoulder, with a wince.

"This just adds to the long list of reasons to kill him," he growled.

"We need to go," I whispered urgently, tugging at Drayzen's arm. But there were no shadows. He looked up, noting the same thing. We were stuck.

A fire lit his eyes as his lips curved, revealing both his fangs. "Ready to fight, little kitten?"

"Are you crazy?" My eyes widened.

"We can take them," he said, determination flaring.

He was definitely crazy.

"They're weak. Most of them won't even make it off that boat."

"Look at them!" I pointed as they continued marching towards us.

"*I* have martem. They don't have any here." He raised a brow, power igniting in his eyes as little wisps of silver danced in them.

"What do you—?" His smirk accompanied my realization.

Here. We were in The Fading.

43

"WE ABSOLUTELY CAN*NOT*TAKE THEM."

"We don't have a choice. Not yet anyway," he said, pointing upwards. Clouds began to blot out the sky from the east, moving towards us from the direction of Death's island. "The gods can only interfere so much. Autyr is sending them our way. We just have to wait until they reach the sun."

I glanced back at the approaching soldiers, then back to the sky, then the soldiers—the pit in my stomach only grew. There were two of us. And I didn't even consider myself useful. I had some training, months at best, but against Fae warriors? Fighters hundreds of years old?

I stood no chance.

"They're weak here, look."

Drayzen tilted my chin to the army. Some of them were already toppling, creating a pile of bodies. They tried to maintain formation, marching straight over, but half of them stayed down.

Ten crossed over the middle ground and unsheathed their swords, the glistening golden metal reflecting the unforgiving sunlight.

Drayzen stood, unsheathing his own sword, the black stone hilt fitting perfectly in his grip. It was similar to Cade's, this one having two snakes wrapped around its hilt with black and plum diamonds throughout their scales.

He grabbed a dagger from his boot, handing it to me, but I didn't take it. I stayed there, frozen.

This was insane.

He kneeled, locking his midnight eyes with mine. "Mar," he whispered, his voice distant through my thick fear. "Hey." The silver swirls in his eyes calmed as his thumb grazed my cheek, pulling me back to reality. "Stay here, okay?"

"You can't take them all," I gasped.

"You're in for a real treat." He smirked, pushing back the hair that fell over his forehead.

And with those words, he dashed forwards.

His speed was faster than anything I'd ever witnessed, surpassing both Humans, Fae, and Cade. Even without being able to shift, he effortlessly moved between the soldiers, cutting them down one by one. His movements were precise, a skill only centuries of training could have taught him.

I stood, my mouth wide open, because he was incredible. None of the soldiers managed to land a single hit on him and he cut a path through them. His black clothes stained with blood but none of it was his.

Drayzen thrived in the chaos and in a matter of moments, the first wave of soldiers were dead at his feet. I watched as he kneeled, wiping the blood from his sword on one of the bodies.

He was a deadly beauty on the battlefield, one I couldn't keep my eyes off of. He looked back at me, his eyes warm as a small laugh escaped his lips.

The soldiers that could still stand advanced. There were about thirty who made it close to Drayzen. But it didn't matter. He resumed his deadly dance, slicing through them effortlessly.

Azral stood atop the pile of fallen, his eyes locked on Drayzen.

I looked up at the sky, praying the clouds would move faster. Drayzen seemed unfazed—even with two arrow wounds—but he'd tire eventually. *Right?* How long could he keep this up?

I adjusted my tilting crown, meeting Azral's glare. There was no trace of emotion on his face but his piercing emerald stare bore into me.

I looked down at the dagger Drayzen gave me, my hand still trembling, but then it stopped. My fear disappeared with the realization that we might win. That I could fight.

I scanned the weak army, then a coughing Azral. *He's weak here, too.*

And that could be my one chance, my one advantage to make him pay. For his lies, his words, for everything he'd done to me, everything he took. I looked at the fallen bodies, the blood that coated the once barren land.

Drip. Drip. Drip.

The memory of the first life I took flashed but only for an instant. It didn't cripple me anymore, it only fueled my anger.

This was the monster he created.

I lifted the dagger, leveling it with my eyesight, pointing it straight towards Azral.

In the corner of my eye Drayzen gave me a feral smile. His approving nod was all I needed. I sprung into action, running for the closest soldier. I whirled, swiftly cutting through the vulnerable gap in his armor near his neck. Without hesitation, I turned. Another soldier grabbed my free hand. My heart ratcheted. But I hissed, baring my teeth and with my other arm, I plunged the dagger straight into his eye. He fell back. Metal armor *clanged* with the other fallen bodies.

"Ew," I whispered, as his blood sprayed across my face. I swiped at it and when I opened my eyes, Drayzen was before me. His stupid smirk sent unexpected flutters through me, even in the midst of this chaos.

"You're hurt," I gasped at the blood leeching through his shirt. I could smell it, too, as a breeze rolled by, carrying a hint of pine with it.

"I'm fine, Mar." He brushed my loose hair aside.

But I didn't believe him. I grabbed his arm, inspecting the wounds. My thumb rolled over blood-stained skin but there was no cut, no mark. My brows furrowed, looking back at him.

"I told you, I'm fine." His eyes shimmered with silver.

How strong were the Denazin that they could heal that fast, or was Drayzen just that much stronger?

Our attention was drawn to the approaching group of soldiers and this time, they were led by Azral. They marched amidst the sea of fallen bodies, steadily towards us.

Drayzen looked to the sky and I followed. The clouds were still too far.

"I'm growing tired of this," he muttered, sheathing his sword. "Wait here."

And before I could stop him, he was off with lightning speed.

Even though he couldn't shift, he still cut through the soldiers in a blur. I watched warily as those smoky tendrils grew from his fingertips. He no longer used his sword and as a soldier approached, he lifted his hand, a trail of black smoke grabbing the soldier's helmet. In an instant, Drayzen was on the enemy, teeth sinking into their neck. Blood sprayed as the body dropped to the ground.

My heart jumped as another one came running from behind him. But before he could swing, the inky smoke grabbed onto the sword, throwing it and the guard across the battlefield.

Holy—

Drayzen was a blur of smoke now and I spotted him just as he slipped behind a crouching Azral. Drayzen tapped on his shoulder, relishing the moment, blood dripping from his smile. Azral spun but Drayzen only smirked before sinking his fangs in. He tore through his neck and pulled away. Blood and flesh coated his grinning mouth before he was a blur again.

He appeared by my side as he wiped the stain from his face.

"Disgusting," he muttered.

The approaching soldiers came to a halt, their attention shifting to Azral now fallen to the ground.

"That should hold them off for a moment." Drayzen smirked, a dangerous wicked thing.

Those hopes were shattered as I watched anger boil in Azral's eyes. He rose to his feet, a malevolent smile plastered on his face. The soldiers followed his lead, encircling us.

Drayzen growled and in a flash, he launched himself at the army, ripping off their helmets and tearing through their throats. One by one, in an inky, he dispatched them.

I tried to keep up, slicing my dagger through the weaker looking ones. Some of them fell on their own, the power of the land coming to our advantage. I looked for my next opponent but I froze, my eyes locking with the male before me.

His breath kissed my nose as those emerald eyes lowered on me. A sight I once loved now glowed with twisted delight as blood trickled from his mouth.

"Are you going to kill me, too?" Azral coughed.

"Yes." I hesitated. The truth burned, searing as it left my lips.

He grabbed my arm. I didn't let myself think as I plunged my dagger into his chest and twisted right through his heart—through our memories, through my love that cruelly lingered.

His grip on me loosened, his hand falling away from me.

I bore into his eyes. They flickered with something unrecognizable before he let out a chilling laugh. My brows furrowed but my rage disappeared as searing pain surged through my chest. Warmth seeped from my body. I glanced down. The hilt of a golden dagger plunged through my heart.

And the hand that held it there...

No.

The hand changed from the tanned complexion of Azral to a pale hue I'd only just come to know. The dagger's hilt slowly faded from gold to a silvery black.

No.

I looked up again, my eyes wide. Because it was no longer Azral who stood before me.

It wasn't Azral I drove my dagger into.

It wasn't Azral who drove his into me.

Panic filled the midnight eyes I met.

"Drayzen?" I coughed, his name barely escaping my lips as blood dribbled from my mouth.

I turned to find Azral across the field. He was on the ground, still bleeding from his neck, laughing through blood as the deadly sound echoed.

It was unheard of for a Fae to be able to use their martem in The Fading.

But with whatever ounce of strength he had left, Azral had done just that.

I fell into Drayzen's arms. My dagger still stuck in his chest. "Are you okay?" I coughed through the metallic taste in my mouth.

He didn't answer, though. His frantic eyes looked at the sky, back at Azral, then back at my chest. His hand shook above the dagger.

"No," he seethed.

I shivered under him. It was getting cold. Not even the blood pooling around me was enough to keep warm. I looked up through blurry eyes and saw the clouds close in.

Shadows surrounded us.

44

THE SHADOWS DWINDLED AS DRAYZEN GENTLY laid me on the couch in the sitting room of the cottage. My bloody hand fell over the side, leaving a trail of red over the fabric. My crown fell as my head hit the cushion. The clang of metal on the wooden floor was like a ticking clock.

It was fitting this would be where I die, Death's home.

"Hey," Drayzen whispered, his hand cupping my cheek as he sat on the floor next to me. I tried to offer a reassuring smile but it was stifled by a violent fit of coughing. More blood spilled from my mouth and I weakly moved a hand to cover it.

"It's okay, you're okay," he reassured me. His voice was a delicate mix of calm and terror. He carefully brushed hair behind my ear before placing his hands over my heart.

I looked at his chest, placing my hand on the spot I had stabbed him. The dagger was gone, replaced by blood from the already healed wound. I pushed back the hair falling over his face, leaving a line of blood on his forehead.

"I'm okay." He nodded. "You're going to be okay too." He nodded again, lying to the both of us.

I'd come close to dying too many times to know I was not okay. My body dropped to a chilling cool but I knew it wasn't Drayzen's power. No this, this was death.

And there was nothing I could do this time. No one was coming to save me. I could only lay here and watch Drayzen's fear-filled eyes dart around the room.

"What happened?" Cade thundered as he stormed in.

Finally, some sort of emotion from him. If only it didn't take me dying.

"Oh my—" Violet's hand flew to her mouth as she dropped to her knees.

"It's fine, she's okay," Drayzen lied to them. He turned his attention to me, his touch anchoring me to this life.

"Drayzen," Cade rasped above me.

Another gasp echoed, followed by Sovanni and Thysa. Both looked shocked and unsure what to do. Tears welled in Sovanni's eyes. "No," she breathed.

"*She's fine,*" Drayzen growled, baring his fangs. "She's going to be fine."

But I didn't believe him. And it seemed no one else did either.

The pain that had consumed me gradually faded; the ache in my chest where the dagger had been numbed. My head felt heavy, as if being pulled into the calming darkness. I drifted in and out of it, like a fragile presence teetering on the edge of the abyss.

That was not a good sign.

Drayzen's voice pierced through the haze as he lifted my head. His midnight eyes pulled me back. "Stay with me," he whispered, his words a fragile plea.

Violet, her face painted with tears, reached for him but before she could get close, he pushed her away, his fangs bared with a warning growl.

The truth was unfolding before us all and Drayzen refused to accept it.

This reality was undeniable—I was dying.

Struggling to summon my remaining strength, I called to him in my mind, hoping he could hear my final words.

Would he still be able to reach me here, after I succumbed to the final darkness?

Drayzen?

His gaze snapped to me but he didn't answer. Shadows encircled his body, swirling with his mounting fear. "You will *not* die on me," he seethed.

He lifted my head, pulling me into his side as he raised his wrist to his mouth, biting down. He pushed his wrist to my mouth and whispered, "Drink."

"Drayzen," Cade roared. "You cannot do this, the consequences—"

"Screw the consequences!" Drayzen growled.

"They won't allow this! You'll be killing her!" Violet pleaded.

Drayzen looked back at me, his eyes void of emotion. "I've killed her either way."

Silence veiled the room.

"I need you to drink, Mar." He pleaded with me, raising his wrist closer to my mouth.

Realization washed over me. *Yes. Yes, his blood.* That was what would save me, that would heal me. My lips brushed his soft skin and with what little strength I had left, I drank. But I didn't get the taste I'd come to long for; it wasn't silky and cool anymore. It was metallic and it burned as it trickled down my throat, tainted with a hint of rust and decay.

I coughed, shoving his wrist away, his blood mingling with my own.

I looked up at him as everything around the two of us blurred.

I couldn't see how Thysa held Sovanni. I couldn't see Violet sobbing in the corner. I didn't hear Cade screaming at him to stop.

I could only see Drayzen.

He placed one hand on my chin, the other on my neck. "Do you trust me?"

And there was no question. "Yes, I trus—"

45

Drayzen

AMARA'S NECK SNAPPED BETWEEN MY HANDS.

The breaking of her spine echoed in my ears and the room dropped to a chill. The air carried the smell of burning lavender, a scent I knew all too well—the scent of death.

"Autyr help us all." Cade dropped his head.

Vi's sobs stopped in the corner.

The Fae females watched in horror and they were right to be afraid.

"What did you do?" Sovanni rasped.

Amara's lifeless body laid next to me as I turned my head. My tone chilling in a way even I didn't recognize. "I Turned her."

I sat for what felt like centuries, waiting for Mar to wake up. I tried reaching out to her mind, searching for any fragment of a memory, anything that could bring her back. But I was met with nothing, emptiness—a void where her life once resided, a void I'd found comfort in for so many years.

It'd been hours. The sun already dipped below the horizon. "She should be awake by now," I seethed. Vi's hand gently rested on my shoulder, an attempt at comfort, I knew, but I recoiled, pushing her away and rising from the floor.

Rage consumed every fiber of my being as my martem surged through me. Shadows danced around me, filling the room with a chilling darkness.

"Drayzen." Violet's voice was a mere whisper compared to the overwhelming power that took over.

"Autyr!" I growled. "Autyr!"

Sovanni and Thysa gasped, clutching at each other.

"Get them out of here," I snarled.

Violet shifted before them, ushering them out of the room and shutting the door behind her. I turned to my brother.

"It's too late," Cade muttered. "This—what you've done—it's not the natural order of things."

"It never is!" I hissed.

"The balance—"

"Get out of here," I commanded. Teeth bared. Anger unbridled.

But before he could move, the shadows intensified. I felt a sudden drop in temperature, colder than what my own power had created.

Still, a cynical smirk curled on my lips as I turned to face the newest male.

Behind me, I felt Cade sink to his knees, his usually calm heartbeat accelerating as he kneeled.

The God of Death was in the room.

"Fix this," I growled, my eyes narrowed on him.

He stood tall before me but not much taller. He looked down, dark long hair falling over his face. Black stubble contrasted against his pale skin. His power rippled around mine, pulsing with intensity as he met my stare with his own deep blue eyes.

"Is that any way to greet me?" Autyr purred.

"Fix this," I growled again.

"She's dead," Autyr stated calmly, his voice unwavering as he looked at Amara.

Dead.

His words, that truth, shattered through me.

But it was a truth I refused to accept.

"You've done it before," I shot back. "Let her Turn."

Autyr only laughed. He stood before Mar, observing her with a critical eye. "It's a shame, what they've done to her." He kicked the golden crown on the floor.

"Let her—" I started. But I paused, realizing what I needed to do.

Taking a deep breath, cool air brushed my throat as I bent down, my knee meeting the unforgiving floor. I kneeled before Autyr, an act of submission I had never granted anyone.

Not even him, my creator.

"Please."

Raising my eyes to him, I found no trace of emotion on his face as he watched me. "Stand up." He motioned with his hand. "Begging does not suit you."

I obeyed, pushing myself to my feet. He stepped past me, toward Mar's lifeless, cold body. Silent moments passed as he stood over her, his piercing gaze fixed on her face. Blood streaked her pale, white waves, but her familiar scent—vanilla and mint—lingered in the air, haunting me. He flicked a strand of blood-matted hair from her cheek with a deliberate gentleness that made my jaw clench.

"You were successful in turning her." He said to her body before turning back to me. "You didn't need to beg." *Maybe not, but for her, I would do anything.* "She's just taking a little longer to wake up." Autyr smirked.

"But Drayzen." His tone darkened. "You just created something no one could have imagined." He turned back, placing his hand on Mar's bloody chest. "This, my dear boy, is just the beginning."

Darkness engulfed the room. I squinted through it, trying to see what was happening, but in a fleeting moment, the chill lifted, the shadows receded, and Autyr was gone.

I reined in my own power, drawing the leftover veils of shadows back to me as I moved for Mar. Her wound was closed, leaving only the pools of blood around her.

Cade stood next to me, examining her with equal concern.

I placed one hand gently on her cold cheek and ran my fingers through her hair with the other, searching for any sign of life. I called to her in the darkness, trying to help her find her way back to me.

And then, I heard it—the faint flow of blood coursing through her veins. I tried to stay calm, brushing my thumb against her cheek. A wave of relief washed over me as her eyes slowly fluttered open. She surveyed the room; her face contorted with confusion. Her gaze flicked between me and Cade, who now kneeled beside us.

"Hey," I whispered.

Her heart no longer beat but the blood in her veins raced around her body as her eyes widened.

"Where are they?" she rasped.

"We're right here." I brushed the hair behind her ears, trying to steady her panic.

"No, no!" she yelled, pushing me away. "Where did *they* go? I wasn't done talking to them!"

Cade looked at me, confusion clouding his face. "Who are you talking about?" he asked. And I was just as confused.

"They told me how I can get my power back," she said to him, her eyes still frantic.

Her missing soul. "Who, Mar? Who told you this?"

She froze and her scarlet eyes locked onto mine. "My parents."

Amara's story doesn't end here.

PRONUNCIATION GUIDE

CHARACTERS
Amara: ah-mar-ah
Azral: az-role
Sovanni: so-vaan-ee
Thysa: th-ee-sa
Erixx: eric-ss
Isidore: ee-sid-or
Lettie: let-ee
Drayzen: dray-zin
Saigus: say-jus
Melenyz: melineez
Autyr: aw-tear
Nyrah: near-ah

PLACES
Zandar: zand-are
Kaluth: kal-ath
Solyrus: sole-eye-rus
Lunhayven: lune-hay-vin
Menasai: men-ah-sigh

OTHER
Illion: ill-ee-ahn
Danriel: dan-ree-al
Denazin: den-ah-zeen
Drakai: drah-k-eye

ACKNOWLEDGEMENTS

There aren't enough ways I can express my gratitude to my parents for their unwavering support of my (often) crazy ideas. Mom, you have been my #1 fan and best friend since day one. From reading early drafts to pushing me to meet my deadlines, I could not have done *any* of this without you. Dad, thank you for always supporting me and encouraging me every step of the way. I loved sharing each step of this process with you and your support throughout means more than I can ever put into words.

To my editor, Erin. I seriously could not have done this without you. You came into my life when things were hectic, and you literally saved this story (and my sanity)! You helped me see a different side of this and for all the better. There are truly not enough thank yous I can give you for this.

To my incredible BETA readers. Every time I hit the send button to you my heart raced. Sharing your life's work with others can be a terrifying experience, but you all made it the most magical journey for me. You pushed my creativity to new heights I never thought possible, and you all made it that much more special.

To my artists, you brought Amara (and her friends) to life for me. Watching my characters come to life through your eyes and talent has been an indescribable experience. I had envisioned getting artwork done for this book, but you all truly surpassed my expectations. Not only with your talent but with your heartfelt support as well.

And finally, to the person who listened to me talk about this story endlessly for the past three years, to my best friend, the love of my life. Thank you for patiently listening to me rant about this and these characters for countless hours. Thank you for supporting me and lifting me back up when I thought I couldn't do it. Thank you for pushing me forward and making sure I never gave up. And most importantly, thank you for loving me. Trevor, I love you always and forever.

Kitty Aldrin is a reader turned author who found herself unable to leave the realm of fantasy books.

While she's not weaving threads of magic and romance, you can find her spending time in the beautiful sunshine state with family and friends.

Check out her website and socials to stay up to date on all things Kaluth!

kittyaldrinbooks.com